What readers like  ystic

An inspired an... ...elho—a
proportions. This is re...
work of fiction designe... ...on a visceral journey that results in
personal awakening.—Mark Botvinick, *Professional Screenwriter.*

This book is destined to become a bestselling spiritual classic. I stayed up late at night reading it—I couldn't put it down! I found myself cutting and pasting insights from the text to refer to again and again. Nothing short of a masterpiece. It's GREAT! —Alexis Neely, *Bestselling Author, Mom, and Blogger.*

I think this is a superb piece of writing. I have read over a thousand novels, and I have one thing to say: **This is a good book.** It's the sort of book that will save someone's life. —Beth Wiskochil, *Vermont.*

This book kicks some serious spiritual ass.. The story is impossible to put down— I was completely hooked just a handful of pages in. Even when I did set it aside, it lingered in my dreams.. I was really on the journey, and I didn't want it to end! I'm reading it again, savoring each moment. So good. So, so good. —Bryce Widom, *Professional Artist.*

Ross Hostetter's **Keepers of the Field** is an engrossing story that takes the reader on a fascinating journey of self-discovery. Hostetter weaves leading edge spiritual wisdom and sophisticated cultural insight into an exciting tale of mystery and enlightenment. **I highly recommend this jewel of a book.**
— Steve McIntosh, author of *Evolution's Purpose,* and *Integral Consciousness and the Future of Evolution.*

This may very well be the first great spiritual adventure story of the 21st century—a book that will offer hope and real help to anyone who is on a personal spiritual path. It's just beautifully done. I loved it!— Jeff Salzman, author of the blog *The Daily Evolver,* and Senior Teacher at the Integral Center in Boulder.

I don't really know where to start except to tell you that your book has changed my life. I could literally feel energy jumping from each turned page. My mind was sucked in by your dynamic narrative and my spirit is infused with the layered wisdom (myth, metaphor, and sermon) that saturates your wonderful story IT IS A P-H-E-N-O-M-E-N-A-L BOOK!!— Marc Pollock, *Businessman.*

Oh my gosh, I love your book, absolutely love it. I was reading on the plane coming home and afraid that I would finish it! Thinking, I don't want it to end! — Adelyn Jones, *Creator of the Frequency of Love Project.*

A terrific book that plumbs the depths of human potential, and points the way to an enlightened wisdom for all.— Ken Wilber, *The Integral Vision.*

KEEPERS OF THE FIELD

A Spiritual Adventure

ROSS HOSTETTER

Text: Copyright © 2014 Ross Hostetter

All rights reserved. Except as permitted under the U.S Copyright act of 1976, no part of this publication may be reproduced, distributed, or transmitted or stored in any form by any means, without the prior permission of the Author.

Published by Unitive Publications
Author's Email:
ross@fieldworkschool.org

Snail Mail:
P.O Box 21213
Boulder, Colorado, 80308

**We'd love to hear from you.
Contact us to arrange for Ross to drop in to your book club.**

Cover Art: Copyright © 2012 Bryce Widom
Used under license.

Back cover photo by Melissa C. Hostetter
Back cover photo Copyright ©Ross Hostetter, 2012
All rights reserved.

Hostetter, Ross, 2014
Keepers of the Field: a novel/ Ross Hostetter.—1st edition.

Summary: This novel is a spiritual adventure story—the journey of a man-child named Charlie Smithson who decides to leave the pinnacle of success and risk it all to become a true man. Charlie is led deep into the wilderness by a guide named Moses, where he encounters the mysterious forces of 'The Committee,' and is trained to become a Messenger and a Keeper of the Field. He is then abandoned, and must go on alone toward an encounter that will either destroy him, or bring him to enlightenment.

Book website:
http://www.keepersofthefield.com/

ISBN: **0990301400**
ISBN-13: 978-0-9903014-0-0

Library of Congress Control Number: 2014939222

1. Spirituality—Fiction. 2. Mysticism—Fiction. 3. Self Help—Fiction. 4. Enlightenment—Fiction.

Jennifer —

For My Family

All the best to you —

Ross

Contents

Prologue 8

Part One: A Call and Answer 11
   1: Starting Where You Are 12
   2: Someone Who Answers 20
   3: Concentration Practice 26
   4: The Invitation 36
   5: From Another Reality 46
   6: Resistance 56
   7: The Answer 65

Part Two: Leaving Identity Behind 71
   8: The New Journey 72
   9: Turning 'Till You Come 'Round Right 80
   10: Free Attention 91
   11: Explorer's Eyes 98
   12: Leaving Identity Behind 110
   13: Sunday Morning 117
   14: Sunday Evening 122
   15: The Swamp 129

Part Three: Choosing the Path 139
   16: Meeting the Guide 140
   17: Going Light 152
   18: Gaining the Initiative 164
   19: Freeze-Dried Purpose 176
   20: Dreams within Dreams 186
   21: The Competitors 196
   22: Manhood in Chains 210

Part Four: Following the Guide 225
- 23: The Soul Friend 226
- 24: The Pearl 238
- 25: Making Fire 243
- 26: First Things 251
- 27: Taking God's Perspective 262
- 28: A Journey to Somewhere 274
- 29: The Quickening 297
- 30: The Turning of the Wheel 303

Part Five: The Night Journey 311
- 31: Her 312
- 32: The Music 324
- 33: Alone 330
- 34: Potency 340
- 35: Deconstruction 348
- 36: Baptism 354
- 37: Choosing Life 364
- 38: Losing the Way, Finding the Way 373
- 39: No Bottom, No Top 386
- 40: Enlightenment 391
- Epilogue: The Return of Charlie Smithson 399

A Call to Action 405

Acknowledgements 407

Prologue

The water glistened as it poured from the long hair clinging to her back as she ran barefoot down the weathered wooden boards of the dock and into the air, turning back to smile at me from the apex of her leap; spinning with her toes pointed and her arms captured in a dancer's pirouette before she disappeared into the cold blue water.

"—*If she is the one, the Field will mark her body. The Messenger has always been marked, as you well know, Cronus.*"

I felt the ridges of the old scars on my left hand—the pathway of the currents of fire that had flowed into me the night when I was marked and given my true name. A pattern, like the delicate branching of fern leaves, flowed up from my fingers and flared into spirals that intertwined my forearm.

"I know. She will be strong enough. I see the light around her."

The girl's head emerged with the audible exhale of a diver coming up from the deep. The water was thick against her shoulders as she swam toward the shore.

"—*She will be tested. And she is so young, Cronus. She might not survive.*"

'Her innocence will protect her. I will protect her. She is the one. She will discover who she is, and accept the mission for which she's been made."

"—*But you must not impose; you must not demand. The Rule forbids it. She must be the one to choose, and choose three times, just as you did.*"

"Yes."

I walked toward the steep grassy embankment that lined the shore. There was a book with a worn leather cover in my back pocket. Inside the book were pressed leaves of aspen, and flowers in the form of stars within stars. A title was carved into the cover, now barely visible to the eye: *The Field Book*. The book held the written wisdom of The Committee—wisdom that was still in the act of being created. It could be said that the book was alive.

I reached down the embankment and extended my hand to the girl as she struggled up the slippery slope. She looked up at me and smiled as our eyes met. She had trusting eyes, with no guile. She reached up her hand. Our palms were less than a foot apart. In a moment, there would be no going back.

"*—Be careful, Cronus. Be sure. When your hands touch she will be changed. It is an awful thing, the greatness that you ask of her.*"

IT WAS NOT ALWAYS THIS WAY. There was a time before I was Cronus, the servant and messenger of The Committee—a time before I accepted the work of evolving this world through the power of love, link to link. There was a time when I maintained the illusion that I was separate and divided—a time before I was aware of the Field.

But now I am linked to this world cell to cell; I am this very world come alive. I have lost all desire to escape, and I will not leave until the work is finished.

It began a generation ago.

I was not so different then, in the beginning. Like this girl, I was just a child.

SHE REACHED HIGH and our hands touched. The feeling passed between us, and her eyes became pools of light. My body remembered the first touch of a Messenger; the penetration of love, as if I'd been sick all my life and suddenly been made well; like I'd been asleep and suddenly awakened.

I pulled the child up the embankment, and we stood smiling into each other, leaping into the joy of growing and irreversible unity.

I am Cronus, the twenty-third Messenger. I have claimed my true name. I am the custodian of the Field Book, and a Keeper of the Field.

This is my story.

Part One:

A Call and Answer

1: Starting Where You Are

> The spiritual journey starts with the realization that there's nothing more to wait for. The conditions are already perfect. There is no 'something else' that needs to happen before we begin. We start exactly where we are. After all, whether now or later, this is the only place we can begin.
> ...*The Field Book.*

IN THE BEGINNING, my name was Charlie Smithson. I played baseball.

In the summer months before my tenth birthday, I was the back-up right fielder for the Structo Fabricating Little League squad. Structo was one of the few machine shops still open below the smokestacks of our town—a once-thriving enterprise that now faced the world as a ramble of dirty windows and corrugated siding with rusty holes that leaked sparks from the grinding wheels inside.

Our coach was the last of Structo's metal-bending men. He'd stood with his feet just this side of a painted yellow line since '68, doing the same bend on the same endless roll of hot-dipped steel for twenty years' time, ascending at last to the hydraulic press where he'd stood for six years more. The big press could punch a hole through an inch of carbon-steel plate, and Coach never got tired of watching his heavy metal being impaled. The press job was skilled labor—a dollar thirty-six cents more per hour at union scale—and it earned the man a work station by the window where he could watch what was left of the river as it flowed past the gauntlet of discharge pipes and leaking tanks that sloped down from the chain-linked yards of the factories that lined Water Street.

His beer buddies called our coach "The Turk" or just "Turk" because of his ceaseless burning of that smelly Turkish tobacco with a camel on the pack. Turk insisted on his "God-given and Constitutional Right" to smoke everywhere, even in the Little League dugout with children present. Any suggestion that he modify his behavior for the health and welfare of children was met by The Turk with a lowering of his broad head and the downward compression of his brow in a practiced threat display that puffed his over-large chest and cheek-sacks full of righteous outrage; an outrage that he indulged in daily as an orienting emotion fueled by fuzzy images of a well-armed mob of Turk-clones storming the State House in Springfield to lay down their lives together in defense of their right to hack, spit, and enlarge their fifty-six inch waistlines.

Just for emphasis, the big man made a habit of pinching one of his coffin nails continuously between thumb and forefinger, to bear it before him with the burning end poking into the air like a fuming candle that trailed glories of toxic blue smoke in sheets and whorls. The Turk saw himself as a torch-bearer for the Structo Way, and he carried the Camel aloft into our weekly competitions as both a symbol of personal freedom and as a sacred Olympic Flame. How such a man could remain a Little League mentor was explained by a loophole in the Summer Rec. League Guidelines that allowed the team's sponsor to name the coach. No one was left at Structo to take the coaching job, so Turk leapt at the opportunity to boss somebody else around for a change and imbue young men with the proper values.

Turk's coaching strategy revolved around two central concepts. The first was his idea of 'barehanding' the ball—not using the glove to field, but instead stabbing at hot grounders with the gloveless open hand. Turk's mission was to eliminate the oh-so-sluggish transfer from glove to throwing hand. In theory, this would allow us to pick off more of those streaking runners with a quick, snappy throw.

Second, and more importantly, Turk had filled his mind with the idea that our season's success rested on his ability to confront the umpire about every questionable call. He believed in his heart that the man behind the mask could be entrained by shouts, false charges, and other timely challenges to make all close and not-so-close calls in favor of the Structo side. All those close calls going our way would add up to quite a sum over the course of a season, giving our squad a significant statistical advantage.

THE TURK SCHOOL OF BAREHANDED FIELDING AND UMPIRE CONFRONTATION was a boon to our opponents. By stabbing unsuccessfully at routine ground balls, our infield leaked a reliable stream of errors to the outfielders, who actually managed to pick up the hits with an open hand as they dribbled to a stop in the bumpy grass of the Rec. League field. Over time, the outfield unconsciously crept closer to form a second infield. This made us tragically vulnerable to a well-hit fly ball. But our real problem lay not with the base-clearing hits booming off the bats of our opponents. It was Turk's feeble emotional intelligence that doomed our squad to the cellar.

With confrontation on his mind, Turk had begun, starting last winter, to mechanically memorize the rules of Little League baseball as he watched his press pound steel. Those rote efforts had brought him to the single intellectual achievement of his lifetime—a nearly complete mastery of every minor technicality contained in the Blue Pocket Edition of the Little League Rules, which Turk carried as a Bible in a back pocket next to his Zippo lighter.

When the season opened, Turk proceeded with a simple plan. He first established a clear line of sight to the home plate Ump. With his narrow eyes locked on, he then settled into the role of coon dog with the hapless volunteer umpire serving as treed coon; subject to all of Turk's bay and bark and the persistent bug-eyed stare-down of a very large man with a smoking unfiltered in his hand. There was no peace possible in Turk's self-made umpire war, because both sides of the war were generated in Turk's own mind. And he was not without his weapons.

I GOT A pretty good look at The Turk from my seat on the bench. He had a hard time remembering a belt, and whenever he bent over, the top of his hairy white ass cheeks would ride out over the waistline of his blue Little Dickey work pants. That ragged little rule book would be there, fart-gassed and pressed hard but ready as a pistol in a greased holster—ready to be whipped out and shaken in a bellowing charge toward the home plate Ump with the rule book in one hand and a glowing unfiltered in the other. This was Turk's John Wayne charge to glory, with reins in his teeth and both hands full of manhood, bawling emotion down the third-base line.

When Turk reached the plate, he began to make offers to the Umpire: offers to "take it outside," "to settle this like men"—and, as the situation progressed, to "pound your fucking face in." These typically did not impress the Ump as statements which should come from one with authority over nine-year-old boys, and the Turk's charge would always end with the big man standing in humiliation on the bumper of his truck, out in the parking lot behind my personal warm spot on the bench, where all his energy would melt down, and he would collapse into an embarrassing stream of emotionally choked sounds and whimpers; a mess of whining garble that an untrained ear might interpret as a pathetic attempt to redeem himself and continue coaching the squad.

OF COURSE it wasn't always this way. I could remember a place where we once lived in the city, a place with polished floors and rugs with fringes with a big bay window that I could lie in and watch the snow as it fell to the streets and out on the big water in the distance. I was small, no more than three and a half years old and hiding under the table in the dining room. I could only see their feet under the lace of the tablecloth; the polished wing tips of my father and the black high heels of my mother. The feet were circling each other. I was on my knees in my boy-velvet Christmas pants and jacket, with my kneecaps tight together and the hard black heels of my buckle shoes biting into my bottom. My mother's black heels spun and paced and the wingtips shifted from side to side.

"You've lost it all, you stupid shit!" she said. "Who's going to pay the bills on this place now? You don't have any idea what it costs to keep a child!"

There were more words that came out in a raw flurry, raising welts in the air. The word 'money' was the hardest, loudest, and most frequent word.

"Don't talk to me like that, bitch! You've never done a single thing but sit here drinking while...."

There was a sound of a palm hitting a man's face, then the harder, sickening sound of the return blow. I could see the knees of my mother on the carpet. I dared not reach out to touch her.

THAT WAS THEN. Now we were here. Mom and I had moved to Prosperville to be closer to her parents. It wasn't my fault. At least that's what my mom kept telling me. "It's not your fault, Charlie, it's not your fault," she would say as she combed the knots out of my hair before bed. I heard her words, but I couldn't figure out what 'fault' was, or why it mattered. I only knew this: having me around was not what my Dad had in mind. I tried to imagine that he was alive in some kind of way—that there was some connection between us—but all I could remember about him was his shoes.

I was with The Turk now—a man to be with once every week at game time, and twice more at practice. To her credit, Mom made it to every outing and sat in the bleachers, doing the very best she could. Still, her best couldn't help me with baseball. In Prosperville, I needed a man for that. Mom's hair was a wreck most days, and she was too tired from working her jobs and too overwhelmed with her own thoughts to do anything except sit. She would stare out at the lights as she ate her popcorn, her mind somewhere far beyond the game. We'd go home and she would sit alone in the dark. I could see the ember of her cigarette moving slowly up to her mouth and back down to her ashtray—up and back as the ice of her drink clinked softly against glass. She certainly had no energy to challenge anyone or anything, especially someone as big as our coach. It was just the way things were, she said. "Just the way men are," she said. So with that, I was officially on my own down here in the dugout next to the Turk. I had to find a way to deal with it. Everyone finds a way to deal with it. And my way of dealing with it was to become quiet little Charlie, the reserve right fielder.

QUIET CHARLIE was a doe-eyed boy, a nice boy who wanted to please everybody if he could only find a way. I was well-liked by my grade school teachers. I helped my mother after dinner. I sat still in class with both feet on the floor with the very top button of a check-plaid shirt buttoned up high. The curves of my cursive exactly touched the top, bottom, and dotted midline of my wide-ruled tablet paper. I was lousy at baseball even though I tried to do everything just as I was told—really tried to get a ball to stay in my glove or make just one throw that didn't end up in the dirt at the catcher's feet. I was a kid who hadn't given up the game, even though I was watching it through the chain link and smoothing dirt with my sneakers.

I had a problem with baseball that I couldn't solve, and I needed some help. You see, every time a fly was hit in my direction I'd flush up with excitement and involuntarily run forward to meet the ball. And every time, I would be stopped in full stride by the sight of that ball cruising high overhead, only to land just a couple of feet from the exact spot where I'd just been standing. My leaping, open-mouthed attempt at a catch served only to make me look more spastic before running to dig the ball out of the grass next to the outfield fence as the batter rounded the bases. The outfield boundary was a faded red snow fence made of wooden slats, put there because the town didn't have money for anything else. Soft rye grass grew into long, slender seed-heads beside the fence.

It was all quite natural. And the thing about this, the really pathetic thing, the thing that made me a true right fielder—was that I'd come to believe nothing about my situation was wrong. Everyone but me knew our team just sucked, that Turk was an inbred and instinctual loser, and that my position as Structo's second-string right fielder was the sorriest spot on the worst team in the league. Right field was where they sent the kid with no arm; the kid with no glove. And I was even a step down from right field. The second-string right fielder was the bottom of the bottom. He was the kid who rode the pine for the first two-thirds of the game, to be sent out reluctantly in the seventh for the two and a half innings he must be allowed to play under paragraph 14(a) of the Summer Rec. League Full Participation Guidelines. His teammates then could only pray that a ball would never come his way.

I WAS A RIGHT FIELDER because it was natural for me to be there on the bench, out of the action, in a uniform three sizes too big with the peeling iron-on letters of the Structo Fabricating name on my back. It was natural for the town to have no money for baseball, and a field that hadn't been improved in two decades. It was natural for the place to produce a coach like The Turk as an example to children; natural to demonstrate and entrain bad habits at every opportunity; natural for the town to just go along, dying a day at a time. I didn't know any different. And why should *I* try to change anything? "It's just the way things are meant to be," I heard. That's what I said too, and I believed it.

There's a perspective that one develops from this position, especially when you don't worry about it: everything is fine if you don't let yourself believe anything's wrong. I played last-string right field for Structo as a sleepwalker; happy just to watch the fascinating spirals of Turk's second-hand smoke waft through the dugout, happy to give a little pepper and yell out "hey batta-batta" from a seat on the bench, and to smooth the dirt with my sneakers until I was sent out to play for two and a half innings in right field—there to watch the balls go over my head, then run to dig them out of the lush green rye grass that grew, untrimmed, against the faded red snow fence that marked the boundary of my Little League world.

BUT SOME DAYS were different. Sometimes in the middle of a game an uncomfortable thought would come to me in the clearest way. *It shouldn't be like this, Charlie*, the thought said. *There's something better that could happen here.* I was spending my summer sitting next to The Turk, letting his smoke pour across my face in absolute and passive acceptance, listening to his foul mouth, looking at his morbid body, and becoming more Turk-like a bit at a time by force of contact. *If I could only stand up for myself like he does*, I thought, *things might be different.* But I had no idea where such a power could come from. I was waiting there for something. I didn't even know what I was waiting for.

So there on the bench, I did the only thing I could do. With every slow, smooth curve of the toe of my Converse sneaker in the dirt, I was letting my mind go quiet, and in that quiet mind I was sending out a prayer. I was silently, secretly, praying for a miracle. And then, on the twenty-second day of June, at the bottom of the seventh inning, that miracle turned up.

2: Someone Who Answers

There are no miracles; only messages from another place on the path.
> ...*The Field Book.*

I'D JUST LET ANOTHER BALL FLY OVER MY HEAD during our fifth game, and was running in from right field to get my one chance at bat. A man was leaning up against the chain link fence that paralleled the right field line. His image flickered twice then became solid. I'd never seen anyone like him before. *Probably from out of town visiting relatives,* I thought. He had a jaw with no fat under it, and I could see the veins in his forearms. He wore a clean white T-shirt tucked into a trim waist, faded blue jeans, and a worn red ball cap.

"Hey kid."

He looked straight at me with his chin down and motioned to me with the fingers of his left hand. I felt powerless to resist him, and he looked so much like a real coach that I ran right over. But I didn't make it, at least not all the way.

About four feet from him I ran into something midstride.

I'd heard of alien force fields, like bubbles or invisible shields that space-beings put out around their mother ship to protect it from lasers, cosmic rays, and other space stuff. I was still young enough to believe that such things were possible. But this was different. I felt a circle around this man that was both fierce and loving at the same time. It felt like a boundary—a boundary to another world.

The man picked his head up slightly, and for just a moment, a glitter of light flashed out from under the shadow of his cap. The light was coming from his eyes, his intense eyes that were blue as a robin's egg around the edges and fading to liquid blue-black in the centers. I'd seen color like this once before in the deep middle of a clear Midwestern summer's sky above my Grandpa's farm, just as the first star was coming out at twilight. There was a small black dot just above and between his eyes, like someone had marked him there.

"Would you like to come in?" he asked.

I didn't know what to say. He was waiting for me. There was a small leather-bound book in his right hand which he closed and transferred to his back pocket. I could just make out the title carved with a leather-working tool into the cover: *The Field Book*.

Maybe the book has something to do with baseball, I thought. *After all, baseball is played in a field.*

The hand that had been holding the book stretched out to me palm upward, but the man didn't reach across whatever was separating us. He was inviting me in, but I would have to take a step across the boundary to get to him. There was something about this man that required me to make a decision and take action. It was a single step, but without that step nothing was going to happen.

My right foot moved, and I felt all of the fierceness melt away. My ball glove fell from my left hand and came to rest on the ground. I was less than two feet from him. For just an instant, I felt as if I'd been sick all my life and suddenly been made well. I stood there before him.

He held me in his gaze, and then spoke.

"So let me ask you something," he said, smiling at me.

"What?"

"Are you tired of missing those fly balls every damn time?"

I'd never had an adult talk to me like this before. His eyes were on me, and I couldn't move. I heard myself start to talk.

"I *am* pretty tired of it to tell you the truth. It's no fun."

"You said it. So if I told you about something that would change things—would you actually do it?"

"Whaddaya mean?"

"I mean if I told you a secret about how to catch—something you could do that would let you catch any ball that came your way, any time, maybe even *every* time—would you do exactly what I tell you? Actually do it and not just talk about it, pretend you've done it, or make excuses?"

"I guess so."

"I need to hear a 'yes.'."

"OK. It's 'yes,' I guess," I said, not knowing what I was getting myself into.

"OK. And, well … would your answer be the same if I told you that this thing might really cost you?"

"Like how much?" I asked.

There was a gray toy safe on my shelf back at home nestled between a hard-bound version of *Daniel Boone Wilderness Scout* and a purple rock from Michigan. Inside were six black cat firecrackers that my mom didn't know about, two five dollar bills, six ones, five quarters, five nickels, and a dime. I'd been saving those seventeen dollars and sixty cents for more than a year.

"Like giving up who you are," he said. "That's how much."

That didn't seem so bad. I was relieved that I was not going to lose my whole seventeen-sixty! Giving up 'who I was' didn't seem like such a big deal to me. I was only nine years old. I *wanted* to be somebody else.

"You got a deal," I heard myself say.

"I'll consider that a promise."

He motioned me closer, leaning forward to whisper. "My little brother, from here on out, *all* of the time, *no matter what…*" he said, leaning still closer, now right in my ear "Watch … the … ball … watch the ball, then *watch the ball some more*. Don't you take your eyes off it, for *any* reason, *no matter what*. Do just this one thing, and let everything else take care of itself."

He pulled upright.

"Ya got it?"

"I think so."

"So when are you going to start?"

I just looked at him and shrugged. He smiled at my hesitation.

"Always off in the future, isn't it?"

He knelt back down and looked at the ground, rubbed his cheek, then turned and pulled on my elbow.

"Do you want to hear a secret? I'll tell you one, no extra charge," he whispered.

"What's that?"

He sat back on his ankles, folding his hands in front of him.

"Listen. Whether it's tonight or a hundred years from now, there's only one place and one time that you can ever actually do anything, see anything, or realize anything. It's the most important moment in life."

"When's that?"

His eyes softened and he smiled gently at me.

"I offer this moment. Right now. And what could shift *right now* that will create the next moment, and then the next, and the next, which is ..." he paused ... "now a moment that has just arrived."

He stood up, reached forward, and put the first two fingers of his right hand gently against my forehead. I felt my mind shift outside of itself. For an instant I believed ... no ... I *knew* that I could watch that ball, no matter what. Of course I could do it. It was already done. Then he took his fingers away and the feeling left me. I just stood there, looking into his blue eyes.

"Ya got it?"

"Yes, I think so," I said, not knowing what had just happened.

"So whatcha gonna do?"

"Watch the ball?"

"And when are you going to do it?"

"Right now?"

"Alright then!"

The man stepped back, and I was outside again. Some kind of boundary went up between us, but it was softer and not as fierce as before.

He doffed his hat with his left hand and pointed the cap toward the Structo dugout. He smiled and bowed to me with his right palm upraised. I picked up my glove, turned, and ran back to my teammates. The other squad had already taken the field, and I was holding up the game. I sat down and looked back to the first base fence where the man had been standing. He was gone.

I turned to Jimmy Rice, sitting next to me.

"Did you see that old guy there by the fence next to first?"

"I didn't see anybody. I thought you were over there taking a pee."

The dugout cracked up.

I looked back over to first again. Strange. I'd just been talking to a man, a real ball player, and made a promise to him. I was sure of it.

"Hey, did anybody see that guy I was just talking to?"

The only answer was the pandemonium of headlocks, wedgies, and goofballing that was our typical dugout deportment. No one had been paying any attention. But surely Mom would have been watching me, worried that I was talking with a stranger. I called her down from the stands and asked her if she'd seen him. Again no. Between innings she'd been buying one of her greasy sacks of Pops-Rite corn and had seen nothing. Scanning the bleachers, I saw no one but the grab-bag of parents and siblings who were always at our games. He was just gone, as if he'd never really been.

I sat down on the bench. *So how would anyone know what I'd promised, or whether I was doing what I'd said I'd do? Who'd care anyway?* I could just forget about it, and there would be no consequences as far as I could see. It seemed pretty stupid—worrying about some silly promise. The grey-haired man wasn't even my real coach. My real coach was The Turk, sitting down at the end of the dugout flipping open his Zippo.

I watched Turk light up another one, then snap his lighter closed with a flick of his fat wrist. That man out of nowhere—the man with the sinewy arms and flashing eyes—what if *he* were our coach? Would we be on the bench laughing at farts, karate chopping each other, and not caring whether we won or lost? I had a feeling it would be a lot different. Everyone would either leave the team or start down a road that led to something—something like becoming real ball players. As it was, nothing would happen. Nothing. I could just coast along, finish the season, and that would be it.

I turned my eyes to the field and watched the ball as it made an elliptical arc around the pitcher's back and was released. The man had told me to watch baseballs as they flew around the field. I'd made a promise to do it. I glanced over at The Turk as he exhaled a blue cloud through his nostrils like an overweight dragon. He then picked a piece of tobacco off of his tongue. I turned my eyes back to the field as the ball dropped out of the catcher's mitt. And with that, I began my summer of watching.

3: Concentration Practice

Once committed to the 'yes,' all of the rest is just working out the details. Each step taken, by itself, is fairly simple and easy—it's the hesitation and doubt that makes it difficult. It's all quite easy if you are willing to drop yourself, your past, and your future, and simply do the next thing now.
  ...*The Field Book.*

THERE ON THE BENCH, I didn't have much else to do. Each game I'd come and watch the ball. I watched the ball as it left the hand of the pitcher, and followed its line into the catcher's glove. I watched The Turk mindlessly rub a ball in his hands like he wanted to erase the lacings. I watched the foul grounders come toward the dugout, making little craters as they hopped, and watched the little rooster tail of dirt behind them as they rolled to a stop. It didn't take more than a few innings to realize what a bit of heavy lifting I'd taken on. Despite my desire to create something more interesting, at bottom there was absolutely nothing more to watching the ball than watching a ball. Nothing.

Of course it's not so hard to watch the ball *some* of the time. I could do that without much problem, then go back to drawing pictures in the dirt of the dugout floor. But to watch the ball *all of the time, no matter what*, like the man told me to do: *that* was a whole different thing.

To *never* take your eye off the ball was hard. It was boring. Just watching, and *only* watching the flight of *every* pitch and throwback.

Exactly following the path of every hit and never looking at the runner—never going to the bathroom, or turning to talk. If I watched the ball properly, I couldn't do anything else. What's more, I was failing at this one simple thing.

As hard as I tried, I couldn't watch for more than three minutes at a stretch. I started to itch. A rogue bee buzzed my head. I had to pee. The sun was in my eyes. I started to use the word 'damn' just like the man on the sideline. I must have taken my eyes off the damn ball six hundred times.

Watching got so hard that the very fact that it *was* so hard began to make it interesting. *Some unseen force is trying to stop me from looking at the ball and keeping my promise*, I thought. I was sure of it. So I started to play a game that I made up. After I'd reached a point when I was sure I couldn't last another second, I'd count five more breaths and keep watching. Sometimes I would look away right after the fifth exhale. But at other times I would break through and be able to watch for many minutes more. My body could watch forever—the problem was in my mind. I was in a hardball staring contest with myself as both winner and loser. I watched from the dugout, and watched from right field when I got a chance to play. Then slowly, like a growing thing, something started to happen.

I started to see the ball.

Instead of a boring white thing being thrown and hit around, the ball became a pattern of color. When the ball was hit hard from underneath, the red stitching spun backwards, turning the ball the slightest shade of pink in flight. The thrown ball was a tight red spiral changing depth and size in the air as the ball came in or away. I saw for the first time that the ball moved through different arcs even before it left the thrower's hand. From the travel of those arcs, I could begin to tell *before* the ball was released whether the throw would be high, low, or off to the side.

During warm-ups, I stopped thinking about catching the ball and let myself watch the stitches rotate toward me. If I concentrated, I could watch those stitches all the way into my glove. There would be a ball just sitting there in the pocket, caught. Yes. Caught.

I began catching more of what was thrown at me, even the hard grounders bouncing right in front. Hard grounders had terrified me since the time in practice when a hard-hit ball bounced wild into my face just below my left eye. Jimmie Roberts had been hit in the nuts by a hard one-hopper while playing shortstop in our first game. He lay there in the dirt, trying not to put his hands down there in front of everybody. After the inning, he sat on the bench next to me throwing up with his white face down between his knees.

Since spring, Jason Lott, our big second baseman, had thrown balls right at my feet just to see me close my eyes and jump away. But now Jason's mean throw was a reddish-white comet a foot and a half long, making a fascinating impact crater right in front of me. If I put my face *forward* to watch it better, right into the danger zone, my glove automatically came up at the perfect instant to grab the ball. If I could see the ball, I was protected by reflexes I didn't know I had! I fielded four in a row that Jase threw at me, catching three, and knocking the other one down in front of me. He then gave up on the one-hop game and started throwing bullets as hard as he could. I caught those too, except the wild one he tossed twelve feet over my head.

During a game against the Kiwanis squad, I fielded a line drive cleanly on the first hop, and got the ball almost back to second. The next game, a fly ball was hit hard to me. My legs jumped at the crack of the bat. I saw it coming out with a little under-spin on it. *I can see it. It's getting bigger. But ...* Damn. I was running up again. I made my highest and most spastic leap yet, but watched the ball sail three inches over the top of my glove. It ended up in the seed-heads by the fence like all of the rest. An easy out turned into a stand-up triple. Turk said nothing to me when I came in, but it was clear that for the rest of the season I was getting nothing more than my allotted innings in the outfield, and one at-bat per game. I didn't care. Sitting on the bench gave me more time to watch the ball.

August seventeenth arrived, and with it the last game of the regular season. We hadn't won a single game all summer, so there was no chance that we'd be involved in the playoffs over the Labor Day weekend. Four of our thirteen players were gone, three on vacation, with Ricky Edwards out due to injury from a treble hook he'd put into the palm of his hand while fishing up in Wisconsin. With only nine players, The Turk *had* to put me in. And not just for two and a half innings. The whole game. I stood out in right field with my knees flexed as we played Symco Battery, giving a little pepper, yelling "hey batta-batta," ready to field. I watched the ball and waited. There was no action in right field all game.

Yet at the start of the final inning, our depleted Structo squad found itself in a most unusual position. We were ahead with a one-run lead. I'm proud to say that the score was made by yours truly. At the top of the third I'd come to bat with no one on base, and watched the spirals of a slow curve ball come right into the sweet spot of my twenty-eight inch Louisville Slugger. No vibration. Just a cracking sound so sweet and satisfying and beautiful—the ball springing away and sailing just left and over the second baseman's head for a clean single. Even The Turk waddled up off the empty bench and clapped with the two fingers that weren't holding his Camel. After a walk, a dying quail hit to right, and an overthrow, I arrived. A little leap left the dusty impression of my sneaker right in the center of home plate, a place no sneaker of mine had ever been before.

IN THE BOTTOM of the ninth—the final inning of the season—I was still in right field defending our one-run lead. The inning went pretty well for us, with the first two batters going down one-two. But now, at the final out, the string unraveled for our pitcher Teddy "Mac" McElvay. He hit the wall at what must have been his hundred and twenty-eighth pitch, and his arm turned to rubber. He bounced a few weak pitches in front of the plate, and then threw a couple at the umpire's head. Two batters in a row took a walk. Turk was too much of an idiot to bring Jason in from second base to throw his bullets and give Mac the break he deserved. Yet wild Jase could have been his own disaster. He could easily have hit three batters in a row, or thrown it over the backstop to lose the game for us in the end.

And so with two on and two out, Bobby Roberts came to bat. Bobby was a good kid. He lived a couple of blocks north of our house, and came down on winter weekends to play Legos with me in the basement. A quiet kid. Big. A ten year old going on fifteen, already weighing about one-fifty, with peach fuzz and a need for deodorant. He didn't mind hanging out with me. He was above the crowd. The best cleanup batter in the league. He could do whatever he wanted.

I knew what was going to happen before Mac released the first pitch. I watched the arc of the ball traveling in his hand as it came around behind him to be released high as Mac fell forward, trying to force it over the plate. A weak, fat fastball with no spin at all high up in the strike zone. It would've been a changeup had Mac established a real fastball first, but that hadn't happened. Bobby started to swing but then hitched back, waiting for it to come. A late swing would launch it toward the weak spot in the defense and the closest outfield fence. That was right field, and me.

I was moving before the sound reached me. I could see Bobby's open stance and the ball hanging on the fat of the bat, like it was being slung forward instead of hit. It cleared the infield, rising hot, a three-foot streak picked up by the weak lights of the Rec. League field. A little over-spin as it turned in the air over to my right, getting bigger. I could pick out the slow rotation of a red string that had been jarred loose. There was nothing in my mind but quiet.

I barely felt the old snow fence as I hit it, going clean through the faded slats, stumbling just a little but not enough to break my watch on the ball. I saw it fall, now big as a grapefruit, and heard the soft sizzling sound of a ball slicing the air not five feet away. Left foot down ... one full stride ... then the glove reaching—a four-inch leather pocket traveling gently through space at a dead run five feet off the ground towards a meeting place: the only place in the universe, at the only instant in time, where the small pocket and the falling ball could ever come together. I slowed down and looked at the ball nestled in my glove, realizing for the first time that a baseball had beautiful, tiny, cell-like patterns on its leather surface.

THE SILENCE was broken by a full, happy sound from the infield rising toward me on the night air. I could hear Mom cheering, and the boom and bellow of The Turk, our coach and mentor, his fat, powerful fingers wrapped into chain link; ramming and rattling the dugout fence like a gorilla in a cage. "Fuckin-A! Fuckin-A, did you see that? Fuckin-A!"

I was too much aglow, in love with everything, with the deep evening wrapped around me and the game ball in my glove, to care much when the plate umpire ruled the hit a home run. His contention was that the ball had cleared the park, and could not have been reached by me but for a construction defect in the playing field.

Had an archangel appeared bodily with a flaming sword, Structo could have found no better advocate and defender than now materialized in the unlikely body of The Turk. All that he was, all that he had, and all that he might become was committed at that moment to me and to the cause of preserving Structo Fabricating's only win of the season. He'd finally found something honorable to fight for.

The fracas found its epicenter in front of home plate, pulling everyone out of the stands. I could not have cared less. The win didn't matter. Bobby and I smiled across the diamond at each other. We both knew just how well he'd hit that ball—and that just this once, this one time in my life, I'd caught it better. That was enough. I slipped away with the ball in my glove and jumped over the third base fence to be alone and look up at the stars.

I WAS LEAPING a little—running easily—the great moment already being re-remembered and magnified when a shadow moved in front of me out of the deeper shadow of a blue spruce that stood in the lawn next to the diamond. I tried to pull up, but ran right into a hard belly with my forehead. It was him. The man in the ball cap.

We were beyond the arc of the Rec. League lights, but his eyes were alive as if lit from inside.

I stood there with my heart racing, feeling a strange kind of fear with joy all mixed into it. Something was about to happen.

He smiled at me. "It seems that you've done well, my little brother—a good bit better than some of the others who at first seemed to have greater potential. I knew you had a chance when I saw the light around you there in right field."

"You saw a light around me?"

"I did indeed."

I just stood there, not knowing what to say, and wondering who the "others" might be.

He pointed toward the field. "Just look at all of those folks arguing about a silly game, and not one of them even remotely curious about the only thing here of real interest."

"What's that?" I asked.

"How you came to catch that ball, of course!"

I turned my head for an instant to watch The Turk flail his arms like a giant and flightless blue bird in the infield.

I turned my head back, and the man was forty feet away, with one hand slung casually over his head and the other in his pocket. I'd been looking away for no more than four or five seconds. Nobody could cover that distance that fast without making a sound.

"How did you do that?" I demanded.

"Why don't you pitch me the ball," he said.

I took the game ball out of my glove and threw it to him. Even though it was nearly dark, he caught it deftly with one hand and slung it back to me. I watched it glimmer into my glove, and he motioned for me to throw it again. We started to play catch. Each time he would throw it a little harder, and I would throw back just as hard.

"I came back to ask you something," he said, taking a short wind up.

"What's that?" I asked, huffing from effort.

"I was wondering if someday you might be interested in doing some real training, something a bit more intense and interesting than just watching baseballs."

"You mean like becoming a pro player?" I asked, getting excited.

He chuckled. "Your future does not lie in baseball, my little brother. One catch hardly qualifies you for the big leagues, and your real talents lie elsewhere. I had something a bit different in mind."

"Like what?"

"I can't tell you."

"Well why not?" I asked indignantly.

"It's because I have to *show* you, or rather set up the conditions where you might be shown. I can offer no guarantees. It's not up to me in the end. But I *can* say that some powerful men and women—people who could have anything on this earth—have considered the chance that I am offering to be the one thing, the only thing, of any real value in this world."

He snagged another ball effortlessly with his open hand. I was throwing really hard now.

"So what did it feel like to catch that ball—how'd it happen?" he asked.

"I don't know. It just happened. I opened my glove and there it was."

"Yes, of course. You have that now. Like the first little trickle of water beginning to mark a channel in the desert, something that might become as vast and beautiful as the Grand Canyon in the end. A good start, but only that."

Something about that comment made me throw the ball as hard as I could right at the man's head. He stepped to the side and caught it like it was a feather. He walked up to me, signaling that our game was over.

"So Charlie, I've got to go now."

"How is it that you know my name?"

"I know a lot about you, Charlie. More right now than you know about yourself."

"Who are you anyway? I don't even know who you are!"

"Well hmmm ..." He sat there for a minute with his head cocked, scratching the back of his head. "Who *I* am ... will be determined entirely by who *you* are, Charlie. Whether I like it or not, your mind will turn me into whoever you need me to be. I'm here to serve you, and that's it. I'll become the person you need; the person that gives you permission to take the next step. I'm here to help you remember what your soul has already decided."

"You mean something like taking the training?"

"Well, that would be a big next step, if you want to take it on. It's really up to you. The choice is always up to you."

"I still don't know who you are! And what's this training going to be like anyway?"

He looked at me quizzically. "Well ... I think for you, kid, it might very well be a wilderness training—the wild is a place that holds great concentrations of power. It's a good place for friends like us. Yes, I think so … definitely," he said, as if settling something in his mind that he'd been debating. "The deep wilderness for you Charlie. A journey across water. *She'd* like that. I'll lead you out into the wilderness someday Charlie, if you want to come. Up north, I think. You can meet her there."

"So what are you saying … are you going to be like Moses leading me into the wilderness?" I asked, remembering a lesson from last week's Sunday school.

"Not bad. That's closer to being right than you might think," he said. "Very good. You've decided who I need to be for you."

"But I don't even know your name!"

"We'll since you've come up with it, you can call me 'Moses' if it suits you." he said laughing. "Yes, 'Moses' it is. That's alright isn't it?"

I hardly knew what to say. And who was *she* anyway?

"So I'll call for you when the time is right—when you're ready for the next step—OK?"

"When will that be?"

"This sort of thing doesn't happen on a schedule Charlie. It will be just the right time, when you've developed enough. An inconvenient time. Some time when you have something to do with your life that seems much better, and therefore the opportunity to make a choice."

"How will I know it's you?"

Moses laughed, rolling his eyes and waving the baseball in the air.

"Perhaps the gentleman will require a written invitation …" he said mockingly, making an exaggerated bow. "Yes of course, an invitation! Look for it—a formal invitation in the mail—it's already coming to you!"

He stepped back, and fired the ball into the evening air with a powerful snap of his arm. The ball went up like it was leaving the planet. In a matter of seconds it became less than a pinpoint in the night sky, tiny but illuminated, like it had joined the stars. The ball hung in the air, floating around. Then it started to grow bigger. It was coming down, right toward me, faster than any ball ever thrown.

The voice of Moses was already faint, shouting at me from a quarter of a mile away. "Watch the ball … watch the ball, Charlie! Right here! Right now!"

I stood underneath the rocketing ball, wobbling with my mitt up, not knowing whether to attempt a catch, or turn and run like hell. I had the oddest feeling that running wouldn't help—that the ball would follow me wherever I ran. It was coming, coming down, and there was not a damn thing I could do about it.

4: The Invitation

In every one of us there's a voice that tells us we are destined for some great thing. It can begin with just a whisper, an impulse to evolve. A journey into the fullest possibilities of being human might begin this way.
...*The Field Book*.

Springtime in Chicago, sixteen years later.
THE SLOT in the door of my refurbished Chicago brownstone needed oiling, and screeched open as the mailman struggled to jam a fat bundle through it. Today's delivery landed with a thud on the new forest-green flooring created to mimic real Italian marble. A half-dozen glossy home décor catalogues scattered on the floor, along with a couple of bills and invitations from credit card companies. A rectangular package separated itself from the rest of the mail and skidded across the floor to rest against the buffed edge of my loafer. It looked out of place without a label or tape, wrapped in brown paper and tied with twine the old fashioned way.

"Anything interesting in the mail?" she asked as she leaned forward into the mirror, her eye almost touching the glass as she extended her eyelashes with a small mascara wand.

"Not really" I replied, picking up the brown parcel. "Just some catalogues and stuff."

"You wouldn't mind if I grabbed a couple of your *Architectural Digests* to flip through on my way to the airport, would you?" she asked.

"I'm planning to get my own place next year, and just can't wait to start decorating."

"No problem."

The parcel was heavy for its size; solid. I turned it over. The right hand corner was covered with Canadian stamps. The name 'Charlie Smithson' was written in a small, careful hand. There was no return address—just two carefully drawn circles overlapping one another, with the constellation Ursa Major, the great bear, drawn within and pointing to Polaris, the northern star. My fingertips tingled as my hand moved across the parcel. *Could this be from him?*

The woman put down the mascara and pulled out a glossy lipstick, which she began to apply to her open lips in a series of slow accurate strokes. I watched her through the open door of my bedroom, forgetting for a moment what I held in my hand. My head was pounding from too many Mojitos last night, and I was having the hardest time remembering her name. She was one of the first-year law students from out of town for a round of interviews at the firm—I was pretty sure about that. Right now she was leaning into the mirror dressed in black heels with no stockings and a strapless black 'Miracle Bra' that pushed her breasts up high and together. *You shouldn't have done this—especially on a Wednesday night, Charlie,* I thought. *You were supposed to be interviewing her.*

I pulled lightly on one of the strings of the parcel, then stopped for fear of what the package might contain. *It's been nearly sixteen years.* I couldn't remember the features of his face, although I could still remember the energy around him: it's fierceness on the outside and gentleness once inside his field.

"You said that you could take me to the airport this morning," she said.

I looked down at my watch. It read 9:15. My disciplined personal schedule required that I be in the library at 10:00 sharp—no later. Finals were over, and everyone else was just relaxing for a week in preparation for graduation. But Professor Wills had asked me for my analysis of a new Supreme Court precedent, and I was planning to do that today. I spent almost every free day in the library, whether I had an assignment due or not.

"Just where are you from again?" I asked.

She snapped the lipstick wand into its holder, and rolled her eyes to look at me in the mirror with a single upraised brow.

"I'm from New York, Charlie, which you've obviously forgotten, and in case you're worried, I'm not going to take the job you offered me when you were drunk last night. I had a better offer in San Francisco before I even got here. I'm just out here for dinner, cocktails, and sex courtesy of the Thompson Group, it seems," she said, rolling her wrist upward toward the ceiling. "You don't even remember my name, do you?"

I looked down at the floor.

"You don't mind if I call you a cab? I forgot that I had an appointment this morning. I'd be happy to pay for your trip to the airport."

"No problem," she said, turning to the bedroom to gather up the rest of her things. "Someday when you're President, I can say that I screwed you then decided to take a better offer. And by the way, my name is Heather."

Maybe I could be President, I thought, rolling the idea around in my mind as I dialed up the cab. After all, I was number one at Northwestern Law School and would be reporting to work at the Thompson Group in less than a month. *That's a pretty good place to start*, I thought.

"It'll be here in five minutes," I said, putting down the phone.

Thompson had promised a window office on the sixty-fourth floor of the Hancock Tower with a beautiful view of the lake, a six-figure starting salary, and a personal secretary. I'd just signed an impossibly expensive rental agreement on this North Shore townhome based on my anticipated earning power, and the maître d' at the Signature Room on the 95th floor of the Hancock already knew my name. *Why couldn't I be President?*

Heather shimmied into a little black dress, sleeveless with padded shoulders, and finished her ritual with the placement of some long dangly earrings. She would cross and uncross her shaved legs dozens of times today inside that form-fitting black tube, each re-arrangement an opportunity to enjoy the subtle shift in energy that her legs in those heels could produce in any room.

"Can you zip me?"

"Sure."

She turned her back to me, pulling her hair to the side. I flipped the parcel onto the couch and reached down to touch the zipper at the base of her spine.

You've done this too many times before, Charlie. You know how empty you always feel when they walk out the door.

I zipped Heather into her dress. She extended her chin to offer me her cheek. She had insufficient reason to kiss me directly and risk messing up her lips this early in the morning.

"Bye then," she said, picking up her bag and walking toward the door.

She turned once to look over her shoulder, offering me her neck for just an instant.

"See you in the White House."

"See you then," I replied.

I heard Heather's heels mince down the front steps of the brownstone, the door of the taxi closing behind her, and the sound of the car pulling away. I stood for a long time, listening. Now there was only the sound of the morning traffic on the street outside, broken by muffled snippets of conversation from the sidewalk.

I looked around for a moment at the confines of my luxury residence. I'd chosen this home in part because of its hardwood floors and tile that could be spotlessly maintained to a high gloss. My sparse modernist furniture was hard, with clean aesthetic lines. A dozen well-sharpened yellow number two pencils were in their round holder next to the phone, tips up. A small collection of loafers and Johnston and Murphy wing tips were in my closet, with a cedar shoe tree in each shoe to maintain the original shape. I had three high quality suits in the closet along with about nine other outfits, each on a plastic hanger spaced evenly apart. I felt that this was the best way to do things, and I expected nothing but the best from both myself and from others around me.

I reached down and picked up the parcel. It was the first thing not mass-processed that had come through my mail slot since I'd moved in. I weighed the parcel in my hand.

I have Moses to thank for all of this, I thought. *Without him, none of this would have happened.*

It all started a few weeks after my big catch, when school began, and I showed up for the first day of class in fifth grade. When Mrs. McIntosh passed out the first assignments, I looked down at my papers. I looked at those papers for a long time and concentrated. I looked deeper at the combination of letters, and felt a cone of silence come down and wrap around me. I was safe inside the cone.

Then, as if it were happening of its own accord, the edges of the papers began to glow with the slightest yellow and blue color. And just like that, I could see almost all of the answers written there on the page before I even put a pencil down to write them.

It all was so was simple: up in front of the class Mrs. McIntosh was using the greenboard and her chalk to throw a ball to me. She was pitching slow and easy. I could see that it was all a game. Each classroom day was a small window through which information was coming. The teacher would open a window and hand information through it. I would catch the information, polish it, and hand the information back through my own little clear window—my homework papers and the weekly test. It was easy. I really didn't have to think all that much. I could just focus my attention, feel the cone come down, and enter into a quiet, ordered world where the straightness of my lines, the neatness of my paper, and the rightness of my answer mattered to someone.

Over the years, many windows passed between me and the teachers. I didn't know where it was all going, but I just went with the flow. Despite much talk about challenge and independent thinking for 'gifted' students like me, what most teachers in Prosperville wanted was to hear their own words repeated back to them as truth. They never got tired of it. Adopting the teacher's perspective meant that I was smart; it meant I was good.

I began to receive papers back that had the number 100 written in red on the upper left corner. Next to that number were comments like

"Good job!" and little smiley faces. Report cards came back to Mom with glowing columns of A's. Gradually it began to mount up: hundreds of polished windows, thousands. Each window building on the next; each slightly more complex. It was a game of pitch and catch that required concentration, focus, and a willingness to repeat just what I'd been told.

In the beginning of this new game, I thought about Moses a lot, and thanked him every day for my new powers. He'd done something when he'd touched me on the forehead—some part of him had passed into me that caused good things to happen. But gradually, I came to think about him less and less. After all, *I* was doing all the work. I was the one who was gifted. Sometime around junior year in high school, I stopped thinking about him altogether. About that same time, I'd come to believe that all my talents were self-created.

I became 'the smartest kid in Prosperville.' At least that's what the man at the Rotary Club said when he presented me with a five-hundred dollar scholarship my senior year. A full ride to Illinois State University came next.

At State, it was four years of A's, except for that creative writing class with the long-haired teacher. He sat there with his feet up on the desk, asking us to get in touch with our "muse" and create something original that had "emotional depth and complexity." I was lost. In a panic, I went outside the class and found a book entitled *The Elements of Mystery Writing*. There was a formula to follow, and I turned in a mystery story of one hundred and twenty-eight pages. The story was "trite" "formulaic" and "clichéd," according to the long-hair. But my story was also complete, neat, turned in on time, and not plagiarized. I got a 'B+'—the only one in my college career. I still graduated summa cum laude.

I received another scholarship to Northwestern Law School in Chicago. Nothing there was that much different, except at Northwestern, all the seats were filled with other smart kids like me. It turned out that "thinking like a lawyer" was a lot like "thinking like the instructor." The windows had to be even clearer, with information returned back exactly as spoken from above, in exactly the same verbal sequence. It took longer to learn everything, and I devoted every moment—sixteen, seventeen hours a day—to the lines of words passing through the windows. It became my whole life. But I was good at it. Better, in fact, than everyone.

I broke things down into their easy parts, and mastered them one by one. The throw might look complicated, but if I broke it down into pieces—a bunch of easy throws—I could handle just about anything. The "complicated fact patterns" on the exams were nothing but facts from five or six cases put together in a single scenario. My answer was five or six polished windows passed back to the instructor; just what she had said when those cases were being discussed in class. I should know what was said; I could just close my eyes, let the cone come down, and then open my eyes. The first few words of the lecture were already there on my paper. All I had to do was point my pen and follow the lines. And now, the rewards were really starting to arrive.

I PULLED THE STRING on the parcel, but it would not come loose. I flipped it over and examined the binding. The string was tied in the back with a perfect square knot, and the loose ends were not loose but neatly lashed with smaller string and secured by knots that I recognized from my Boy Scout days as clove hitches. Someone had tied the package like they were securing it against a high wind. I took a butcher knife out of the drawer, cut the string away, and unwrapped the heavy paper.

Inside was a clear waterproof map-case—a clear folder of heavy plastic that was rolled closed and sealed with a Velcro strip—the kind of carryall that whitewater river guides use to keep valuable things dry. I opened the case and began to remove the contents. The first thing out was a ragged and water-spotted map. The map was deeply creased, and worn so thin in places that there was nothing but holes where some information once had been. I gingerly held it up. In the topmost margin there was a hand-made drawing of the constellation Ursa Major, known by most everyone as the Big Dipper. The Dipper was pouring its contents toward another smaller star next to which was the careful notation: "Polaris, the North Star, Constant Friend and Guide."

This was a topographical map of a vast wilderness area without roads, bridges, towns, or buildings. A maze of blue and brown lines representing streams and hills snaked around spills of blue that ranged from the size of a freckle up to an area as big as my hand. These were lakes. In places, comments were written in ink: "Good trout," "night wind campsite," "not this way." The largest comment, marked in thick black ink with a different pen, was an arrow drawn to a thin lake shaped like a ribbon, with one large word: "Here." There was no road leading to the place, only a dotted black line indicating a gravel road—Highway 67—which ended abruptly about ten miles from the ribbon-shaped lake. I would have to walk overland and paddle across several other lakes to get where the map was directing me to go.

I put the map on the coffee table and again reached into the pouch. My hand came to rest on a compass, a water-filled navigation tool with a scratched surface. It was in about the same condition as the map; they obviously had been used together over an extended period. I held the device in the palm of my hand, and watched the red end of the needle slowly come around and settle in one direction: north. *This map and compass are navigation tools for a guide,* I thought. This outfit had been used and re-used by someone who'd actually been to the places on the map and made careful hand-written notations for the benefit of the next user. This was not a second-hand map; it was first-hand knowledge. I instantly sensed that I could bet my life on the cryptic statements scratched onto its surface. They could be relied on as fact.

There was more. I shook the pouch, and out fell the final object. It was a small book with a worn, soft leather cover, slick and smudged in places from hands that had held it in the out-of-doors. It was a book of thick rag pages filled with words and images. Three faded words were tooled into the leather cover.

I fanned the soft pages. The book smelled of the thin soil of the forest floor, of sweat and spring air. A pressed white flower in the form of a star within a star fell out of the book onto the tile. The book was filled with other pressings and objects: aspen leaves with twirling stems, a small sprig of white pine still seasoned and resinous, flattened leaves of wild spearmint. The pressings had been waiting inside the book; waiting to release their breath. Their fragrance now rose from the pages. I closed my eyes and imagined a place where one could smell the pine and spearmint just by walking over the ground—where the footpaths released the scent as they warmed at midday. A feather from a great owl, with its quiet edges, drifted out of the book and onto the floor between my feet.

I gathered the fragile pressings, and set them gently on the end-table next to me. I held the book in both hands, feeling the softness of the cover. I opened the book to the first page.

Inserted there was a piece of birch bark, upon which was drawn an overly-elaborate crest—a knight's helmet with feathers coming out of the top and vines trailing down to form a border around the page. In the center of the page were written these words in calligraphic script:

—A FORMAL INVITATION—

To Awakening
To Adventure
To the End of His Way of Life

Issued personally to:

Charlie Smithson

From The Committee
-&-
Moses, Servant and Messenger

At the bottom of the bark-paper, in less formal writing, were these words:

"Gear up for a wilderness canoe trip. We're going deep, if you're up for it. Bring only what is essential. You are the first essential. All else is secondary. Come now."

IT WAS HIM. My body began to remember the moment those years ago when I'd caught the ball. The sense of being outside of time, the total quiet, the magical result, and the peace that followed; not caring if we won or lost—the simple joy of focus on the ball, and afterwards the voice of the man in the ball cap, stepping out from the shadow of the spruce tree: "Perhaps the gentleman will require a written invitation ... yes of course, an invitation! Look for it—a formal invitation in the mail—it's already coming to you!" Yes. "It will be just the right time," he'd said; an inconvenient time.

I stood in the brownstone in stunned silence. The invitation had at last arrived.

5: From Another Reality

The Committee has a rule about the path. According to this rule you must be given a real choice. You must decide. The door to the path is always open, but the will to walk through it—the will—so fragile, so precious, so fleeting.
...*The Field Book.*

I LAY DOWN on the couch, with one hand on my head and another on my belly and closed my eyes. I could feel myself running in slow motion through the snow fence, my legs moving on their own through the summer night wind, one step, then another. I could remember the love, the overwhelming love, when I'd first stepped into the presence of Moses.

It had been a long time since I'd felt those feelings. The part of me that could feel the deep peace had gone underground, into shadow, and no longer had a life in the day-lit world. *That was the best part of me*, I thought, *the open-hearted part that wanted to play a hit and catch game that took me outside the fence.*

The part of me that could feel the deep peace had been long submerged by another world that did not have the right mix of air for it to breathe. With my hand feeling the breath rise and fall in my belly, I began to drift. I'd been thinking so hard now for such a long time. I'd forgotten what it was like to feel.

"—*If you let yourself feel, Charlie, what do you feel?*"

"I feel like I've driven to the wrong house, crossed its threshold and started to eat a long dinner with a family I don't know. All of the scenes in this house are strange and confusing. Every molecule in my body is exhausted to tell you the truth. I'm over-focused. I've become nothing but a concentrated mind working in a windowless room, waiting for the next instruction—a kind of machine that has no soul inside. My life has become a process of learning more and more about less and less. There has to be something more."

"—*Yes. Tell me.*"

"There's a part of me that's become uneasy, glancing at the side door, looking for a way to escape. My brain's been clogged by data and images, of polished rooms and polished people, that have me in a trance. I'm living someone else's life. I've been wishing for something else, but I'm afraid to find out what it might be."

"—*That's right. You've mastered a practice technique, Charlie, but forgotten the purpose of the game—the reason why you practice. You've lost the ability to feel the path. You have to do something about it, Charlie. You have to do something or the best part of you will. . . .*"

I sat up, snapped the Field Book closed, and put it back on the new coffee table. Just now there'd been a woman speaking quietly to me inside my head. I'd been talking with her like she was here in the room with me. *It's that crazy book that's putting weird thoughts in my head.* That book is dangerous. It's better to keep that book closed.

I went to the kitchen and made myself a cup of strong coffee, and sat back down on the couch to scan the business section of the *Tribune*.

Why should I listen to some woman in my head? I thought, perusing an article about North Shore condominium sales. After all, I was set. In just two weeks, I'd graduate. Everyone would be there. Even though she was too sick to make the trip to Chicago, Mom would be there in spirit—so proud of me and what I'd accomplished. I would walk across the stage as the Alpha student, number one in the class, move my tassel, reach for my diploma and handshake, and bask in the reward and applause.

All of the top kids like me already had their jobs lined up and were heading to important judicial clerkships and positions with the major firms. We were starting to work; now that real money was to be had. It was time to enter the 'real world': to begin the intense and detailed task of ingestion and production of great stacks of paper; to fall asleep on top of books of case precedent in the office at two a.m.; to pay the weighty tolls on the long road leading to the mantle of partnership. But in time, the best of us would succeed. We would come to own powerful personas capable of entering some domain and dominating it. We would become substantial. We would have 'names'.

And then, there was the book in front of me.

The compass needle was on the coffee table on top of the old map, pointing north—a direction so clear and simple that there could hardly be any answer except a 'yes' or a 'no.'

"*—The first step will destroy all other possibilities,*" I heard the quiet voice say.

That's strange. Why would I think that?

I took up the book and jammed it in my back pocket. I walked out of the brownstone into the early spring air, and headed to the library to finish my research for Professor Wills.

USUALLY the confinement in my favorite cubicle on the third floor at the back of the library was enough to create the concentration necessary to attack a deep stack of legal reasoning. The cubicle offered three close, quiet walls surrounded by many tons of hardbound books. The library was empty and almost clear of the smell of fear and caffeine that always accompanied the week of testing at semester's end. It should have been a good time to work, but the Field Book was uncomfortable in my back pocket, and I'd made the mistake of pulling it out and putting it on the shelf of the cubicle. My hand kept creeping up to touch it.

The book felt old. It was written entirely by hand, and from the variations in penmanship I guessed that there might have been as many as a half-dozen contributors. *This has been passed hand to hand,* I thought. *Some group has worked together to create this.* There were blank pages in the back.

The Field Book had sections with headings that made little sense to me, like "Deconstruction," "The Movement of Energy," and "Enlightenment." The pages were smudged with fingerprints at the edges where they had been handled in smoke and firelight. *There's effort behind this; intention.* It was clearly an old manuscript. *It feels like a sacred book*, I thought. *This could be the only copy.*

Everything was quiet. Turning the pages, I stopped at random to read some of the entries:

> The Field promises nothing except itself, which is sometimes called the Truth.

And then:

> ...contact with a limitless, penetrating love, a radiant, endless field of love, connecting everything. In that moment, we see that we are actually *within* this vast and beautiful living thing, not at all separate as it seems....

This is one of those old manuscripts like they uncover out in the desert, I thought. But ... no. This was different. Some of the entries looked quite recent. *This book is still being written.* It has energy that I can feel when I run my fingers across the cover. This isn't old and dead. *It's alive.*

I closed the book and put it back on its little cubicle shelf. "This is getting ridiculous, Charlie," I said aloud. Some strange guy turned up at your little league game when you were a kid. You happened to make one good catch. It could have happened to anybody. To turn your life around right now and follow some stupid arrow to a spot on a moldy map is laughable. Think about the years of hard work you've put in already. You're finally set. *Don't blow it.*

I sat staring at the Wills research all day and into the evening. For some reason, the cone of concentration did not descend as it always had before. There was no glow around the pages. I sat there until almost midnight and accomplished exactly nothing. As the library was closing, I put the Field Book in my hip pocket and walked toward the door. The thought of Moses and his invitation sent chills up my spine. How in the hell did he know where I was anyway? Somebody calling himself 'Moses' was probably a freaky stalker, playing some kind of sick joke to ruin my life. *I should call the police and have the package fingerprinted.* I walked past the night clerk, through the turnstile and into the night.

The Brownstone was within walking distance, and the streets were well lit. Even late at night, nothing had ever happened on my walk home before.

THE STREETS WERE EMPTY. A few folks like me who had worked too late scurried by the occasional couple staggering home with arms draped around each other. My route down East Chicago Avenue and up Van Der Rohe Way took me past the Hancock Tower, rising a hundred floors high. The corner offices near the top were magnificent, with views stretching twenty miles over the lake.

On the street level, there were small plantings of trees with flower beds that lent some softness to the concrete cityscape. A gardener was working one of the beds with the cowl of a white sweatshirt obscuring his face. *Strange. It's awfully late to be gardening.*

There was something about the man that made me uncomfortable, and I almost crossed the street to avoid him. *But why? There's no reason not to walk home the way I want to,* I thought. I decided to take bigger, bolder strides and just get past him. I looked down as I hurried past, and saw what he had in his hand. *He's working the ground with a sickle. That's not the tool for a flowerbed.*

I took an even larger step, and then I heard something fall with a slap on the concrete. The Field Book had worked its way out of my back pocket in response to my over-striding. I turned, and the book was lying on the sidewalk ten feet behind me. The man in the white cowl had stopped his digging. He'd turned away from the dirt and was crawling across the sidewalk on his knees. A black hand reached out toward the book lying on the concrete.

The bony hand appeared disembodied as it emerged from the white sweatshirt and came to rest on the top of the Field Book. *Just turn and leave it, Charlie,* I said to myself. *This is how things go wrong. That book is not worth your life.*

The man stood up slowly, his movements speaking of age and wear. He held the Field Book in his right hand and the curved tool in his left. I could see bare outlines of his muscled face in the shadow cast by the streetlight, but his features were still obscured by the white cowl. He extended the book, using his open hand like a platter. *He's going to cut me when I reach out to take it,* I thought.

The man stood there, unmoving, with ten feet separating us. A cab went rattling by, then another going the opposite direction. It was then quiet in the street. The man simply stood with the book outstretched, waiting. And then, a voice came from inside the hood.

"Perhaps the gentleman will require a written invitation to step forward and take what's his."

I was shocked by the words *written invitation* coming from the lips of the man. How did he know what was in the book?

"Who are you?" I demanded, ready to either run or start shouting for help.

"Who do you need me to be?" he asked.

I was in no mood for this conversation.

"Are you the one who sent this book to me? Have you been stalking me?"

With this question, the man reached up and pulled back his hood. The streetlamp cast a stark shadow across his face. His skin was deeply lined. Although the face was old, age was not the only tool that had cut its flesh. The face was *carved*. Deep lines had been scoured with a tool, perhaps the one that he held in his hand, with deep black ash from a plant or animal pushed into the intricate wounds. Spirals and vortexes swirled in patterns around his forehead and down his cheeks. His right eyelid was closed, but his left eye—fixed on me—was luminously clear, dark, and bright. There was no eye inside the lid that was closed.

"I am the one who is extending it to you now," the man said.

I stood there, not knowing what to do, transfixed by his face. It was a face that did not belong in a Chicago street. It was a face that did not belong in this century.

"What has been offered is something that must be claimed—must be chosen," the man said. "Even the promised land had to be taken by force in the end. If you will not claim your birthright now, then when will you claim it? If not here, then where? If this teaching is not for you, then for whom *is* it meant?"

"You're in league with him, aren't you? You're part of the group that wrote that book!"

The man took three steps towards me, and extended the book until it was just touching my chest.

"I believe you dropped something, sir," he said, pulling his cowl back up around his face, bowing slightly.

I snatched the book from his hand. The white, five-petaled flower that had been pressed inside flew out and fluttered down onto the street. I turned and ran toward Michigan Avenue. At the corner I glanced backward. The man was standing bareheaded in the light. His cutting tool was on the ground, and he was holding the white flower in his left palm. His right hand came up to the middle of his chest, palm outward, right at the level of his heart, making a sign. His five fingers were spread wide, trembling, and stretching toward me.

I rounded the corner and broke into a run.

THE STREET in front of my house was quiet when I got home. I looked left and right as I fumbled with the lock. No one was on the street. It was good to feel the big oak door close behind me; to hear the click of the deadbolt; the turning of the doorknob lock; and the slide of the chain.

I put the Field Book into the top drawer of my dresser along with the map and compass, slipped off my clothes, and took a long hot shower, letting the steam rise around me in an attempt to wash away the memories of the man in the street. No success. I felt like his face had been carved into the back of my brain. When I closed my eyes, his luminous eye was still upon me. *Who would scar their face into such designs?*

I got out and toweled off with one of the plush new color-coordinated towels that had come in a brown box a couple of weeks ago. I wrapped the towel around me and padded out into the bedroom. *Tomorrow I'll send the parcel back where it came from.* The problem was, I had no idea how to send something back to a place on a wilderness map marked 'Here.'

I walked quietly across the bedroom, and slowly pulled open the top drawer of the dresser. There was the book and the crinkled map. The compass gave off a slight glow, as if lit from the inside. *Probably some glow-in-the-dark camping thing,* I thought. And then as I watched, the floating needle started to move. It vibrated slightly and then swung off its direction. The needle came to rest pointing straight at me.

I jumped back with a start, and the towel dropped to the floor. I leaned forward, feeling a hot churning—an energy circling like a spiraling ball just below my navel. The compass was connecting to the churning, and I could feel my lower belly quiver and move just as the compass was moving. And then we started to turn. The red needle began to swing to the right, and rotate slowly. My body was pulled into the turning. The face of the compass began to glow lighter and brighter until the room was filled with a soft white glow. The needle came to rest again for an instant, pointing at me, then around in a circle a second time, and then a third.

With each slow rotation, my body became lighter and hotter, as if I were being opened. I was being pulled apart: a trapped energy was becoming free. Again the compass went around, with more pain and more opening. I clutched my belly, clawing at it. What was once solid flesh now felt as if it had turned into a liquid pool of energy that could move on its own.

My body began to fill with energy. A white-hot gel moved up my spine and into my head. It filled my skull and poured into each of my teeth. The energy then moved down my spine and into my organs and bones, and flowed down my arms and legs and into my hands and feet, lighting up my toes. I stood there growing lighter and hotter. The energy was taking me over.

There was a place at the base of my skull where all of the sensations were now being concentrated. Some power had taken over my breathing—there was a delicious sense of *being breathed.* My belly was rising and falling like an ocean, the molecules and cells filling up with joy, brimming and burning softly with light.

I staggered backward, falling onto my bed.

I lay there with my arms outstretched unable to move. My body was pulsating. I don't remember closing my eyes, but no one can dream with their eyes open—at least that's what I'd come to believe.

As the dream began, my bedroom and the brownstone were gone.

I was in a prison of long tunneled hallways. Each hallway was encased in hard, shiny tile on bottom, top, and sides, without doors or windows. The hallways were clean swept and well lit in artificial light, all on the same level and all completely empty. I was free to walk anywhere, but couldn't escape the long hallways, all of which were either dead ends or passages that led to more of the same. I wandered through the halls trying to find a way out. Not a sound could escape. Every sound and ray of light was contained and bounced back. I was perfectly safe. I could wander forever—forever 'free'—yet never outside the hallways.

I walked. There was nothing else to do. Finally a hallway opened to a low room containing other prisoners. Dark men were dressed in white prison suits with deep white cowls obscuring their faces. The dark men were being led upward through a door in the ceiling to another level of the prison. Their hands were bound behind them. *They're not escaping, just moving to a different level,* I thought. The new level may be better, but might be worse.

I tried to sneak into line and go up with them. I approached the line, trying to sneak into the back unnoticed. It was then that he turned his head. Slowly the cowl fell, revealing a lean face with one eye gone. The face was carved in intricate patterns—patterns that moved as his face moved. His eye was steady, looking at me. From under the white garment, his left hand appeared palm outward—a silent 'no.' The hand then moved and pointed down a hallway that I'd not yet traveled, one that led steeply down a curving path into the earth. Its end could not be seen. This was my way.

I took the curving path. The path led me deeper into the bowels of the prison, until I reached a great room at the bottommost level. It was the boiler room of the vast complex, with high ceilings and huge metal tanks filled with compressed steam. The air was filled with heat and a sense of quivering, explosive energy barely contained behind thick metal.

In the room stood a woman in flowing white whose face I'd not seen before. All around her was a feeling—a sense of ferocious intensity and great love mixed together.

I walked down a flight of stairs toward her. *This woman is master of the place—master of the prison. She has the keys.* As I descended toward her, two crossed badminton racquets appeared on the wall, arranged like a decoration for some athletic club. I took the racquets off the wall, and extended one, handle-first, toward the woman. I felt cocky and confident.

We stood apart. The woman was bemused and loose, ready to game with me at any level. I looked over into her eyes. They were intense blue eyes with light around the edges that grew deeper toward the center. I was drawn into her eyes, but could not hold her gaze. The eyes made me want to hide.

"I'll play you for my freedom," I said.

"I'll play you for your life," she replied.

A high net appeared and the game began.

I served a shuttle. The return stroke was swift. The woman leapt into the air, twisting and coiling, coming over the top of the net with her leading hand above and already behind me, her racquet cocked in the other. In one effortless flashing motion she let the racquet fall, smashing me to atoms.

There was no pain.

A CLEAN BREEZE now flowed around me, billowing my hair. I leaned back with arms stretched wide and looked into a limitless blue sky. The prison was far away on the horizon, a castle of low white stone fading into the distance. My liberator sat at the stern of our open wooden boat, comically using the racquet as a tiller. We were both filled with joy. Her beautiful eyes were smiling at me, and I could look into them now without fear, without hiding. I'd made it out. *I'm outside the walls forever.*

6: Resistance

No one wants a man who's never leapt forward; who clings to narrow gains; or spends his time longing for the past on his hands and knees, weeping over a bowl of dust.
   ...*The Field Book*.

THE PIERCING LIGHT of the midday sun was coming through the skylight in my bedroom when I opened my eyes. I'd never slept this late. I tried to move, but my limbs were pinned flat to the bed. With some effort, I was able to move the fingers of my hands and regain the feeling in my arms and legs. I sat up on the edge of the bed. *Holy shit*, I thought. *One step deeper into that dream, and I wouldn't have ever awakened again.* I'd never experienced a dream like that before. I was *awake* inside that dream. I could move and talk and make choices in the dream world just like I could in my ordinary world.

I walked on stilts over to the dresser. The map and compass were still in the drawer, but the Field Book was gone. *Strange.* I was sure that I'd put the book in the drawer when I got home. I staggered into the kitchen, using the walls for support, and made a carafe of dark Colombian coffee in a new French press—another accessory that had recently arrived in a box at the door. I began to scour the house for the book. I didn't have to look long. The Field Book was resting in the middle of the coffee table, perfectly aligned with the morning paper next to a small white envelope. The book was open. I picked it up and read this passage:

There is inside each of us a design for completeness, something that is whole. We have been implanted with this design since birth, and it rests in our soul as a seed. This seed contains a code, a packet of information about an *Imago Dei*, a unique image of the divine—one clear facet in the infinite diamond.

Your divine image is inside of you, working to change you, moving you. It wants to become visible; it wants to grow. Sometimes the seed will send a message— a call to do something that will carve you away from what you consider 'normal.' When you hear the call you must follow it, even though you don't know where you're going. Your divine image knows what it needs. It will lead you into situations— into an ecology of circumstances—that will begin to unfold your mystery, your way of bringing heaven to this earth. This is why you're here, why you've come.

Imago Dei, I thought. *That has a ring to it.*
I opened the envelope. Inside was the five-petaled flower that had fallen to the street the night before.

A SHOCK OF ADRENALINE went up my spine, down the outsides of my arms, and into my hands. I went to the door of the brownstone and flung it open. There was no one there. I slammed the door and pushed over the deadbolt, turning the bottom lock as well. *I've had enough of this,* I thought. Books that move under their own power; carved-faced men in the street; bodies that travel through a dream only to be smashed to atoms. Enough.

I took a big swill of coffee, went over to the telephone and dialed the police.

"Chicago nine-one-one operator number forty-nine. Where is your emergency?"

"Well ... I'm in my living room right now."

"And just where is your living room located sir?"

"I'm on East Elm, near the lake. It's a brownstone," I said.

"And what is the nature of your emergency?"

I paused, unable to formulate an answer to this simple question.

"Are you in physical danger, sir?"

"I don't know. I'm not sure. I might be."

"Is there someone in the room with you now, sir?"

"No."

"And just what is happening in your living room that's caused you to call nine-one-one this morning?"

"There's an envelope with a flower in it on my coffee table that wasn't there last night."

There was a long silence on the other end of the line.

"I see, sir. If you can provide me with your name and the exact address, I'll send an officer around sometime this morning to speak with you."

"That would be great."

I gave her the information and hung up the phone.

I strode into the bedroom, stuffed the map and compass back into the waterproof pouch, and did the same with the Field Book and the little envelope containing the flower. I took the whole kit out the back door into the garage, threw the pouch into the trash can, slammed the lid, put a heavy box on top, and then piled on three more boxes until the trash can formed the base of a tottering pile. "Who asked for you anyway?" I shouted, and turned my back to the trash with my arms crossed, breathing hard in anger.

I went back into the living room, sat down on the sofa, and picked up the newspaper. There was an article there about geese migrations—how this time of year the birds were heading back north. The scientists were speculating about why the geese made a trip of over a thousand miles back into cold country, when they could just stay in the warm south and raise their chicks. The north was simpler, they said. Fewer dogs, skunks, and other predators to threaten the nests and the chicks, and thousands of rocky islands on the lakes where the geese could be alone. The north was a place to incubate eggs and to grow fragile things before they could take flight.

Admit it Charlie. For a couple of years you've been secretly asking for something to happen that would change everything; and now the possibility is presented.

At bottom I knew that the invitation from Moses would come someday—an invitation to a journey into the wilderness: something wild and risky. A life that might be filled with moments like the one in right field, moving without effort, running back, watching something fall perfectly into my glove at exactly midstride. I'd been secretly hoping for something that might carve me away from my tidy and predictable life—a life where I got just what I planned to get and nothing more. *I should be careful what I ask for*, I thought, *especially when I am asking from the heart, when I'm all alone. Someone might be listening.*

THE DOORBELL RANG. I unlocked the bolts and was greeted by an officer.

"Are you Mr. Smithson?"

"Yes."

"I'm Officer Mallory. The dispatcher sent me over here in response to a nine-one-one call? Something about a flower in your living room?" he asked in a deadpan voice.

He already thinks I'm a nut case, I thought. *Maybe I am.*

"I know this is hard to understand, but there was an unusual man who threatened me on my way back from the law library last night."

"You say he threatened you?"

"Yes."

"And just how did he threaten you?"

I thought for a moment. "Well, he picked up a book that had fallen out of my pocket and handed it back to me."

"I see."

"And he had a sickle in his hand that he was using to weed a flowerbed near the Hancock Tower."

"Did he threaten you with the sickle?"

"No, not really…" I said in frustration. "Ok, maybe I shouldn't use the word 'threatened.' He scared me. That's what happened."

"I see. Could you describe the man?"

"He was a dark man in a hooded sweatshirt who had tattoos all over his face and one eye gone. If you saw his face you would remember it for the rest of your life."

The officer opened a folder that he was carrying, and pulled out a picture.

"Would this be the person?"

There, in eight by ten color, was a photograph of the carved man.

"I knew I wasn't making this all up!" I said excitedly. "What is he, some criminal I bet—a stalker?"

"Well not exactly. The department had no record of him whatsoever until a few hours ago. As the beat officer for this neighborhood, I took this picture of your man at two a.m. this morning when I was on patrol."

"You met him yourself?"

"Yes."

"Well, what was he doing?" I asked, wanting to know all of the details.

"He was sitting cross-legged on the sidewalk right there," the officer said, pointing down at a spot on the walkway a couple of feet from my front steps. "He was mumbling something with his arms stretched out and his eyes closed. When I asked him what he was doing, he said that there was someone 'carrying a potential' whom he was protecting in the dream world. He said he was helping the person find a way to his 'guide' and receive the vision that he needed to continue on his mission. I don't suppose he was talking about *you*, was he?"

"Why didn't you arrest him?" I demanded.

"Well, Mr. Smithson, we still have to have probable cause to arrest someone in the city of Chicago. He had no weapon, no drugs, and was not technically on your property. Until just now, the department had received no complaints about him. If a vagrant can't produce an ID, I'm authorized to take a picture of him and set up a file. That's what I did. I can't arrest people for mumbling or sitting on the sidewalk at night, no matter how weird they look. It costs the city a lot of money to put the street people up in jail, courtesy of the taxpayers. And he seemed unusually gentle, even docile to me—no immediate threat. I asked him to move on, and he did."

I stood there in disbelief. "Did he tell you what his name was?" I asked.

"Not exactly, but that's not so unusual for the mental cases and freaks on the streets. They give themselves weird names all the time. This one said that he was a member of 'The Committee' and 'the teacher of a man called 'Moses.' That's all I could get out of him. Does this ring any bells for you?"

I stood there in disbelief. *Since that book arrived, I've entered into a whole new world.*

"Do you want to press charges, Mr. Smithson?" the officer asked.

"Yes ... no—I don't think so. I have to take a minute to sort it all out."

"No problem sir," the officer said, reaching into his pocket to hand me his card. "You call me if you change your mind or if the man bothers you again."

"I will. Thank you."

The officer turned to go. "You might be interested in this, Mr. Smithson. After I took your friend's picture last night, I ran the photo through our database to see if we could come up with any information about him. We have quite the research capability, now with the internet you know, and links to law enforcement all over the world."

"Yes, and what did you find out?"

"Our researcher came up with a painting by a Czech artist named Gottfried Lindauer painted in 1885. Lindauer was famous for painting chieftains and Shamans that lived in a group of islands we now call New Zealand. One of the men Lindauer painted was a one-eyed Shaman who had no name."

"So what does this have to do with the guy that was at my doorstep last night?"

"Nothing really, except for the fact that the face in the portrait and the face of the man on your sidewalk were identical down to the last chiseled curve—give or take a hundred twenty-five years of age. It's wild what the freaks these days will come up with, isn't it? You don't often see tattooing that deep."

"Yes, wild," I said, remembering the churning ball of energy in my body last night.

"And there was another strange thing."
"Yes?"
"You probably won't believe this."
"Try me."
"As I was climbing back into my squad car after I'd asked him to move on, I looked up and saw him down on the corner, just as he was turning south on State Street. He was holding out his hand, with his fingers outstretched, and I felt something shift in my back. I've had low back pain every day for the last twenty years, and at that moment, it just disappeared. Completely gone! I haven't felt this good in I don't know how long. Pretty weird, huh? My back just popped back into place, right at that instant. It's been a pretty good morning for me so far."

"Congratulations," I said. "Glad you're feeling better."

"You'll let me know if anything else happens, right?"

"I will officer. Thanks again," I said, and closed the door.

I WALKED TO THE COUCH, and my knees nearly hit the floor as I collapsed under my own weight.

This was the moment I'd been secretly hoping for; that I knew for years was coming. Powerful allies were arriving at every turn. They were already opening me, changing me. The last time I had said 'yes' to an invitation like this, there had been a shift in the trajectory of my life that was wonderful beyond anything I could have hoped for or imagined. I was given a new chance at life then. Now, it seemed, I was being given another one.

I felt a sudden and complete loss of energy. The wind that had been filling my sails was gone. I felt as if an elemental field had shifted under my feet. After years of doing just what the system around me said I was supposed to do, I was now being presented an opportunity to do something completely different. I was being invited into something big.

"—*Not big, Charlie; limitless. Unimaginable capacity ... unimaginable currents of clarity and power....*"

Doubts. Fears. *I don't know what's good for me*, I thought. I don't have what it takes to do something like this. Only a fool would do something like this.

"*—That's right, Charlie, only a fool has what it takes to begin a quest and see it through.*"

I was hearing the voice again. There was someone inside my head talking with me, using some different form of communication.

"*—If you weren't a fool, you would refuse the Call right now, Charlie. But of course, doing the 'reasonable' thing might have its own consequences, like being bored and tired for the rest of your life, and always wondering, what if. . . .*"

"You can't seriously be thinking about throwing the opportunity presented by Thompson back in the water," I said to myself aloud. *I've worked so hard for that spot at Thompson.*

The Thompson firm had treated me quite well and had graciously invited me into their exclusive club. I was on their 'authorized list.' There was a sturdy plastic card with my name on it, numbered and duly issued, waiting at the reception desk. The magnetic security information on that card allowed its owner to open the firm's sealed mahogany doors and cross a threshold into a privileged world. There were many other high achievers wanting to cross that invisible magnetic line into the world of power and money—plenty of bridesmaids waiting in the wings to get married to Thompson. To back out of the marriage now would mean that I would be taken off the 'authorized' list, perhaps forever.

"*—But listen, Charlie. Can you see a different view? What if the Universe is keeping a list of* outbound *threshold-crossers, also considered 'authorized' and well qualified; those with enough energy and courage to leave and follow their best impulse into the unknown? The possibilities of the universe expand only through those who risk something new. The universe won't inspire an act of profound courage only to abandon you in a ditch and laugh in your face.*"

What she was saying had a ring of truth. There could be other ways to look at what was happening. Maybe my life story didn't have to end in those polished mahogany rooms of the Thompson firm.

"*—Yes, Charlie, your wildness* can *stay alive. That's all we're promising. You can join a legion of men and women who've simply walked out the door, and on the way out, thrown off placards that they've been carrying without knowing it;*

placards that read: 'This Life is for Sale: Mind Included for No Additional Charge.' There's some new signage under construction for you, Charlie. What do you think it might be?"

I stretched out on the couch and closed my eyes. Even though I'd slept until noon, I was exhausted by the inner conflict and had just gone limp. I began to drift off again into sleep. As I was dropping off, I remembered a black and white photograph of a freedom marcher, walking for his civil rights down the main street of a southern town in the sixties. The marcher had a placard on his back. His placard read: "I am a Man."

7: The Answer

The first moments of creation always bring joy to the Field. Many of your problems simply disappear in the light of your deliberate and terrific refusal to respond with anything but your deepest, highest, richest answer to something that is yet unknown. Move forward. Find out who you're intended to be. You already have the means at your disposal.
...*The Field Book*.

WHEN I AWOKE, the brownstone was in deep quiet. It was just a few minutes before three in the morning. I'd slept another twelve hours. Smiling women had been in my dreams. They were trying to talk to me, but their voices were muffled and far away.

I'd never been up quite this early, at the time when everyone else was in their deepest sleep. *It's a good time to listen*, I thought. I made a cup of black coffee sweetened with sugar and heavy cream. "Nothing's going to happen unless you take action, Charlie," I said aloud. The floor of the brownstone seemed unusually far away in the darkness of the quiet hour. I felt like I was on a scary platform with a bar in my hand, getting ready to swing out into unknown space.

I went out into the garage, off-loaded the boxes from the top of the trash can, and pulled out the guide's bag. I unrolled the waterproof closure, and looked at the contents. Everything was still there. I took the map out of the case, and spread it on the hood of an old car.

There were two cars out in my garage. One was a shiny new black Volvo that I'd leased in a no-money-down deal. The other was an old '69 Dodge Coronet 500. The Dodge was an antique—my first car—that I'd bought with the scholarship money that the Prosperville Rotary Club had given me.

Earlier this spring, I'd driven the Dodge to a recruiting picnic hosted by the Thompson firm. The relic looked out of place next to all of the Mercedes and BMWs. One of the tax partners saw my 500 (it was hard to miss it) and began to loudly opine over his chardonnay "that the car one drives speaks clearly about one's egoic 'drive,' the primal motivating force behind all action." According to the partner, a crappy old car spoke to the world about a drive in horrible disarray; a psychic embarrassment on public display.

The next weekend, I went and leased the Volvo, making yet another promise to make a large monthly payment based on my expected salary at the firm.

The new black Volvo was the *right* kind of drive—sleek, powerful, and fully equipped with many safety features. It didn't matter that I might be indebted to the Volvo Company for the rest of my life, and that the car might just be driving me, not the other way around. I'd get used to all those payments, year after year, forcing me to toil in ways never really chosen or imagined, and forget the simple pleasure that I'd felt when I'd driven the 'five' for the first time; the feeling of moving across the earth in a miracle of invention I'd paid for in full with good cash money.

In the spring of my senior year in high school, I'd bought the car from Mrs. Fenwick, a nice grandma who lived next door to our house in Prosperville. She didn't want to take any money for it, but I'd talked her into the five hundred dollars. Her husband, Mr. Fenwick, had bought the car the day before he died. The 500 was Dodge's low-priced muscle car of the late sixties, with poor steering, weak brakes, and as much engine as they could possibly cram under a hood. Mr. Fenwick had emptied his savings of twenty-five years and bought the car for cash with the idea that he and the Mrs. might take the 'trip of a lifetime,' the Great American Road Trip down Route 66—and come to rest looking at the Pacific. He had no plans beyond that moment.

According to Mrs. Fenwick, Mr. Fenwick drove the 500 home with all the windows rolled down and his elbow resting on the polished blue of the door, his tie loose, and his sleeves rolled up, with the car's whitewalls turning in perfect circles and the fins and chrome gleaming shiny new. He parked the big muscle car in the driveway for all the neighbors to see, then went to bed, and died in his sleep. Mrs. Fenwick said that he was smiling when she tried to wake him the next morning.

Grandma Fenwick had let the car sit in her garage for thirty-two years, afraid to drive it herself and afraid to sell it for fear that the new owner would follow Mr. Fenwick off the mortal coil as soon as the engine fired. Her brother came from Indianapolis a couple of times a year to drive it around the block, charge the battery, replace the crumbling hoses, and keep the vehicle in running condition. It took some talking to convince Grandma Fenwick to hand over the keys. But at last she relented, and after thirty-two years of idleness the Dodge turned over after a long whining crank that reverberated off the walls of the Fenwick's garage, leaving a long black imprint on the concrete—a brushstroke of carbon that poured out the tailpipe from the force of first combustion. The 500 would leave this distinctive carbon autograph on every garage, driveway, and parking lot she would ever visit, a fresco laid down in loving layers as I juiced the throttle, her own artistic statement that would defy the most potent efforts at scrubbing and eradication.

I survived my first night with the 500 in possession, and had made it through every night since. When I backed the car out of the Fenwick's garage, its odometer had recorded just fifty-eight miles traveled.

The Dodge was a relic from the last of the tailfin era, and ran with no maintenance other than the occasional oil change. I had no doubt that the car was designed in Detroit by a team in white lab coats who all wore heavy black plastic glasses that accentuated owl-like eyes peering through a half inch of polished telescope glass. The 500 reflected this aesthetic down to its smallest feature. It was a joke in the book of any modern professional.

She had conservative fins, not too tall or sharp; dark blue, so as not to stand out; heavy as a truck with a half-inch steel body and not an ounce of plastic. No air conditioning, no radio—a relic from an era when these were options considered an excessive indulgence by some important percentage of the Midwestern consuming public.

Maybe it's the world of that tax partner that needs updating, not my 500, I thought. Updated to a world not quite so trapped in the controlling forces of all those ego drives; a world where there was an exit door marked 'freedom.' I looked at the old Dodge and began to see its potential. The key was in it, along with about three-quarters of a tank of gas. Wilderness roads would not hurt it much, and I could ride it till it dropped without having to worry about damaging a lease car I didn't really own. I could simply get in, turn the key, and start heading north. *Old Mr. Fenwick would like a trip like that.* He would like to have his Dodge driven to the end of the road by a young man who would then set out into the wilderness to a place marked 'Here.' If his old 500 could carry that polite neighbor boy to such a place, he'd be happy, even though he'd paid $3,076.00 in 1969 dollars and only received five hundred bucks back for his shiny new car thirty-two years later.

Still, the car was old and bone ugly. *Only a geekish loser would drive something like this,* I thought.

"—So Charlie, what would it take to change that thought? Is there something different you can see in the Field, is there another 'field of view' that's more benign, more gentle, a bit more loving toward yourself and the vehicle that's carrying you?"

Well, sure.

I was comfortable in Mr. Fenwick's old car; something solid and stable in a situation as strange and new as this one. *The car does have its unique brand of geekish élan.* The 500 had survived the junkyard long enough to reach a point where she was 'new' again, and could draw stares, if not the same kind of admiring stares old Mr. Fenwick got when he drove her home on the last day of his life. There were no others like her on the road. The car had lived long enough to turn the corner back to cool.

Only an amazingly cool, totally confident, and self-directed person has what it takes to step in and drive a 'five' like this one, especially on a quest for a future so wild that it is beyond his current imagination, I thought.

"—All right. That's a much better interpretation."

I went back into the brownstone and began to make calls from my cell phone, knowing that I would only get voice mail at 3:30 in the morning.

To the administration office: "a family emergency has come up and I won't be attending graduation. Please mail my diploma to...."

To Mom: "I won't be attending graduation. I know that you weren't planning to come anyway, so I decided to take a well-deserved vacation before I start work."

I was shocked to realize that there were only two calls to make about my graduation. I'd been so holed up in my drive to be number one that I'd hardly made any real friends. Maybe there were not so many people cheering me on as I'd imagined.

I scrolled down to the number of the hiring partner at the Thompson firm. *I can't deal with all of this right now*, I thought. *If I keep thinking about all of this, I'm going to get too scared to move.*

"*—Just right, Charlie. If you wait until everything is perfect, it probably will never happen.*"

I went to my closet and put a change of clothes in a duffel bag. I could figure what I needed for a wilderness camping trip later. I went out to the garage, opened the door of the 500, and squeezed in. I took the cell phone off of my belt, closed the device, turned it to the lowest level of 'off,' and then took out the battery. I turned the key in the Dodge. She turned over after a couple of cranks, leaving her signature imprint on the garage floor as she roared to life.

Part Two:

Leaving Identity Behind

8: The New Journey

There exists in every one of us the voice of a fool that tells us we are destined for some great thing. Sometimes the journey begins when the sun is shining, and the fool lifts his head in an angle of delight to soak up the rays. In his hand is a fragrant flower. All that he carries for the long journey is tied in a little napkin on a stick flung casually across his shoulder. A long coat billows like a set of false wings, embracing the mountain air. A study in rapture and grace, he is about to walk off a cliff. The beauty has caught him, and he doesn't realize where he is. There's a little dog barking at his heels, trying to give some sort of warning. It seems the dog has more sense than the man. The current version of that man is about to die. This is how it starts.
...*The Field Book.*

PULLING OUT of the driveway was easier than I thought it might be—no different than any other time. *If I focus on the next step, just the next one, it might be all right; one moment at a time.*

I was on a divide. On one side of the divide was paralyzing fear, and on the other was tremendous excitement that might be converted into energy and harnessed for the adventure ahead. I didn't know which side of the divide I was going to fall towards. It could go either way.

The sky and the roads were clear. I drove over broad and empty expanses of elevated highway, going out of the city against the first strands of the incoming rush hour. The light was growing on the blue horizon of Lake Michigan to my right. The first red rays of dawn were lighting the city from the top down. Its glass and stone were mirrors to the sunrise, catching light like snowcaps. I'd been living here for three years and had never before seen the beauty of the place.

The compass rested on the seat next to me, its needle swinging freely; crossing back and forth along a center line that marked magnetic north. *It's just an adventure,* I told myself. *You'll be back here before you know it.* But my gut knew something different was happening. My body was pulsing energy down into its parts, down my legs, and into my hands.

"*—Yes, Charlie. Your body is remembering what your soul is here to do.*"

Who knows, I thought. There just might be a miracle up this road.

By seven a.m. I was across the state line and into Wisconsin. For the first time since childhood, I was starting a day without a schedule. For years, my eye had been 'on the ball'—I had been controlled by task lists, time frames, classes, interviews, and due dates. My schedule had been a hard shell that had already begun to reshape my body, hunching it over and making my shoulders rise up around my ears to push against its weight. Now, without my husk of plans and deadlines, I was much lighter and could simply look around.

Moses had given me no instructions about how to get to the place on the map marked 'Here,' so around ten, I decided to leave the freeway. I took a left and began to wind north on roads that had a rhythm, roads that turned with the hillsides and made stops at every place folks had gathered to form a community. It seemed that each small town had risen up to assert a distinction. The towns were celebrating wholesome and gentle things.

A town offering the lure of the "world's biggest six pack" (six huge storage tanks, three abreast actually filled with beer) certainly seemed to have its priorities in order. Many places were 'capitals'—world epicenters that no one else in the world knew about. There were bratwurst capitals, cheese capitals, loon capitals, and musky fishing capitals. I glided past a massive fiberglass statue of a walleye, created by local boosters to stake down their claim as one of Wisconsin's great walleye capitals. Doubtless the town had borne witness to a thousand afternoons where 'the boys' would meet at the Tailfin Tap for a couple of Pabst Blue Ribbons after a long day of Lindy-rigging. On good days, limits of fish would swim in the live wells of the boats parked out front.

Plumpness and happiness seemed synonymous here. Everywhere were images of a gentle life trajectory focused on the production, harvesting, preparation, ingestion, and digestion of food, with cheese and beer forming the base of the pyramid. *It's no crime to be twenty-five pounds overweight here*, I thought. *I can relax here.* It's also quite alright to be, well, forty over. Anything less and you'd be buying your jeans in the 'slim' section of the store downtown.

I STOPPED at a roadside stand selling hard cheese, crisp apples, and dried venison, to ask where I might buy some items for a wilderness camping trip. I was directed to a discount place just outside of town. I drove over, parked, and walked past racks of women's bras, the enormous aisle filled with chips, another wide aisle filled with soda, and a third filled with candy. The sporting goods were in the back.

I was met by a man standing behind a glass counter filled with guns and knives. He was immense; six-foot-five and three hundred pounds of muscle. He stood wide-footed underneath an even more immense moose head that once belonged to an animal with antlers twelve feet off the ground. There was a strong suggestion that one could bring down such an animal personally by means of any one of the weapons on display. The man was an obvious participant in the thrilling drama of the hunter-prey relationship, and both man and moose seemed to be close descendants of pre-historic ice age steppe dwellers. In just a few hundred miles, the people and the animals had grown larger with more mass in ratio to their surface area, perhaps to be better protected from the cold.

He was a man with fur, fully bearded from the bottom of his eyes down to where his three-inch chest hairs poked from his white T-shirt. He was wearing red flannel over the top of the hair, but I had no doubt that the thatch continued down his body unabated. He was haired on the back of his hands. His forehead was also dense with mashed hair, clearly showing a ring where a stocking cap had been in place for many hours, its contour line showing above his protruding supraorbital ridges and uni-brow. Dark eyes examined me from under the brow.

"Can I help you?" he asked in a high and cheerful home-town voice.

He is not going to spear me. Thank God. His body may be Neanderthal, but the soul inside belongs to a small town Wisconsin Lutheran. He stood ready to sell me a high velocity weapon, several knives, and a handgun with hollow point bullets with the same the perky attitude and downright friendliness of a church deacon serving banana crème pie at the social.

"I'm going on a camping trip," I said.

"What kind of a trip?"

"Whaddaya mean?"

"I mean car camping, backpacking, hunting ... canoe?"

"It's going to be a canoe trip."

"How long you gonna be out?"

"Don't know."

"Are you going with an outfitter?"

"What's that?"

"I mean a guide, an outfitter, don't ya know."

"I'm not sure. I think so."

He looked at me quizzically, but he came from a culture where this might not be anyone's business, and he was reluctant to intrude.

"Well, what kind of gear do you need?"

I remembered the injunction on the invitation from Moses. I was to gear up for a wilderness canoe trip, and bring only what was essential. I didn't know enough about wilderness camping to know what was essential and what was not. "I need everything," I responded.

With this he took a step back, put both hands behind his head, arched his back, and gave me a cockeyed grin. I was a nut case.

"Well, so ... how much money do you have to get everything?"

I pulled out my wallet, and peered into it, sorting through a couple of business cards and random pieces of paper.

"Well ... I have thirty-seven dollars in cash...," then I remembered, "and a new line of credit on this Chase Visa for twenty-two thousand."

I'd forgotten that I was a good credit risk, and right in the heart of the young high-consuming profile most desired by a credit card company hoping to make a shit-pile of money on high interest consumer debt.

"Let's see it."

"What?"

"The card."

I handed over the Visa, glimmering with a hologram of a dove ascending into flight. *Perhaps the damn thing is associated with freedom after all.*

He took the card, punched a few numbers on a machine, and made a phone call while I looked over the gleaming forty-five calibers, nine millimeters, and three-fifty-seven magnums.

In a couple of minutes he handed back the card.

"You're good!" he said with a tone of pleasure and surprise. "So well ... do you want me to pick out some stuff for you?"

"That would be great."

He stepped out from behind the counter, wheeled a huge orange shopping cart into place, and began to walk down the aisles with me in tow.

Sporting goods of every description were raked off the shelves into the giant wheeled basket.

"Need a tent?"

"Yes."

"How 'bout a sleeping bag?"

"For sure."

"Are you going to shit in the woods?"

"Excuse me?"

"Do you need a shovel?" he asked, somewhat impatiently.

"Sure."

On we went through the bug dope, tarps, ropes, lanterns, headlamps, paddles, and cook gear. The man unhooked the biggest aluminum frame pack in the store and put it into a second cart that he now pulled along behind him. We were snaking like a consumer choo-

choo train through the store with an Extreme Alaskan Outfitter Pack taking up most of the caboose. It was good to know that I would have four thousand seven hundred cubic inches of storage space on my back.

The Extreme Alaskan was decked out with its own rifle-holding pocket and drink tube clip to accommodate a hydration bladder (sold separately). The man also fixed me up with a smaller 'day pack' for essential items to keep handy at all times. The day pack was to be carried on my belly to counterbalance the weight of the Extreme Alaskan. Apparently, his plan for me was to go out into the woods looking something like a pregnant mom two weeks past her due date, who could somehow navigate the wilderness trails despite the inability to see her feet.

The single most expensive item in the cart was a handheld Global Positioning System Navigator on sale for $335.99. It stayed in simultaneous communication with no fewer than three space satellites at all times, pinpointing my position anywhere on earth within three feet. "Impossible to get lost with a GPS," the hairy man said. "You'll never need a map and compass again." It occurred to me that Moses might have sent me the old map and compass after trading up for his own electronic navigation gadget, but somehow I doubted it.

We paused at an aisle filled with long poles, nets, and hundreds of packets of gleaming plastic lures of every description.

"Are you going to fish?"

"I guess so."

"What are you going after? Musky, trout, perch...."

"I don't know."

"So a good all-round rig then?"

"Yes."

"What test line?"

"Just pick something."

"Ever fished before?"

I remembered a tangled reel and a catfish on the bank of the Prosperville town pond.

"A couple of times when I was little."

"Let me fix you up then."

Lures of every description fell into the cart, along with several hundred yards of high tensile, low stretch monofilament, a heavy fiberglass rod, and an open faced spinning reel. The hairy man was a fountain of knowledge about fishing, showing me drawings of the improved clinch knot; issuing stern warnings about intestinal worms carried by trout; revealing the deadly peril of the translucent 'Y' bones in the backs of northern pike that could catch in your throat and choke you to death; and warning of the dangers of aquatic parasites in untreated water. It was all vital backwoods information.

"Hard to break these Ugly-Sticks," he said, as he picked the heavy black rod out of the cart and whipped it violently with his meaty hands.

I backed away from the thrashing and upset a stack of duck decoys. I scrambled to pick them up.

"Sounds good, sir," I said with my arms full of plastic Drake Mallards.

"Have any camp food?"

"No sir."

We made a detour into the food section of the store. Boxes of pop-tarts, Swiss Miss hot chocolate, instant coffee singles, granola bars, trail bars, and many other single-wrapped high fat and high carbohydrate snack foods fell into the cart.

He tilted a knowing head toward me.

"This is the sort of stuff to eat out on the trail," he said. "You burn up a lot of calories and need to keep your energy up—and all this goes great with those thick moose steaks!" he said, giving me a wink.

"Here's your supper!" he said, piling on a two-week supply of freeze-dried dinners in shrink-wrapped foil into the trailing cart.

"You'll hardly notice the taste after a couple of days," he said. "As they say, 'hunger is the best sauce'!" He was just so darn chipper about everything. It was hard not to get enthused about the chance to put all of this great stuff on my back and carry it into the deep wilderness.

We rounded the last aisle.

"So that's about it. Do you need a weapon?"

"I don't think so."

"Well, there's lots of critters out there...."

"I think I'll take my chances."

"Do as you please ... we have a special running on the thirty-ought-sixes ... hell of a gun for the price."

I looked at the mountain of stuff already in the cart.

"I think I'm good."

"Good enough then! I'll ring you up."

In a few moments I was in the parking lot, trying to keep a cart with two hundred pounds of gear from wheeling into one of the other parked cars. I owed the Visa Company an additional two thousand, four hundred twenty-five dollars and sixty-seven cents. I also had a slip of paper given to me by the furry man with directions to a spot that told me where I could rent a canoe and a car-top carrier in a town just up the road.

Forty-five minutes later, I had a gleaming seventeen-foot aluminum canoe on top of the 500, strapped down in front and back with red elastic tie-downs. I could just peek over the packages to watch a vibrating strap in my rear view mirror that struggled to hold the canoe on top of the car.

The boat gave the 500 a new double prow. The car had developed a low, sensual moan of wind through her new rigging that grew to a fierce shout of mismatched harmonics as we accelerated, then died to a quiet hum around sixty miles an hour. The 500's body was vibrating as the wind strummed the new rigging and cut across the lines of the boat on top, and had developed a skating motion down the road that threatened to put us in the ditch. I put the compass up on the dashboard in an attempt to influence the car to move in a straighter line. The bow of the boat lined up with north on the compass, and the sideways motion calmed a little. Whatever was up this road, I was now determined to keep going.

"*—Faith doesn't have anything to do with believing propositions, Charlie. Faith is about taking the next step. Anyone with enough faith to simply take the next step has most of the right gear already.*"

I worked the 500 through a series of 'S' curves that wound around newly-planted fields and hillside terraces of green grass. I could only hope that the lady in my head was right.

9: Turning 'Till You Come 'Round Right

> Growth within imperfection is the promise of the spiritual life. The bedrock of conscious evolution is to walk fearlessly within that which is imperfect.
> ...*The Field Book.*

IT WAS GROWING DARK as I approached the Minnesota border. The open fields were becoming fewer, and the road was darkened with dense pine on either side. A small finger of the great boreal forest, the Taiga that bands the globe across Scandinavia, Russia, and Canada had reached down to this northernmost point in Wisconsin. All the houses were small, tight little dwellings with windows set ten feet above the ground so that the view would not be obscured by drifts of snow. Every house had four or five concrete steps up to a little concrete porch, designed so that on winter days the front door could be opened above the snow. Tire chains hung in the garages. Everywhere was the reminder of the long season, the winter. A bumper sticker on the car ahead read "When hell freezes over I'll ice fish there too." *Loving the winter makes you belong here,* I thought. Right now, I was just visiting.

My back-country route wound its way to a point where it paralleled the interstate for a few miles. After being off the big highway for half a day, I now felt assaulted by its rush, glare, and point-to-point directionality. Had I stayed on the 'big road' I might have 'been there' by now, but since I was not quite sure where 'there' was, or when I needed to be there, my speed of travel didn't matter all that much.

A city was up ahead, and from the frontage road I could read the high wattage highway signs that announced its presence. *I think I'll resist. I know what they're trying to do.*

The signs were attempting to influence me well in advance of my arrival at the city's limit, so I would exit my high-speed transit at just the right spot, slow down to a stop, and land at a designated Formica counter. A pleasant and mutually beneficial interaction would be made over that counter, involving just a small portion of the remaining balance on my Visa. The signs reminded me of my great hunger and thirst, and promised that all my longings would be satisfied by eating myself into a high-fat, two thousand calorie processed food coma in less than thirty minutes. There were well-lit motel chains, clean and cheap, with a high carb and caffeine breakfast included in one low price. The porn on the TV that would prey on my loneliness when I latched the door would be an additional $14.95. One could get addicted to these things. In fact, that's the business model.

On the left, there was a painted wooden sign, carved to look like an Indian arrow. It advertised Bill and Edna's cabins for rent on the shores of beautiful Loon Lake. The sign announced a four star rating by the American Automobile Association. The pointer was weathered, but still hung straight on its hinges. Its letters were hollowed out by a wood carving tool that left little scoops in the cedar. Just below the arrow were the words "Quality since 1955". I turned down the gravel road and wound back into the woods.

The road needed grading and was pocked with deep holes filled with water. I could only hope that the cabins weren't in the same condition as the road. What was down this road would depend a great deal on the intention and integrity of Bill and Edna.

In one of my college business classes I'd learned about a man named Kemmons Wilson who'd taken a family road trip across America in the early fifties, and was appalled by the filth of roadside accommodations and the huge variation in their quality. In response, he opened a motor hotel he called the Holiday Inn, named after a song and dance movie. The Inn, and other motels like it, eliminated all of the problems and guesswork for travelers by putting an identical motel in every town, with each room an ultra-clean empty box that was exactly the same. Travelers could go from spot to spot and have a repeatable, safe, and clean experience. The system took the risk out of traveling.

No risk, but not much reward either, I thought as I bounced down the rutted road. There might still be some really great places well off the beaten path, places with porches, pines, tire swings, and lake breezes; places I could afford with my thirty-seven dollars in cash and still have something left over. Bill and Edna's quality cabins might be a spot like my grandmother talked about, a spot booked in advance for decades by the same people who returned again and again to recapture the simple joy they felt when they were younger. A place to exhale, to laugh, and to play canasta; where one could learn the good fishing spots and keep them secret, and feel the glow of a few cans of Schlitz while resting in the summer breeze on a porch smelling faintly of perch and pine. I imagined talking into the night there, talking about simple things that were good to know: how to cook fish, build a house, or can the vegetable garden. Somehow, the kids never managed to drown during all the years, despite the rickety docks and deep drop-offs into dark blue water where you could dive head-first but never reach the bottom.

Loon Lake appeared suddenly out of the pines, just a grey shimmer in the fading light. It was nearly dark, and there was no humming light to disturb the parking area. An 'A' frame cabin had an orange glow inside, and the word "office" was carved into a lacquered pine railing. I got out of the 500, put the Field Book in my back pocket, and walked toward the office. Everything had the look of something built by hand, and built to last. Heavy field-cut pine trunks had been stripped and shaped with a draw knife and notched with an axe so they interlocked at the corners of the house. Other logs bore the marks of having been worked with an adze. The logs were left textured, and were interesting to examine. I'd seen the same surface texture copied by the 'designer looks' of many smart dwellings featured in the catalogues that came through my mail slot in Chicago. But here the look was natural. It was just the way the logs turned out after they'd been worked by hand.

There was a soft sound of flowing water from an open aqueduct coming down from the hill behind the camp. *Spring water coming into the cabins.* Six structures were facing the lake, all with screened porches and outdoor fire pits. *The porches are positioned to catch the prevailing breeze.* All the cabins had an unobstructed view of the sunset, which was now nothing but soft pink glow reflected on the still surface of the lake. A beautiful dock of hand-hewn planks, worn by generations of bare feet, extended into the lake. A couple of smaller swim platforms were anchored further out. Canoes and john-boats were stacked in racks over to the right, and a neat row of ten-horse Evinrude kickers hung on an outbuilding. Shavings and sawdust were mixed into the sand on the ground. *So quiet here. So peaceful here.*

The aluminum storm screen banged as I knocked on it, conveying something louder and more insistent than my actual intent. Lights came on, and a woman's round face opened the main door, then the screen.

"Can I help you?"

"I'm looking for a place to spend the night, and I wondered if one of the cabins was available."

"Oh dear, you didn't drive all the way down here from the highway, did you?"

"Well yes," I replied, unclear about how else one could get here.

"Well the cabins aren't ready yet. I'm not sure that we can open this year at all, to tell you the truth."

I looked at her, not knowing what to say.

She propped open the storm screen with her sturdy body. I didn't say another word, but within five minutes I knew the whole story.

—Bill had mysteriously lost all of the strength in his left side just after Christmas. He'd always been such a strong, good-looking man.

—He was now up at Mayo's in Rochester having some tests run.

—She'd just come down for the day to get some more clothes and supplies and would be driving back first thing tomorrow.

—Ed Bridges—a pretty good carpenter who'd been renting each summer for twenty years said he might be able to come up from

Rockford to get the cabins ready, but Ed was having a hard time getting off work.

—There was so much to fix from the ice-storm, and she had her hands full just taking care of Bill. She couldn't rent the cabins in their current condition.

—She'd cleaned them herself every spring for the last fifty-four years just to know the job had been done right. It was hard to find good help, someone willing to scrub the corners of the windows and leave them sparkling without any streaks. You had to get up on a ladder to get those cobwebs out of the ceiling corners, you know, and move all the furniture to get a proper cleaning. The pilot lights were not even lit, so no hot water. The cabins hadn't been opened since October; no telling what was in there. But it would be a shame to drive all the way back to the highway this time of night. Had I come far? Had I had dinner?

"You must be Edna," I inquired.

"Yes, Edna Robertson," she replied.

"I'm Charlie Smithson," I said, extending my hand. "I'm up from Chicago today, on my way to Canada for a canoe trip."

She took my hand, grabbing three fingers and shaking them.

"So do you think I could stay in one of the cabins down by the lake? I have my own stove and a lot of camp food. I have a sleeping bag, so no need for linens and all that. I'd be happy to sweep the place out for you. What do the cabins rent for?"

"They're fifteen dollars a night in the off-season. But I couldn't charge you. They aren't ready."

I thought about the thirty-seven dollars in cash I had left to get me the next six hundred miles north. There was no evidence that credit cards had ever been used at Bill and Edna's. From the look of things, the five-percent surcharge the card companies took off the top would probably consume Bill and Edna's entire profit margin.

"How 'bout I give you ten bucks, sweep out the place, and try to light the pilot myself. I'll leave it clean and get out early in the morning so I won't hold you up."

"Well it would be a shame to make you drive all the way back to the highway. But the rooms are nicer up there, you know."

"Why don't you let me be the judge of that," I replied.

"Well alright. But I've never rented a room out in this condition. They're not ready. You'll probably never come back."

She's right about that, I thought. But my return doesn't have anything to do with the condition of the rooms. I couldn't envision a return trip, only a one-way trip to the spot on the old map marked 'Here.'

I offered the ten. She took it reluctantly, shaking her head, and with a sigh put it in the open mouth of a stuffed largemouth bass. A little sign that said 'tips' hung from the bottom jaw of the fiberglass fish. Some invisible line Edna had defended for many years was being crossed. She was a woman with four-star cabins, even if the rating man was last seen forty years ago. It was a matter of pride. First Bill and the loss of his left side. Now the cabins not ready for the first guest of the season. She was on a muddy slope, sliding down.

"The cabins aren't ready," she said, now only to herself. She took a key from a hand-made rack, grabbed a flashlight, and led me down a sandy path.

HER UPPER ARMS swayed back and forth as she descended the path, the skin hanging wrinkled and loose. She moved with an uneven gait that spoke of hip pain on her right side. Her bulky body settled from side to side, stepping wide with each stride to balance her weight on the uneven ground. A fall would be a devastating event, with all of her weight crashing down on joints grown brittle. Despite her age and obvious limitations, I already had the feeling that I could depend on Edna; that she would take on any task that needed to be done, no matter how thankless. Edna impressed me as someone who had been doing good things for others for a long time. *She can feel what others are feeling and know what they need*, I thought.

Edna talked to me over her shoulder, a steady stream of banter, telling me that the cabins here were all different and hand-made by Bill when he was younger. He built them after the Korean War to fit on the site so that the old-growth white pines could be saved. Did I notice the pine next to the parking area that was over five feet across? It was a hundred and fifty years old, she said. To build the cabins, Bill harvested trees from the woods all around the lake, clearing the forest by taking only the pines that were stunted or beetle-killed. He lopped the limbs with his axe and hauled the trunks out of the woods and across the lake in winter with a team of roan Morgan horses. There's a right way to do something, you know. Did I know that? Number Six is her favorite, with the best view of the lake. This camp has been their home since '55, she told me. She was just nineteen the day they started here together.

It was clear to me that Bill and Edna were coming to the end of their line. *There's no way that she can run this place alone and compete against the franchises,* I thought. Not with their well-strategized business plans and the clean rooms available any time of the day or night, three hundred sixty-five days a year. Bill and Edna's four-star cabins will soon be road-kill on the modernization highway. In fact, with Ed gone, they're finished already. It's just a matter of playing out the final chapter of a book already written.

"*—Sometimes in the death of a thing, its beauty glows more brightly,*" I heard the voice in my head say.

She stopped at Number Six, inserted the key, and tried to open the door. It wouldn't budge.

"Can I give it a try?" I asked.

"Be my guest."

I put my shoulder to the door as hard as I dared, but the door was lodged tight. As I pushed, The Field Book fell out of my pocket onto the ground. *That book seems to have a mind of its own,* I thought.

Edna reached down and picked the book up. I turned and looked at her. She held it in her hands and fanned the pages with a faraway look in her eyes, remembering.

This is not the first time she's seen that book. I looked down to the book and back up into her face.

"You've seen this before."

"Yes, I've seen this book before," she said casually. "It looks like more has been written since he was here last."

"Who was here—was Moses here?" I asked excitedly.

She laughed. "Moses! So *that's* his name now. My, things seem to have gotten awful high-falutin. If your 'Moses' is that handsome man with the blue eyes you'd never forget, we're talking about the same fella. He went by the name of Eddie Taylor when he was here."

"You knew him?"

"Thirty years ago he stayed a whole winter right here in Number Six. He sure knew how to repair an outboard motor. He worked with Bill most of that winter bringing in logs for the big dock. He was the best hand we've ever had around the place. We were sorry to see him go. He left here to find his 'teacher.' Said he had some questions that needed answering."

I looked at her. I now knew that there was something more than chance behind my impulse to follow the arrow down here to Bill and Edna's.

"We're in the same business, you know—your 'Moses' and me."

"And what business is that?" I asked.

"Showing people what they need to see."

The stooped woman in front of me straightened and looked hard at me. The light from the cabin illuminated her from behind, obscuring her face and giving the appearance of a halo. In this light, Edna suddenly appeared as a much younger woman—a beautiful Norse woman—with high cheekbones and long blonde hair streaming down shoulders that were thrown back and erect. Edna reached out and touched me on the forehead with two fingers in just the same place Moses had touched me those years ago on the ball field. As she held her fingers there, a vision arrived.

I SAW A CREW in the bottommost room of an ocean liner, shoveling coal into an immense furnace belching noise and heat. Edna was down there with them, like a strong Norse goddess, stoking the fire. Well-dressed men and women were on the deck above, basking in the sea air, doing business, dancing, eating, and smiling. The engine crew had no interest in such frivolity. The crew's work was down below. They accepted the plain conditions of their confined space and their duties there.

There was a red telephone hanging on the steamy wall of the engine room. The telephone line was linked directly to the ship's Captain. An identical red phone was up on the bridge in the wheelhouse right next to the wheel, the highest point on the boat. The Captain knew that if the turning rotor stopped, everyone on board would soon know just how far they were out at sea, and how vulnerable they were, adrift without forward motion in the vast ocean. With no forward progress, even a gentle roll of swell would make the passengers sick. With a storm wave, the boat would go under. Should the red phone ring, the Captain would drop everything—every plotting and navigation—every conversation in mid-sentence—to answer the call.

The Captain knew the importance of the engine room and those who worked it. The engine crew knew their importance, too. So the crew stayed, turning at their station at the bottom of the boat. They had pride.

As QUICKLY AS IT CAME ON, the vision vanished, and there was a stooped older woman standing outside the door to Number Six.

"What is *that* supposed to mean, Edna? What are you trying to tell me?"

"When a vision wants to arrive it arrives," she said. "That's the way of such things. Your vision is for you to see—for you to interpret. You have to find its meaning on your own."

She turned the key of the lock again, and the door opened as if it had never been jammed. "That's better," she said, and moved into the room.

"Bill and I have done the best we could here," she said as she bounced the springs of the bed and ran her finger across the counter, checking for dust.

"Do you mind if I ask you a question?" I asked.

"Go right ahead."

"A couple of days ago I received an invitation from some 'committee.' You might think I'm crazy—but I think that I'm taking more than a canoe trip. I think I may be on some kind of a special journey that this 'committee' has invited me to take, so I can become someone or do something now that I can't see or understand. It could be that ... well ... I was wondering ... are you one of them? One of the people on the Committee?"

Edna looked me in the face and laughed. "Oh heaven's no, Charlie. I really don't even know what you're talking about. My work has been here, with Bill. But what you're talking about seems a lot like

~ 88 ~

something Eddie would be involved in. He was always interested in connections with people with special powers."

"And that's not you? If you don't have special powers, what just happened when you touched me on the forehead?"

Edna laughed again. "That's just a different way of using your mind, Charlie. Whatever you saw was just a picture of your own thoughts about me and the place we have here. From the look on your face, it seems like you saw something good. I'm glad. It's true I can help people see what they need to see from time to time. But my real work is not with visionary experiences. My real work is friendship: just being here for people who need me."

"Friendship," I said. "Sounds like you've been a pretty good friend to a lot of people."

"I've been called that. It's a station—a place to stand. I know my place." She leaned on the counter and smiled softly at me. "You know Charlie, not everyone has to go on some big vision quest. You can learn to love someone right where you are."

"Yes. I understand that."

"There will always be plenty of people to love. And if you see Eddie—the man you call 'Moses'—you can remind him that he doesn't have to become a person with special powers to live a 'spiritual' life. He spent all of his free time here meditating, watching his mind, and trying to focus his attention. Real life will offer plenty of practice, if you ask me. All you have to do is wake up in the morning, accept what is, and work to leave the world a better place by the time the sun goes down. With each day of service, you turn a little bit into the light. Like the old Shakers used to say: *"To turn, turn, will be our delight, 'till by turning, turning we come 'round right."* That's my way. It's really not that complicated."

"I believe it."

"You could get a big head otherwise. Just because unusual things are happening to you doesn't mean that you are better than anyone else."

It occurred to me that Edna was likely to make it to heaven. *The occasional can of beer won't be held against her,* I thought. Bill will be waiting there for her to arrive. She'll have no problem turning to the light.

Edna turned on a switch above the gas stove. She smiled and touched my cheek with the back of her hand. "And remember this, Charlie: The path of service grounds the spiritual life. Service draws the energy of spiritual beings to the earth. They follow its scent like a beacon. With their help, you don't have to work so hard here. We're not alone, you know. Remember that. If you need help, and your intentions are good, just ask for help and see what happens."

With those words, she left the cabin and headed up the path. I was left alone in a cold room with no television, no radio, and with old sepia photographs of smiling men with dead fish hanging on the wall. I had to sit down for a moment. I had the clearest feeling that the last three days had already shifted my future; that the lines of possibility would never again converge in the same way. *The first step has destroyed all other possibilities*, I thought, just as the voice had said.

"*—Yes, and this is only the beginning.*"

10: Free Attention

The ultimate promise of practice is that the sensation of a separate self will be diminished or eliminated. A sudden, complete, but usually temporary loss of the illusion of the separate self has traditionally been known as 'Ecstasy' from the Latin *ex-stasis*, literally: "to be or stand outside oneself." Over time, Ecstasy can become more and more ordinary—the way things simply are from day to day.
...*The Field Book*.

THE SHORE OF THE LAKE was just a couple of steps away, and there was a gentle sound of small waves. I went back to the 500, and dug through my gear for a sleeping bag, some food, and my new stove. I put the compass and the Field Book in my pocket.

I returned to the cabin, and after forty-five minutes of fumbling with directions, spilling white gas, and burning myself, I managed to get the stove lit. Within a few minutes I had boiling water which I poured into a foil bag where a meal of cheese-flavored instant rice, dried hamburger meat, and powdered peas re-hydrated. In ten minutes the hot metal bag produced an offering that could be considered a form of human food. It was cheesy, fatty, and dry all at the same time. To say that it was "tasteless" would be a compliment. It tasted worse than any meal in memory.

I threw the foil bag into the trash with only a couple of spoonfuls eaten, and rolled out my new bag on one of the single beds. The room was quiet except for the sound of waves against crushed stone, hitting and receding.

The place smelled faintly of fish and rotten wood. A wooden table in the room was hollowed out by the friction of thousands of plates, hands of cards, and the scraping of dominoes. No television, no radio. The only things to look at were the wooden beams on the ceiling.

I tried to lie still and rest, but I couldn't quiet my mind. More strange things had happened in the last twenty-four hours than had happened in the twenty-four years that preceded them. There was a lot to process, but I couldn't focus my mind on any of it.

I opened the Field Book. Toward the back, there was a section of 'definitions' laid out like a small dictionary. One of the passages was on the subject of 'Free Attention.'

> **Free Attention:** The capacity to become relatively free of internal distractions, needs, wants, desires, worries, fantasies, fears, demands of the body, plans, expectations—all of the gaggle of things in one's mind and body. Free Attention is a moving 'state,' and can be easily lost, then consciously regained. Consistent free attention is rare in human beings, but nonetheless can be trained by interruption of the impulse to act in the usual conditioned way, thus opening the seeker into a relatively expanded state of mind in a given moment.
>
> Training the state of free attention is called 'Practice' and may take place through a variety of tools. These tools include simply breathing and watching the demand pass; conscious attention to a distracting signal combined with active re-interpretation of what the stimulus means and requires; seeking vertical alignment with one's best nature and connection in love with our fellow beings in a moment of anger, jealousy, or other negative emotion; insertion of a prayer of gratitude for the triggering event and the wisdom it

has to offer (a form of turning the other cheek in love to all that is arising); or the willingness to simply witness one's own pain and that of others in a given moment without reacting.

'Practice' typically involves many thousands of interventions over a period of time spanning many years, a process known by many names including 'becoming free,' 'transcending the false self,' 'waking up,' 'the work,' or simply 'practice'. As practice progresses, moments of free attention can accumulate into sentences and paragraphs that are often described as flow states, or 'being in flow.'

In advanced stages of practice, sustained states of free attention may be achieved in which the practitioner can be described as being 'fully present' or more accurately, 'In Presence.' This state opens opportunities to see vastly more of what is real, and reality becomes fresh, intensely vibrant, and interesting. Practice diminishes internal pre-occupations (sometimes referred to as 'illusions'). As illusions diminish, so does the sense of a 'separate self'.

Awareness of perspectives that are beyond or outside of the 'separate self' come on line. To stand in awareness outside the self is sometimes called 'Ecstasy.'

I closed the Field Book. The waves outside were breaking gently on the sand. I began to drift. The gentle sound of waves was pulling me deeper. It was then that I realized I was not alone.

MICE TRY to move quietly. They're very old ancestors of ours that have managed to live through assaults from T-rexes, devastating meteor strikes, and all the eons when home was an ice ball. They've succeeded by living in holes, staying low, moving quietly at night, having lots of babies, and running like hell.

A hard tile floor is a challenging surface for a mouse. It's a loud and slippery veneer for a creature that has to take a lot of steps and can't retract its claws to move quietly. No doubt a tile surface makes mice exceedingly uncomfortable. They're dangerously exposed there compared to the much safer places within the walls.

It's natural that the first one should foray out with just the shortest frantic scamper. But where there is one, there's always more.

Of course, Edna *had* said that the cabins weren't ready. "No telling what's in there..." she'd said. And yet I found myself bolt upright in bed, experiencing a terror. There was something about that sound, that frantic scampering of little claws—the darting motion right beneath where I was sleeping—that created an uncontrollable skin response, a flush of sick, sweaty heat as if they were already on me, in bed with me, and crawling over my face and in my hair.

There were more of them. They came from everywhere, scampering over the tile, hopping and jumping. They were in the walls. These mice did not seem to understand the rules. They were collectively failing to understand that I loved them, truly, as one of the dear, sweet creatures of this earth. I recognized them as innocent and furry little cutie-pies with beautiful wide dark eyes and with little pink blind babies to be nurtured in nests of grass and fed special mice-milk. I loved mice. They were among my favorite cartoon characters.

But the mice here did not understand that my deep compassion had its limits. They failed to understand that at the moment when they put their little hard claws inside my human habitation, the cutie-pies instantly morphed into loathsome disease-carrying vermin-criminals whose trespasses against my human habitation carried a sentence of death, right now, by any means necessary—usually by the breaking of their little necks with loaded steel wires—or the agony of poison as they barfed and crapped their bleeding guts out while crawling away for water.

"— *Humans are a confusing species...*" I heard the voice say.

I was frozen in terror. I had to get over to the light switch, which meant stepping on the floor. I leapt over to the wall and smashed the switch on. One of them ran across my foot. I was sure that one was crawling up my leg. I made it back into bed, frantically shaking out my sleeping bag and searching for crawling things.

Where was that god-dammed shovel I'd just bought? I was ready to bash them in self-defense, ready to stomp their little brains out if I could only get enough courage to put my feet down and get my shoes on. But there would probably be at least one already down in the toe of the shoe, maybe more than one, ready to frantically claw my toes, biting my appendages bloody to the bone. The whole colony would then follow the blood-scent and start feeding on me in waves from the toenails up.

I stood up on the bed and looked up to one of the rafters. I made a leap for it. The beam was the size of a mid-sized pine, exactly what it was in 1956 when Bill cut it down and used it here as the main brace for Number Six. It was shellacked, slippery, and too big to grip. I found myself falling in terror back into the sea of swarming mice.

Except ... well, there actually were no mice on the old twin that Edna had lovingly cleaned and vacuumed all of these years. There was only that old unfinished book, with the passage about 'Free Attention.'

> "The capacity to be relatively free of fear by interruption of the impulse to act in the usual conditioned way, thus opening the seeker into a relatively expanded state of mind ... Freedom ... Ecstasy...."

I was on my knees on the bed, clutching the sleeping bag around me. Breathe. "Free space." "Out beyond conditioning." "The ability to see from a different and new perspective." Three breaths. Seven. Ten.

At about the fifteenth breath, it occurred to me that I had never actually heard of a human death from a field-mouse feeding frenzy. I had heard of rat bites, but not mice bites. It also dawned on me that I was at least five hundred times bigger than the average Wisconsin mouse. Twenty breaths. My breathing produced a little free space to observe that the mice were on the floor and in the walls, but were avoiding the bed, taking the long way 'round to make sure they didn't come within arms-length of a killer like me. They were moving just as fast as they could into the room, then back out.

Finally it dawned on me. The mouse-pack and I were gathered together here at Bill and Edna's on the last night of a long winter. All of the seeds in the meadows were long gone, and not enough tender spring shoots had come up to nourish the clan and feed all of those blind mouse-babies. Sitting in the middle of this room—just a short, dangerous scamper away—was an immense and concentrated food supply still warm, apparently abandoned, enough to fill their starving bellies, enough for all of them. It was even flavored like cheese.

I started to watch them at work, daring the slip-sliding floor and full lamplight to jump in and ingest a few grains of dehydrated rice, then jump out to carry a glob of the mush to the walls, where they disappeared into invisible cracks. They were attacking the bag from all sides, tearing feeding holes, trying to make quick work of such an unexpected and God-sent treasure.

> "…Conscious attention … active re-interpretation of what the stimulus means and requires; seeking vertical alignment with our best nature and connection in love with our fellow beings in the moment…."

I had invited the Loon Lake mice to dinner in the woods. The mice of this lake had not read the rules of swank urban townhomes. They were still playing by the basic house rule of planet Earth: nothing goes to waste. Abandoned food belongs to the wide world, and the earth has taught its creatures to take it, use it, and break it down for the good of everything else.

Even with this realization about the proper way of things, I was still not ready to put my bare feet down on a floor running with clawed animals that might leap up my leg. The sound of all of that scratching was everywhere. To walk across that floor and pick up a wastebasket containing live jumping mice seemed more than I could accomplish just by breathing. My skin was still crawling with all of the scratching and hop-hopping; the sounds were making my jaw ache, and a knot was forming between my eyes.

I took a big leap up and came down on the green tile with a hard bang that exploded two mice out of the wastebasket. They ran for their lives to the walls. This cleared the basket for pickup and a bolt out the door. I put the basket outside, closed the door tight, and leapt back into bed. The scent of the freeze-dried meal was still in the room, and a half-dozen of my roommates raced around in crazy circles looking for the treasure. But in a few minutes they were all gone. Apparently one of their sentinels had found the stash outside. They all must have learned about it conterminously through some sort of mouse telepathy that humans have still to understand.

As the place started to quiet down, I realized that I'd never shared my space with any other living thing except other humans and well-behaved animals whose genome had been extensively modified. To change that pattern was too much to ask of me in one day. *A human dwelling excludes all others*, I thought. No uninvited life, not even a bug, is welcome. *Humans have learned to fence the entire living world out, and fence themselves in.* Perhaps there are other ways to live, but I couldn't think of any. *I've been in this pattern too long*, I thought.

I dropped off to sleep with the sound of the waves, and with the Field Book upside down on the floor. I doubted that I'd passed my first test in the art of 'Free Attention.'

11: Explorer's Eyes

Imagine a fool with full consciousness—an explorer if you will—who is fully deliberate and fully responsible for his actions, and who is simply taking the next step along a path into the unknown. Such a wise fool is fully lost—he doesn't know where his path is leading. Yet the wise fool is never lost because he has no place to be lost from. For him, there is only 'here' right from the beginning. In this place, is the fool not free?

...*The Field Book*.

AT PRECISELY SIX-THIRTY A.M., there was a loud bang on the screen door of Number Six. A paper plate covered by a large dome of tin foil emerged from around the corner, held in a plump hand. The hand was connected to Edna. A wholesome smell filled the cabin—bacon, for sure, and probably eggs and hash browns to boot.

"Did you sleep well?" she asked.

"Well enough, I guess. I had some company earlier."

"I can see that. There's bits of shredded foil all over the yard. I told you the cabin wasn't ready."

"My fault really."

"Well, it's never a good idea to leave smelly food out at night up here in the woods. I should have told you. When you get a little further north, you're going to have to hang everything. Bears, you know. In '59 a mother and two cubs broke into Number Four, which had an open ham inside. Ripped the door down just like it was paper."

"Thanks for telling me," I said, grateful for the fact that she'd not given me that piece of information to feed my imagination last night.

"Haven't seen a bear up here this winter, but I hear that they're making a big comeback up in Minnesota, with all the hunting regulations and such. Bill faced that momma down bare handed and chased her out of there. There wasn't much that he couldn't handle in his prime."

I could imagine a north woods Dan Boone, standing between Edna and Number Four, ready to give it all if necessary.

"He's been a good man," Edna said, wiping a bit of moisture from her left eye. "I wasn't all that bad, myself, back then. Bill was always calling me 'The Miss America of the Lake Country.' Isn't that a nice thing to say?"

"Very nice. No doubt you were the Miss America of the plains and mountains as well."

She stood for a moment with a faraway look in her eye, remembering. As the morning light struck her face, I could see the beautiful Norse bone structure underneath her wrinkled skin. The skin was still soft and unblemished. My impression of her beauty was something I would have liked to have conveyed to her, but I couldn't find the words.

"I have to start for Rochester. Bill will be looking for me before nightfall. He worries if I'm driving at night. The old goggles aren't quite what they used to be," she said, tapping the side of her head.

"I hope you like Canadian bacon. Had to use it up along with the last of the eggs. No sense letting it spoil. They won't let you bring in your own food up at the hospital. I boiled some potatoes and put some cheese on 'em. And here's a thermos of coffee for the road. You can keep it. It belongs to the Adamsons, but they haven't been back to claim it for six years. I suppose it belongs to the camp now, and I don't need to hold it for them anymore."

She unwrapped a heaping meal from the tin foil and put it on the worn wood of the table.

"I won't take anything for it, especially since you had to live with all of those critters last night."

I didn't know what to say. I'd moved into a world running on a different currency than the $5.99 latte culture I'd left just a couple of days ago. This world was one of unspeakable natural generosity that simply assumed that I would be ready for a lumberjack breakfast and an unannounced family chat at six thirty a.m. After all, the sun had been up for almost seventeen minutes.

"So will you close up and put the key under the mat of the A-frame? You can take your time, but I would appreciate a cleanup of all of that scattered mouse trash out in the yard. And if you could, it would really help if you would take the trash up the road and put it in one of those big dumpsters. Everything that's food will be dragged out and eaten here. It's a mess."

"No problem," I responded.

"You take good care now. By the way, just where in Canada are you headed with all of your new gear?"

"I don't really know. I am heading for a lake in Ontario where my trip is going to start. That's all I can tell you."

"Are you planning to meet Eddie there? The man you call Moses?"

I'd assumed that Moses would be at the place at the end of the road to meet me. But there was nothing in his invitation that promised he would be there. To get to the place marked 'Here' I would have to paddle and portage into the woods for at least ten miles. I had no idea what to expect.

"I can't say. All I can say with certainty is that he sent me an invitation to end my way of life, and an old map with a spot marked 'Here'."

"Sounds just like the fella. He was always full of mystery; always seemed to be part of a group that he would not speak much about. Probably that 'committee' you were talking about last night. If you see him, you can give him this."

She held out a long necklace of beads.

"It's a 'Mala'—one hundred and eight beads made of seeds of the Bodi tree. I don't know much about all of those eastern religions, but I understand something good happened under that tree a long time ago. Eddie left the necklace here all those years ago. I've used it most every night—gotten used to saying my prayers with it. But you're here now, and it's time for me to let it go. If Bill passes, I may be moving on to follow him. We've been together for a long time you know."

I took the necklace.

"Wrap it up around your forearm. That's how Eddie used to wear it. It sure did draw some stares thirty years ago, I can tell you that."

"Thanks, Edna. I'll give this to Moses with your regards if I see him."

"Well good luck to you. Looks like you have a good car. They don't make 'em like they used to."

And with that, Edna turned and walked up the path.

I PICKED UP MOUSE-CHEWED FOIL in the 'front yard' for a half-hour, loaded my gear in the car, and closed up Number Six. I walked up to the A-frame with the key, and put it under a mat with the words 'Welcome to the Camp' circling the image of a frisky Walleye. The sound of small, moist gravel crunched beneath my feet as I walked to the 500. I turned for one last look at the lake.

There. On the dock, unmistakably clear, was a young girl. She stood with the morning light glowing against her skin, looking at me with a steady gaze. A band around her arm was interwoven with three strands of gold. She lifted her arm slowly, turning her wrist over in a dancer's gesture. She bit her lip, and gave me an inviting, winsome smile without guile; then turned her body while continuing to look at me sidelong, as if beckoning me to follow. The girl then exploded into a barefoot sprint down the dock, like a long jumper running so smooth and so fast that it seemed her feet did not even touch the boards. She leapt high off the end of the dock and turned again at the apex of her leap to pull a deep breath through her nostrils—her black hair spinning wide—to smile at me again in just a way that said, "Ain't life grand?" and then she was gone. Not a splash, not a ripple. She simply vanished, leaving something that shimmered the morning light at the end of the dock like a handful of deep magic cast into the wind.

I ran down the dock and stopped at the final weathered board, peering down into the blue water. There was nothing there but my own reflection, broken by small ripples in the surface of the lake. *What the....*

"*—She's part of one future, Charlie, one future. Just one of many potential futures that you might decide to participate within.*"

"I felt so attracted to her," I said aloud. "I felt like she was my own...."

"*—Nothing's predestined, Charlie. Why don't you go back to the car? You still have a long way to go.*"

I turned back to the 500, got in, and turned the key. There were things that were happening that I didn't have the ability to understand. I was beginning to believe that the very fact that I couldn't understand them was important; that I was like a child again, swimming in a world that was far wider than any label I could put on it.

"*—Yes, Charlie, 'beginner's mind' is a wonderful state to be within. In this mind, you don't have to change anything. All you have to do is look around.*"

I WOUND BACK up the gravel road toward the interstate and dropped the trash at a fast food joint with Wisconsinites standing five deep at the counter, then got back onto the long highway north. The 500 was still swimming with the boat on top, but under control in a gentle side-wind. It was still a long way from Loon Lake to the end of the road and the place on the map marked 'Here.'

The car was running well. Edna's coffee was hot, black, and wonderful inside one of those old glass thermoses that would keep it warm all day. As I sipped coffee out of the metal screw-top with the window rolled down, I was filled for just a moment with a calm and manly feeling of riding well-mounted into new country; something I imagined the old explorers or adventurers might have felt as they moved into undiscovered country with their eyes lifted up to a fresh horizon.

In forty-five minutes I crossed into Minnesota, "The Land of Ten Thousand Lakes," most of them long deep slivers and potholes formed by the advance and retreat of glaciers that had scoured the land down to the granite bedrock to melt and leave vast pools of clear, fresh, drinkable water. I kept to the back roads, and the country was getting quieter, with the towns further apart and pine forest stretching out to the horizon.

This journey northward was a journey into simplicity. Where there had been fifty different kinds of trees further south, here there were ten, now seven, now five. The north is ascetic by its very nature; spare and cool. It's an alert place that requires its inhabitants to focus. One cannot risk being unprepared in the north. The killing cold is never all that far from your boot-tops.

With each mile north, I felt that I was winding the clock back to an earlier springtime. I could feel myself moving deeper into this springtime; a season of long light, a long and deep springtime that would never really become summer; only a deeper springtime with a nighttime sun. I imagined other life-forms moving with me into the window of light. Birds were taking flight by the tens of millions. The whales were coming north in the Pacific—surging up the currents by the millions of tons, abandoning the equator. Even the butterflies were flocking from Mexico, unable to make the long journey in a single generation, but rather in waves of propagation that pushed northward to produce the final generation that would make it to Ontario.

As I moved 'up map' I felt myself becoming simpler. With each mile things were being left behind: the need to worry, the need to talk, other needs.

As we moved past Bemidji, the 500 was finally getting her chance to run the open road, and was purring and finding her groove. We were both responding to the cool air and quiet highway, moving through forests free of oak and hickory, forests filled with the scent of pine and the flutter of the first birch leaves on their stems.

When we turned toward the border at Crookston, the road became a two-lane blacktop with no oncoming cars. I stopped, parked the car in the road, and walked out into the woods to smell the forest. There was a spring scent, a warm welling from the forest floor—the same delicious clean scent that had come up from the guide's bag I'd opened in my townhouse. *I'm getting closer.*

I put my tongue on the roof of my mouth and let the spring air circulate. *It isn't just one smell, it's five or six mixed together*, I realized. I'd never parsed a scent in that way before. The quiet and the lack of external stimulation was forcing my attention to go a-looking into new sights and smells. I was coming to appreciate the value of solitude as a generative state of immense possibility.

THERE WAS JUST one small town left before I crossed the imaginary boundary between the United States and Canada. The village was nothing more than a few small houses at a crossroads, and I pulled into the only gas station. A lanky man who'd been sitting in a rusty metal chair rose up and, without asking, began to fill the tank with regular. I went into the station, where a woman sat at the counter reading a local newspaper, drawing on a long cigarette, and blinking her right eye as the smoke curled into it. She had fishing licenses for sale, and the place smelled like she might have a tank of minnows somewhere out back. There was a sparse collection of snacks, and a good supply of canned herring past its expiration date stacked on faded red Formica shelves. The place didn't look like it saw much traffic. An assortment of greasy wrenches was strewn around an open red toolbox next to a trash can that dripped with used quarts of Pennzoil.

I went into the men's bathroom, a small single-stool arrangement with a tile floor that was starting to separate from the concrete below. It had no knob or lock, only a hole in the door where a knob could have been. The door did not shut completely, and there was no way to hold it closed and at the same time have much chance of landing anything within the confines of the toilet bowl. I had the oddest feeling of being watched through the cracked door, but the cashier was looking down and had not moved a muscle. The smoke was still drifting around her eyes.

I examined her through the crack. I was beginning to look at every person now as a potential member of the 'Committee'—some divine being that was here on earth to come to my aid. As I watched her work the newspaper's puzzle, I was ready to see and meet her as an agent of the divine, regardless of the shabbiness of her external surroundings and the fact that I was pissing into a brown toilet.

"—*That's right, Charlie. Every person is an image of the Divine. So nice that you are beginning to practice the art of seeing the Divine everywhere, all the time, no matter what.*"

Right at eye level there was an 'adult novelty' dispenser with products on display in little glassine windows. I resisted the temptation to deposit two quarters and turn the crank, despite the lure of a small picture of a beautiful blond with her head thrown back in a state of high arousal. Her eyes seemed to track downward to where I was peeing into the bowl. She was certainly the best thing in the bathroom, as there was no hot water in the tap, and only a dribble of cold to wash my hands. No towels. I wiped my hands on my pants.

On the way back to the cashier, I passed a few bags of chewy gumdrop candy that had been manufactured to imitate sections of an orange. All of the slices were covered with big crystals of pure sugar, and two-pound bags were on sale for seventy-five cents each. I was not much of a candy eater, but for some reason I had a strong, almost compelling impulse to buy a bag. *Maybe I should trust my instincts*, I thought.

I laid the candy on the counter.

"That'll be $25.73 with the fill-up, gumdrops, and tax," the cashier said, barely looking up from her diffident, dead-end preoccupation with the crossword puzzle.

I looked down at the puzzle. She was struggling to fill in a four-letter word beginning with 'E.'

"Try 'Eros'," I said. "It's a Greek word for intense longing, the desire for something higher and better."

She filled in the horizontal line, cocking an eye up at me with an expressionless nod. I paid for the gas and gumdrops, a transaction which left me $1.27 in cash for the rest of the trip. It didn't matter. I was almost certain that would be enough to make it to the place on the map marked 'Here.'

FIVE MINUTES LATER I was waved across the Canadian border by a pleasant-looking man in a brown uniform. I was crossing the longest peaceful boundary between countries in the world. I knew from my history classes that our last battles with the Canadians had been fought back in 1812 and were now mostly forgotten. *Strange how my country has to fight other countries before we can become friends with them*, I thought. I wracked my brain to think of a single close ally we had not fought savagely before we became friends. Not one. *Maybe we're due for a personality change,* I said to myself.

Once into Manitoba, the blacktop took me out of the forest and on to the flat prairie. The vast and empty wind-swept steppes, naturally sown with generations of low and hardy grasses, were now replaced by endless fields getting ready for their seeds of wheat. The sun was setting across a black earth just turned. Ice glistened in the furrows, making long red bands that strobe-flashed ribbon after ribbon of sunset as I drove past. The quiet and vastness of the plains triggered a decision to drive all night if I had to. *It would be hard to sleep inside walls tonight,* I thought.

AROUND TEN I reached the garish lights of Winnipeg, topped off the tank using my Visa card, then took a road north and east out of town that led back into the forest.

The road grew darker. On each side was a dense blackness of short jack pines. The shoulders disappeared, putting the road on the level of the trees and creating the sense that I was burrowing through the woods. The blacktop ate the illumination from my headlights, their light now only a small moving pool bordered by thick fences of living wood. Edna's coffee thermos had been empty for several hours. The white centerline had also disappeared, and I found myself driving down a black tunnel. I looked down for a moment to check my progress against the faded map Moses had sent me, and then turned my eyes back to the road.

No. Please no. *Not out here in the blackness.*

There was a shape on the road, right on the edge of the light-pool cast by the headlamps. She was standing in the middle of the road sixty feet ahead; now fifty, now forty. The light-pool wreathed around her. Her muscular arms hung loosely at her sides. Glittering eyes were deep set in her face, and small twining horns emerged from her head. I thought I saw a bow in her hand, with an arrow notched. She was smiling, looking right through the windshield at me as two tons of Detroit steel hurtled towards her.

My foot moved from the accelerator to the brake. Too slow. The 500 shuddered violently in a four-wheel lockup. The canoe lurched sideways and down, and the smell of burning tires filled the car. She was right on the front bumper, not moving, just there, smiling. The rapidly decelerating Dodge seemed to move right through her. I couldn't tell whether she was over the car, under it, or had simply disappeared.

And then I saw them.

Three full-grown does. They were leaping in slow motion. The first had already cleared the road, moving from left to right, her head disappearing into the jack pines on the passenger's side. The second landed on her forelegs just out in front of the car; then instantly gathered in the middle of the road for another bound. She exploded with the noise of the locking wheels, and launched off the road in a rainbow arc that carried her into the forest. Then, the third and last: she was already in mid-flight. Her huge brown eye drifted across the front grill right at the level of my own, and then her body filled my entire field of vision. I instinctively pivoted the 500 slightly to the right, buying a couple more inches. Her trailing rear hoof met the upper-right corner of the windshield with a sound of a sledge driving a post. The glass broke into a little starburst pattern about four feet from my head. It concaved into the passenger cabin, but held. She was gone. The whole scene disappeared into the forest.

The 500 was wheezing painfully from somewhere underneath as I brought her to a stop. I pulled the door lever and raced back with a flashlight. I was sure that I would find a body, but there was nothing on the road. I walked slowly down both sides, shining the light a few feet into the forest, searching everywhere. Nothing. I could see the place in the middle of the road where the skid marks began, a swerving 'S' of heavy black. There was no blood or any other sign. I was sure that a woman had been there. I had seen the glitter of her eyes just before impact. But there was no impact. She'd simply disappeared.

I walked back to the 500, which sat askew in the middle of the road. The car was enveloped in a dusty fog that smelled of burned rubber and oil. The engine was still running. Less than ten seconds had passed between the moment the woman had appeared in my headlights and the deer's trailing hoof hit the windshield. All of it could have been a dream; but there on the windshield was the starburst of broken glass.

I ran my hand over it from the outside, feeling its sharp ridges. *There's no questioning this.* A second sooner to the point of impact, a couple of miles-per-hour more, and the two-hundred pound body of that deer would have come right through the windshield into my lap. Had the woman not appeared in my light pool, I would now be lying in the front seat of the 500 with the deer, both of us chest-crushed, and the canoe pointed into the forest and the blackness on either side.

I felt the adrenaline drain out of my body. A limp, rubbery feeling spread down into my fingers and toes. I slumped into the driver's seat. There on the dash was the compass, barely disturbed. It was emitting a glowing light, and its needle swung freely to the north. The Field Book was there on the seat, open to this:

> One sign that you are on the right path is that you will encounter help unlooked for. The Field is something that is behind us, in front of us, through us, enveloping us—all things without exception. Your intention bends the gravity contours of the field, creating a path from all dimensions of the Cosmos to your door.

I put the car in gear and began to move slowly further into the blackness. I didn't know what else to do.

WITHIN A FEW MILES, the road crossed some imaginary line and the smooth blacktop simply ceased. Abruptly the highway became a track: a carving through the woods made by some huge machine that had done little more than plow once through the forest then back again. Trees were strewn akimbo on their sides, their fan-shaped roots upturned and clutching rocks. Boulders the size of washing machines littered the roadway along with a variety of lesser stone. This was not a summer road, but rather a lane made for passage after several feet of snow had covered the rocks. It was likely that machines and men had crawled up here looking for oil or metal, and found nothing. The trees this far north were too small and crooked to entice a logging operation.

I was sure this road was the dotted line on the worn-out map sent to me by Moses. There was an end to the line, and past that end, the wilderness.

IT WAS THREE A.M. The track was becoming so rough that I began to contemplate leaving the car and walking with my gear to the end of the line. The road was washed with little watercourses, many of them flowing vigorously. It was an odd feeling to drive upstream, then motor down small waterfalls on the other side of the hills. The 500 was moving no faster than I could walk, but at least the car was carrying the gear. I decided to put the car in first, go with the flow, and let the 500 carry the weight as far as it could. I was still in relative luxury at four miles per hour.

At last I reached a hillside that was no more than a tumble of stone. There were a couple of red marker flags at odd angles indicating the end of the road. The 500 was really limping now, making a strange whining sound as she slowly released a buildup of steamy pressure. Her all-steel undercarriage had been scraped hard on the boulder road, and she had accomplished a great feat in these last few hours. It was a proud display of reliability, but now it was clear that we could go no further together. An early dawn was beginning to spread a gray half-light all around the wilderness. There was not a sound out here except for the distant call of a loon and the sighing of the 500. I'd come to the end of the dotted line.

I walked up the boulder hill with the map and compass. It was a relief to get out of the car and stretch my legs. There was a breeze coming over the little crest. It was there: the water. The sound of waves on a gravel bar, and a distant shore layered in mist. I was at the end of the road. Somewhere out there was the place on the map marked 'Here.'

12: Leaving Identity Behind

> Who you think you are is a lot less interesting than who you actually are.
> ...*The Field Book*.

A SMALL SPIT of black gravel that sparkled with little pieces of quartz made a pebbly beach at the end of the road. It crunched gently under my feet, leaving wet footprints that slowly filled with clear water. No jagged rocks here—just a gentle slope into crystalline depths. I took off my shoes and walked in ankle deep, feeling the refreshing coolness. I felt thin and stretched from the long night of driving.

There was no sign of a person, camp, or boat. I looked around to see if there was some note somewhere. Nothing. Only the shimmering blue water, the gentle breeze, and the sun coming up over a beautiful spring day.

"He must be out on the lake somewhere," I said aloud, squinting at the horizon. "Somebody's bound to be here in a bit."

I walked back to the car and began to unload my gear. The 500 was covered in dust, and made small cracking sounds as she cooled off. The car looked a bit forlorn with her right eye caved in, like a fighter that had gone the distance. Her chances of starting again were poor, but that was a problem for another day.

I spent the next hour and a half taking camping stuff out of its packaging and trying to find ways to cram it into the two packs I'd purchased. Most of the stuff was encased in sealed thermoplastic bubbles that were designed to resist opening from any angle. I needed wire cutters, a strong utility knife, and a pair of heavy gloves. I felt fortunate that my wrists survived with only a single bloody cut from the sharp plastic edges. The process left several cubic yards of thermoplastic trash sitting in the back seat which would remain intact beyond the next ice age.

I tried to get most of the food and gear into the big pack, but it wouldn't fit. Overstuffed, the Extreme Alaskan weighed at least eighty pounds, and with effort I could dead-lift the sack onto the hood of the car, and then shoulder it from there. My smaller, lighter day pack with 'essentials' like my first aid kit, the global positioning device, and some high carb snacks weighed around twenty pounds. My packs contained only what I believed to be the bare minimum.

I heaved the heavy Alaskan up, nearly busting the straps, then walked up the hill to drop the big pack onto the gravel bar. I clomped loose-limbed down the boulder-field a third time to retrieve the canoe. I slid the boat off the car onto my shoulders. It seemed light compared to the big pack, and was easy to carry up the little hill. I'd rented a wooden carrying yoke for ten bucks that was screwed in as a substitute for the middle thwart. The yoke allowed me to get under the middle of the canoe and carry it solo, balanced on a couple of hard pads which distributed the weight across my shoulders. My legs were eager for a workout after the long drive, and I tottered up the hill with seventeen feet of aluminum on my shoulders. It came down with a crash on the gravel bar.

A hundred sixty-five pounds of boat and gear lay there on the beach, and I turned to make a final trip back for the small pack. The guide's map and compass, my flashlight, watch, wallet, car keys, and the Field Book went in its outside pockets. I tried to power up my cell phone in one last attempt to call my voice mail, but the battery was nearly gone, and there was no reception. I felt the loss of this link—that the last physical connection with my old life was being severed. I was on my own now, at least for a while. I locked the car, shouldered the pack, and walked slowly up the hill carrying the paddles and a life jacket in the early morning light.

I slumped the small pack down onto the ground, and put my butt on the damp beach with my back against the warmth of the metal canoe. I turned my face to the nine o'clock morning sun, drifting. I let my belly relax and felt my breath float in and out as the sun's rays moved through the thin red membranes of my closed eyelids.

Small waves washed gently on the gravel. A warm spring wind was blowing with very low humidity. I could hear tiny springs of snowmelt dripping off moss and lichens on the north faces of the cliffs and in the hollows of the pine bowers that were still in snow. The morning sun was coaxing the aspen to trust that the time had come; that the days were long enough; that the warm south wind would hold; that the wide earth had again made its full journey around the sun. These living beings of the forest, which could not swim or fly but only sway and slowly bend, would soon be pointing like arrows directly into the glowing warmth. Their tops would then begin to open. Millions upon millions of glistening and dancing panels were about to burst from the branches to collect the astonishing abundance of free-falling energy and light.

I spent a few minutes drifting there, letting all of the tension drain, moving to the edge of a dream state, resting. Then the wind shifted, pulling coolness out of the forest and across my chest. My eyes opened slowly in soft focus, and there it was.

It could not have been there before. I'd looked all around. But yet, there it was, right at eye level, stuck on a protruding twig of aspen not twenty feet away.

I walked over and pulled the note off of the branch. It was written in small, careful letters.

"My heartfelt congratulations on making it this far. So we begin!"

"A few 'rules'—helpful (perhaps essential) for this stage of your development and this stage only; rules that are designed to be broken when you have applied them fully and begin to rely on them overmuch; rules that are dangerous for you and everyone else if you stop half-way, and eddy-off to join the legions of puffed-up people who have rule-knowledge and nothing more. Yet, with all dangers known, we begin with 'the rules' in the classic, traditional way. Yes. These rules have been designed by the Committee to give you freedom. They bring life, and the power to create in the phenomenal world from a place of passion, service, and deep bliss."

Rule Number One: 'Going Light'
(A rule pertaining to freedom and joy around physical possessions.)

Everything Necessary to Take the Next Step—Present.
Everything Unnecessary—Absent.

A note to the user:

"Walk in trust that what will be needed for the step following this one will arise at its proper moment. One and only one 'luxury item' with no purpose whatsoever except the expression of your joyfulness must be carried as well. No exceptions. The highest quality is strongly recommended."

Then in a hastier cursive, this was written at the bottom:

"This means leaving four-fifths of the junk you've brought, including your wallet, phone, watch, money, and keys. You won't need them where we're going. Meet us at Ribbon Lake whenever you can get there."

"M."

"Well, I'll be damned," I said aloud.

He'd been here in the moment while I was resting. It had to be—I could *not* have missed seeing that note. Yet, there were no footprints on the soft beach except my own. I waded thigh-deep into the lake to look down the bank for a canoe. Nothing. Was he standing there under that aspen, writing a note while I was sleeping? It was creepy to think he might have been looking into my packs.

Anger began to rise up my spine. How rude to pull me all this way to the end of the road then not even have the courtesy to meet me! I slapped the note with the back of my hand. *And all of this yap*—giving me rules. I had not formally agreed to *anything*. I should be asked first, and asked politely. He should be asking for my consent before bossing me around!

I had half a mind to put my stuff back in the 500 and head back to Winnipeg. I could be there by nightfall, back to somewhere where they used credit cards, and where I could have beer and sleep all of this off in a clean bed. I looked at the faded guide's map. Ribbon Lake was less than an inch away. I probably could be there by the end of the day as well.

Well I've come this far. Might as well give the gear some use, and at least get to the place marked 'Here.'

I turned to my gear, holding the note in my left hand. There was a canoe weighing about eighty pounds, and more than a hundred pounds of other gear in addition. I could not see parting with a bit of it.

I was going out into the wilderness, for Christ's sake. And from what I could remember, the motto of every good Boy Scout was "Be Prepared." No telling what I would run into on the way to Ribbon Lake.

This gear had been carefully selected by an experienced salesperson at a trusted discount retailer. I was fully confident that I had most of the gear I needed: the gas, the stove, the dried food, the first aid kit, the global positioning system, the emergency flares, and a sea-dye marker so I could be spotted by a float plane in the event of an emergency.

After ten minutes of careful analysis, I came to my conclusion. I would comply with the new rule about 'going light' by leaving the shovel behind. With a big wooden handle and steel blade, it was one of the heaviest things in the pack. The ground was too rocky for digging holes anyway.

I unzipped the little pack, pulled out my wallet and keys, and also removed the Field Book. "Sounds like I could put you into the 'non-essential' category if I wanted to," I said aloud, looking at the oily cover of the book and the silly birch bark invitation from Moses stuffed inside. It would serve him right to leave it behind.

I walked slowly down to the 500 with the shovel, the Field Book, and the rest. I unlocked the car, threw in the shovel, put the Field Book on the passenger's seat, and opened the glove compartment.

The wallet, my watch, and the last of the money went in.

I locked the compartment, leaving the Field Book on the seat, put the keys under the fender, and turned to walk uphill. My legs were walking in molasses. I was walking away without the identification that I'd been carrying every day of my adult life.

Dangerous. Very dangerous. Jesus. *This is a mistake.*

My ID, my credit card, my watch, even my library card—the whole kit—was absolutely essential to navigate the world. They were sitting back there abandoned. I could feel the pull of them at my sleeve. Without my watch, I couldn't know what time it was, and whether I was on schedule. Without those papers, I was walking into the world naked for Christ's sake, leaving behind the identity that I'd worked so hard to establish. Without those plastic cards, there was no way to prove who I was. Without them, my identity was subject to change.

"It's a trap. I'm trapped," I heard myself say aloud. Yet I didn't know where the trap was—the place at Ribbon Lake where I might be by the end of the day? Or the place in Winnipeg that could appreciate the value of little papers and plastic, and give me a warm bed in return?

"*—We understand that you have an identity abandoned in the glove box, Charlie. It's your 'cover story,' and it's awfully important to you at the moment.*"

That voice again.

"*—That story determines whether people approve of you, hire you, live with you, and love you—does it not? It determines whether you are 'in' or 'out.' And even more important, it determines who* you *will let in or cast out.*"

"I have a story that does all that?" I asked aloud.

"*—Oh yes, Charlie. Your mask! Yes, yes. Your 'persona'—that bag of old stories and selectively remembered truths, half-truths, quarter truths, and outright lies that you open up at parties and interviews, hoping for approval. You've worked a young lifetime on that story, and it's pretty darn good, as such stories go. But what would it be like to live free from your story? What would that be like? How liberating would that be, Charlie?*"

"What am I doing talking to someone inside my head?" I shouted. *I should be back in Chicago adding the next chapter to my story like all the rest of my friends.* I didn't like the fact that "I" was being abandoned in a dusty old car at the end of a Canadian dirt road. No, not at all!

I turned and walked nine steps back. I unlocked the car and grabbed the Field Book. I fished a pen out of a cubby in the driver's side door, throwing clutter around, agitated that it was taking me so long. He'd said one luxury item, no exceptions. I guessed the little Field Book, a quarter full of still-blank pages, was the item.

I locked up the car again, and ripped a blank page out of the book. "Left for Ribbon Lake, May 2." Signed, "C. Smithson". Then a postscript: "Keys under fender."

"I'll be back before you know it," I said to the trees, knowing it was a lie. I folded the paper twice, put it on the windshield, and walked away.

I WALKED OVER THE HILL, leaving my identity behind. I pulled the canoe into the lake, arranged the packs and pushed off, sloshing a gallon of water into the boat and almost tipping it over as I pulled my boots in. There was a surge up the back of my spine, a little thrill. I was entering a world that was not divided by fictional segments of time or by groups of people stacked and ranked. This new world could care less about papers in a glove box or what those papers might say about who I was. This new world was the real world, beckoning and billowing up her skirts at me on a beautiful spring day.

13: Sunday Morning

You have chosen to observe the God that is right in front of you with a limited clarity, the way you might look at a picture in a gallery, or an animal on display at the zoo. You are an observer, a customer, someone separate from the divine to be pleased or displeased by the display, always thinking you are in control. This is a grievous error. You have forgotten that you are within God, the creation. That creation is the big part, and you the small.
...*The Field Book*.

I GUESS IT HAD TO START on a day that felt like Sunday in the park. It was one of those days with a gravitational pull into itself; so gentle a day that any loving nurse would open the hospital windows and wheel her invalids out to feel the sun. A little south wind was blowing with very little moisture in the air. This was an early spring day, excited by its powers, that was jumping ahead thigh-deep into summer. The light was clean. It fell like light on a mountain: dappled, bent, and shimmered by the first buds of aspen around the lake. Through the aspens, the light fell like thousands of tiny droplets out of the head of a gardener's can.

Everything was gentle that morning. "God's green earth," my Grandmother would have said. The heat was moving the air, lifting moisture from the cool water, slightly veiling the big sky and open horizon. This was a day to worship the sun. As I paddled across the lake, I found myself in the middle of a fantastic Sunday morning in the biggest and most beautiful park imaginable.

It seemed silly to listen to the vague sense of foreboding that was climbing up my back as I pushed further out into the water. The day was just too nice for such things. I was young and full of strength. The little spit of gravel at the end of the road disappeared behind me as I put my back into the paddle, switching from one side to the other to stay on course, surging across the lake.

The sun was high when I reached the far shore and attempted my first portage through the woods. The route to Ribbon Lake followed a chain of shallow pools, each connected by short carries across land. There was a clear trail showing signs of boot prints. The tracks were fresh.

I struggled at the portage, feeling a slight twinge in my back as I muscled the canoe up onto my shoulders. There was no way I could carry all my stuff across in one trip. My gear weighed more than I did. No big deal. The portage was a mere forty yards, and I could see the other lake after just fifteen steps. I took one trip across with the canoe and walked back; a second round-trip with the big pack; then a final walk across with the small pack, paddles, and my life jacket. Five crossings total; two hundred yards of walking to move forty yards toward Ribbon Lake.

On the other side of the portage, the water began to narrow into a beautiful chain of smaller interconnected lakes. Other than the boot prints, there was no sign of any person. I'd made it into the wilderness, and this warm Sunday morning was a day to fall in love. This was the most beautiful temple I'd ever seen, a place made just for me.

I moved through the chain, paddling with my shirt off to soak up the rays. I began to feel quite pleased with myself; I was now a woodsman. I knew the names of some of the plants from a botany course I'd taken as an elective back in college, and was silently ticking them off in my mind. I'd gotten 'A's' in earth science; I was practically a professional naturalist. The exercise of paddling was really no strain at all, just a vigorous stretching of muscles ready to be used. Each stroke of the paddle produced a sizzling arc of droplets that fell into the boat. The light and water danced together.

The lakes unfolded before me just as they appeared on my high-tech global positioning device. It was comforting to be in such intimate communion with a web of satellites quadrangulating my exact position on the surface of the earth. *No chance of getting lost with this baby,* I thought. I was glad that the furry man had outfitted me so well. I knew *exactly* where I was. These woods were not so different from a clump of trees in any city park. I'd spent a lot of time in parks. *Nothing here to be afraid of.*

From my botany class, I'd learned a lot about nature, and was ready to tell myself all about it. I proceeded with textbook definitions of the things passing around me: flora, fauna, boreal forest, coniferous trees of the genus *Pinus*, in the family *Pinaceae*. *Poulus tremuloides,* the 'quaking aspen.' "Nothing like knowing the Latin name to show that you've really grabbed hold of something," my botany teacher had said. I could pass any challenging short course in memorization. I felt amazed at my powers of recall, especially considering how little sleep I'd had in the last couple of days.

How pleasant it is to be here naming and noting in the womb of nature, I thought. This is easy. Not so different than being at home in Chicago in front of a big screen, watching the digitized flight of a bald eagle. I can sit here enjoying nature in my comfortable canoe chair, eating my processed food out of foil bags, and thereby participate in the grand design of creation: its birth, life, and death. I was ready to name the stars should they be out tonight. I already knew the big ones: Vega, Antares, and Daneb. I could name the constellations in which they sat. The vast expanse of interstellar space was pre-organized into the shapes and forms of my familiar terrestrial world. The spheres all revolving around *me* in a kind of a literary world where I could simply open nature's book, have a good read, then close the opus at my convenience. And the best part—the really good part—was that all of this vital knowledge was so learnable, so teachable, and testable. I could classify, name, record, number, and note. *That* was the way to get hold of the important stuff.

It was great to be part of the ecosystem.

I WAS INTO my third lake when the light on the waterway began to slant, coming now in shafts divided by the tall trees beside the water. The air was filled with an early mayfly hatch that rose up spinning thick and golden in the afternoon light. It seemed like I'd traveled fifty miles. I looked down at the GPS device. I was less than a third of the way to Ribbon Lake. My shoulders started to slump, and my breaths came in big sighs from my belly. There was tightness behind my eyes. I began to think that I might have overdone it, pushing out this far all in one day with so little sleep. The lake was getting weedy and shallower.

I could see no place to camp on these shores. The banks were all covered by a dense wall of reeds. The GPS showed all of these lakes to be open bodies of water instead of shallow reed-beds. I put down the GPS for a moment and took out the guide's map. There was a notation that I had not noticed earlier next to the entire chain of small lakes that led to Ribbon. It said: "Not here."

One more medium-length portage would take me into a bigger lake that might have open water and a place to camp, and I had enough energy to attempt one last portage. I bent down to pick up the canoe, and nearly fell into the boat as I leaned forward. The mosquitoes were bad here, and were joined by a thick swarm of biting black flies. The skin between my shoulder blades had changed. The skin now felt thick and stiff, and I couldn't move my back without a crackling pain.

I flipped the boat on top of me, splashing heavily sideways, and falling forward into the water, banging my knees on rock, dumping the boat, and swamping it full of water. I pulled the canoe to shore, and stood at one end to flip it over and get the water out. I managed to shoulder the boat on my second attempt, and took a couple of steps in the water with the load on top of me. All the weight was pressing down on a few square inches of shoulder, and those shoulders were screaming at me.

It's him I have to blame for this.

The portage started with a steep ascent up a little hillock. The small rise was a force resisting me. Each step required a deliberate flat placement of my foot, a bend of the knee, and then a hoist of the weight with my thighs. I could only move six inches a step. The intense leg presses were knocking the wind out of me. I slowly ascended, pushing uphill inches at a time with the blood pounding in my ears. *I hope my heart will stay in my chest.*

I neared the end of the portage and could see the surface of the big water through the trees that promised relief from the pain, a good camp, supper, and sleep. The water ahead was sparkling gold as its surface caught the light. The surrounding woods were starting to cool as afternoon shadows crept into the forest, but it was still a warm day on the surface of the lake. I took my five trips back and forth across the portage.

On my last trip across, I didn't have to look back to know what was happening. I could feel it at the base of my spine. The wall of the wilderness was closing up behind me in the dark shadows of the late afternoon. This wall had been closing up behind me all day, but now it was getting closer. Soon the wilderness would overtake me, and I would be in it alone when night came to the forest.

14: Sunday Evening

If you only knew the beauty of who you are, you would beg for more light to illuminate every corner of yourself. The light of awareness is a miracle, and the awareness itself heals. When we've begun in earnest, we commit to the light's revelation—whatever it reveals—fully, unconditionally; open and curious. Yes, yes, and yes again to whatever arises—yes.
...*The Field Book*

As I cleared the portage, the swollen places on my shoulders where the carrying yoke and pack straps bit into my sunburned skin were just a small sub-sensation in a much louder symphony of pain that reached into all layers of my muscle and bone. I dragged the loaded canoe into the water stumbling from exhaustion.

On the backlit LED screen of my GPS device, the lake looked like it might be a good place to camp: a scenic spot with a small river running into it on the north end. The guide's map had offered a different opinion. Looking out, I saw nothing but a shallow, weedy marsh stretching into the distance, with a small patch of open water near the middle. A forest of thick reeds covered the banks on all sides and the lake was hemmed in tightly with impenetrable stands of black alder. There was no visible open space on the shores; no place to camp, to rest. Going on was not a possibility now. I could go no further today. I was already pressing my luck, exhausted, stumbling, and becoming careless. My knees were bleeding.

Only two hours of daylight were left, and I couldn't set up the tent in my canoe. The only campsite possibility was a mournful fourth-choice location sitting in the center of the marsh on the edge of the open water. It was a big domed-shaped boulder, without soil or a flat spot to lie on.

"This is total bullshit!" I said aloud. It had been such a long trip getting here. The sense of excitement that had filled the morning had faded completely. All I wanted to do was to collapse in a heap and have someone else cook my dinner and take care of me. But I was no longer in a place where such a thing was possible, and thinking about my plight only made things worse. Nothing was going to happen unless I did it myself.

Sometime in the last few hours there had been a radical shift in verbs. Just two days ago, I was one of the millions of people on the planet who described their day with words like fly, drive, fax, study, order (as in dinner), ride, call, analyze, and shower. I had moved five miles into the wilderness and two centuries back in time into a world of different verbs, all of which described back-breaking labor. Pull. Carry. Paddle. Push. Walk. Climb. Lift. Balance. Hoist. Load. To move, to eat, or even to sleep in a place like this required more effort in a day than I was used to expending in a month.

If that son of a bitch had just met me at the end of the road, both of us could have paddled, and we would have been in the clear waters of Ribbon Lake by now. We could have spread the work, I thought.

I'd just left a world where numbers of people meant obstacles: a hassle, a longer line, a crowded expressway. In this different country and different time, they meant real help. I could now see that a tribe was a working cooperative focused on the task of staying alive. To live outside of the tribe, alone, was not a long-term survival possibility. Something in my body—one of the older places back at the base of my brain—knew this as a fact. My body was saying that it was dangerous here, dangerous to be alone. My low brain wanted to panic, but I choked the panic down. The wisdom of the older part of my body said that it was time to start a heavy adrenaline flow to get me back to the tribe. But panic would not help me now. The more advanced, strategic part of my brain knew that a body chemistry change would not even carry me back over the last portage. I was here, stuck in the weeds, too tired to move.

Something unasked-for was now starting to happen. A deep sadness—a loneliness—was coming up from the depths. The sadness was a powerful feeling that I could not control—a feeling bigger than I was; a feeling that could swallow me alive.

This is the belly of the whale, I thought. I'm being led into the belly of the whale.

I HAD TO MAKE CAMP. I paddled out to the egg-rock. It turned out to be slightly bigger than it looked from shore, with a shallow indentation in its top about four feet long and two feet wide that might keep me from rolling into the water.

I unloaded onto the rock and began to set up camp. I had two segmented fiberglass poles in my pop-up tent kit that were strung together with a long elastic shock cord. Once out of the bag, the poles clicked instantly into wiggly filaments ten feet long. Pushing the squirming poles through the nylon tent sleeves and fastening them into grommets was a job for at least two people. I strained the tenting to the breaking point and finally made a structure that caught the wind like a sail. Tent stakes were useless. Any kind of breeze would blow me right off the rock.

I rolled out my sleeping bag, and threw the Field Book inside the tent along with a couple of energy bars. I unpacked the gas stove and boiled a quart of water. I'd carried in about three pounds of sugary hot chocolate, so I made myself a triple cup. I instantly felt better, but had no enthusiasm for a freeze-dried meal. The sun was just at the top of the trees.

"Maybe there're some fish in this lake," I said, envisioning flaky and delicious fast food: Alaskan Pollack fish burgers all hot and oily and cut square to fit on a nice sesame bun. I had no realistic idea what it would take to catch, clean, and cook a fish.

I managed to rig my rod, and with help from the how-to pamphlet that came with the reel, I tied on a fancy white lure with a shiny blade, a pink tail, and three sharp hooks. "Guaranteed to catch anything that swims," I said aloud, reading the slogan on the lure's package.

I cast the lure as the sun dipped over the trees. The spinner ran about three feet, barely sinking out of sight when it was slammed by a small pike no more than ten inches long. I reeled the fish in quickly, unhooked it, and threw it back into the water. The pike looked inedible: a thin wriggly mass of small teeth and bones. The hairy man had warned me that a pike was a primitive fish with 'Y' shaped bones sticking upward into the meaty part of its back. These could easily lodge inside my throat, choking me to death with springy tines.

The next cast barely hit the surface before the spinner was hit and hit again by a school of tiny pike. The lure was a third their size, and they were too small to hook themselves on their first try. It was clear to me now that the lake was overpopulated, and the fish were competing with tremendous fierceness for any bit of potential food that hit the water. I reeled in another tiny fish and released it. My hands were now covered with slime, and the mosquitoes were starting to announce themselves.

Hoping for one fish of edible size, I cast out further into the open water. What was probably the biggest pike in the lake hit the pink tail of my spinner, and the fish inhaled the lure down into its gullet. I pulled it in, flopping and slippery. There was no way to free the fish—all three of the sharp treble hooks were down its throat. I wrestled with the thing, trying to stick my finger down its mouth to free the hooks. I got one hook free only to catch another barb in the soft flesh of the pike's throat. The barbed hooks were doing their job. The only way the lure could move was backward into the fish.

My index finger was being shredded by tiny pike teeth, and finally in frustration I gave the lure a yank. A ribbon of bright red blood poured out over my hand and forearm. The lure was out, but a red fish gill was hanging on one of the trebles. I'd ripped the fish's lungs out, and his mottled green color turned grey-white there in my hand.

On the scale of all that humans do, have done, and will do against the natural world, the death of this tiny pike in its overcrowded home world was no big tragedy. A biologist would say that half the fish here could be removed, and it would do the place a favor. Probably a big pregnant mother had swum in one spring when the creek at the far end was swollen, laid her eggs, and thousands of her offspring had come alive only to be trapped and cut off in this weedy enclosure. But in my weakened condition, killing the pike, and watching it die in my hand unnerved me, and brought up a racking sadness which teetered me on the rock. I threw the fish out as far as I could into the weed beds, where he lay in the last light of day with its white belly facing up. It was then that the sun went down.

When the sun fell below the horizon, a wave descended on the rock. My sunburned face and neck came alive with a dozen stings hitting at once. I frantically slapped at them with my slime and blood covered hands. All this did was butter the bread for the plasma drinkers. I rushed down to the water, nearly breaking my rod as I stepped on it, stumbling and furiously splashing water over my face and hands. I fled into the tent and closed up my little world against the mosquitoes, thankful for this tiny bit of human, separated space. Without it, I would be dead by morning.

INSIDE THE TENT the small shelf was just big enough to keep me from rolling into the lake if I lay flat on my back and didn't move. I was exhausted. I could only lie and listen to the buzz of tens of thousands of tiny wings. There were four or five mosquitoes on every square inch of netting—buzzing, poking, and probing their beaks into the tiny holes, looking for any opening. The sound was making my arms and back itch even though I knew that they were not inside.

I stared up at the nylon, but was too tired and miserable to sleep. After half an hour, I switched on my headlamp and felt around for the Field Book.

In a section called "The Fool's Journey," this was written:

> The training stage of spiritual life is about cultivating the willingness to welcome the light, and the wilderness is a great illuminator. It tends to show us exactly every weakness, and builds on every strength. There's not a corner of the room it will not reveal. Most people don't love themselves—all of themselves—enough to be open and curious about what starts to arise when they are placed in an environment that

begins to deconstruct the small, dense self. This
deconstruction makes room for something new. Most
people run from difficulty and pain, going from pillar to
post, drink to distraction, and drama to death to avoid
revelation at all costs. But in the wilderness, there is nowhere
to hide. The lights are on. The best part of ourselves has
chosen and brought us to a place where we can't wriggle out.

And then, on the next page, these lines appeared, written in a different pen and color. I had the oddest sensation that the entry had been made just today. But of course this was impossible. The Field Book had been in my pack until just a few minutes ago.

And by the way, the revelation does not happen in an
'ecosystem'—some place outside us. The world is not an 'it,'
a place from which we are separate, that we can name, order,
and classify to please ourselves, and then think that we have
come into some important kind of knowledge. The healing
always happens in a place that knows us, the very place from
which we are made, that loves us, that is giving its whole life
to help us—it is so proud of us—its magnificent creation.
The healing happens in a very special place. It's a place called
'home.'

I TURNED OFF the headlamp, and my body finally gave over. The dream came again.

Again, the long tunneled hallways, the endless walking with no escape. Down and down into the boiler room vibrating with barely contained raw energy. And they were there again, the blue eyes, waiting. But now they were deep-set in the calm face of a huge silver-gray she-wolf, who was circling me in a sandy ring.

"I'll fight you for my freedom," I said.

"I'll play you for your life," the animal replied.

I tried to gain an advantage, but she rushed in, twisting and coiling into the air, coming over the top and behind me, falling with fangs open onto me, smashing me to atoms. There was no pain. A clean breeze then flowed around me, billowing my hair. I leaned back with arms stretched wide and looked into a limitless blue sky. The prison was a low castle of white stone fading into the distance. The blue eyes were now in the face of a woman at the tiller of a boat. The beautiful eyes were smiling at me, and I could look into them now without fear, without hiding. We were both filled with joy.

15: The Swamp

Perhaps the greatest spiritual gift is the gift of failure. Failure teaches us that we need something greater than ourselves. If we seek great teaching and great learning, we will choose to put ourselves deliberately into situations where failure is almost certain. Failure creates a point of vulnerability that makes us receptive to something new, that opens us to a new way, a new teaching and possibility. When we attempt the impossible, we invite failure and are forced to become faithful, believing in the growing, believing in the process, believing in the guide.
    ...*The Field Book.*

I AWOKE THE NEXT MORNING, still in the presence of the dream. I lay motionless in the crook of the rock except for my breath which rose and fell on its own. I was being breathed. There was something or someone else inside me, breathing me, making my chest fall up and down, and taking deep, effortless breaths from my belly. These breaths were powerful draughts of air, delicious and nourishing. They had a cleansing effect on my nervous system, and washed the stress out of my body and mind. Every part of my body was completely still, watching the breathing. *These breaths are like food*, I thought to myself. *If I could learn to breathe like this all of the time, I could live for two hundred years.*

I rolled the dream around in my mind. I was afraid that the dream was telling me that I was about to die. Yet the feeling of the dream was different. The dream felt hopeful. I felt like the dream was trying to tell me that there was cause for hope and that it was possible to somehow change and get free. I had no idea how this freedom could happen. And then I tried to move.

There was a reason that only my breath was moving. The rest of my body could not move. Every inch of me felt like it had been hammered with a rubber mallet. There were sore spots within aches within stiffness within pain. The skin between my shoulder blades was like red crackling paper. My back had conformed to the contour of the rock, which had twisted my spine into an unnatural shape that popped and ached into alignment as I elbowed my torso out of the indentation. I managed to sit up. The sun was already two hands above the horizon. Thank God the mosquitoes had left with the eight o'clock sun.

I unzipped the mosquito netting and stood up. This simple act brought some relief, and my body began to re-align. The pike had disappeared from the edge of the weed-bed where I'd thrown it last night. On a half-submerged log about forty yards away, there was a beautiful bird with an eagle's beak and sharp talons ripping off chunks of the fish and raising its head to swallow them. I immediately felt better, seeing that the osprey was there treating itself to an easy breakfast. Some good had come from my senseless killing. *Maybe this is a place that will allow me to make a mistake and not be too angry*, I said to myself. Back in my lawyer world, there were no second chances. At the Thompson firm, there were no forgiving margins; there was no room to fail.

I had no appetite for breakfast, and no energy for the task of pumping up the stove or cooking. I filled my two-quart aluminum canteen with water, and put four iodine tablets in the container per the instructions on my water safety kit. It would take fifteen minutes for the water to be chemically altered in a way deemed fit for drinking. The prospect of dragging four pounds of tasteless hot liquid around with me all day could not have been less appealing, especially in an environment where I was floating atop billions of gallons of crystal clear water. Even in this reedy lake, I could see straight to the bottom. Yet according to the Hairy Man, water safety in the backwoods was incredibly important. There were microbes everywhere that could kill me. I wondered what all of the deer and moose and beavers were drinking out here. Maybe they were all just dying slowly of microbe poisoning and didn't know it.

With the water soaking in its chemicals, I reached into the small pack for one of my single-wrapped granola bars, and out fell the slip of paper that I'd pulled off the tree yesterday. There was something written on the back that somehow I hadn't noticed before. It was another 'rule.'

RULE NUMBER TWO: 'GOING FORWARD'
(A rule relating to freedom of movement and rapid forward progress toward wherever you are going on 'life's pathway.')

ONCE A QUEST IS UNDERTAKEN, THERE IS TO BE NO GOING BACK TO SOME EARLIER PLACE OR TIME.

A note to the user:

"To look backward with your precious awareness robs you of the power to create what is next here and now, and works against the great intention of the universe—to evolve and create a future different from the past. This rule is designed to help you end repetitive cycles, seize the moment, and leave the past behind. When new opportunity is at hand, there is no reason to turn back to wash the dead. Let the dead bury the dead. You are moving forward."

Then this postscript:

"Out here, this means that there is to be one and only one trip across any trail, crossing, or passage, with no exception. This requires everything to be carried at once—no carrying the canoe across and then going back for the packs. If you obediently follow the first rule about 'going light,' your life support system is at its minimum and is not capable of being divided. Safety rests in having everything accessible, all of the time. Also, you will be able to begin to flow across the land, and to move here like you belong instead of crashing around like a blind rhino."

"M"

I was beginning to feel freaky about all of this writing. At Ribbon Lake I would find out just who was behind all of this.

I PACKED UP. This process took over an hour. I shuffled and reshuffled, but the stuff just wouldn't fit the way I'd packed it on the hood of the 500. I stretched the nylon of the Alaskan to the bursting point. My food was getting crushed. I ended up tying my tent and sleeping bag on the outside, even though they might get soaking wet there.

Finally I shoved off, with the canoe listing slightly to one side from the weight of the gear. *Boy, am I happy to be out of this shit swamp hole. We'll try only one trip across the portages today, and see what happens.*

Seated in the stern, I pulled out the old paper map to cross-check my position. Whoever had been the map's previous owner had marked the passage to Ribbon Lake with small blue lines indicating the portage trails. The route, as marked on the old map, followed a series of unnamed lakes north of Ribbon, with about a half dozen medium-long portages between each of them. The route then curled back south and a little west like a fishhook. The tip of the hook pointed into Ribbon Lake on its eastern side. It looked like at least two days travel at the rate I was going. *Too long and too hard*, I thought. I pulled out the GPS device for a second opinion. "Here, look!" I said aloud.

Clearly there was an easier way. The west end of Ribbon Lake was not that far from where I was now. *I can take the stream out of this weedy lake and then right here ...* pointing to the lighted screen—I could carry my stuff less than two hundred yards to that little stream that flows right into Ribbon from the west. The route was so obvious and simple I wondered why it was not marked on the guide's map. It would save me five portages and a day and a half of travel.

IN THE STREAM at the end of the reed lake the water became so shallow that I had to step out and drag the canoe. Thank God I didn't have to unload it. The sky was changing, and the air was growing rapidly colder. Low gray clouds filled the space above me. A cold misty dampness was setting in, making the forest close and intimate around me.

As I sloshed up the narrow creek, I felt for just an instant that someone was behind me. I swiveled my head to see who was there. No one. Only the wind. I turned back to pull the canoe up and over the rocks. I heard a twig snap, then a footfall so soft that it might have been nothing but a branch brushing the ground. I stood up and scanned the northern shoreline. "Who's there?" I yelled. Silence. I peered into the bushes, but the black alders on the shoreline were so thick that my gaze could only penetrate a few feet. I was sure that something was there. Someone was watching me.

I cleared the little river and climbed back into the boat, pushing swiftly across the water to get clear of the narrows and to put some distance between me and the northern shore. I couldn't shake the feeling that there were eyes focused on my back as I moved away. *Maybe it's nothing. Don't start to imagine things, Charlie. Don't even turn around. Your job is to stay focused and get to Ribbon Lake as soon as possible.*

I paddled to the spot just north of the little creek leading into Ribbon Lake from the west. "There it is," I said to myself. On one of the trees there was a fresh blaze—an axe mark still oozing sap. "Yes!" I said aloud, looking at the GPS device in my hand. This mark was right where it should be, right at the point where the screen indicated the shortest route would be. There was even a path up out of the lake, wide and clear.

But something in my gut was feeling strange about this. There was something about that oozing mark on the tree that was giving me an odd feeling; like the tree was trying to tell me something.

What's the tree saying? I asked myself.

It's saying "no" Charlie. "No."

But this is clearly a trail. What's the big deal?

I got out, and briefly considered leaving my packs and canoe to go on a little scouting mission and confirm that my plan would work. However, leaving my gear would violate Rule Two, and I disliked the idea of getting separated from my equipment now that safety was an obvious issue. I decided to take it like a man, gear up, and carry everything to the little river at once. It was only two hundred yards or so. *I should be able to see the stream in a couple of minutes*, I thought, and I can rest if I get tired and take it in stages. Besides, spending two lonely and mosquito-filled days taking the long way around didn't feel that good in my gut either.

I tied my lifejacket to the back seat, and wedged my paddle and the spare between the yoke and the front thwart. *I won't need this water—it's too heavy,* I said to myself as I took a couple of deep drinks of iodine liquid, then poured the rest out on the ground. *I can fill up again at that little creek when I get there.* Going this short distance without water will save me a few pounds right there.

I put the GPS device into my pocket so I would have it handy. I slung the big Alaskan onto my back, and then put the little pack on my chest, double packing. I couldn't see my feet, but at least I had everything. And then there was the canoe. It came up on the first try, staggering me. "Jesus, this is heavy," I said aloud. I was loaded like a mean mule, and the weight was bearing down to the point where the power of my diaphragm could barely lift my chest enough to draw a breath. Yet, I was able to take a step, then another and another. I was moving. *Just a few more yards,* I said to myself.

I walked a hundred steps, crushed under the weight, but following comforting axe marks that appeared on trees every twenty feet or so. There was no real trail on the ground. The trees were getting smaller with more space in between. The axe marks disappeared, and the trees opened into what appeared to be a meadow. *At last! Some flat easy walking,* I thought. And then the ground underneath me began to move.

My right foot sank up to the shin and the five yards of ground in front of me wobbled slightly. Then my left foot went in up to the thigh. After that, I simply vanished.

I WAS STILL UNDER THE CANOE, with my head in the yoke and the rest of my body fully submerged. The packs were bobbing slightly in a thick jelly-like substance dense enough to support them easily, but through which they could not move. I was spitting small black and green particles that were already fully up both my pant legs and inside my shirt. A cold sweaty panic raced down the back of my arms. *This is going to take me,* I thought. It's a pit like the pits that trapped the mastodons and saber tooth tigers. *I am probably standing on their petrified carcasses right now.* I began to struggle violently, getting deeper in.

The air was foul under the canoe from my panicked breath, and the small space started to fill with mosquitoes. *I need to get this damn canoe off me. It's going to push me into the pit.*

I managed to roll the canoe to the right. The boat sat up as if it were on dry ground, its weight easily supported across its seventeen-foot length. The canoe was not sinking me—just the opposite—it was the one thing I had that could hold me up. Most of me was underground, and without the canoe to pull up on, I might have been stuck there forever. I wiggled out of the chest pack, tossing it into the canoe, and then grabbed the carrying yoke. With a lunging effort I got a grip on the gunwale on the canoe's far side.

Take it slow now, Charlie, slow hard pull.

The pit did not want to let go of my feet. I pointed my toes like a dancer and pulled. My knees felt like they were going to come apart. One inch, two. I was coming up slowly with a slurping sound. The muck let go of my torso, and I pulled my waist over the boat. The weight of the Extreme Alaskan on my back rolled me over like a tortoise with a heavy shell, and I flopped back-first into the canoe, a motion that levered my legs out of the pit like a high jumper clearing the bar. I fell into the canoe, panting. Every fold of my skin was covered, and every orifice of my body had been individually invaded by a wet jelly made of tiny black, brown, and greenish particles. It was not water. It was not land. It wasn't a pit either. "Holy shit," I said aloud. "What *is* this?"

I twisted my shoulders to get out of the heavy pack, and hand-walked myself to one of the seats, with my feet still dangling out of the boat. I reached into a slimy pocket for my GPS device. No luck. It just wasn't there. Panicking, I shoved my arm shoulder-deep into the muck, and my fingers made contact with the wet plastic of the device. The jelly was holding on to it just like everything else. The device came slurping up without its battery cover. Sticky particles had covered it inside and out. I pressed the 'on' button. Nothing. I banged it against my wet palm. Still nothing. The device was toast. There had been another GPS on sale at the discount store for a hundred bucks more. *That must have been the waterproof model.* This one was now a wilderness paperweight.

I dug into my pack, pulled out the map, and looked at the narrow band of 'land' that separated me from the little stream. There were markings on the map: many small blue tufts of grass. I slowly unfolded the paper, looking in amazement. There were little blue tufts everywhere on the map—vast stretches of them bigger than many of the lakes. I looked down to the faded map legend in the lower-right corner, and found a little blue tuft-mark and the word next to it. "Swamp," I said aloud.

I looked out onto the 'meadow.' The open field was a living black sucking swamp. A few weak, waterlogged pines and several dozen cedars were somehow growing in the wet. The GPS had shown this area as land. The dedicated high-use buttons, UBS interface, treasure hunt game, and barometric altimeter were apparently not designed to distinguish swamp from land. I stared at the old guide's map. There were hundreds of blue blotches (the lakes) and a few ribbons of river. Lakes and streams filled up almost a third of the map space. Another third was filled by the little blue swamp signs. Only about a third of this wilderness was dry land.

I was becoming educated. This was first-hand experience of the dominant flora of the great northern wilderness—the living, green-black, sucking swamp. No telling how deep it was, but it was surely deeper than I was tall. I tried to scrape the muck away from my skin, but it wouldn't leave me. The particles were so fine that they caught in the tiniest folds of the skin, staining it like green-black fruit juice. This was a wet compost bin, in slow decomposition since the last ice age. Billions of rotting tons of the muck were suspended in other countless billions of gallons of tepid green mosquito rainwater. The swamp oozed blue in places, as if droppers full of oil had been squirted onto the surface.

I looked out at the swamp. About forty yards away there was another ax blaze, clear as day, on an old cedar. "It can't be more than a hundred yards," I said to myself. This is the path to Ribbon Lake. *Just hang in there.*

OVER THE NEXT FIVE HOURS, my education continued at a rapid pace. Nothing else did.

My first lesson was that measurement in artificial units, like feet or yards, meant nothing here. Units of measurement could not give forewarning about the difficulty of the passage, which was the only information that mattered.

How long was a yard? Sitting inside the canoe loaded with gear, I could gain a yard by using the paddle as a push-pole, but only if there was a grassy tuft or log to push against. The swamp-surface did not permit a glide. I pushed the paddle to the breaking point, then sat.

How long was a foot? Pushing did not work over parts of the swamp that were more like land, and I was forced out of the boat, crawling forward on my knees, holding onto the canoe for support; then sinking and being grabbed by sticky slop; happy now just for inches as I slowly pulled my gear forward.

How long was ten yards? There were little islands of nearly solid land where I could get footing; so it was back on with the packs and up with the canoe. I could stagger forward over these islands four times as fast as the push, drag, and crawl; but the stagger always ended with a step off an unseen ledge. At the edge of most islands, I walked into swamp that was more like water and just disappeared.

There was no sign of the creek anywhere. *I should have intersected it hours ago*, I thought. *I should go back and look.* "But for what Charlie, for what?" I said aloud. "You've crawled over every inch of this ground. You would have seen the creek if it was there."

By late afternoon, I was well beyond being brought to my knees. The mosquitoes, black flies, and the crawling things in the swamp had taken me down much lower. The flies were unlike any flies I'd ever encountered—they bit and chewed small pieces of my flesh, preparing my skin for others of their kind to take the feeding deeper. The space under the canoe was a windless catch-haven for the bugs. Their beaks and mouths were probing everywhere; up my pant legs and through my shirt. But the worst part was that my head had gone wrong. My ears had become so hard and large that I could no longer touch them to the sides of my face. My neck had become a single grotesquely inflated lymph node. My body was swelling in a futile attempt to slow the circulation of toxins from the beaks and biting mouths of the insects.

My system was being overrun and was dangerously close to shutting down.

I had been five hours without water. The empty canteen dangled uselessly at my side. Drinking the oily slicks pooling on top of muddy flecks of swamp-shit was impossible. I would be drinking slime. Dehydration was chalking my throat, and my breath was coming out in a thin whine. The swamp was spinning.

I'm going to die out here. I'm going to fall in, go under, and die. There's no end to this place. Night will come, and I will literally be eaten alive.

I dragged the boat a few more yards to a bit of dry land with a single small green pine growing on it. I looked out at the swamp and saw something that gave me a glimmer of hope. Not more than fifty feet away, a ribbon of open water was showing.

After a brief panting rest, I resolved to make the supreme effort. I could see a pathway to the ribbon of water if I stepped perfectly with the weight: my right foot on that submerged log, then my left on the grass—a few steps on the floating moss, then a bit more dry land....

I put the packs on and crawled under the canoe to a crouched position. I managed to lift all the weight with a massive squat thrust and ran forward with the boat balanced on the middle of my back, bent over ninety degrees and facing the ground, panting and whining through tears. In this position it was impossible to keep the bow more than a hands-width above the ground, while the stern jutted wildly into the air.

Impact.

When the front of the boat hit the cedar stump, I experienced a slow collapse, folding over sideways with my head wedged in the carrying yoke. My feet were still firmly planted, sinking into the black oozing mass. These combined physical forces worked to bend me over, stretching me at the waist and neck like the latest version of a swamp Gumby Doll. The top of my head was buried in swamp shit. It was then, bent in that obtuse angle, through the steam of my breath and the small window of clarity left to me, that I saw the boot.

Part Three:

Choosing the Path

16: Meeting the Guide

> No one can come to God except through God. The goal of any great teacher is to light the way to this realization.
> ...*The Field Book*.

WHAT UNFOLDED, as I sank into the mire, was the image of a man. I couldn't place his age. His boots were well-worn Wolverines, with red-topped heavy wool socks protruding from the footwear. The legs of a sturdy pair of canvas pants were tucked into the socks. He was wearing a thick wool shirt with a white T-shirt underneath. The cap on his head was the kind that might be worn by the turret gunner of a B-52—a leather arrangement with Elmer Fudd wool earflaps tied together at the top. The cap was cocked jauntily to the side just above one eye. His eyes were an electric blue, like the edges of the sky in deep summer. Between his eyes was a small black mark that might have been tattooed onto him.

He was there, as if dropped fully formed from above, reclining in what appeared to be total comfort and luxury on the fan-shaped roots of an upturned cedar in the middle of the hell-hole swamp. He sat with one of his arms stretched around a root behind him, his feet out and crossed at the ankles, appearing for all the world like some northern-tier James Dean with a whole theater to himself, sitting in the best seat in the house with his arm around a beautiful date. He looked at me with a bemused smile on his face.

The man reached into his shirt pocket with a smooth motion and pulled out a small bag. Again his hand went into the pocket and a packet of rolling papers emerged. He opened the bag, and out of it flowed the appealing scent of strong, rum-soaked tobacco, which he shook onto a little gummed paper. He rolled the tobacco up. A kitchen match came out of another pocket. He lifted up his knee, stretching the canvas pants, and raked the match behind his thigh. The head burst into flames, and he casually lit the cigarette. The sweet and pungent odor of its tobacco mingled blue and white with the late afternoon air. The mosquitoes immediately lessened. The man took a deep draught and exhaled. He offered the unlit end to me inquiringly, then seemed to answer his own question. He leaned back and took another drag.

The smoke drifted lazily in ringlets around his cap and into the Canadian air. He held the cigarette next to his forehead, and looked at me sideways as if trying to figure out what to do. He then began to speak.

"The Field must really love you, Charlie Smithson. Putting you into failure this deep this soon; why, this can't be much more than the middle of your second day here, aren't I right? Most impressive! Quite a good omen! Really quite hopeful. I had some hopes you know, but I could hardly have expected help like this to come so soon."

He sat there on the snag, moving his eyebrows in crazy circles, giving me sidelong glances with winks and idiotic grins. I began to form the impression that I'd come all this way to meet the village idiot of the northern lake country. Then, in a sudden movement, he leapt off of the snag and landed with both feet in the swamp next to me. He knelt down in the muck and sat on his heels with his hands relaxed in his lap. He began to speak again.

"I want to engage you in a deep inquiry," he said, crouching down close over my face. "There's an important question to be asked and answered at a moment like this when one's very survival is on the line," he said in a soft and serious tone.

He paused and leaned closer, building dramatic intensity.

"So, Charlie...?"

Another pause.

"Charlie, who's the leader of the club that's made for you and me? M-i-c-k-e-y M-o-u-s-e?"

That was it. He stood up, bounded back to his cedar snag, and let his body fall out into uncontrollable heaves and fits of laughter. I stared at him, dumbfounded from my vantage point in the swamp shit. He sighed, chuckled a few more times and settled back to smoke. His whole spirit emanated mirth and delight. The man appeared ready to wait there indefinitely, enjoying his look at a filthy tear-stained kid with a swollen head swarmed by mosquitoes. But he'd picked the wrong kid; I was in no mood to play games.

A flash of anger filled me with energy. I threw off the canoe, wriggled out of my packs, and staggered up to my feet to face him.

"I suppose you think all this is some kind of joke!"

"Well, you have to admit it's not bad," he said.

"I suppose you lured me all the way out here just to have a good laugh, didn't you!"

"I actually don't recall personally recommending the swamp route … especially with all this gear. My, my! It certainly seems that you have come prepared for just about anything … except perhaps the place here in the swamp where you actually find yourself."

"I didn't come all the way up here to be laughed at! I've given up *everything* to get up here, following your stupid map and stupid rules. I could be back home getting ready for a six-figure job! What the hell am I doing here anyway?" I asked, turning away and snarling to myself. I turned back to face him.

"You're him, aren't you?"

"Who's that?"

"You're Moses—the guy that showed up at the ball field all those years ago after I caught that homer hit by Bobby Roberts."

"Well, I believe I've already said that I am willing to be whomever you need me to be, Charlie—that's my commitment to you. Whomever you need me to be to give yourself the permission to take the next step. You can call me by any name you like. Right now, I'm the permission that you cannot yet give to yourself. The permission to do the things that you—Charlie Smithson—want to do. If you didn't want to leave that life with your fine job you wouldn't be here. I'm just operating as the part of you that's not yet strong enough to execute the steps toward your own highest intention. If you want to call that part Moses ... well, be my guest."

"Well, how the hell are you helping me by laughing at me, and making me into some kind of joke?" I asked. "I was within a half hour of dying out here—I'm completely dehydrated, bit to pieces by bugs, my throat is closing up from the worst allergy attack I've ever had— and all to get to some stupid place where *you* said I should show up."

"I think we're already at the place we need to be, Charlie, well started on our journey. And about the laughter—well. . . ."

He sat in bemused contemplation for a moment.

"Before we had our little chuckle, I believe I was witnessing the fearsome sight of a full-grown man, whining and moaning through tears, grossly overburdened by his own security structure to the point of paralysis, and ready to give up and die in a stinking swamp."

He put the cigarette out, then tore the butt to pieces, scattering bits of tobacco to be recycled by the swamp.

"And now look at you," he said, raising his arm palm-up to put me on display. "Standing upright, asking questions, getting information ... a bit more like a man, wouldn't you say? That flash of anger served you pretty well, don't you think? Not the highest of energy states, but a good bit higher than that whining self-pity trap I found you in. One step at a time, Charlie; one step at a time. Progressively higher and wider. Anger can be a big step in the right direction. But we're likely to do better than a flash of anger before it's over. Much better, I would think, don't you, Charlie?"

I stood there, flummoxed.

"I want to get out of here," I said.

"To *where*, is the question. Wasn't it Ribbon Lake? Wasn't that where you were headed by means of this 'shortcut'?" he asked.

"Yes," I replied. "That's where your stupid map said I was supposed to meet you."

"Well you're three-quarters of a mile past the little creek that flows into Ribbon and about fifty yards to the north right now," he said. "Nothing in the direction you were heading except six more miles of swamp."

He casually flipped his wrist to the south, the path of certain death.

"When I picked up your trail, it looked like you fell into the creek that leads into Ribbon from the north about four hours ago. Little creeks and swamp—they all look pretty much the same this time of year."

"I was a dead man then," I said, turning pale and looking in the direction he was pointing. My gut convulsed with the thought of the struggle: the thousands of mosquitoes and black flies, the slow exhaustion, the confusion and agony.

"Good," Moses said, observing my face. "Good for your body to remember where you are, and what's at stake. My hunch is that if you'd listened to the wisdom of your body in the first place, you wouldn't be here."

I remembered the sense of foreboding which I'd ignored when looking at that oozing ax-blaze. My gut had registered a clear 'no.'

"How did you know that I'd be trying the shortcut?" I asked.

"Just a hunch, Charlie, just a hunch. And by the way, those blazes mark a *winter* route. Seven months out of the year this place is frozen solid and flat as a pancake," he said, pushing his boot-toe several times into the wiggling surface of the swamp. "Easy walking then, and great for snowshoeing. All roads change with the season, Charlie. The cycles of the earth are in control here, not us."

Both my head and *my gut were right*, I thought. The trail *did* mark the path to Ribbon Lake—just not today.

He paused for a moment.

"So what do you want to do with this gear?" he asked.

"Well ... you could help me carry it."

"That's true," he replied, scratching his head and looking absently down and to his left.

"I apologize," he said. "It seems that I'm responsible for luring you out all this way only to tell you that you have another choice to make. It's a choice that's going to determine everything we might do together from this point forward."

Shit, I thought, *not this again*. "What kind of a choice?" I asked, in no mood to delay one minute longer. I wanted out of this swamp.

"Hard to say for sure, Charlie. But before we do anything—would you indulge me? I want to review the 'rules' with you, and make sure that we have an agreement, a baseline about what we're going to do with our intention."

Here we go again with all the rules, I thought as I slapped a mosquito on my cheek, leaving a splat of blood about the size of a dime. I waved away two more that were drilling into my forehead.

He looked down at me and smiled as if he had just read my mind. "I think this might go better if you are temporarily relieved of some of your discomfort," he said.

Yeah, discomfort. More like agony if you ask me.

"Pain is a great teacher, but panic will prevent you from hearing what I have to say. Why don't you come up here and sit with me for a while." He patted a spot next to him on the cedar snag. I couldn't see how moving five feet would change anything, but I climbed up out of the swamp and sat down.

Getting my feet out of the muck felt wonderful, and there was a little nub on the cedar that fit perfectly into a spot just below my right scapula that had been in spasm for the last two hours. I pushed my back against the nub, moving my shoulder around and letting the wood dig into the soreness.

Moses reached down behind him and produced an aluminum cylinder that he extended towards me. Beads of cool moisture had formed on its surface. The container displayed the same design that was on the upper-left corner of the package that had arrived at the brownstone—two carefully drawn circles overlapping one another, with the stars pouring into the North Star drawn within.

I took the offering. Clear, cold spring water poured down my throat, cooling down every part of me. I drained the container in one long breath, taking big swallows and letting the water pour down my chin and neck. No drink had ever tasted so good.

"Better, yes?"

I could only nod in reply. My attention was diverted by a cloud of bugs swarming around the funny hat that Moses had on his head. The bugs formed a ring around the crown of the hat, and didn't seem interested in feeding. As I watched, the swarm turned from a ring into a spiral. I stood there, watching a distinct rising spiral of insects. *He must have some special kind of bug dope,* I thought. Then I realized that the mosquitoes had stopped biting me as well. My body began to cool a bit. The swelling had reached its peak and was now subsiding.

I looked up to see that a bug-spire had begun to form directly over my own head, and that my swirl was starting to intertwine with the swarm above Moses to form a spiraling helix pattern. *Must be something they do in the late afternoon*, I thought. *Some kind of a mating ritual like the dance of the fruit flies.* Moses sat looking at me calmly.

"Can I offer you anything else?" he asked.

"I'm good. At least for a moment."

"We have a moment. Wonderful! Let's proceed, then. We were about to review the rules, were we not?"

I nodded.

"So back where you came from, there are rules for everything, right? Rules for crossing the street; rules about what to say in polite company; how to dress, speak, write, and act—more doctrines, protocols, commandments, and laws than we could recite from now to midwinter. So here, I've given you three rules, and that's it. Nothing particularly complicated. Everything else is really a matter of personal choice, everything else just a decision you can make or not make, with consequences freely accepted."

"So, I guess I could kill you right now if I wanted to," I said, reaching into my pocket and pulling out my folded red Swiss Army knife (the 'Ranger' model with nineteen separate utility functions) that somehow was still in my pocket after five hours in a swamp. "Killing's not in violation of any of your rules."

"The choice to make that attempt is available to most every human at any moment. But what's preventing you from trying to kill me is your rule, not mine."

I looked into his eyes. Calm and clear. *He could die right here, and it would be no big deal to him*, I thought. *He's ready to go. He's made peace with this life and is looking forward to the next. It's something that gives him power.*

"So do you remember the rules?" he asked.

"First rule: Everything necessary; present. Everything unnecessary; absent. One luxury item, no exceptions. Second rule: There is to be no going back or pining for an earlier place or time. One and only one trip across any passage," I recited.

"Great!" he said, then cocked his head, waiting. "What about rule number three? Did you miss it?"

"There was no 'rule number three.' There was one piece of paper, with a rule on the front and a second on the back."

"Look again."

I reached down, lifting the small pack by its strap, and pulled out what was now a wet wad of paper. I gingerly unfolded the note so that it would not break apart in my hands. I was ready to show him that there was nothing there. And yet, there it was. At the bottom of the backside there was more writing.

"This wasn't here yesterday," I said emphatically, pointing to a smeared paragraph.

"Maybe you were just not ready to see it," he said.

Impossible, I thought. *I can read a piece of paper.*

"There are big resistances to this sort of work, Charlie. The part that's in control wants to stay in control. It's pretty amazing what the controller will let in or block out to protect itself from the forces of change. It's likely that you will have to come to terms with that controller before it's over."

I waited. The writing was definitely there. I almost expected more script to appear as I was holding the wet paper.

"So what does it say?" he asked in the impatient tone of a five-year-old about to open a present. "The tension's killing me!"

I held the paper up into the light and read this aloud:

RULE NUMBER THREE: 'ACCEPTING THE BURDEN'
(Acknowledgement that every decision involves a price.)

ONCE A BURDEN IS VOLUNTARILY UNDERTAKEN, IT MUST BE CARRIED JOYFULLY, GRATEFULLY, AND CONTINUOUSLY UNTIL THE GOAL IS REACHED.

A note to the user:

"The pain of the burden is simply the thing that is arising. Willingness to accept the pain that always comes with the creation of new capacity is the key to all rapid forward progress. All strength is created out of an interaction with weakness. With the right understanding, pain is not suffering. We only delay the task and induce more pain by resisting or trying to avoid the pain. Deal with whatever arises. Watch what arises and get free. This is easier, of course, if you're in love."

AFTER I READ THE WORD 'LOVE,' the paper began to drop away out of my hand, and wet chunks of it began to fall into the swamp. I could just make out the final postscript as the paper melted in my hands.

"*...Here, this rule requires that you shoulder all of your gear at the beginning of a portage, and not put it down until you reach the end of the trail. You will find that you can take steps with that gear that you now consider impossible.*"

The last of the paper fell away and was absorbed by the swamp as if it had never existed.

"So whaddya think, Charlie?" Moses said, now more serious and quiet. "These three..." he paused searching for the right words, "these three 'suggestions about conduct' I have offered join together and form what my teacher called 'The Rule.' Three rules together form The Rule under which we travel."

"I'm not sure what it all means," I said.

"It tends to unfold over time. I thought it important to give you The Rule exactly as it was passed down to me, so I had to write it down to be sure. The Rule doesn't really 'mean' anything. The important thing is *what it does*. The Rule outlines an attitude toward the small part of the universe that is within your control. Apply it, and things happen."

"What sorts of things happen?" I asked.

"Two small things usually happen; and sometimes a big thing, Charlie. The first 'small thing' is that you will begin to move toward your goal with more ease, and without all the excess weight and awful self-pity weighing you down. Then, once you're moving, a second thing starts to happen. People and forces begin to show up to help you. When people see honest effort, they naturally reach out to help. But you have to move Charlie; you have to get out of your old broken car and push if you want to get help from the people passing by. If you apply The Rule, you are showing the universe that you're willing to do what it takes to get somewhere. Then things start to show up to help you get there."

"Are those the small things?" I asked. All of it sounded pretty big and important to me.

"Well, yes," he responded.

"It sounds like you're about to tell me the big thing," I said. "Let's hear it."

"So here's the big thing." He looked away as if searching for words.

"The Rule works to make space, to un-tether and un-grip: to make free. You grow smaller, and something else grows greater." He had taken an interest in his fingernails. He looked up from them to me.

"Ok, Charlie, let me give it to you straight up. If you're lucky, The Rule will break you into a thousand bits out here. You will break under the burden you have chosen to carry—the suffering you have intentionally created by obedience to the best part of yourself."

Obedience. Suffering. Those are words out of the past, I thought. Neither suffering nor obedience sounded that good to me.

"You'll come to learn that you can't follow The Rule under your own power, no matter how hard you try. You're going to need the help of something else—something bigger than yourself. Finding that bigger thing is the ultimate lesson, the reason for The Rule. When the power that's bigger than yourself comes up out of the ground to meet you and takes up your burden, The Rule has served its purpose, and you'll be free."

The sun was starting to throw long shadows across the swamp-meadow and glistened off the wings of the flies crisscrossing the air. I remembered last night. A dinner bell had rung when the sun dropped over the horizon. The ring of that awful bell was less than an hour away. Countless tiny beaks would then rise up off the swamp to hone in on anything warm, searching for their blood meal. The daylight bugs that had almost killed me today were only the scouting patrol of a vast army waiting to arise in the dark of night. We could not, *must not* be in the swamp when it happened. I was sure that Moses knew this. Yet he waited there, loose-limbed, as if we had all the time in the world.

"So can we go now? Are you willing to help me with some of this? We're about to be eaten alive."

To my dismay, Moses seemed in no hurry at all. Surely he knew that we could not camp here. The swamp was getting darker and scarier by the minute. Within an hour there would be no way that we could find our way out; at least none that I could see.

"I *could* pick your stuff up and carry it for you, and I am *most* willing to do it," he said with complete sincerity. He seemed kinder now than before, like a porter at a five-star hotel willing to cheerfully carry however many bags any diva might bring in. "There's a little ridge of high ground about two hundred yards in that direction," he said, pointing west, away from Ribbon Lake. "The path is pretty well cleared out by some snowmobiles that came in here last winter," he said. "With both of us carrying the load, we could be back to where you started and be setting up camp in about half an hour. With any luck we could pick up a breeze to keep the mosquitoes off for a few minutes while we cook some supper. I'd be happy to make supper for you; you're probably a bit tired."

"Well, what about Ribbon Lake? We can't be that far."

"Right again, Charlie. Not more than about a ten-minute walk, I would say, right through there..." he pointed to a darkening spot in the trees. "We can hit the south shore and paddle across to what's next."

"So what *is* next?" I demanded.

He reached into his pocket, pulled out the tobacco, and began to slowly roll another of his rum-smoke cigarettes, oblivious to my anxiety. He lit up his smoke. "The problem is, Charlie," he said exhaling, "if we go in that direction (pointing to Ribbon Lake), you'll be making a choice; a choice to be curious enough and bold enough to take the next step *without knowing what's next*. Giving your utmost and highest—the best of your effort—to something still unseen is a definition of faith, Charlie. Faith is a wonderful attribute—it's a strobe-beacon calling out to the universe. You'd be surprised what shows up in response."

I stood there with nothing to say.

"Let me put it to you as plainly as I can," he said. "I can't carry *anything* for you if we move to Ribbon Lake. You will be deciding to go

~ 150 ~

forward, in faith, under The Rule, accepting the consequences. You'll be walking with the intention of becoming free."

He finished half the smoke, put it out, and put the butt in his pocket. "I don't want to influence your decision, but you should know that if you apply the principle of 'going light,' you'll be able to carry all of your own stuff for ten minutes without much problem, even as tired as you are. You have to learn to carry your own load before you can be of much help to anyone else. Self-responsibility is the first step to freedom, Charlie."

I was finished. I just needed to get to water, and be out of the swamp. Going forward under The Rule or back to where I'd started did not matter that much to me at the moment. I had no real desire to do anything but collapse in a puddle and be taken care of.

"I'll go to Ribbon," I heard myself say. There was a tone of finality in the phrase that belied how little I cared. I guess there was some small part of me, faintly glimmering, still ready to see what was next. It answered for me.

17: Going Light

Full engagement and full relinquishment in every moment:
This is the dance of dances.
      ...*The Field Book.*

"VERY WELL THEN," Moses said. "A deep bow to the part of you that's made a decision. I can't carry your load now under any circumstances, but I can help a bit without doing much harm. May I?" he said, pointing at my two swamp-slimed packs.

"Be my guest," I said, too tired at this point to care.

Moses jumped down from the snag and leapt cat-like across the top of the swamp. The man could move. He heaved my big Alaskan up on his back, and put his forearm through the smaller one. He ran with the heavy weight, his feet moving so fast that they danced across the wobbling ground to a little island where a few pine trees had managed to take root. I hadn't seen the island there. *Leave it to him to find a dry spot covered with nice pine needles in this hell-hole*, I thought. I followed, staggering my way across.

Moses opened the packs, shook everything out, and began to rapidly sort through every item, opening every container, and peering into every pocket in the fading light. He was making two piles. Into the first, he put nearly everything that was in the pack. Gas, grate, stove, spare pants, underwear, freeze-dried food, flashlight, flares, camp shoes, T-shirts, axe, saw, clothesline, tarp, fire starter, insect coil, comb, razor, folding camp seat, lighter. . . .

"Hope you're ready to lose some weight!" he said, throwing a twenty-dollar pack of energy bars into the pile.

I lurched over to the growing pile, unwilling to let my food supply go that easily. I tore open one of the bars, consumed it, and opened another, nearly choking on the sticky stuff. Moses swiveled his head, and arched an eyebrow high over his left eye. From somewhere he produced a second canister of water exactly like the first, and threw it over to me.

"A high carbohydrate diet has been linked to several debilitating medical conditions," he intoned.

I looked straight back at him, stuffed the last of the second snack bar into my mouth with my index finger, and washed it down with several gulps of cool water while I prepared to open a third. The calories were hitting me in a rush of good feelings.

"What's this?" he asked, holding up the bag of gooey orange-flavored candy that I'd bought at the dead-end Texaco station.

"Just something I picked up on impulse on the way here," I said.

"You picked this up yourself—it was not something recommended by some guy in a discount store?"

"Yes. That's right."

"How did you feel when you bought it—what did the impulse feel like?"

"Well, kind of like I was watching someone else buy the bag, absolutely certain that I needed it for some reason I didn't know then and still don't know now." I had no idea why he was asking me all of these questions about something that obviously belonged in the 'leave it behind' pile.

"I only spent seventy-five cents on it," I said. "It's nothing."

"Yet it's the only thing you actually bought yourself, for reasons beyond your understanding..." he said, musing, not really talking to me anymore. "It might be important for reasons we cannot yet foresee."

He placed the two-pound bag of candy in the pile of stuff that was coming with us. Go figure.

AT THE END of ten minutes there was a pile of gear almost three feet high to be left behind. There was another pile that could be put into a five gallon bucket. Moses looked at the wasted G.P.S. device. "Another stroke of luck!" he said as he threw it away. "Now you'll have to start looking at the real world to find your way. The Field wants you to look, Charlie; it wants you to look deeply into the world around you. You can be sure of it."

He then started to dig into the 'kits' of things I'd brought. The forty or fifty fishing lures in my tackle box were reduced to three. There was still some daylight left. A shaft of light hit Moses, lighting up his face. The creases around his eyes were deeply scored. *Old*, I thought. *Older than he looks at first glance.*

He opened the first-aid kit, counted bandages, and carefully evaluated every item. Two-thirds of the kit was put into the big pile. Tent stakes: gone. Extra paddle: gone. Life jacket: gone.

After twenty minutes he'd finished sorting, and put the items from the small pile into the big Alaskan pack. The smaller pack was now completely empty, and it went in the pile to be left behind. My tent and sleeping bag could now fit easily inside the big pack. He lifted the Extreme Alaskan with two fingers.

"Better, don't you think?" he said.

"You're not planning to leave all of this stuff here, are you?" I asked.

"No, not at all," he said. "*You* are the one that is going to leave it. I'm just sorting it for you so we can finally get out of here."

"That's close to two thousand dollars' worth of gear." I said, looking at the big pile.

He looked at me with an expression of indifference. "How much would you say your life's worth, Charlie?"

This was no time to argue. I put the Alaskan on my back. It felt more like a kid's backpack with a few schoolbooks in it than a life support structure for the wilderness.

"Aren't you forgetting something?" he asked.

"What's that?"

"The luxury item. The one thing brought for the pure pleasure it brings to you. It's part of The Rule, remember? One luxury item—no exceptions."

"I remember."

"So what will it be?" Moses asked pointing to big pile.

I noticed that Moses had put the Field Book in the unessential pile. There was so much in that big pile that would make life more comfortable. My back was aching from all of the carrying it had done in the last couple of days. I looked lovingly at the folding canvas camp chair.

The Field Book was so different from the rest of the gear that it stood out like a nugget in a miner's pan. It was clearly the thing of greatest value. "I'll take the book you sent me," I heard myself say. "You must have spent years writing all of that stuff. It would be a shame to leave all of your wisdom in the swamp."

"If it's wisdom, it's held by us collectively," Moses said. "Wisdom exists independently of me or you. It arises out of a collective level of consciousness. It's already inside us all, and it is our *own* truth that we recognize when we hear it. We reinforce this pre-existing truth by articulating it. Sharing wisdom makes what is already real *more* real. The truth is literally realized—made real—as it passes between two people," he said.

"I gave the Field Book to you, and let it go completely when I dropped it in the mail. Giving a gift should feel like dropping a clay pot off a ten story building. You just let it go, knowing that it's gone for good. The book is yours now. You can do with it what you want." He took the volume out of the pile and handed it to me.

I took the Field Book, feeling the softness of its worn cover. "This seems like a one-of-a-kind manuscript, all handwritten, like it's some kind of an original."

"Just right, Charlie. It is one of a kind. The only copy in the world is sitting right there in your hands."

My fingers started to tremble. I felt like I had just opened a jar in the desert, and had taken out an ancient manuscript that had the power to change the world. I was frozen there with the book in my hands. *What am I supposed to do with this?*

Moses noticed my trepidation, and started to chuckle. "Actually what you have in your hands represents a kind of failure," he said. "Probably best not to get too wrapped up in its importance."

"A failure?"

"Yes. There's been quite a debate among the members of the Committee about it—whether or not a book like that should even exist."

I looked puzzled, so he continued.

"Some members of the Committee came to realize that the Field surrounding us humans was still too dense for their work to be received. So the mechanism of a 'Field Book' was proposed, to help clear the Field a bit—a bit of writing designed to break through the crust and clear away some of the topsoil so that the work could proceed."

"And this is that book?" I asked, holding the manuscript in my left hand.

"Yes."

"So what's wrong with it?" I asked.

"The Field Book uses the mechanism of language, Charlie," Moses said. "Language is dualistic by its very nature. The way language 'makes sense' is to point to something that *is*, which can then be seen only in contrast against what 'it' is *not*. Language was born out of the perspective that we are separate. It's not all that helpful for describing things which are *One*."

Moses continued. "We've also ingrained the bad habit of using things written down as 'belief systems'—locked-down domination devices invented by a separated mind, a mind that's already high on its drug cocktail of believing, belonging, and superiority. The book that you hold in your hand—it could do nothing but point into the light on every page, and still be used as a tool to justify killing somebody. It's happened before you know, and more than once."

I again looked down at the manuscript. I was not so sure that I wanted the thing now after all.

"So what do you want me to do with this? Why have you given it to me?" I asked.

"The Committee has allowed one copy. They have permitted me to write down a few things that might be helpful in the right hands. They have chosen to put the Field Book in your hands, Charlie, for good or ill."

I stood there, astonished, not knowing what to say. I simply stared down at the cover, and then glanced up and into the beautiful eyes of Moses. They were softer now, no longer laughing at me.

"The Committee, despite all of its powers, also has limitations, Charlie. You should know this. Sometimes they need a messenger. They've picked you as a candidate, Charlie. They've seen something in you that you have yet to see in yourself. There are high hopes. Yes. But of course, you are not obligated to do anything. And there is much to do before such a possibility is even considered. I have already said too much."

So that's it, I thought. *They want me for something. Wasn't it Moses that signed his name 'Servant and* Messenger'*?*

"So it's time to go, Charlie," Moses said. "The Field Book is in your hands now, released into the world. I've done my part. We still must reach Ribbon Lake before nightfall."

I ruffled the pages of the book. I'm sure that I was imagining it, but the pages seemed to have a magical quality, like they were reading my mind. *I can open this book right to the place that will offer the guidance I need,* I thought. I had the sense that a page could simply appear freshly written if a reader needed to hear something badly enough, and then disappear in the same way. *He's not telling me everything about this book,* I thought. *This book is no failure.*

It was then that I remembered. I pulled up my dirty shirt-sleeve to reveal the Mala beads that were wrapped around my forearm.

"Do you remember these?" I asked, unwrapping them and holding them out to Moses.

Moses beamed. "Edna," he said. "How is she?"

"She's well," I said, somewhat taken aback that Moses was not more surprised to see the necklace after thirty years. "Bill has taken a turn for the worse, however. He's in the hospital at Rochester, and may not last that much longer."

"I'm sorry to hear that. He was one of the finest men I've ever known."

"That says a lot, coming from you."

"I speak the truth; that is all."

"Well, Edna said that she might be following Bill to the other side if he goes that way. She wanted to give these beads back to you—so here they are. She said she's used them with her prayers most every night." I turned my hand and extended the necklace to Moses a second time. "She has good energy, you know. The necklace might help you."

"No doubt it will. No doubt. I accept this from you, Charlie, and from Edna, as a gift from the earth." Moses lifted the beads to his forehead in clasped palms, and then wrapped them around his left wrist.

"Aren't you just a little surprised, that of all the people in Wisconsin, I met the one person who knew you, and who wanted to return a gift to you after thirty years?"

"I'm delighted, Charlie, but not surprised. I gave this mala to Edna all those years ago as a gift to her highest intention—I poured it into the river. Things poured into the river always come back to you in time. *Always* Charlie. And sometimes a hundred, even a thousand-fold. If you don't believe me, look at this necklace on my wrist, and the fact that you are here as well. If that is not a thousand-fold return, what is it?"

I smiled at Moses. I was beginning to see how things worked in his world.

"And now, since you've given this to me, I am overburdened by luxury items. I can have only one you know," he said. "The Rule no longer applies to me, but I've chosen to once again place myself under its conditions to be in solidarity with you," he said smiling.

"So that leaves me with an item I would like to give you," he said, reaching to an inside pocket and pulling out a gleaming cylinder. "You can have this pen to go with the book. Use both of them as you see fit."

What he passed to me was more like a magic wand than a pen. Across its middle were five rings of polished silver wrapped in bands around a warm glowing stone. The cap unscrewed easily and forged to the bottom with an audible click. The pen flowed down to a golden nib. I put it in my right hand and felt its balance. It seemed to belong in my hand. Holding the pen made me feel like my hand was worth something, that something good was destined to flow from both hand

and pen. I could feel the energy of Moses in the instrument. And like everything around him, it was in some way *alive*.

"Wow," I said, reading the inscription just below the screw cap—'Handmade in Germany'—sounds like something important."

"Just the location of the manufacturer," Moses said. "What looks like stone on the barrel is actually pine sap—the tears from trees like the ones here, tears that flowed about forty-five million years ago and became a kind of stone. It's amber. I hope you like the gift and that it serves you well."

I opened the back of the Field Book, and signed my name. The fountain pen laid down a beautiful line.

"Wouldn't that black plastic pen in my map case be more practical out here?" I asked. "Seems like nobody in their right mind would bring anything like this on a camping trip."

Moses just smiled. "What's 'practical' is what will produce the intended result with a minimum of effort, in a direct line. In my view, it has nothing at all to do with what someone might consider 'prudent.' Prudent people are concerned about what they stand to lose. What I consider practical is something that puts you on the path to gain. What's practical is what triggers the courageous part of you to say 'yes' and take action."

He doffed his hat and waved at the gathering mosquitoes. It was more like he was conducting an orchestra of tiny whining wings than making an attempt to wave them away. "So tell me, Charlie, how do you feel about that pen and the Field Book?"

I liked the feel of the pen. I liked the potential of it. And I liked the book, even though it contained more wisdom than I had the capacity to absorb. The blank pages were calling to me in a subtle way, something that said: "You can add something. Make your mark here, Charlie." I felt that whomever gave me these gifts believed in me; that they had faith that someday I might be worthy of gifts like these. I was glad that the manuscript and the writing instrument were coming with me.

"I like them. They make me feel like I could do something special."

"Quite practical then. We'll consider the pen and paper a single luxury item, since they are part of a single function, like a matchstick and a head that combine to get a fire started. Treating them as one thing won't violate The Rule, in my opinion. Besides, the interpretation of rules should bend in favor of generosity, don't you think?"

"Right."

I put the two items in the black waterproof pouch, which also held the map and compass.

"Generosity is a quality the soul never regrets," he said.

Moses bundled all of the remaining equipment in the tarp I'd brought, and tied it up by the corners like a stork package. He found a tussock of swamp grass and pulled it up. The roots held a wad of jet-black swamp-muck. He used the tussock as a paintbrush, and painted a large 'O' on the tarp. Near the top of the 'O' a space was left open, like the start of a spiral. Moses then tied a stick to the end of the nylon line I'd brought, and threw the stick with the line attached high over the limb of one of the pines. He hoisted the bundle a couple of feet off the ground, and tied it off. "That should keep it," he said. "That mark will tell whoever comes by that they can take whatever they want. That's alright with you, isn't it?"

"I'd be happy to share anything I have," I replied, not knowing why anyone would come to this swamp for gear in the first place. I sure had no plans to come back here.

Moses turned from the cache. He was now ready to get underway. *He's just closed the door, and that's that,* I thought. *He's already forgotten what's in that pile, and the fact that he once owned this beautiful pen.*

"LET ME SHOW you how to pick this up," Moses said, moving back to the canoe. "It's fairly simple if you use mechanical advantage. First, grab the gunwale closest to you, then 'walk' your hands up the yoke. Grab the far gunwale with your left hand like this…" he said, reaching across the canoe. "Then slip your right arm underneath, cradling the boat, and use the fulcrum of your arm at the elbow to do the lifting." He moved the eighty-pound weight easily with his bent right arm. "Rock it a couple of times to build momentum, and lift it with an impulse from the ground up through your thighs, up and over like this…." The canoe was on top of him easily, and he adjusted his shoulders so that the boat rode flat and floated easily atop him.

He's going to help me, I thought. *He could carry it so easily.*

He flipped the canoe off and set it down soundlessly on the swamp. The bugs were starting to come out in all of their ferocity, but I still remained unbitten. He pointed to the canoe, beckoning me with a smile. "All yours, Charlie," he said. "Just ten minutes. Let's try ten minutes of impeccability here in the last light of day."

I wobbled over to the canoe, and managed to get the boat balanced on my thighs. I rocked it and made an attempt to get it up. My timing was wrong, and I dropped the boat from the level of my shoulder, making a muddy whack on the surface of the swamp.

"Good to practice on softer ground before making the lift over sharp rocks—the going does get a *bit* slow with a hole in the bottom," Moses observed, pulling out his smoke.

I tried again, and the canoe came up with no strain on my back. I immediately sank six inches into the ground. The combined load of pack and canoe was still over a hundred pounds.

"You'll have to move your feet faster." Moses said. "It's a dance. Look ahead and plan four or five steps in advance. You'll have a better chance of staying up."

I stood in place, staggering sideways and using a little forward motion to keep from sinking. *We're really leaving all that gear in the middle of a swamp,* I thought, *really leaving it behind for good.*

"I'm right here behind you," he said, pushing up slightly on the stern to even the boat on my shoulders. "Look up ahead."

It must have been the way the sun hit the top of the swamp in the final light of day. Perhaps it was my exhaustion that was making me see things that weren't really there. But for just an instant, as I looked out from under the canoe, I swear I saw her, the same young girl that was racing down the dock at Loon Lake, turning her head to smile at me, her hair spinning in the wind, dancing on the surface of the swamp. I looked across the swamp after her. There were spots that were emitting a soft glow, showing little landing places for my feet. The girl disappeared ahead, dancing into the fading light.

I began to move, hitting the first four spots, and making more forward progress in thirty seconds than I had made in the last two hours. Moses walked behind me. I couldn't see him, but I felt as if he had his arms wide open and outstretched, following me. He was doing something with his mind that was balancing me, keeping me upright so I wouldn't fall. I could hear him singing softly, a familiar tune, but something that I could not quite place. I tried to remember the song, but it was like trying to remember the sequence of a dream. I started to leap across the surface of the swamp.

Something quite new began to happen. All the physical pain and exhaustion were still there, but layered over and around the pain was a surge of energy, an emotional fierceness flaming up with single-pointed intensity, like some inner Commander was urging me forward. A force—a powerful guide—had just arrived to take up temporary residence inside of me. As I leapt forward, I began to tap into him. No. It's more accurate to say that *he* was tapping into *me*. The Commander felt like an archetype from some other dimension who had suddenly chosen me as a vessel, and was coming alive inside me. I had swirling images of myself alone in the wilderness moving in power, risking everything, calling out and being answered. . . .

SUDDENLY THERE WAS A LIGHT up ahead. It was the surface of Ribbon Lake through the trees. Nine minutes had gone past. *The arc of the universe*, I thought. Maybe the universe *did* come to help me in the swamp because I was in there trying, even though I was panting and whining through tears. Maybe it saw me in need, stuck in the muck. *Maybe the universe didn't call me up here just to laugh in my face after all.*

It was firm ground now down to the lake, scraping small branches as we went.

"Walk out into the water," Moses yelled. His was voice further back in the woods than I thought it would be, as if he'd been delayed by something. "Take the canoe down by reversing the steps you followed to get it up." I did as I was told, and the canoe slipped softly onto the water.

Just as the bow touched the surface, I again had the distinct feeling that there was a pair of eyes on me—that I was being watched from the trees. I turned to scan the shore, but could see nothing in the gathering darkness.

We loaded the canoe, and moved in darkness north and east across Ribbon Lake, with Moses paddling in the stern. The moon was rising over the eastern horizon, and threw enough light to cast a shadow of the canoe on the still surface of the water. We moved across the water for half an hour, with Moses doing most of the work. With encouragement from him, every few moments I stopped paddling and dipped my cup into Ribbon Lake to take a drink without any iodine. The lake tasted wonderful.

"I think there was something following us back there," I said between gulps.

"The forest has many eyes," he replied, but would say no more.

As we moved up-lake, I began to see a light coming from the northern shore. It was obscured by the trees, but was growing brighter.

We rounded a point, and the source of the light came into view. "How's that for something in the middle of nowhere," he said, pointing across the lake with the blade of his paddle.

I looked across. Nothing could have prepared me for the sight that reached me from across water.

18: Gaining the Initiative

The separated self has a hard time knowing its purpose. It will change the course of an entire life to gain approval, and then want something different in the end. It proposes a life of constant need no matter how much you have. It just goes on and on like a hungry ghost. As an antidote, we propose that you find a place where a column of light is walking down a line of trees and look at it. Then look at it again.
...*The Field Book*.

MY EYES FOLLOWED the gleam of light across the rippled surface. It was an electric glare—bright, white and powerful—coming from a dozen arc lights arranged in bright rows, each connected by thick black wires to a bank of humming generators. Large green tents were arranged military-style, and shimmered in the glare. Dozens of men were moving about the camp, each wearing a brightly colored kerchief. The camp was divided by kerchief-color: some wore blue, others red, orange, or green. A small flag snapped in the breeze in the center of the encampment. The banner was a circle of bright blue arrows pointing outward in all directions, with a large orange "I" in the center.

"What the hell is this?" I asked.

"This, Charlie, is the encampment of the 'Strategic Self Transformation Initiative.' They have hired me as a consultant on 'local conditions.' I, in turn, have agreed to waive my fee in order to place a person of my choice in the program."

I guess I know who that is, I thought.

"So what did you have to do to get me in?" I asked.

"The standard fee for entrance to this program is one hundred thousand dollars," Moses replied casually. "It's only open to ... what's their wording ... 'high potential individuals willing to make a substantial investment to become elite units of productivity.' Those guys over there—the ones running around in neck scarves—have signed on to do whatever it takes to make it into the 'utmost tier of success.' That's the mission."

I felt a knot growing in my stomach and a tightness and resistance running down into my hands.

"...About that feeling in the body that you said I should have listened to when I took that path into the swamp?"

"Yes, I remember."

"I'm having it now."

Moses immediately stopped paddling. I swiveled around in the bow seat to face him.

"So what are you going to do about it?" he asked.

I was wishing that I'd chosen to take the other way out of that swamp. We might be camping somewhere nice right now, enjoying dinner in the cool night breeze. So far, this 'transformation' business didn't seem like all it was cracked up to be.

"I'm trusting you—I'm here to find something and I don't know what it is." I replied. "I don't know what else to do but take the next step."

"You always have a choice Charlie—we take in information and we must decide. Fear is a piece of information, but fear is never fully right, as you have already observed."

"All I can say is that I'm trusting you."

Moses focused his blue eyes right on me. "I present you with opportunities Charlie, that's all *I* can say. The opportunity across the lake is one that many consider 'golden.' There are people in those neckerchiefs that could change your life. There's money there: power, connections, and the ability to get things done. The Initiative is building human capacities, and they're creating bonds that will last for life, or at least that's the plan."

I looked out at the encampment. We were drifting closer. Moses seemed unconcerned with the scene across the lake. He stayed focused on me. "Things won't end here with us if you decide to turn down this opportunity. The direction you choose is not all that important. It's *owning* the choice that's important—accepting all of the possibilities and consequences of the choice without complaint—including the consequence that this opportunity might never arise again."

The boat was headed toward the camp—sliding effortlessly across the water under its own power. *I'm already on his path*, I thought. *For some reason he just wants me to keep choosing it again and again.*

"We're almost there," I observed. "I guess we should find out what they have to offer."

"Indeed," he said, taking up his paddle and putting his back into a powerful stroke.

"But don't expect me to interfere with anything here. Just take in this place as a piece of the puzzle, and learn what you can from it."

WE CAME TO REST with a gentle sound of sand grains flowing across the smooth belly of the canoe. I looked up and saw the banner of the Initiative snapping in the wind, illuminated by the cross-beams of four bright spotlights pointing upward. The air had been stagnant and swarming in the swamp where we'd been standing only a few minutes ago. But here the breeze was fresh and insect-free. The cliffs of the lake were acting as a wind tunnel, concentrating the prevailing westerly wind and accelerating it across this lake point. *Unusual.* All of the other big lakes ran north/south in the direction of the glaciers, but this one was bounded by steep granite cliffs running almost exactly east/west. *This has to be the only spot in a hundred square miles with enough night breeze to keep the bugs back,* I thought. The sandy point was open, flat, and big enough to handle a large encampment. *Maybe these guys know what they're doing.*

A man bounded across the beach to meet us. He was balding and had the paunchy look of someone old for his age. The man was immaculately dressed in a tan trout shirt with multiple pockets; pleated pants tucked into jungle boots reaching almost to the knee; and an Aussie-style outback hat hanging from a lanyard. A purple kerchief was knotted at his neck. I would later learn that the purple kerchief meant that he was a leader of the Initiative, a member of the fully initiated 'Alpha Group.'

"Nice campsite you've found for us, Mr. Taylor. Finding this is worth half your fee. We can stay on task here all night long if we want to. Only problem is that it's hard to get the planes in and out down this narrow lake. We're almost out of steaks and ice, but we'll manage, we'll manage. And who's this? Is this the newest pivotal high-performance shift-point about to meet his destiny?"

I looked sideways at Moses, wondering now about everything "Mr. Taylor" had said so far. It didn't seem like there was much need of 'The Rule' if steaks and ice could be brought into the wilderness by floatplane.

I staggered up out of the water and held out my hand. "Charlie Smithson," I said.

The man stood back and looked me up and down. There was not a square inch of my discount store outdoor outfit that was not covered in swamp shit. I felt inadequate and improperly dressed. There was a small voice inside of me saying that this feeling of inadequacy was exactly what the man wanted.

Despite his close examination, the Alpha Man had not yet *quite* looked me in the eye. It was so easy to look into the eyes of Moses. It was almost impossible to stay out of those blue eyes—there was a sense of deep compassion behind the eyes, a sense of ease, like all was seen, and all was accepted. Moses was *present*. There was no program running behind his eyes, no other place to be. But this man's eyes were different in a way that I wouldn't have noticed had I not spent the last few hours with Moses. It seemed like there were a dozen schemes, projects, evaluations, and strategies going on behind the eyes. *He's trying to figure out how I will fit into his world*, I thought. *Trying to see whether I am a 'yes' or a 'no.' He'll decide it in a blink.* I already had a strong feeling that I was a 'no,' and that the decision was irreversible.

Nonetheless, there was nothing in the way the man acted that confirmed any of my suspicions. On the contrary, as he stepped toward me, he was nothing but an expression of great welcome—like he'd been waiting all of his life for just this moment of greeting. His face beamed with the broadest smile I'd seen anywhere in real life. He had the expansive air of a Bible preacher embracing the pimply kid who had just responded to his altar call. He glanced up into my face, not quite focusing, then honed in on my outstretched hand. His right hand fell on mine like a falcon hitting prey. His elbow flew up to shoulder height—a move that allowed him to get his big deltoids, triceps and trapezius muscles into the man-to-man shake. With my hand clutched in his powerful grip, he pulled me close. I could feel his breath next to my right ear, a slightly sour breath from a belly full of too much rich food, too little sleep, and a cigar about this time yesterday. His left hand pounded my back. Every motion of the greeting announced that I was a returning prodigal son, and part of me was responding favorably to it. Yet there was something about it. Something that was so, well, so *professional*.

The man pulled back, still gripping my hand with an outstretched arm, and looked me up and down like an uncle who was admiring just how much I'd grown. Finally his eyes locked into mine, and he pulsed his grip with a tremor as he wobbled his head excitedly. It was the look of a birthday boy with a big cake in front of him. He seemed so darned pleased. Yet, I could not quite tell whether he was pleased with me, or pleased with his flawless completion of the final step of a multi-step greeting process that he'd learned at some seminar that promised to teach you how to convert an absolute stranger into a best friend in sixty seconds.

"Charlie Smithson!" he exclaimed. "Just so proud to know you. Mr. Taylor has told me so much about you. Can't wait to have you as part of our team. I want to welcome you to the most successful executive training program in the world. Only the best for the best, Charlie. And we have the metrics to prove it."

"Well, thanks—I hardly knew what to expect," I said, giving Moses a sidelong glance. "And you are...?"

The man let go of my hand. His genuine surprise bordered on shock. How could anybody showing up at his camp not know who *he* was? He glanced at Moses. "Well I see that you have not been fully informed. No problem, no problem. We take 'em any way we find 'em. Tommy Rankin's my name. Again, a pleasure to meet you, sir."

"Back at Yale the folks gave him the nick name 'Tommy Gun' for the way he used to pitch baseballs and mow down batter after batter," Moses chimed in.

I remembered wild Jase, the second baseman on the Structo squad who loved to throw bullets right at my nuts. *This is that same bullet-throwing kid who somehow made it to the Ivy Leagues.*

"Indeed that's true. I'm the Gun," Rankin said, smiling and taking a big fake windup to pitch an imaginary ball right at me. "True, true. But that's not what we're here to talk about, is it Charlie? No sir. What we're here to talk about is you! This is the place for *you*, Charlie, more and more and even more you until you get everything you want, everything you need, everything that you *by-God deserve*, and…" he paused. Inhaling deeply, he dropped his voice into a stage whisper. "Until you Charlie, become a 'person of personal destiny.' That's what we're here to do Charlie. Achieve destinies! The question is, are you ready—are you ready to catch the ball and run with it for the rest of your life? Are you tired of missing the ball all the damn time, Charlie? Are you ready to do something about it? Are you ready to *meet your destiny*?!!"

I looked again at Moses. He stood impassively, leaning on a paddle, taking in the scene. Tommy Gun's speech was a lot like the one that Moses had given me on the right field line so many years ago; yet it sounded so different coming out of the 'Gun.' The words were similar, but they aimed at a different place.

My reverie was broken by the painful thump of a fist hitting my breastbone.

"Front and center, Smithson," Tommy said, as he backed up with his fist cocked. He moved his feet and bobbed his head like a bantamweight prize fighter. "No time to be daydreaming when your destiny is on the line." *If I knew the first thing about boxing, I could step in, give a little head fake and clock him to the ground*, I thought. We'd then see what *his* destiny was.

The Gun continued to move his feet and bounce his shoulders boxer-style. " So let me ask you, son, what's the *number one* thing you want out of life?"

I hesitated. Tommy froze in his boxer stance.

It had been such a long day. The lift that I'd felt in the presence of Moses that had carried me out of the swamp; the feeling of the presence of the Commander; the vision of the beautiful young girl ... all were fading now as my heels sank into the sand. The sugary snacks I'd stuffed down in the swamp were no longer sustaining me, and my blood sugar was crashing. Just by putting my feet on the Gun's beach, I guess I'd somehow given him permission to immediately confront me.

"To be happy, I guess," I finally replied.

"*Wrong!*" he said.

Our interaction was starting to draw a crowd. Five or six guys my age gathered on the sand point, all of them in garb cloning Tommy's and each with a different color kerchief around his neck.

"Happiness in not a goal, Charlie. Everybody knows that," the Gun said. "Happiness is a *result*. Happiness is what happens when you are aligned with your purpose and working toward your goal. It's a state that comes and goes like the weather," he said, looking up and flipping his wrist at the sky. "Nothing you can really control—so forget about it!"

Something about this sounded right to me. I'd heard it said that if I looked for happiness, I would never find it, but if I focused on something else, like helping someone, happiness would come and alight like a butterfly on my shoulder.

"I see some of the good sense we have to offer here is already starting to resonate with you, Smithson," he said. *He's good at reading people*, I thought. He has a skill. Still, I couldn't shake the feeling that the Gun was maneuvering to gain an advantage. *Advantage.* Yes. *That* was his thing. He could teach me the art of gaining an advantage, if I wanted to learn it.

"We're going to get you a purpose before the sun sets tomorrow, Charlie, and we've got just the process to do it." The Gun said. "That purpose will be the foundation upon which everything else is built."

The Gun then raised his voice and began to address the entire assembled group, signaling that my personal session with him was over. Only later was I to learn that his personal attention was considered quite valuable.

"We have a busy day tomorrow, starting at 4:30 a.m. gentlemen, so I suggest that you all get a good night's sleep. As you know, the statistics from past programs tell us that only half of you will complete the program. Many will be weeded out. Only the strong survive!"

The Gun finished with his clenched fists in the air, looking right into me. The group began to disband and head for the tents.

"Mike," the Gun said, gesturing to one of the guys. A young man about my age came over. He looked as if he'd spent the last seven years pumping iron three hours a day. "Smithson, this is Mike Kimmel, Green Team leader. Kimmel, Charlie Smithson." Kimmel put out his hand without fanfare.

"Welcome to Green Team, Smithson," Kimmel said. "We have a team meeting every morning at o-seven hundred just after breakfast. Tomorrow you're excused so you can give one hundred percent focus to the purpose exercise. Looks like you need to wash up, and get some chow. You'll have to work hard to stay with us. You're almost three days behind already."

Kimmel moved over to the canoe where Moses was reaching inside of his pocket for the butt end of the smoke he'd rolled back in the swamp. The Gun turned and walked up the beach.

"Tobacco is not allowed in the beachfront area as you know Taylor, but I see that you have not formally come ashore," he said, looking at the water lapping around Moses' knees. "Tomorrow we need you to scout routes for the ordeal passages. We'll need those routes in twenty-four hours."

"No problem," Moses replied, lighting up. I looked over to Moses, wondering what the hell. His face was impassive, but still glowing softly with light and kindness. Moses seemed oddly uncritical of the Gun, and appreciative of Kimmel, who started to unload the canoe.

"Is this your gear Smithson?" Kimmel asked, pointing to my pack.

"That's what's left of it."

"Have you brought any cell phones, navigation systems, or other portable communication devices with you?"

Not any that would have survived the swamp and the sorting by Moses, I thought.

"No," I replied. "I left my phone at the end of the road two days ago, and my GPS washed out."

"Yeah, I heard from Taylor that you decided to drive up here and paddle in. Wow. That's a first. But it's good that you left your phone anyway. We don't allow com devices here. Keeps you focused on the program. I assume that you have your schedule cleared for the next four days or so?"

The question took me by surprise. I'd not thought about when my training might end.

"I'm free for the next four days," I replied, not knowing where else I could possibly go at this point. "So how did everybody else get here, if you don't mind my asking?"

"Did you get *any* information about this program Smithson?" Kimmel asked, glancing over at Moses.

"I was told the name of it about fifteen minutes ago as we were paddling up," I replied in a voice loud enough for Moses to hear.

Kimmel stood there, amazed. He cleared his throat and began. "This is one of the best known and most rigorous executive training programs in the world. There's hardly a corporate boardroom in the country that we haven't touched in some way. Flights from any place in the continental U.S., Europe, and Canada were paid for as part of your admission fee, Smithson. We all met up in Winnipeg three days ago and flew in on float plane charters."

I looked over to Moses, who had now put out his smoke. He turned and walked up the beach without as much as a word. Looking into his back as he walked away, I felt a growing rage. *He'd known about the flights, the floatplanes, the start date and everything else, yet decided to send me that mangy map so I could drive all night and walk through hell just to get here three days late.* It would have been nice, polite at least, to give me a description of this program and the chance to make a choice. I'd driven through Winnipeg just three days ago and could easily have hooked up with this crew to fly in here and get started like all the rest. *And what's this crap about an ordeal.* I was already in an ordeal, not having slept but four hours in the last three days. The slight slope of the beach looked like a mountain to me now. There was nothing left in my legs. I couldn't carry my pack or the canoe one step further.

Kimmel picked up my pack. "Going light, I see," he said balancing the pack on a couple of fingers. "Always a good idea. No matter though—you won't need any of this gear for the duration of the program. I guess you weren't informed that everything would be provided for you."

That *would have been nice to know too*, I thought as I visualized the big pile of equipment I'd left in the swamp.

Kimmel noticed how tired I was. "Let me take that for you Smithson. You'll feel better after some steak and a couple of cups of coffee. What you have to do next will involve sitting and thinking, but not much else." I willingly handed Kimmel the pack, and he shouldered up the canoe without much problem. We walked up the beach together, past a sign in loud block letters:

PLAN TO SUCCEED!
THE PRICE OF SUCCESS IS ALWAYS CHEAPER THAN THE
COST OF FAILURE!

"We change the sign every six hours—something new to inspire you four times a day," Kimmel said. I liked Kimmel, even though I'd never had any friends like him. I sensed that Kimmel genuinely enjoyed helping others move forward. He was generously carrying my gear, which was more than I could say for Moses. The steak sounded great, and the idea of fresh coffee more than fabulous. The reverence I'd developed for Moses was already fading a bit as we stopped at tent seventeen.

Kimmel unshouldered the canoe, and put it keel-up next to the tent. "There's a bag for the soiled laundry under the bed," he said. "Your bunk is the one on the bottom right. You can keep your gear under the bunk if you like. The other three guys in your tent are Abrams, Ramsey, and Smith. We get clean clothes here every morning, and there are two sets of clothes on your bunk. We're re-supplied by floatplane every forty-eight. We've got hot water from the generators and showers down at the end," he said pointing with his free hand. "Not bad for this far out in the boondocks, I have to say, and it will only get better if you complete the program."

"Do you mind if I ask you a question?" I asked.

"Shoot," answered Kimmel.

"What was the Gun talking about when he said that only half of us would complete the program?"

Again, Kimmel looked amazed that I could ask such a question. But as I stood there, he realized that I really didn't know. So, like a professional, he answered in a straightforward way that acknowledged that I needed the information.

"Like Mr. Rankin said, this is a date with personal destiny. It is the most rigorous executive training program in the world. This phase of the training involves a lot of physicality, so men and women are segregated to keep competition fair. We hook up later in the more cognitive portion of the training. This stint here in the wilderness is just the start of the program—it weeds out those who are unlikely to qualify as exemplary leaders. Failure to complete any aspect of the training means you're out. Focus and drive are the fundamental building blocks for everything that comes next, so we feel it's best to begin by weeding out those who can't cut it."

"So half of us will not get to the next phase?" I asked.

"That's what typically happens. This is a self-selecting peer group of unquestionable winners that we call a 'Cohort': the fused members of an elite group. Plan to be one of them."

Kimmel's straightforward answers were refreshing. Everything in his world was logical, crisp, clear, and directional, with all outcomes pre-determined if the right steps were taken in the proper sequence. The idea that I could become an 'unquestionable winner' in just five days' time, and have a group of lifelong friends committed to my success seemed like a great result. I nodded to Kimmel, signaling that I understood him.

"And by the way, since you've picked such an unusual strategy, most of the guys here already think you are some kind of a nut case. You may have to work extra hard to earn their confidence. I personally respect your strategy though—it takes guts to stand out and walk in here alone. I wish you the best of luck."

Kimmel ducked out of the tent. Standing there in silence, I felt betrayed by Moses. He'd led me here to a training where I was already an outcast.

I dragged my pack into the tent and stripped off my filthy clothes. It was a comfortable tent with an eight-foot peak and solid wood floor. *Must have brought this in here last winter*, I thought. *These guys are probably the ones that created the shortcut across the swamp.* I looked at my naked white body in a shaft of light pouring through the tent opening where the flaps didn't quite come together. My tent-mates were somewhere else. Nearly every place on my skin was covered with particles of slime. I looked down at the cot with its clean white sheets. I don't remember falling into the sheets, only the deep dreamless sleep that came afterward.

19: Freeze-Dried Purpose

> Discovering who you are is something that must be realized by direct experience. The gift might arrive spontaneously at a time and place that can't be predicted. It also might arrive after long years of 'the work' of clearing the mind, surrendering the will, and opening the heart. Even then, who knows?
>
> ...*The Field Book*

IT WAS STILL THE MIDDLE OF THE NIGHT when I felt a hand on my back shaking me awake. It was Kimmel. I was freezing from head to toe; naked in the cold Canadian air. I could hear a light drizzle of rain on the tent fabric.

"Hey man, you have to get your ass out of bed or you're going to wash out before tomorrow night," he said. There was a strong smell of coffee in the tent. Through my half-lidded eyes, I could see a column of steam coming from a huge metal cup. Everything in my body wanted to pull up the wool blankets and crawl under the clean sheets. Kimmel kept shaking me.

"Triple espresso dude. Now get up and drink it before these other guys get up. I felt sorry for you last night coming in with that kooky guy Taylor. I know that he's paying your tuition and all, but in truth he's not quite with the program. But really, Smithson, I can't keep helping you or my own ass is going to be in a crack. I can't show favorites 'cause all these guys deserve an equal chance." He pulled me up and put the mug under my nose. "Now chug this down, shower up, and get a good breakfast. Then report to tent seven. Get a purpose and get back with Green Team this afternoon."

THE CASCADE OF WARM WATER, mixed with the sudden clarity brought on by the jolt of caffeine, induced a temporary sense of well-being to every cell of my body. *This is not going to be so bad after all.* Still, I was confused as I soaked my head under the delicious hot stream. Why the elaborate invitation, the rules, and the hassle with the gear only to lead me here? This program did not seem consistent with anything that Moses was teaching. And as much as I liked Kimmel, his idea of 'getting a purpose' by lunch time seemed more like picking out a new dress shirt than uncovering a life-altering insight. I'd always imagined that a purpose was connected with something higher, something that my soul was here to do in this life so that it could be released and move on to some higher ground.

I bent my head over and watched the streams of water flow around my ears and down onto the floor. For just a moment I had the clearest feeling that some deep beauty was waiting out in the wilderness beyond the camp, that someone impossibly powerful was moving out there—right now—in the stillness of this early morning. And then, as clear as if it were yesterday, I was nine years old next to the blue spruce with Moses. He'd been debating something, and finally had made a decision. "The deep wilderness for you Charlie," he'd said. "*She'd* like that. I'll lead you out into the wilderness someday, Charlie, if you want to come. You can meet *her* there."

I snapped out of my reverie with the sound of the Gun yelling through a bullhorn.

"Cohort Number one-oohh-threeeee! It's time to meet your destiny! So drop your cocks and grab your socks. It's daylight in the swamp!"

Only the Gun could come up with something that stupid to start the day. I put on the clean outfit provided by the Initiative, and walked to the mess tent past the sign that now read:

BELIEVE IT IS POSSIBLE!

Everything here ended with an exclamation mark: *Like they couldn't find a way to make what they were dishing out taste good enough*, I thought. Tabasco on everything was the answer.

As I entered the mess tent, the Gun had already taken the podium to deliver the daily inspirational message that was to begin precisely at 5:45, as posted on the daily schedule written with careful letters on a white board behind him. Many members of the Cohort had the chiseled looks of semi-pro athletes, yet a good number of them looked not so different from me.

The breakfast was better than anything I'd expected. Heaps of fresh salmon, poached eggs, toast with honey, and an endless cup of good coffee. Now we're talking. I was impressed with the flawless execution of the Initiative. It sure beat any of the food that was left in my Alaskan backwoods pack.

Up at the front of the room, the Gun cleared his throat and began.

"So, Mr. Smithson, let me ask you the same question I posed to you last night. Just what is it that you *really* want?"

I sat there, speechless, staring at my beautiful food. The crowd grew quiet and uncomfortable. Most of them were looking down, smoothing the floor with their boots, then glancing up at one another and exchanging knowing smiles. *All of them must know what they want*, I thought. *I am the only one here without a clue.*

"Don't know what you want, Charlie?" the Gun asked, for the first time more quiet and knowing. "Well, you're not the first, not the first. Even *I* sat there speechless like you when my mentor asked me 'The Question.' I know what it feels like to be purposeless. Just leaves you kind of hollow inside, doesn't it, Charlie?"

I didn't respond. I had to admit that I was confused, deeply confused, and becoming more confused with every passing minute. With Moses suddenly gone, I had no defenses. I wanted to ask Moses whether he thought it was OK not to know exactly what I wanted, to just be open and curious, not knowing. It took all of my energy just to hold the gaze of the Gun, not look down to the ground, and have him defeat me openly.

"So we've found your problem and we're going to start to work on it, Charlie. Because here's the deal, and I want all of you to remember it," the Gun said, crouching a little and bringing his index finger up to the level of his right eye as he swept the room with an all-knowing smile.

He seems like a card shark about to deal a rigged hand that will allow me to rake in all the bets on the table.

"The deal is that *all of you* must decide your life's purpose, and decide it right here and now. Because without a purpose, you don't know your goals, and without your goals you can't determine your strategy, and without your strategy you can't determine the metrics that allow you to measure whether or not you have met your goals. And without those metrics, those measurements, you can't know whether or not you are moving toward your purpose, and without that movement towards your purpose you can never be happy."

He said this all in one long breath. The speech drew nods of approval all around. I couldn't argue with the logic the Gun had laid out for me. I had to admit that it would be great to know exactly what my purpose was.

The Gun finally broke off his gaze and returned to the relaxed and expansive posture that he had used when greeting me last night on the beach.

"Gentlemen, this is Charlie Smithson, our newest and final member. Smithson, this is the Strategic Self Transformation Initiative, Cohort number one hundred and three," the Gun said, now using a voice that would fill an opera hall. "Everyone here has made a date with personal destiny. Like the hundreds of elite graduates who have come before you, you will come to realize that this moment, this very moment, is the *turning point*, the fulcrum of your personal history, the moment when you will find what has been ordained by destiny (and personal choice) to be the thing, the *one* thing that you will do in this lifetime to make *this* a more perfect world. You will find the motivation to do it, be given the skills to execute a plan, and earn the allegiance of one another throughout this lifetime. BELIEVE IT IS POSSIBLE!" He shouted. The group responded with the Marine Rallying Cry, an enthused OOHRAH! which shook the tent.

At 6:30 a.m. I entered tent seven to find my purpose.

By 6:45 I was deep into the 'Patented Process of Purpose' ™ that the Initiative considered one of the cornerstones of their undisputed success. It started with a request for my signature on a three-page legal form that required non-disclosure of any portion of the 'patented process' without express written permission. I acknowledged that disclosure of such a valuable trade secret could and would cause irrevocable harm to the Initiative in an amount incapable of calculation. I was asked to agree to liquidated damages in the amount of two hundred fifty-thousand dollars in the event of a willful or negligent disclosure on my part.

Come and collect it from me, I thought. I'd attended a pretty darn good law school. In my first-year contracts class I learned that liquidated damages were unenforceable if they did not bear some reasonable relationship to actual damages. I also remembered that patent protection was typically not extended to a business process. It was a contract of adhesion (a contract containing outrageous terms presented in a setting where there was no possibility for negotiation), and I was under duress at 6:45 a.m. *This thing will never hold up in court.* I signed the document.

With the legal formalities out of the way, the 'purpose process' began. I was asked to list a half-dozen of my unique, positive, personal qualities. Several were suggested, such as enthusiasm, diligence, energy, creativity, loyalty, and friendliness. It was something like the Scout Law (a scout is trustworthy, loyal, helpful...) only with expanded options.

"Any place for characteristics that I might consider negative, like fear, inability to focus, stuff like that?" I asked.

"Your purpose is always positive, or it's not really a purpose," the trainer informed me.

My trainer was a Gun clone down to the purple sash. He wielded a clipboard and a pen with the outward-pointing logo of the Initiative embossed on the barrel. *A true believer that has drunk the Kool-Aid,* I thought.

I listed my handful of positive personal qualities. I told the trainer that I was intelligent, detail oriented, diligent in completing projects, and a good friend given a chance. The final thing about friendship I sort of made up. The truth was that I *wanted* to be a good friend to someone, but the way that I'd structured my life so far hadn't allowed me the time.

"Now, narrow it down to the two characteristics that you feel are the most important."

"Only two?" I asked.

"Just the two most important," he said.

I chose "being a good friend" and "diligence". He wrote them down. "Very good, Charlie. Now, for the next step."

The next step was to list one or two ways that I "truly, deeply, and profoundly" enjoyed expression of my qualities in transactions with others.

"Is it always in relation to others? Could I just enjoy them on my own?" I asked.

"Your true purpose is always in relationship to others. The universe does not assign a purpose that does not invite you to be in service to others," the trainer intoned.

That settled it. The truth was that I could not think of a single thing I 'truly, deeply, and profoundly' enjoyed' doing for others. I'd been doing nothing but homework for the last fifteen years, for Christ's sake. I sat for a long time as the trainer tapped his pen on his clipboard. Nothing. With the morning light shifting in the tent, I decided to make up something that sounded noble, something that I might like to do if I ever had the chance. *I might as well make it sound as good as I can*, I thought. I took my pad and wrote down that I liked to help my friends with their projects, especially when they were trying something difficult and new. The trainer seemed quite pleased with this response.

"And now for the exciting part," the Trainer said. He hooked the tent flaps of number seven closed and padlocked a small chain around the grommets.

"Now is the time for deep meditation," he said. "The time to visualize your perfect world: a world in which you have the ability to express your unique talents; a world where you will be deeply appreciated. See, touch, and feel your perfect world with every fiber of your being. The universe has created a perfect place just for you and is ready to deliver. Visualize the place that will complete you. See yourself at work there every day for the rest of your life. *Demand* a vision of your future, Charlie, and we will have this completed by mid-morning."

It seemed like a lot of pressure, especially with the requirement that we be finished so soon. It looked like I would have to cut my way out of the tent with my Ranger pocketknife if I couldn't come up with something.

"I am here to support you, Charlie. Take your time," the trainer said, glancing at his waterproof sports watch. He assumed a meditative position, his fingers curled so that the middle finger and thumb just touched, making an oval around his belly button.

"I invoke the universe to reveal the perfect purpose for my brother, Charlie Smithson," he said, closing his eyes and breathing deeply. "Focus on your unique talents of attention, your quality as a friend, your diligence, the other fine qualities that are your unique gifts, and the place where those gifts will be received, with gratitude, by others. This is your 'place of purpose,' Charlie. I am supporting you now."

With that, the tent went silent, except for the sounds of training outside. I could hear the Gun shouting: "Commit to constant and never-ending improvement!" *That's the new slogan for the morning,* I thought.

"Green Team! Commit to constant and never ending improvement!" I heard Kimmel shout as the ranks of the Green Team huffed past the front of number seven. *Must be running in formation.* I was glad to be here inside the tent instead of running around outside with that phrase in my head. I closed my eyes and took a deep breath. I sensed some impatience in the trainer, as if he lacked any real respect for anyone my age that did not already know his purpose.

I put my hands on my lap and took a couple of deep breaths. My mind went blank. Maybe it was the strangeness of the situation or all of the odd events of the last few days. I just sank into the cot. Nothing at all came to mind. No vision. No place. Nothing.

After what seemed like an hour, the trainer shifted, and took up his pen and notepad.

"Anything?" he asked.

"Nothing," I replied. That was not quite true. My mind was full of concern about what we were going to have for lunch. I also was being bothered by some of the mosquito bites on my neck. I must have scratched some of them bloody during the night, and they were starting to itch.

"Sometimes the part of us that does not want our true destiny revealed will try to keep the mind enslaved," the trainer intoned. "Continue to focus on your talents and on those who will receive them, and then imagine the scene where you are using those talents to their utmost capacity. Where are you, Charlie? Where are you?"

The trainer dropped his meditative posture and began to stare at me. Apparently he was used to uncovering life purposes in less than an hour.

"What if I don't know?" I pleaded. "What if it's something that hasn't been invented yet?"

"You will be able to imagine it nonetheless," he replied. The flatness of his tone indicated that the matter was closed. I shut my eyes again.

What if I'm in some process of development? I thought. Would my purpose change if I grew and evolved? Did I *have* to want the same thing every day of the rest of my life?

And what was it that I'd read in the Field Book, something about *waking up* and becoming an entirely different human as a result? I was about to ask the trainer if my purpose could change as I discovered who I was.

As if reading my mind, he said "One purpose, Charlie. If you jump around from flower to flower you will never have sufficient focus to do what is necessary to manifest a purpose. Your one purpose must clear the way for itself. It has chosen you, Charlie. The only question is whether you are man enough to choose it in return."

This seemed so final and so certain that I could hardly argue with it. Maybe it *was* my own inadequacy getting in the way.

I sat in silence with my eyes closed. I could feel the trainer drilling a hole in me with his eyes. Still nothing. A bell rang outside signaling that it was lunchtime. The trainer didn't move. The smell of bratwurst sausages came into the tent from a grill behind the mess hall. I wanted those sausages. And there it was. The vision of Edna's hand coming through the door of cabin number six, bearing that heaping plate of sausages, cheese potatoes, and eggs. I saw the cabins by Loon Lake in need of repair, and Edna walking down the path with pain in her hip, her triceps swaying as she walked.

"I am seeing myself in a group of cabins by a lake where friends gather to restore themselves," I reported, opening my eyes.

The trainer jumped up with a double fist pump. "Yes!" he said scribbling the exact words. "Now just one last step, Charlie. We combine all three of the foregoing elements into one cohesive statement of no more than one sentence that combines the essence of all. This will be the statement of your unique purpose. You will reaffirm and recommit to this purpose each and every day of your life from this point forward." He seemed impatient and ready to go to lunch. Undoubtedly the time of such a master trainer was quite valuable. "Here, let me do it for you—just an example—you can change it if it isn't right."

He scribbled on his pad:

"I create a beautiful retreat environment where I use the power of my friendship and my capacity for diligence to aid others in creation of their innovative projects."

Wow, I thought. *That actually sounds really good.* I had no idea that this was my purpose when I entered the tent earlier this morning. The trainer noticed my surprise.

"Always works, Charlie. Never fails. That's why you pay us the big bucks." He ripped my purpose off his pad. "You can announce it at lunch, and the rest of the Cohort will begin to support you in fulfilling your purpose, starting today. Never take your eyes off your purpose, Charlie, if you want to succeed. Never doubt it. You came here to find this purpose, Charlie," the trainer said in a lowered voice. "We have revealed your Destiny. The Initiative will now bring out the drive to fulfill your destiny, and help you create a world-beating business process to bring it into manifestation."

Had I known that it would be this easy to find my purpose and destiny, I would have done it sooner. I put away all the nagging doubts about something that came this easily.

The trainer unlocked the tent flaps, and ushered me out with an air of self-satisfaction. He had done it again. I could not help wondering whether I would have come up with a different purpose using a different process, but this seemed trivial. I had my purpose; now we could go to lunch.

20: Dreams within Dreams

> We have reached an age where most human problems and solutions are created by humans. The dreams of humans have become the most powerful force on earth.
> ...*The Field Book.*

I ENTERED THE LUNCH ROOM where a meal of sausage sandwiches, fresh vegetables, and potatoes was already in progress. A large beige tent had been placed over a granite outcrop. The flaps of the tent were rolled up to collect a gentle breeze flowing in from the lake. The precise arrangement of the tent and tables transformed the outcrop into a designer setting that enhanced the intimacy of conversation and the sense of being connected to both nature and luxury at the same time. Around the perimeter of the tent hung thirty-one colored placards, one for each member of the Cohort. A sentence was written in flowing calligraphic script on each of the placards that expressed a life purpose. "To use my discipline and physical prowess to teach young people to become champion golfers;" "To use my drive and organization skills to create a company where everyone makes at least a million dollars a year trading securities;" and so on.

I was ushered to the table of the Green Team. In the center of the table was a small green flag upon which the sunburst arrows of the Initiative were embroidered in gold. There was space for eight team members at the table, with Kimmel as team leader making nine. Kimmel handed me a green kerchief to match those already worn by the rest of the team. "Only get to wear one of these when you have a purpose and are ready to move forward toward its fulfillment," he said. I put the kerchief on.

On my left was Abrams, a short Jewish kid from New York wearing thick black glasses. Abrams looked out of place in a wilderness setting, like a city kid who'd never been west of the Hudson River. I had the impression that he didn't want to be here. I imagined that he had been strongly encouraged by a domineering father who had put up the princely tuition with hopes of catapulting his son into the big leagues. The Initiative was a backdoor, a ticket into the sort of success club typically enjoyed only by graduates of Harvard, Yale, or one of the other Ivy's. In comparison to the cost of *that* type of education, the hundred grand required by the Initiative was a relative bargain.

Standing next to Abrams were my two other tent mates, Ramsey and Smith. Ramsey was an inch shorter than Abrams, and his head only made it to Kimmel's shoulder. I disliked Ramsey instinctively before he'd uttered a word. There was something about him. His narrow eyes kept darting around in his flat face—never meeting a gaze or resting anywhere. He looked as if he was checking the scene so he would not be caught off guard if someone pulled a knife on him. His body was not at ease—like he'd been beaten one too many times as a kid, and he wasn't about to let it happen again. Ramsey had the air of someone not quite tall enough, not quite handsome enough, and not quite good enough on those aptitude tests. He was making a big investment here and was not about to be one of the people left behind. *If he has to walk over me to make his success happen, he will be more than willing to do it*, I thought.

Smith, my final tent-mate, was an African-American in his late twenties. He was light skinned, calm, and self-possessed. He exhibited none of the nervous aggression that poured off Ramsey. I liked Smith and was glad to have him on my team. *If there's a way to make it by playing by the rules and giving a solid effort, Smith will end up one of the winners*, I thought. Later I would find out that my first impression was well founded. Smith was a good team member, so good, in fact, that he'd been spotted in the middle manager ranks at General Electric, culled out, brought forward, and offered a fully paid spot in the Cohort as an investment in the company's future.

There were four other guys at our table: Goddard, Wilkes, Ashton, and Roberts. They all were bunked up together in tent eight. These four were striking in that they all seemed so much the same, all junior versions of Kimmel, our team leader, cut from the same well-muscled mode, and displaying the relaxed attitude of obvious winners. They were all slightly bored. The four of them conveyed the impression that this was business as usual, that they had somehow been here, done this. This didn't make any sense to me—this program did not seem like something anyone would do multiple times. There was something odd about all this, but I couldn't put my finger on it. Yet I was sure of one thing: If I had to out-compete the four guys in tent eight, it would be damn hard to do. I felt like the winners of the Green Team competition had been sorted already, and I wasn't one of them.

I shook hands all around and endured the bone crushing vice-like grips of the alpha guys from tent eight. I sat back in my chair nursing a growing resentment toward Moses. He had led me up here into a lion's den, and it was clear to me that I would wash out. I'd come all of this way just to have another experience of being second string.

My trainer stood up with a placard edged in green and rang a small gong with a wooden mallet.

"Charlie Smithson! Are you ready to add your life's purpose to our collective intention?"

Immediately the room went silent. All eyes turned to me.

"Do you want me to announce the purpose we've come up with this morning?" I asked.

"That would be the idea," the trainer said holding up the placard. My purpose was already written in script, but the lettering was too small to read from this distance.

I stood up to recite my purpose. Suddenly everything went blank. My newly-discovered destiny was not stored in the same part of my brain that had the job of remembering the name of the person I'd just met or the number of the parking space where I'd left my car. It was a piece of information that was just not connected to anything.

The room stared at me. The phrase just wasn't there. I could feel the flush rising up my neck and into my face. I turned my eyes to the trainer, silently begging him to help me out. Finally he broke the silence.

"Sometimes one's purpose comes at such a level of depth that the conscious mind has a hard time retaining it," he said. It was another one of those phrases said in deep tones that got deeper near the end of the phrase. *He's practiced this,* I thought. *He's taken some kind of class in the art of making authoritative statements that everyone in the room will accept as true.*

I thought back to the three or four statements the trainer had made in tent seven, all with this same voice. Not one of his statements about the nature of one's purpose and destiny could be proved or disproved as fact. The formula seemed to be this: (1) statement that could not be proved wrong; plus (2) air of absolute certainty; equals (3) The Truth. *Wow, what a racket. These guys are in the* belief *business.* Something created out of thin air is stated authoritatively as a fact. The fact becomes progressively more and more real as it is restated and reinforced a thousand times, then acted on. *But what the hell,* I thought. *If you come to believe something and act as if it's true, isn't that thing more likely to happen?*

The trainer saw that I was drifting. "Let your conscious mind hear this, Smithson, and come not just to believe it to be true, but to *know* it to be true. Your destiny is..." he looked down at the placard, "to create a beautiful retreat environment where you will use the power of your friendship and your capacity for diligence to aid others in creation of their innovative projects. Now, Smithson, WHAT IS YOUR PURPOSE?"

I recited the phrase as best I could. The bell rang again.

"Two minutes of silence while the group holds this intention in its field of collective manifestation," the trainer said. The room went into silence. The only sounds were shuffling feet and one sneeze.

After two minutes the bell rang again.

"I hang this purpose where it can be affirmed by all!" the trainer said as my purpose joined the others. The group let out a collective 'OORAH!' with a guttural explosion of breath, then went back to eating. Apparently the Cohort had done this thirty-one times before over the last few days. I completed the Cohort as number thirty-two.

I sat down and retreated into my meal. I was happy that my table seemed hungry and was eating in silence. My third bite into a delicious bratwurst sandwich was interrupted by a stinging slap on my back.

"Glad to see that you have decided to get into the hospitality business, Smithson!" the Gun said. "Not so different than the business we've gotten ourselves into, is it, Kimmel?"

"You're so right, sir," Kimmel said. "Helping people bring their innovations into the world is our mission in life."

The Gun continued. "We have a lot to teach you, Smithson, a lot to teach you. If you make it through our training, living your purpose is virtually assured, and you will bask in unwavering clarity for the rest of your life."

All I could do was nod and smile meekly up at him. I honestly could not tell if I was being given the greatest gift in the world or a death sentence. I had to admit that 'unwavering clarity' would be a huge step up for me. There was something appealing about having everything all buttoned up: the idea of a pre-determined life that would make me complete, whole, and perfect; a life just lying there on the ground for me to find it. *Wow.* I wanted to find Moses and ask him about my new purpose. I scanned the room of multi-colored kerchiefs and khaki outfits. Moses was nowhere to be found.

I finished lunch and walked back to tent seventeen for the thirty minute 'reflection period' that was allowed in the busy schedule of the Initiative. *The Field Book talks about purpose too,* I thought, sitting down on my bunk. *It just seems to be coming from a different place.* The ideas on the placards around the mess tent were not necessarily wrong; they were just, well, *small*. Moses would probably say that my purpose was to serve something larger, bigger than myself—something that would take me over in the end. As far as I could tell, Moses and The Committee were entirely focused on the health and expansion of something they were calling 'The Field' and the balance of everything in it. It was clear to me that they wanted me to be a *vehicle* for some change in this Field that might shift the whole world. I just didn't know what it was.

As I lay down on my bunk, a woman's voice entered my mind.

"*—You can't yet know until you've seen the Field,*" the voice said. Then nothing.

I closed my eyes. I was even more confused than I was earlier this morning. *I can't keep this up much longer.*

IN MY PREOCCUPATION, I hadn't noticed that I was not alone. A man cleared his throat, and I looked over to see Abrams was on the bunk opposite me as I came in, his thick black glasses resting on his forehead.

"Grooved on your purpose man; sounds definitely do-able," he said in a thick Bronx accent.

"Thanks," I replied.

I sat up, reached into my pack, and pulled out the Field Book and the pen that Moses had given me. *I should at least write down my life's purpose, so I can remember it next time I'm asked.* I didn't want to be embarrassed again. As I unclicked the cap of the pen, Abrams gave a low whistle.

"Wow, you must have money to burn bringing something like that out here in the woods," he said.

"Why, is it something special?"

He looked at me and snorted. "Something special? Do you know what you have there?"

"I guess not."

"Well, did it just fall into your hand or something?"

"Something like that."

"Well, in case you're not bullshitting me, it happens to be a Graf von Faber-Castell. Looks like one of their limited editions. Mind if I have a look?"

I handed the pen over to him, and he examined it carefully.

"Yes, definitely a limited," he said, handing the pen back to me. "I should know. My family's been in the jewelry business in midtown Manhattan for three generations. That pen retails for about three thousand in our store, but it takes a special customer to buy one. Most people want more gold and jewels on the pen if they spend that much money for it. They're just buying flash. That Faber-Castell is one of the few top-ends that you can actually write with. Hell of a gift if you don't mind me saying so."

I looked at the pen in astonishment. I guess I hadn't done so badly trading my dime store gear for something like this.

I turned to one of the blank pages of the Field Book to write my purpose with one of the most expensive pens in the world, and then stopped. *The Field Book is a collective truth, pointing to something.* I should understand more about what the book is pointing toward before I make my first entry. I should wait until I'm clearer.

I carefully tore one of the blank pages from the back, and used the page to write down my purpose. The line from the pen flowed clear and dark—a river of ink on thick rag paper that made bends and eddies and tiny pools. Just the lightest touch was all that was required to make the line come alive and bend across the page. I finished the entry, clicked the cap, and put the diary and pen back in my pack. *Where's Moses?* I thought, lying back down. *Why did he lead me here?*

AT PRECISELY ONE-THIRTY P.M., a loud gong sounded outside. The thirty minute 'reflection period' was over, and it was time to start another afternoon of rapid movement toward massive individual and collective transformation by means of the Initiative's unique proprietary process. On the south end of the commons the inspiration had changed again. The sign now read:

I KNOW WHAT I WANT!

This was to be the mantra that all thirty-two of us would recite over and over again during the next six hours. The loud affirmative statements of the Initiative were designed as an all-points bulletin to any objecting parts of the psyche that might dare to reach up out of the depths of the unconscious and sabotage the fine plan made by my cerebral forebrain cortex. There was a new person and a new way of being on the block, buddy-o, and any objections, resistance, or second-guessing would not be tolerated. Every cell of the body had better get with the program or else! The Green Team gathered around the sign.

"Alright Green Team, listen up," Kimmel said. "All of you have now successfully completed the life visioning process, and we are ready to move on to the next phase of your training. So why is it that you have not already accomplished your purpose?"

The team stood around in silence, and then Smith spoke up. "It's because we haven't been clear enough about our purpose?"

"Just right," Kimmel acknowledged, snapping his fingers and pointing into the air. "And what else?"

"Because something is stopping us?" Abrams offered, looking sideways at Kimmel.

"Right again, Abrams," Kimmel said. "There are obstacles to the fulfillment of your purpose that exist both internally and externally. Inside, there are all of your unconscious fears: fear of success, fear of failure, and limiting beliefs about who you are and what you can accomplish. And on the outside there are all of the conditions that must be overcome to get to the prize: getting the money, getting the right people, getting the time." Kimmel shifted into oratory mode. His words were delivered with absolute certainty. "We will deal with your internal blocks to success before you leave this encampment. Over the next seventy-two hours of intense focus and training, you will come face-to-face with all of your fears and limitations and will defeat them in open combat. As you identify your fears, you will embed a positive mental affirmation that will take the place of whatever is stopping you. Fears and inaccurate beliefs will never again have hold of you.

"Then, after completing the wilderness phase of your training, you will return to civilization to develop a comprehensive plan. You will develop a linear timeline of achievable action steps expressed in our patented 'next action' format. You will then proceed to accomplish these steps in sequence, a process that will be supported on an ongoing basis by the Initiative and by the fellow members of the Cohort. Visioning, overcoming resistance, working the plan. One step, two steps, three. It's just that simple. Your success is already here. 'I know what I want'!" Kimmel exclaimed, pointing to the sign.

Toward the end of Kimmel's speech, my mind began to drift out into the pines that surrounded the encampment. This was a spring day, and a warm wind was coming from the south. I wondered whether any Native Americans had stood here on this sandy point before the Initiative arrived. I wondered what they might have thought, standing on this beach in skins and moccasins, looking deep into the forest and up into the shifting sky. *They were in a world larger than themselves*, I thought. I was almost sure of this. *There would be mystery, and stories about fire in the sky.*

"Let's stay with it, Smithson," Kimmel said. "One of the things that we are here to teach you is how to stay focused. You can't get there if you don't focus, focus, focus!" He said emphatically. "So let's get in double file and get some exercise. With each outbreath you are to affirm your purpose using the 'I am' statement of ten words or less that you have created to support your new way of being."

I guess I'd been drifting when the instructions about the 'I am' statement were issued, but the statement wasn't that hard to come up with. "I am successful. I help others achieve their purpose," was in my mind as we started to jog.

"The endorphin state that we will achieve over the next ninety minutes will communicate the truth of your affirmation into every cell of your body," Kimmel said as he picked up the Green Team banner and bounded across the granite.

TEN MINUTES LATER it was clear that one of the techniques of the Initiative was to pound affirmations into us at a breathless pace. We ran in circles around a rocky outcrop behind the camp. Up and back again, up and back again. Each circle came back to the middle of camp and past the sign shouting 'I KNOW WHAT I WANT!'. I dutifully recited my affirmation with every outbreath, but the phrase kept drifting away from me. How could I accomplish my purpose if I could not even keep my purpose in my mind? Doubtless this was the lack of focus that Kimmel was talking about. I could not help but notice that we were running around in circles, not really going anywhere. There was a huge wilderness to explore in every direction. But we were to stay on focus and run on course, reciting our chosen purpose.

On each loop out of camp, my eyes scanned the forest for some sign of Moses. He was simply gone. "Out scouting," Kimmel said. "Best not to have him here anyway. He thinks in confusing ways."

NINETY MINUTES LATER, the laggards of the Green Team collapsed in a heap around the banner still held aloft by our team leader. The four alpha guys finished without much problem. They could finish a ninety-minute jog with boots on and still have plenty left for a mile swim and a bike ride. *They* are *the alpha guys,* I thought. Smith was breathing heavily, but had his head up at the end of the run. The winners were already making small talk with Smith, treating him as one of their own. Ramsey would come in last, brought down by a hamstring cramp from over-striding. He was pale-faced with pain and flushed at the same time as he held on with grim determination. Abrams and I had both beaten Ramsey by a few strides, despite walking most of the last loop. I'd been sitting for most of the last three years, and was lucky to complete the run without a serious injury. With each step of the last lap, my body was saying: 'This is it, big boy. The last step. I'm going to quit you now and fall down. I mean it.'

I had nothing to run on but willpower. *If it's willpower that the Initiative wants, Abrams, Ramsey, and I are at the top of the class this afternoon,* I thought. I looked over at Abrams with his black glasses fogged—red-faced and panting—as Ramsey grimaced on the ground trying to massage out his leg. There was not much chance for the three of us.

21: The Competitors

A blessing sent from the heart is not just a sound on the lips, but an agent sent forth into the world, carrying a power. It is the alternative to violence in organizing the world.
...*The Field Book.*

AFTER AN AFTERNOON of lectures and self-motivation exercises, the big gong sounded again, signaling the Cohort to gather. The Gun was there with a bullhorn.

"Members of the Strategic Self Transformation Initiative number one hundred and three!" he said, greeting us through the bullhorn. He paused as if expecting the camp to erupt in wild applause simply because he had opened his mouth. About half the Cohort responded with a weak, OOHRAH.

"Let me say it again: Members of the Strategic Self Transformation Initiative number one hundred and three!" All of us let out some version of the Rallying Cry, which allowed the Gun to continue.

"Over the next forty-eight hours, the Initiative will present to this Cohort its greatest opportunity for self-transformation," he said, pausing for greater effect.

"Over these two days, half of you will come to realize without any doubt, or even the shadow of a doubt, that you—yes, you—are an incontestable *winner* and *champion of your own destiny*. The other half ... well..." he said in a low tone. "The other half will be released to another future."

The Cohort sobered and grew quiet.

"Look to the right of you, look to the left of you. One of you will not be here two days from today," the Gun said. "Only winners with sufficient drive and determination will survive the ordeals that lie ahead. Through these ordeals, you will do things that you now think impossible, and watch the force of your will create *new* possibilities. Your power will expand to capture everything it desires, like an expanding sun embraces and consumes the planets in its system."

He's describing the death throes of a solar system, I thought. But no sense arguing.

"During the next twenty-four hours you will experience an ordeal in the hands of the brutal wilderness that surrounds us. You will experience the pain of this place and come to appreciate all the ways that modern men have conquered nature through the power of will."

A weak OOHRAH came out of the group.

"Completion counts! There are three phases of the ordeal, and failure to finish any phase means that you're out!"

The Gun went on to explain that upon successful completion of the three phases of the ordeal, the winners would fly out together by float plane, rest up in a nice hotel back in Chicago, then begin the portion of the training which involved business planning, project mapping, and critical path analysis. At the end of the training, we would be ready to take on the world.

I was starting to believe that this training could deliver some positive outcomes for me. With this schedule I would be back in Chicago in time for graduation. The opportunities presented by my law degree and a credential from the Initiative would be substantial. Of course, I would have to finish the ordeals to get there.

The teams were dismissed to a beautiful supper of buffalo steak, potatoes, vegetables, red wine, and Dutch apple pie. "Remember the taste of this," they said. "The winners will be back to this kind of feasting in only two short days. Then it will never stop."

The First Ordeal.

The Gong sounded at 5:30 a.m., and we assembled in the commons under the watchful eye of a sign which read:

Ross Hostetter

JUST DO IT!

Each of us was handed a photocopy of a map (no compass), which was a very low quality version of the map given to me by Moses. The map was a different scale, and lacked all of the comments, corrections, and interlineations that made Moses' guide-map so useful. My tent-mates were having a hard time lining up the map with the ground. Ramsey kept turning his paper this way and that, trying to figure out which way was north. *It's hard to use a map that's being twisted around three hundred and sixty degrees*, I thought. The shock of ancient technology was just too much for the Green Team.

I knew my map needed to stay still and get reconciled with the landscape. Knowing which horizon was north was the first step. The last stars were still out at daybreak, and it was fairly easy to find the Big Dipper in the northern sky and its 'ladle' that poured into Polaris, the unchanging northern star. That morning, the Dipper and the northern star looked exactly the same as Moses had drawn them on the corner of his guide-map. I was thankful for the information.

Someone had taken the trouble to cover up the compass rose on the photocopy before duplicating it, so the map gave no indication of the cardinal directions. But whoever had made the copy had forgotten to white-out the names of the lakes. I knew from my couple of days of navigating that maps 'read' looking north: the tops of all the letters—the 'T's' and the open 'Y's'—all pointed north. It was a simple matter of swiveling the map so the tops of all the letters pointed in the general direction of the North Star twinkling beautifully in the morning sky. The map then aligned perfectly with the landscape. There was the north shore of Ribbon Lake running southeast from this point. There was the granite outcrop running straight north out of camp. I knew where I was!

Goddard, Wilkes, Ashton, and Roberts were glancing casually at their maps with the air of those so effortlessly ahead of the curve.

I continued to watch Ramsey struggle to orient himself. Abrams and Smith were not doing much better.

KEEPERS OF THE FIELD

My tentmates have been here for a week, are totally clear and focused on their mission and purpose, but have no idea at all where they are, I thought to myself. *They don't know north from south or east from west.* All of the 'unquestioned winners' would leave here not knowing the name of a single plant, bird, or animal, and nothing at all about the art of living in this place. For them, this piece of earth was nothing but a big workout room, a place to build capacity for lives in the skyscrapers and boardrooms.

I was not so sure that any of us were becoming all that independent here. Right now, we were dependent on the Initiative for everything. *That's just the way the Gun wants it*, I thought. *Convince a customer that they are totally self-directed, while making them increasingly dependent on you for guidance and even their sense of self.* That's the way to get a customer for life.

AFTER TEN MINUTES of map reading, Kimmel collected the photocopies. He pulled out a long rope, eight blindfolds, and eight signaling beepers from a knapsack. We were about to be led out of camp blindfolded on that rope, and dropped off alone out in the wilderness to find our way back to camp using only our wits and whatever information we'd been able to glean in our ten minutes with the photocopy. Each of us would have a GPS device on our belts that would reveal to the trainers just where we were at any given time, so we would never actually be lost. There was a beeper on the device. Triggering the beeper meant that we had given up and were ready to be collected. It also meant that we had failed and were going home.

The Green Team lined up on the rope, and I was the last man on the strand. As the other men were being spun around three times and blindfolded, I had a few extra seconds to look around. All of the rocks around camp were cut with lines, and all of those lines ran roughly north/south. *Lines caused by the southward advance of the last glaciers*, I thought. *That's a good piece of information.* I could also feel the delicious caress of a morning wind on my left cheek. *The wind is coming out of the west.* The heat of the sun, rising in the east, was on my right cheek. I had two feet on the ground and good markers in all directions. *Bring it*, I thought, as the blindfold slipped over my eyes.

WE WERE LED out of camp. I could just see my feet through a crack in the blindfold and could hear Abrams ahead of me, already breathing through his mouth. We shuffled together in the lurching way of men tied together who have yet to synchronize their steps. We walked for at least an hour, with the footing becoming progressively wetter and more difficult.

Kimmel began to drop people off the rope, starting with the lead man. He told us not to take the blindfolds off for ten minutes after being dropped off. They were watching, and any infraction of the rules would result in disqualification. We walked on, and every fifteen minutes another man was released. I was alone on the rope as the last one departed.

Kimmel led me on and on, over rocks and slippery logs. It was hard for me to see what was fair about this. I thought Kimmel was on my side. I was sure that I was much further out of camp than any other member of the Green Team.

Maybe we were moving in a circle back toward camp, and the distances would be relatively equal for everyone, I thought. But I could feel the slight pressure of the wind square in my face. Unless the wind had shifted, we'd marched a distance north and then had turned west away from camp.

After more than an hour, we finally reached a stopping point, and Kimmel took the rope out of my hand.

"I'm leaving now. I'll be looking back to see if you have that blindfold on, so don't try to remove it for at least ten minutes. You have the beeper on your belt. If you can't make it back, just press the red button, and we'll come and get you." He sounded as if he expected me to fail.

"Don't worry about me," I said from underneath the blindfold. "I'll see you back in camp before you know it."

"I hope so, Smithson, I really do. Good luck to you."

I could hear his footsteps disappearing across rock, and the breaking of small branches as he moved off. When the sounds subsided I pulled off the mask.

I WAS ON THE SHORE of an unfamiliar lake. The lake was bordered by a thin line of pines, with reeds extending some fifty feet from the shore. I was sure that this lake was not on the map I'd examined this morning. The sun was high in the sky, and the air here was thick and still. Cold chills ran down the outside of my arms into my fingertips, and my chest grew tighter. *Breathe.* The worst thing that can happen is that you'll use the beeper. *You're not really lost in the wilderness, it just feels that way.* I started to walk, and my panic began to ease a bit. I found a branch that hung down over the lake and tied my blindfold to it so I would have a reference point. I began to move up the shore in the direction that Kimmel had disappeared, but I lost his trail in a confusion of branches. I walked back to the blindfold, and worked the other way down the lakeshore. And there it was. I laughed out loud.

It was a big ugly blaze on a pine tree, seeping sap. There, on a rock, was a scrape of aluminum from my canoe where I'd dragged bottom unloading my gear two days ago. There was no way that Kimmel could have known that I'd come in this way. I already knew this territory—this was the gateway to the stinking swamp. I was not about to go back in there. But what was it that Moses had said about that little ridge just west of here? If I could find the ridge it would be easy walking. The little creek that led into Ribbon from the west would be coming down that ridge. I doubted that I would fail at my second attempt at the shortcut. I could follow the creek, bounce from tussock to tussock for a few hundred yards, and then walk the north shore of Ribbon right into base camp.

IN LESS THAN AN HOUR, I walked into the commons of the encampment. My boots were barely wet. Goddard, one of the winners from the alpha tent, had already arrived back in camp and was lounging next to the Gun, who had just finished writing "BANISH NEGATIVE THINKING!" on the camp sign. The phrase was taken from a list of hundreds of such phrases he kept on a yellow pad.

I touched the Gun lightly on the shoulder. He spun around in shock.

"What the hell are you doing here?" he exclaimed.

"I just walked in from the woods. I thought that was what we were supposed to do."

"Well, right..." he said hesitatingly. "Right, right!" he said again, now collecting himself.

"Goddard, it appears that Mr. Smithson has somehow managed to come in second in this morning's exercise just behind you. Well done, Smithson, well done. My congratulations to you! Now if you will excuse me, I have some business to discuss with Mr. Kimmel."

He departed quickly. As he walked away I watched his elbow rise to the level of his shoulder as he pointed a finger and pounded the keys of a communication device. *Unhappy with something*, I thought.

I was glad to take a breather. There was nothing to do but lounge and let the rest of the Cohort trickle in. I walked over to a room-sized boulder and leaned my back against its warm uneven surface. Its bumps and nodes felt great on my back, like a hot rock massage. I sank into the surface and closed my eyes, letting my breath move through me. I let the breath flow up into my nose, feeling my tongue touch a spot on the roof of my mouth just behind the teeth. I circulated air into the area behind my eyes, and then let the breath cascade down into my body to my belly where it gathered up bits and ribbons of tension. After another in-breath, I watched the breath move out across a slight constriction of my throat. My jaw dropped open, and the breath left softly with the sound of air moving through open lips that had no care about any sound at all, as if fogging an imaginary mirror. Three breaths ... seven ... ten. There was something about the air in the woods that made breathing easier. The parts of my body being touched by the breath began to let go, to say 'yes.' I sank deeper into the rock, resting and opening.

Various members of Cohort 103 began to trickle into camp. With my eyes closed, I could hear them panting. A slightly sour smell of sticky sweat with notes of anxiety and panic came through my nostrils. *If the hunters of the tribe came in smelling like this, it would be a sign that the whole clan was in trouble*, I thought.

I opened my eyes, and the inspirational phrase 'BANISH NEGATIVE THINKING!' came into soft focus. *Hey there. All of my negative thoughts were gone for just a moment.* I would not call it banishment though, nothing quite that violent. I just opened my body up to let the northwoods air into it, and there were no thoughts to struggle with. The thought of banishment would have been its own negative thought that could have attracted other negativity. *Better to let it all go*, I thought, *and then invite something wholesome back in.*

THE DAY STRETCHED into afternoon, and the men came out of the wilderness increasingly muddy and tattered. Their eyes were wide with relief upon seeing the camp. The tan trout shirts were ripped by branches, and red welts bulged from foreheads, necks, and throats. *They've been running through the woods in all directions, tripping and falling*, I thought. I guess the exercise was harder than it looked, especially if you were lost from the first moment.

Most of the Cohort made it back. Abrams was one of the last afternoon stragglers to arrive, and he was soaked head to toe in sweat. His body was limp with relief as he came into camp, knowing that he would not have to fly out on the floatplane with the trash and empty wine bottles tomorrow.

At suppertime, our Green Team was still missing two members. One was Ramsey. His narrow eyes were still out there somewhere, trying to make sense of the valleys and ridges and match them up with the mental map he had turned in circles earlier in the day. The second missing man was Ashton, one of the alpha boys from tent eight. I was surprised that Ashton had not had an easier time of it. He was not alone. Each of the other three teams was also missing one of their alphas from tent eight.

Just before seven p.m., the camp caught sight of Ramsey. His tattered image was waving to us from a little point on the other side of Ribbon Lake. How he got there, God only knows. Apparently he was completely lost, but somehow had found the shoreline and proceeded to walk around the lake, knowing that the camp had to be on the shore somewhere. It was clear he had no idea where the camp might be, and had just taken a fifty/fifty chance of turning in the right direction. He'd lost the bet, and had marched the long way around.

When Ramsey finally struggled into camp, Ashton was still missing. Then, as if on cue, Ashton came into camp with Kimmel. Ashton's shoulders were slumped forward; and his hands were hanging from limp arms as he walked head down. He'd triggered his beeper. In quick succession, three other alpha guys were brought in by their team leaders and were paraded through camp. *How the mighty have fallen,* I thought. Ashton and the three other losers disappeared behind the mess tent.

The Second Ordeal.
With everyone in, the Cohort, minus the four losers, was again gathered in the commons area. We were informed that there would be no dinner tonight. At dusk we were going back out into the wilderness. We would be allowed water but not food. There would be no flashlights or any other equipment except two kitchen matches per man. We were allowed a rain jacket. We were told not to seek out or speak to each other at any time during the night, upon pain of disqualification.

Each of us was given a ten by ten square of mosquito netting which would be our only shelter. We were to spend the night alone and isolated out in the woods, with such fire as we could make with our two matches. Again we would have our beeper. To press it meant rescue, but elimination from the competition. "The night does strange things and brings out strange fears in people who seem quite strong in the daytime," the Red Team leader said. "Be ready for some surprises."

We were given fifteen minutes to collect ourselves before the second ordeal began. I walked around the mess tent to where the portable latrines stood in a row. Ashton and the three other wash-outs were lounging back by the generators, laughing and drinking beer. *A consolation prize I guess.* At least the Initiative furnished some cold beer to the losers.

THE TEAMS were again led out into the wilderness on a line. Each of us was dropped off out of the sight-line of the others. I was dropped in a densely wooded area away from the windy beach. The mosquitoes were out in earnest. There were thousands of them in the air. God knows what purpose they served in the natural order, maybe food for bats or something. They had no value for a human being as far as I could see. I rummaged around the forest in the growing dark to gather up as much firewood as I could. The wood was wet from the rain a couple of nights ago, and I quickly used my two matches trying to light wet lumber. No success. Without smoke, the mosquitoes were probing me everywhere. I was covered up with a jacket, heavy pants, and a good slathering of bug dope, but still they were finding places where the clothing was tight to the skin, riding there until the fabric was stretched thin by some movement. Then they would attack, working their beaks through the cloth to find the flesh.

Without a fire, I had no defense. I crawled into a fetal position and spread the mosquito cloth over the top of me. The ground was cold and hard. And this night the mosquitos were also joined by a steady invasion of bugs so small that they could easily pass through the netting—the northwoods nemesis called *no-see-ums*—a tiny midge seeking its own blood meal by chewing my skin down to the nerve endings. Wherever the cloth touched my skin or my clothes, a beak or mouth came through and began to probe for a drink. One of my tormentors would find skin every ten minutes or so.

Shit, I thought. *This is impossible.* It was cold and lonely. The bites of the bugs had a way of attacking my nervous system and keeping it in a state of high alert: jumping and slapping to wait and jump and slap some more. It was inevitable that before long my nerves would just burn themselves out and all my defenses would collapse in a pathetic cascade. I got up, hopped around to keep warm, and tried singing to myself. Nothing worked.

There was the beeper on my belt.

The clouds came apart and the Big Dipper emerged. The Dipper had rotated to a position in the sky almost exactly opposite the one it had occupied at daybreak this morning. It was still pouring into the constant, the northern star. On the northern horizon a curtain was going up. Through the trees there was a shimmering veil of green, dancing on the horizon, appearing and disappearing. The northern lights were dancing in veils with the tiny and constant Polaris above.

The shimmering curtains. If only ... of course! Those beds—those enticing, lacy-looking princess beds in the tropics with the mosquito cloth hanging bunched from a central point above.

I pulled a shoelace from one of my boots, then knotted the square of netting in the middle and tied the free end of the lace to a low branch about four feet up. It hung down nicely. I gathered a few rocks and crawled underneath the netting, anchoring the netting with the rocks and pushing it away from me to create a bug-free zone. This produced a cone-space where I could sit with a foot of free space between any part of my body and the netting. The bugs still knew I was somewhere close, and hopped the netting everywhere, but my defenses were now secure. I folded up my rain jacket and put it under my butt to form a cushion, making it easier to sit cross-legged and upright on the hard ground. I turned to face the northern lights, and let my eyes drift into soft focus. There was firelight in the sky, and it had a calming effect on me. For a moment, the soreness of my butt disappeared, and the uncomfortable stiffness in my knees lessened a bit. I breathed in through my nose and felt the breath circulate through my forehead and down into my belly. I exhaled and got ready to sit for the duration. I might not be one of the alpha guys, but I sure knew how to sit and watch in a cone of silence. Moses had at least prepared me for that.

SOMETIME DURING THE NIGHT a beeper sounded down the line, followed by another one a few seconds later. Kimmel passed my mosquito cone with a headlamp blazing. In a few minutes he returned accompanied by Goddard and Roberts, two of the alpha boys. They had buzzed their beepers and were being led out by the team leader. The two, who seemed just so dammed good in daylight, apparently just couldn't handle a lonely night ordeal. We'd been warned about this: the night could reveal an underlying weakness in our psychological armor that could be our undoing.

Watching the alpha boys depart filled me with a glowing sense of satisfaction. My normal reaction would have been to feel sorry for them, washing out in a bug-bitten place like this in the middle of the night. Instead, I remembered their bone-crushing handshakes, and their aloof air of unquestioned superiority. It was just too bad if they did not have the right stuff to make it. I was starting to feel my own little air of superiority. If I could survive this night and the final ordeal, I could become one of the Cohort's 'unquestioned winners.'

More beepers went off throughout the night, and other team leaders showed up to lead members of their team out and back to camp. All of them were Gun-like guys who had shown up so well with so much confidence back in the daylight. The night was weeding out the tough guys and helping some of us who had the ability to wait and endure.

I MUST HAVE FALLEN OVER from my sitting position sometime before daybreak. I would have liked to have met her sitting up, with my hair combed, face washed, and eyes wide open. Instead my face was pushed against the cold rocky ground and I was drooling. My eyes were small, puffy slits when the first light of morning touched them.

She was standing in the light, illuminated from behind with rays of early sunlight. The moist air and patterns of the forest were making shafts of golden light that would last only this first moment and then be gone. She was standing in the moment, her face still shadowed and partially hidden by the backlight that glowed over her long dark strands of hair.

She continued to look deeply into the forest, but must have felt or heard me awaken. I sat up and lifted the mosquito netting so that it hung around my head like a shawl. Her head and shoulders turned first. She looked at me over her shoulder, smiling as if she knew that something wonderful was about to happen. Then her body slowly began to uncoil towards me, her feet moving last, turning around to face me full. She was dressed not so differently than I—dressed man-fashion. Yet her feet were bare, and she was balanced so lightly on the rock—it was as if she were not quite touching the ground.

I was coming out of a dream. There was nothing unusual about a man-dressed woman standing in the forest. *I can open toward her and tell her anything,* I thought. I felt like I'd met my life companion, a deep friend who had nothing in mind for me but the very best she could offer. I was ready to stand up and go a-traveling with her. She was well. Her hands hung easily at her sides. On her upper arm was a band of three interwoven strands. She paused for a moment, assessing me. Then in a dancer's deliberate motion, she turned her palms slowly toward me, raising them slightly above the level of her waist in a gesture of complete openness and greeting. She looked at me across the forest space. No anxiety. No fear. Just gazing at me like a mother might gaze, relaxing after her work is done and looking in love at her young child in the soft light of a summer's evening.

"—*Be at ease.*"

"Yes," I replied.

I'm quite sure her lips did not move. There was no sound coming to my ears except the sound of the forest waking up, the wings of small birds, the cracking of the warming trees, and the larger insects taking flight.

She was in my mind—the same woman's voice that I'd heard driving up in the 500, the voice inviting me to interpret my experience in a gentler way. Words, yes, but more a feeling of certainty and truth that was under the words. Her language was just a carrier frequency. The real communication did not come through my ears or through concepts, but rather came in through the soft part of my belly just below the breastbone.

"—*You are made of this earth. You are part of this earth. You are this very earth come alive.*"

A pause.

"—*Your lover has spoken you into existence, and you are beautiful.*"

She had said it. It was so. I felt ashamed and naked in front of her. Ashamed that I was drooling as I slept, ashamed that I was in this stupid Cohort using the earth as a torture tool, ashamed of the joy I had felt in dominating the other men—ashamed of my plans and schemes about the glories of a separate 'me' doing 'it' to all of 'them.'

"—*Yes. Just right. We are not separate. We are connected cell to cell. Now look down that line of trees.*"

I looked away to the trees on my right. The gold was shining through them, and the wings of insects were illuminated. All the dark and foreboding of night had passed away.

"*—Seeing the beauty will protect you until we meet again. Come deeper into me. He will bring you. There's more. Much more.*"

I broke my gaze down the line of trees to look back toward her. She was gone.

22: Manhood in Chains

> Those with the power *not* to mimic human behavior are invaluable. They set a different example to be emulated. They become new forms, new archetypes. A free human is not just a new idea, but a new *way*, enacted.
> ...*The Field Book.*

THE SUN was at least two hands above the horizon when I awoke in my netting to the sounds of shouting. It was the Blue Team leader waking up the Cohort to lead us back to camp. We lined up. The Cohort's numbers had dropped by eight. No one but me had slept, and the whole group was on edge and exhausted. Perhaps she was only a dream. Yet I felt lifted, drifting on a cushion of air, fascinated by the tousled patterns of Abram's hair as he staggered along in front of me. The rocks in the forest were already catching warmth, and a fresh breeze from Ribbon Lake was on my face. I had no plan now. All plans had been washed out of my body. All I could do was to take the next step.

The remains of the Initiative collapsed in the commons. The Gun was mercifully absent. So was Kimmel.

"Forty-five minutes for some chow and to collect yourselves before the final ordeal—the one that will finally separate the men from the boys," the Orange Team leader said.

There was a table of steaming eggs, coffee, pancakes, and bacon set up for us. Strangely, I had no appetite. I just wanted to spend some time alone and try to sort out what had happened when the golden shafts of first light were in the forest.

I WALKED OUT of camp, and climbed a little hill to a spot where I could lean against a boulder and face east to be fed by the rays of the morning sun. I closed my eyes to bring back the feeling of her, wanting the sense of her to wash into me again. But this spot was not to be the best place for solitude. I wasn't alone.

Down and to my right I heard the low murmur of voices. I moved quietly toward the sound and stopped just behind a large scarred boulder that stood up like a knife blade from the ground. There, in a little grotto, stood Kimmel and the Gun in a heated conversation.

"You know full well what we've agreed to," Kimmel said. "We don't wash out any of the paying customers, only the employees."

"He's different," the Gun said flatly.

"How so?" Kimmel asked.

"Well for starters, he didn't come up with the enrollment money. Paying a hundred grand for the training is a keystone of the practice. When folks pay that much, they have already demonstrated a belief that the training has value and therefore will receive value as a result," the Gun replied.

"Half the kids here have the training paid for by their parents, and it still seems to work for them."

"True," the Gun said, "but their parents aren't that kook Taylor. He's just not in sync with our value system. Do you know what that blue-eyed bastard said to me last night—to *me* of all people?"

"No, what?" Kimmel asked.

"He said, 'Your customers are going to be surprised to find just how unsatisfying getting everything they want really is.' Can you imagine that! Someone lecturing me like that, and telling *me* that *my* customers are going to be dissatisfied?"

The Gun was pacing now, working himself into a froth.

"I'm sick of that Taylor and the kid he came in with. I regret the day I hired the kook and agreed to a trade out. And I'm sure that the old guy has figured out by now that we've rigged the game so that a bunch of losers can believe that they are winners for the first time in their stinking lives. You and I know that once a man feels like a winner, we can teach him how to *act* like a winner. Then he will actually *become* a winner and we will have high-paying customers for life."

Finally this all makes sense, I thought. *This explains everything.*

Despite all the bells and whistles, the Initiative was at bottom nothing but an old-school tribal initiation. I now knew what was going on.

The Initiative had created a training program where a group could coalesce by a process of weeding out the weak—those who didn't have the 'right stuff.' The idea behind such training is to set the bar just high enough so that most will succeed, but still, a few will fail. The loss of those few 'weak' ones creates (for those who remain) the sense that they are part of a corps, an exclusive elite who have been selected, who now 'belong.' It's a deep affirmation for those who make it. A powerful community is formed at a small price. It's an ancient formula for creating a group: unanimity minus one.

The Gun was simply using the proven social formula of the dominator system. He was forming a cohesive clan who defined themselves by those whom they excluded. The old 'outcasting' system was alive and well here, forming a tribe.

I thought back to the moment last night when Goddard and Roberts were being led away. The whole Cohort was watching them in collective silence as they left, released to their experience of 'failure.' *We were actually enjoying it,* I realized. *We were taking pleasure in their misfortune.* I *was* starting to feel like a winner as I watched such big tough guys walk away, unable to endure what *I* could endure.

And now the truth. The Initiative was nothing but an elaborate scheme to make me feel just that way. Only half the guys were actually in the training. The rest were just actors. That explained why Ashton was drinking beer and laughing after he washed out. It explained why all the super-fit alpha guys were in their own tent, so we could not interact with them. It explained why the alpha boys weren't interested in the maps, while the rest of us were studying them like our lives depended on them. Those boys had seen the maps many times before. It explained why all of the obvious winners were washing out while the rest of us survived the ordeals. The ordeals really weren't that hard, and all of them were contrived. Half the Cohort was being paid to make the paying customers believe that they were overcoming incredible obstacles. And it was clear that the Gun did not consider me a customer. He wanted me out.

I continued to listen.

"You know how important this training has been for hundreds of men. You know most of them couldn't make it in a real competition. Our job is to make the losers believe in themselves. We still agree on that don't we?" the Gun asked.

"Definitely a yes there," Kimmel replied. "Perception is reality, and you can't do anything without believing."

"THEY GOTTA BELIEVE!" they both said in unison.

"We both agree that the body chemistry of a winner is different from that of a loser," the Gun continued, "and the best way for a man to feel like a winner is to defeat somebody. Then he's the big buck that's fought off all the little bucks. After the fight, the winner looks differently, acts differently, feels differently, and we both know it. Our studies confirm that his testosterone level will about double, and that's the male motor oil, baby. Not much has changed from the caveman days if you ask me," the Gun said. "Now what are we going to do about that kid Smithson?"

"Well, we both know that he could complete the training with no problem," Kimmel replied. "I found him sleeping like a baby this morning when all the other guys were practically in tears."

"Just my point," the Gun said. "He doesn't know what it feels like to be a loser, and will never be thankful for what we can do for him."

I do know what it feels like to be a loser! I thought. *I know just what it feels like to be the worst player on the worst team in the league.*

I was about to jump out and confront these two, but an image of Abrams and Ramsey flowed into my mind just as I was about to move. Ramsey had put so much into this. There was so much fear in his eyes. He had to succeed. His life could not be founded on another failure.

This might be the only place he could take the long trip around the lake and not come in dead last. I then conjured the image of Abrams in those thick black glasses. I had to admit that it would probably be good for Abrams to call out some small man and lick him. Suddenly I knew that if I were to be the small man that got licked for the benefit of Abrams and Ramsey, it was alright with me.

As Kimmel and the Gun continued to discuss my fate, I moved off quietly, circling back to camp. I was sure that the Gun would come up with some way to keep me from finishing the final ordeal. Actually, the Gun was right. I did not belong in the Initiative.

The Third Ordeal.

Back at the commons the blue team leader was explaining the final ordeal. There were exactly five left in each team now: four paying customers and one actor.

Each of us was given a pack that contained fifty pounds of stone. Each stone was marked with a dot of green, blue, orange, or red depending on the team. We were to be shuttled to a starting point about three miles down the shore of Ribbon Lake. From there we had to carry the pack of stones back to base camp in less than three hours. Parts of the course required the scaling of small cliffs and traversing steep ravines, but the route was not that long, and most of it was flat. A reasonably fit man could walk the course in an hour. I was convinced that Wilkes, the final actor on our team, would be eliminated, and that the Gun had cooked up a way to eliminate me as well.

Kimmel and the Gun reappeared in the commons. There was nothing in their appearance to create any suspicion.

"Check your packs, and especially the straps," Kimmel said. "Both the trainee and the pack must be back in camp in less than three hours, or you're disqualified. And remember this: each man must carry all of his own load the entire length of the course. You have to learn to carry your own load before you can be of much help to anyone else."

This was the same thing that Moses had said back in the swamp. The difference was that Moses was trying to teach me how to carry my life support system in preparation for a real journey, and here the challenge was to carry a pack full of useless stones. I had been assigned pack number four, and it looked fine to me. The team leaders gathered up the packs and shuttled them in a motorized canoe, then came back to shuttle the Cohort to the starting point.

I was asked to lead off for the Green Team. The remaining members of my team would follow in ten-minute intervals.

"You're up to bat, Smithson," Kimmel said as he loaded number four on my back.

The Blue Team leader fired off a starter's pistol. The report resonated for miles against the cliff faces of the surrounding wilderness, and the first wave started toward base camp. I felt fine despite not having eaten in the last twenty-four hours. I felt clear and light, and had already reached the first cliff face when a pistol shot sounded for the second wave. I was scrambling up the cliff when I heard a soft tearing sound. The straps of the pack then separated from my shoulders. The weight of the pack—which was still attached to my body by the pack's waistband—pulled me off the cliff.

The short fall knocked the reserve of air out of my lungs. I found myself gasping painfully at the bottom of the cliff. *Those fuckers.* They must have switched the pack on me. I looked at the straps. Both straps had been separated from the pack at the shoulder point and could not be reattached. The nylon stitching had been abraded with a knife or razor so that just a few threads were holding the fifty-pound weight, and the extra jostling up the cliff face had snapped them.

The starting pistol sounded another report and members of the Cohort began to pass me. Ramsey was by me first, glancing down at me and scrambling up the cliff. He was not about to stop for anything. I started up the cliff, holding the pack like a suitcase, but the rock face was steep and slippery, and I needed both hands and both feet to get up. The swinging pack in my hand made the climbing dangerously unbalanced. I slid back down the cliff, dropping the pack and spilling the green stones. On the way down, the rough granite took a good portion of the skin off the outside of my left leg. The injury put me into involuntary shock for a moment and left me sweaty and weak.

A third gunshot released Smith. He arrived with no suggestions. He scaled the cliff without much problem and was on his way. Abrams followed Smith. Abrams offered a solution: we could try to transport a hundred pounds of stone with his one good pack. His pack was already loaded to the bursting point, so this strategy would involve one of us racing ahead, dumping stones, then racing back to reload and go forward again. When we neared the finish line, I could load my broken pack again and drag it across, while he finished intact with his own load of stones.

I was unsure whether this procedure would violate the rule requiring us to carry our own loads, but I *was* sure that the strategy would effectively triple the length of the course, and run the risk that neither of us would complete the ordeal in the allotted time.

"You go on," I said to Abrams. "There are two ahead of you on their way to finishing, and you will make the third. It's not wrong to be strong and beat somebody this morning."

Abrams seemed genuinely sad that I was not going to make it. He shouldered his pack, and with some effort made it up the cliff. I was glad to see him disappear above me. I knew that Abrams was in no trouble. I was glad that he would have the feeling of being a winner, perhaps just now for the very first time.

Wilkes followed.

"Better hustle up, Smithson. Fifty-five minutes gone already."

He was walking casually. Wilkes had an easy job: to finish in more than three hours, but just ahead of me.

I SAT DOWN at the edge of the cliff amongst my heavy stones dotted with green paint. There was simply no way that I could get the stones up the cliff without a pack. I could wait here another two hours and be picked up by boat. That would be the end of it. Yet I wanted to finish, if only to see the look on the Gun's face when I walked into camp.

I sat down to strategically assess my options. *How about that.* You're thinking like a winner, Charlie: calmly dealing with reality and inviting solutions. "Maybe the Initiative has done me some good after all," I said aloud. I sat at the base of the cliff without any solution for a half an hour. I leaned up against the backpack and let the sun warm me.

What would she *do?* I thought, looking down at the lake. And there it was.

The shore of the lake was thick with greening reeds. *Folk have been weaving straps with reeds since the beginning of history.* I walked down to the lakefront. I tried to break off a reed, twisting it in every possible way. It simply would not break. This was a good sign for their use as pack straps. I took out my Swiss army knife and began to saw away at the stalks.

In about an hour's time, I had woven a rough basket of reeds around the pack and attached more reeds to serve as carrying straps. I picked the pack up gingerly and eased my shoulders into the loops. The pack held the weight and didn't break. I began a careful climb up the cliff. The surface was easy to navigate now with two hands and two feet. *I have an hour left. I may make it after all.*

WITHOUT A WATCH, I couldn't tell exactly what time it was, but I had a pretty good hunch that three hours had not quite expired as I neared the end of the course. I'd cleared all the cliffs and was bouncing along uneven ground, trying to run without breaking my makeshift straps. The reeds were cracking but they were holding. And then I heard it.

A disembodied sound was coming from somewhere up in the trees. It sounded like the speaker of a handheld radio spitting out a stream of processed information. In less than a week in the wilderness, I had already become accustomed to the sound of water on rock, the wings of birds, and the hum of insects. The radio was pollution, a pornography of sound, giving an update on the movement of the Dow Jones Industrial Average.

I looked up and tried to find the source. It was Wilkes, up in the top branches of a big pine tree, holding a portable communication device and checking the news. Apparently reception was a good bit better from the top of the tree. He had some time to kill as he waited for the three-hour limit to expire, at which time he would shimmy down the tree to pick up his pack and limp the distance back into camp. There, he would be officially eliminated from the Cohort according to plan. Abrams, Ramsey, and Smith would be looking on as he came in with his head hung low. "Just too tough," he would say within hearing of the remaining three. The new Alpha Group would watch his back recede while they quietly reveled in his defeat. At least my tentmates would get their money's worth for a hundred grand. Hard to justify spending that amount of money and coming home without your Alpha Male merit badge.

I walked under the tree.

"Hey, Wilkes, what's the news?" I yelled.

The news must have been good, because he was so absorbed in it that he'd not heard me coming.

"Any hot tips for me to call in today before the close of trading?"

Wilkes was a pretty cool customer, but the sight of me standing there with a backpack listening in to his radio show unnerved him.

He fumbled clumsily for the switch, but in his haste he lost control of the device. It leapt out of his hand, and he made the mistake of reaching for it, forgetting that he was forty feet up in the air balanced precariously on a branch.

He started to fall head first in sickening slow motion. Wilkes managed to get his arms out, and his armpits met a dead branch that was too small to hold him. The branch broke with a snap, and he fell the rest of the way, grazing his head on a bigger limb with a sound like the thump of a finger on a ripe watermelon. He landed feet first and began to break from the ground up. There was a sickening pop of his ankle then a splintering sound from the little fibula of his right leg. A bone ripped out through his skin and the material of his pants, and then went back in. A spot of blood no bigger than the face of a pocket watch spread on his pants then stopped. I unshouldered my pack and put my ear down to his face. He was still breathing.

The com device was still tuned to the stock market report, but was now nothing but a raspy stream of static punctuated with words like "up a quarter," "down an eighth." I picked up the device and turned it to the channel marked 'Team Com 1.' The Gun was on the other end.

"What the hell are you doing using this, Wilkes?" he demanded. "Portable com is expressly prohibited except in the event of an emergency."

"This is an emergency, Mr. Rankin," I said calmly.

"Who the hell is this?"

"It's Smithson, Mr. Rankin. Wilkes has fallen out of a tree a quarter of a mile from camp and is unconscious with a compound fracture. I suggest you call in a floatplane as soon as we hang up and get over here with a stretcher immediately."

The other end of the line was completely silent. Then finally: "Will do Smithson."

The four team leaders arrived with the Gun within minutes. I was astounded that there was no stretcher in all the gear that the Initiative had brought out to the wilderness. Kimmel, however, had brought a hatchet and in short order he had taken down two small pines and stripped them of their branches. I emptied the green painted stones out of the packs that Wilkes and I had been carrying. Kimmel put the small pine-trunks through the straps of the empty packs. We shimmied our hands under Wilkes, who was starting to moan and regain consciousness. We clasped hands underneath his body, grabbing each other's wrists. The Orange Team leader held his head. My hands were clasping those of Kimmel, who held my eyes for just a moment before he put his head down to listen to the voice of the Orange Team leader count out one ... two ... three ... lift. All the parts of Wilkes's body came up and onto the makeshift stretcher in unison. The Gun stood about ten feet away from the scene, his face white.

The sounds of floatplane propellers were already echoing loudly off of the south cliffs of Ribbon Lake when we walked in with Wilkes on the makeshift stretcher. One of the packs that supported Wilkes was held together by a weaving of green reeds.

And there, in the commons, stood Moses. He was leaning on a paddle, with one foot in the water, next to our fully loaded canoe that was beached at exactly the same spot where we'd landed three days ago.

The plane taxied up to the sand beach and the physical vibration of high decibel prop wash beat against my chest. Wilkes went in tied to our makeshift stretcher. Kimmel went with him. No one could speak over the roar of the props, but Kimmel looked at me from the door of the plane, then smiled and pointed his index finger toward the sky. He crawled into the fuselage of the plane and shut the door behind him. *That's the last I'll ever see of him*, I thought.

That plane, and others like it, would make a dozen trips here starting tomorrow morning to transport the surviving purpose-filled winners of Cohort 103 back to Winnipeg, then on to Chicago and the world of white shirts, pleated pants, and PowerPoint presentations that I had left barely a week ago.

The tiny aircraft taxied slowly out into the middle of the narrow lake, moving eastward across the surface. It then made a sharp U-turn into the prevailing wind. There was a humming din of huge blades cranking up, and the pitch grew higher and louder. The plane began to move, pushing large white wakes in front of its two pontoons. It slid faster and faster on its pontoon sleds, and then a space slowly appeared between the leading edge of the pontoons and the lake's surface. One foot, two. The sound changed as the plane gained altitude, becoming less laborious and more bee-like. The aircraft turned away, clearing the trees. A glint of sunlight flashed as a wing tilted, turning southward, towards home. Tonight Kimmel would be drinking beer, eating steak, and listening to music. Maybe a woman would be there with him. As the sound of the plane props disappeared to nothing, I thought of my life in Chicago. I felt all the old feelings. I was a kid being left behind at sleepover camp as his mom drove away.

The Gun came up to me, still visibly shaken.

"I was wrong about you, Smithson. I should have listened to Kimmel." He looked down at his feet, and was lost there for a moment before snapping himself to attention. "I would like to invite you to come with us tomorrow into the next phase of our journey into transformation, with all expenses paid. I understand that you are from Chicago, so undoubtedly there will be friends and family there who will support you in your journey toward continued success."

I looked over to Moses. This invitation would put me back in Chicago right on time for graduation, with something substantial to show for it. I turned to Moses.

"Can we talk for a minute?"

"Sure."

Moses and I walked up the beach together.

"If you don't mind my asking you, why the hell did you bring me here to a training course like this? This doesn't seem to be your style."

"I had to be sure," Moses replied.

"Sure about what?" I asked.

"Sure that you have been given a proper chance to turn down what I have to offer you. I'm under a rule just like you are, Charlie. My rule requires me to offer you three compelling opportunities to discern your call. You first chose your path when you left Chicago; once more when you walked out of the swamp with me; and now, a third decision is before you. The road I offer you leads to a kind of death, and only a fool would take it. You must be certain. You must be sure. You should proceed onward with me only if you feel... no, only if you *know* you must."

"So it won't hurt your feelings if I get on that plane and go back to Chicago?"

"Not in the least. I've spent substantial effort to provide you with just that opportunity. If you leave now, I have no doubt that you will become a highly competent and ethical businessman, and that you will make a profound contribution to the world from such a platform."

Moses was speaking with complete sincerity. He was right. I would make a damn good businessman. I was sure about that. I mulled the possibility over in my mind. *What an opportunity.* In the last week I'd learned so much. I already felt loosed from the cage of rote performance that had defined me for years. I felt stronger. *Maybe this stuff about a journey of transformation is more than just talk*, I thought. Time had somehow changed. Time had slowed down while I was moving much faster.

I looked for a moment into the blue eyes of Moses. This was the fork in the road.

I stood on the beach and listened hard as the very faintest hum of the floatplane's engine disappeared into nothing, leaving only the sound of tiny waves lapping the sand beach. I stopped thinking for a moment, and just listened to the waves. They sounded like the outbreath of something alive. I looked over at the canoe, with Moses waiting next to it, leaning on his paddle.

I remembered then. Back then on the first base line, when I was only nine years old—Moses had asked me something about the secret he was about to offer me.

"What if I told you that this thing might really cost you?" he'd asked.

"Like how much?" I'd said.

"Like giving up who you are," he'd replied. "That's how much."

I TURNED, LISTENING to the sound my boots made as they pivoted in the wet sand, and walked back towards the Gun. I had the clearest sense that what the initiative had to offer was just right for Abrams and Ramsey, but that for me it was only a decoy. *I can easily learn all of the stuff taught by the Initiative if the situation calls for it*, I thought. Focused planning and goal setting would be tremendous tools in a context that served something greater than my personal ambition. *Moses can teach me about something bigger*, I thought. *He's so free and powerful because he's tied into something beyond himself.* I had to find out what that greater thing was.

I walked over and stood in front of the Gun. For the first time my eyes could meet his on the level, with no sense of tension or inferiority.

"Thank you very much for the invitation, Mr. Rankin. But as you already know, I've failed to complete the last leg of the ordeal within three hours with my fifty pounds of stone. I think I'm disqualified, and to accept your offer might not be fair to those who have made it according to the rules," I said, looking over to Abrams.

The Gun stood in silence, gripping the clipboard that had become a part of his body.

"May I borrow your pad and a sheet of notepaper?" I asked.

He turned over the clipboard. The words "BELIEVE IN YOURSELF!" were written in large black letters on white athletic tape affixed to the metal clip.

I looked around at the trainees. I was glad for them. Abrams especially. I hoped I would meet Abrams again someday.

I scribbled this note to the hiring partner at the Thompson Firm:

> Dear Sir:
> I regret to inform you that personal circumstances are preventing me from appearing for work at the firm on our agreed-upon date. My deepest thanks for your offer of employment and the many kindnesses you have extended to me. Due to unforeseen developments, it's possible that I may be gone from the Chicago area for an extended time. I have no expectations that the offered position will be available when I return. Thank you again for your consideration, and your belief in my abilities.
> Sincerely,
> Charles Smithson

"If you could put this in an envelope and send it to this address..." I said to the Gun, scribbling the address of the Hancock Tower. "Very much appreciated."

The Gun nodded, and took back his clipboard. For once, he had nothing to say.

In less than fifteen minutes, I'd arranged for Abrams and a member of the blue team to sublease my brownstone and pick up the payments on the Volvo. I felt that I could trust them with a handshake deal. That kind of luxury was well within their means, and they were thrilled to have already found a great place in Chicago where they could continue their work with the Initiative. The keys were in the Volvo's ignition, and the spare key to the brownstone was under a fake rock just outside the garage.

I turned to Moses.

"Are we ready?" I asked.

"I have your backpack and mine already loaded," he said, pointing to my rented canoe pulled up on the sand. "I found the Field Book and the pen on your bunk and packed it away. I just wanted to make sure that you had a choice, and that you made your choice with full understanding. I must not manipulate you or feed upon the trust that your soul offers as its magnificent gift. There's a Rule in the Field Book that prohibits it. You can look it up if you like. It's there somewhere."

"I'll take your word for it," I said, walking into the water, sitting in the bow seat, and pulling my wet feet in. *Looks like I've decided to turn down the secrets of success to learn the secrets of the universe.*

"Let's go," I said aloud.

I could feel Moses push off the sand and settle into the stern. The canoe shuddered and leapt forward with the power of his paddle stroke.

We were leaving. I felt free and light; and for the first time since I'd caught that ball outside the fence, everything was right with the world. She was out there somewhere. I was sure of it.

Part Four:

Following the Guide

23: The Soul Friend

> The entirety of your soul's journey through this life is the master teacher. The journey wastes nothing. Every experience is useful. Interaction with a teacher is but one such experience with a beginning, a middle, and an end. The teacher is just one card in the deck, one more opportunity in the turning wheel.
> ...*The Field Book*.

WE SWUNG OUT into the lake under a blue sky decorated with towering white clouds. I felt free, and was glad to be leaving all the shouting. I'd finally stood up for the best part of myself back there on the beach, and my body relaxed. An important decision had been made, and my body liked where we were going. The best part of me was now moving forward with Moses.

Only now did I realize that I'd been holding an unsustainable level of tension. My thinking mind was exhausted from all of the work of the Initiative, and I was happy to feel for just a moment. My body had been waiting for this—for my mind to catch up with the decision my hands and feet had already made.

I could see that this new situation was strange. I was moving down the lake into the woods, with minimal food and equipment, being guided by a quirky old guy I barely knew. It could be said that I didn't know him at all. I was vulnerable with my back to him, and we were headed into the deep wilderness where anything could happen. But nothing felt wrong. To the contrary—my legs and belly were sending me waves of relief. My body was telling me to trust him. There was a feeling of openness and lightness in the middle of my chest. The sky looked good. Moses was leading me somewhere that my heart wanted to go.

I began to pull hard on the paddle, lifting it high up out of the water in a big wheeling motion above my head, clomping the blade heavily back into the water out away from the boat and then raking the paddle back towards me at an angle, pulling hard with both arms. After a few strokes, my arms were too tired to continue, so I switched sides, continued to clomp, and then began to switch rapidly from one side to the next. I was showing Moses what a good paddler I was. He had picked the right guy to go out with, by golly.

"It sure is nice to stop worrying about the future," I said over my shoulder to Moses. "Out here I can just sink into the 'now,' hang out, and learn the secrets of the universe from a master like yourself."

Moses immediately stopped paddling. We lost our forward motion, and the canoe turned sideways into the wind. It drifted down Ribbon Lake, rocking back and forth, with small waves slapping against the boat's side, rolling us as they came in. Within seconds my gut was responding to the roll, wishing that we could straighten out and not just wallow in the lake like a drift log; I was getting seasick. I tried to pull the boat sideways to get us moving in a straight line, but the wind continued to turn us broadside.

Moses seemed happy just to bob on the lake. The wind was quickening, and it was clear to me that we had a good chance of capsizing the small boat if we did not get going.

"So Charlie, turn around for a second. There are a few things we need to get straight about the 'now,' the 'secrets of the universe,' and 'a master like myself.'"

I swiveled around in the bow seat to face Moses, taking a slap of cold water from an incoming wave as I turned to listen to what he had to say.

"Some people have the idea that getting into the 'now' means to just sit wherever you are with nothing to do and nowhere to go. How are you doing with it?" he asked, looking at me as I gripped onto the gunwales and watched the waves come in.

I was getting more and more disturbed in the 'now'. That lake was damn cold. I could feel its cold coming up through the metal of the bottom of the canoe. I felt around under my seat for a life jacket. There was none. I'd forgotten. The life jacket—something carried only for safety and maybe never used—was in violation of The Rule and was hanging in a tarp back on that swamp hillock.

"So do we have some other choice?" I asked.

"Perhaps we do. For me, being in the 'now' is not about doing nothing, but rather about being present to what is asked of us in this exact moment and being free enough from one's old patterns and reflexes to respond in a fresh and authentic way. You might notice that the 'now' is just one of many species of time. There are multiple species of time, different 'ecosystems' of time, if you will, just like there are multiple species of trees and different types of forest." He opened his hand to the woods around the lake.

"So what would it be like if we could inhabit each species of time," he continued, "in the same way we inhabit the jungles, the plains, and the icy north. What if we could actually move freely from one type of time to another?"

"You tell me," I said.

"Think of it, Charlie—the past, the now, the future—how about simultaneity, all of those times together at once! And what about eternity going on forever; and space-time where time actually changes depending on our speed and the force of gravity? And not to forget old 'circular time'—the snake eating its tail; everything arising and passing away but nothing ever really changing or going anywhere. Then there is our current favorite—linear time—something that can be gained, lost, and wasted—divided up into time segments and ticked off on all of those watches. That type of time did not even exist a short while back—and here it is all over the world! Do you think that's the end of it—the only types of time we can discover and live in?"

I'd never thought about this before. I never realized that I could choose time. I was pretty much stuck in linear time and never seemed to have enough of it.

"So what type of time would you like to inhabit during our 'time' together, Charlie—I'm going to let you decide. Do you want to sit and explore the bliss and beauty of the now? Do you want to imagine and attempt to create the future? Do you want to live in the past? How about trying 'evolutionary time,' Charlie, deep time where the future takes up residence in the present moment and moves it toward something, requiring everything in time's grasp to change, grow, and become something more complex and advanced? What's it going to be? The sort of time we choose can drive a lot of outcomes."

The encampment of the Initiative had disappeared around a corner. We were now completely enclosed by wilderness; like we'd passed some invisible boundary. The modern world had simply disappeared.

I had no idea what to do. I was pretty sure that if I didn't do something, I would, in short order, be experiencing the bliss of the now in the frigid water of the lake. I was nearly certain that Moses would go right along with whatever decision I might make, and would merrily talk with me as we clung onto the boat with all of our gear on the bottom, bobbing along in the icy water until we blew into shore or drowned.

"Let's have enough linear time to get this boat turned around so it doesn't capsize; enough of the future to pick a point on the map to move toward; pretty much hang out in the 'now' so that we can feel some of the bliss I've heard people talk about; and access all of the best of the past, so we don't have to start all over and re-invent the wheel."

"Excellent!" Moses said. "A most popular time selection—a great decision, Charlie! We can officially decide to become 'time omnivores' and enjoy the good health that comes from a balanced diet, eh? Whaddya say?"

With this, he took a powerful sweeping stroke that pushed a volume of water against the back of the canoe. It turned the boat forty-five degrees so that we were running with the wind. All of the rolling instantly stopped, and so did the churning in my gut.

"Really happy that you didn't choose apocalyptic time, Charlie—I was starting to worry there for a minute that we would have to paddle off the end of the world."

It was hard for me to tell whether Moses was joking or serious. I started to swivel around in my seat to begin paddling again, but he motioned for me to stay put, facing him as he paddled.

"So I'm imagining that you think you are going out into the wilderness with some wise old master, some guy who will teach you the secrets of the universe, so you can go back to Chicago filled with wisdom and tell it to the world."

I had to admit that was exactly what I was thinking. "You got it," I said.

Moses looked at me with a wry smile.

"Would it surprise you if I told you that becoming a 'master' and possessing the 'secrets of the universe' is something that I have striven for most of my life? It once was my heart's desire to be seen as a great master and have influence over powerful people such as yourself who would spread my message to the world."

"It wouldn't surprise me at all," I said. "I thought that was who you were."

"Yes...," he said, thinking now to himself. "It would be so easy to turn in this direction, to make you a mouthpiece, a student always under my wing . . . you offer this so freely."

I sat swiveled in the bow seat, looking at Moses. He was looking down at the water and seemed caught in some internal struggle, like some old memory had taken hold of him.

"*—He's being tempted,*" I heard the voice inside me say.

What a strange thing for me to think.

I suddenly had the oddest sensation that there was someone else in the boat with us, just over my shoulder, watching how this would turn out. Such a thing was of course impossible.

I watched Moses as he gazed down into the water. Then suddenly he picked the paddle up and began to balance it on one finger like a juggler, hopping it and re-catching it on his fingertips, rolling his eyes around and smiling like a clown. The man who had been such a powerful presence just a moment ago now looked like an idiot in his silly hat, dancing in his seat, juggling, and humming a little tune. I could just make out a few bars of *'Tea for Two,'* an old song and dance number.

"Indeed," Moses said, throwing his paddle up in the air and catching it like a baton twirler.

He smiled at me, as if relieved of a burden. He looked past me, over my shoulder, with a gaze so intense and withering that I was thankful that it was not directed toward me. Then Moses shifted his gaze and looked at me calmly. His blue eyes were filled with nothing but kindness.

"So one secret that I have to teach you is that there are no secrets, Charlie. And I will never accept the role of master."

I immediately felt the presence behind me lift away. The boat felt lighter and, in an odd way, *safer.*

I looked at him quizzically. "No secrets?"

"None at all. Of course, there are vast realms to be explored, limitless numbers of perspectives to inhabit; limitless things to be seen both inside and outside of us; countless places to see from and countless practices to access it all. But none of it's a secret. The old idea of 'secret knowledge' tucked away in some mountain fastness or dark cave, known only by small communities of the 'adequate' in long robes and heavy cowls, is fading from the earth in this next turning of the wheel. Good riddance in my opinion."

I must have looked disappointed. I was hoping that I would come away from my time with Moses with something that made me quite special. Moses kept paddling, smiling at me with his blue eyes, taking easy strokes that kept the canoe running with the wind.

"In the coming age, all ideas and practices will be in an open exchange. New and better truth will emerge as a result. The lineages that rely on changeless truth from an absolute source are deeply inbred and will die out in the end. They lack the exchange of ideas and practices that make for a healthy system," he said.

"Most 'secret knowledge' is not worth having anyway," he continued, "I should know—I've sought such knowledge all of my life. My experience has led me to the conclusion that secrets appeal to a narcissistic mind that wants to be 'special.' That's not the kind of mind that we're looking for."

It suddenly struck me that I had followed the Field Book up here in anticipation of receiving some great philosophy or secret that would make me special. I wanted some 'high knowledge' so that I could claim it, own it, be 'somebody' and consider myself superior because of it. *I would then become just like the Gun*, I thought, *only with a bit of 'The Wisdom of Moses' added to my competitive portfolio.* Building a spiritualized version of the Gun was not what Moses had in mind.

Moses continued, "It's also possible that this trip will destroy your fascination with 'knowledge', or at least the type of knowledge that comes from the logical mind. The high wind and the driving rain tend to blow holes through the thinking mind—and traveling with me may ruin all hope of returning to the expert analytical mind-scape your law school has entrained in you. But, if it's insight that you seek, I can perhaps offer you something of value. Yet what I offer is not final, not absolute, and definitely not secret. And one last thing. . . ."

"What's that?"

"I am not a 'master.' I do not propose to interact in a way that makes you a servant or a slave; nor have I completed some 'level' of expertise that is final in any way. All I have to offer you is the benefit of the experience I've had. I may be ahead of you in some areas and behind you in others. What's important in determining who's the teacher and who's the student is the sum total of our advancement in the subject at hand, not some arbitrary position. If you cast the projection that I'm your master, you may become blind to important truths about me, and at the same time fail to take responsibility for your own work. Make no commitment to me as master, Charlie. Commit instead to becoming a vehicle to bring more light into this world."

He held up his hand palm first, as if offering something to me. I felt a growing sense of certainty that I'd made the right decision—and that something profound might happen around the next corner. With Moses paddling, we moved easily down the lake looking at each other.

Without breaking my gaze, Moses continued, "So instead of 'mastery,' what I propose is a type of friendship. How does that sound to you?"

"It sounds fine to me," I said. It actually sounded better than I had imagined.

"Wonderful. As your new friend, I have a confession to make."

I waited.

"I have almost no interest in you at all."

I sat back in my seat in stunned silence. I'd never been so insulted in all my life.

"Please don't misinterpret me … it's simply that I must tell you from the outset that I have very little interest in the temporary accident of your personality; the mixed bag of traits that walks through the world under the name of 'Charlie Smithson.' Instead, I hope to be a friend of your soul—your *immortal* soul, if I could use that old term. I would like to be a friend of that soul's highest intention, someone who sees its greatness, and holds a space for your soul to change its shape. Your soul can change its shape through the experience that it has here in this body. Perhaps in our friendship we can exhale a long streaming breath onto the tinder of each other's souls, and make fire. If you like, we can put our whole lives into it."

I hardly knew what to say. I looked across the packs at him as he continued to paddle in easy rhythm. His mind seemed so uncluttered—so clear and bright. I was quite certain that the fellow there under the silly hat was the strangest and most interesting man I'd ever met. My indignation faded as I looked into his blue eyes. *This is going to be more interesting than I thought.*

"OK," I said. "Why not? I'm up for changing the shape of my soul, whatever that means."

Moses smiled. "Yes, indeed. Why not? Too bad we can't think of anything better to do. I'm afraid we're just not as creative as those boys back there at the Initiative, coming up with all those domination games and rivalries and whatnot. But yet, they're offering a valuable service, are they not? The Initiative has a lot to offer in my view. Gaining self-confidence, setting goals, and getting things done has produced many gifts for the human race."

I thought back to Kimmel and the Gun. If one thing could be said for them, it would be that they had a crystal clear direction for every life situation: find a game and win it. For them, this was a win/lose world, and winning was better.

"So I'm not quite sure how to proceed with this new game," I said. "If there's not one right thing from an absolute source, if you're no master, and winning is not the direction—how do we know what's better? How do we know what to do in a given situation?"

"Would you like an example?"

"That would be great."

"Wonderful! So let's call our play 'Mutual Acts of Soul Friendship.' The setting: Ribbon Lake, Ontario, late May. Act One. Let's see ... yes ... how about we call our first act: 'Soul Friends Experience Moving Together in Equipoise.' Sound alright?"

"Just fine," I said, waiting to see what he was going to come up with next.

"So let's start with the basics—how to move. The stroke that you are using. . . ."

Moses picked his paddle blade out of the water, wheeled it high over his head like I'd been doing, and plunged it powerfully back into the lake, raking the paddle back towards the canoe with both hands. The motion rocked the canoe to the gunwale, almost capsizing us in the frigid water, and the bow swiveled off-line forty-five degrees.

"There is nothing at all wrong with that stroke, but it's out of sync with the current context," Moses said as he corrected our course with a few smaller strokes. "That move is called a 'draw stroke'—it's a powerful stroke using everything you've got. A draw stroke is typically not used for forward motion in lake paddling. It's a whitewater river move used when we're headed for a rock and immediate sideways movement is required. If you use the draw stroke in the bow, I have to use a powerful and exhausting 'sweep' counterstroke to keep us in line—like this." He demonstrated, using his paddle to sweep water powerfully against the side of the canoe. Almost all of our forward motion stopped, and the bow pivoted off-line to the right.

"The shoulders tire quickly when your arms are above your head because the muscles that hold your arms aloft are much weaker than the ones that can push and pull at chest level. So the draw stroke—the one that takes the paddle up high and rakes the water—is an emergency move; it will not take us the miles we need to travel over the weeks, months, or years we might be out here."

Years, I thought. *'Years' is a long time.* I looked at Moses. *That's a bit longer than I was thinking of staying.* He ignored my reaction.

"So here's an alternative. Everything in a basic canoe stroke happens at the level of the chest." He demonstrated, propelling his right hand straight out from his shoulder, across his body, and down. The hand on the grip of the paddle stayed below the level of his chin. The result was a smooth motion with enough force to nearly lift the front of the canoe out of the water.

"The paddle is not pulled through the water like you've been doing. Actually the powerface of the blade is *pushed* through the water with the force of the top arm against the grip, using the big muscles of the back in a twisting motion. It's a lot like throwing a short right hook in a boxing match.

"You use the shaft of the paddle as a lever. The hand closest to the water is like a loose, movable oarlock that acts as a fulcrum. The bottom hand guides and doesn't work any harder than it has to. Like Archimedes said—'Give me a lever and a place to stand, and I will move the world.' Here we're just moving a tiny bit of the world's water. And we have chosen to move that water with an economy of motion and very little effort."

His paddle made a sucking sound as it powered against the lake surface. Two small whorls formed at the edge of the blade—small spinning holes in the water that trailed the boat for a few feet before losing their spin and disappearing into the lake.

"So that's one-half of the act of moving together in harmony—how to find functional fit and a leverage point to move with the least amount of effort. The other half of the story is how we can paddle together. We are here together in this small boat and are well-served by working as two forces that are aware of each other and striving to pull together. It's easier for both of us if we paddle in rhythm, putting our paddles in and taking them out at exactly the same instant, always on opposite sides of the boat. This way I counterbalance you, and you counterbalance me."

"Got it," I said. "So our first lesson in soul friendship is discovering the action that's the best functional fit for the situation, counterbalancing to keep on course, and moving forward together."

Moses smiled. "Just right, Charlie. You're a quick learner. Now notice that as we paddle together, we are always off-line just a little bit—never moving in exactly a straight line, but never more than a few degrees off centerline either. The canoe makes no wild swings that must be over-corrected. That's the product of good teamwork—a good team constantly steers and re-balances, but is never far off-center. If we stroke together in counterbalance, more of our effort goes into the forward motion, and less into the steering. Proper counterbalance of forces is one of the things we can explore in our friendship—the dynamic steering of forces within a singularity that appears to be two opposites, but is actually one thing. With the proper counterbalance everything quiets and glides forward."

WITH THE DEMONSTRATION OVER, I swiveled around in my seat, and did my best to apply what Moses had just taught me. Within a few strokes, we were moving faster. I could feel the glide. The work of paddling was being done by my bigger muscles. We were working together as a team, and somehow just the fact that our muscles were firing and resting at the same time in synchronized flow made everything smoother, like a band in the same key and playing to the same beat. Some part of me instantly recognized this as better. Paddling fell into an easy rhythm where our movement was likely to stay for a while. We were starting to 'cut a groove' and create a good new habit.

We paddled down the bends of Ribbon Lake in silence, getting the 'feel' of moving together.

"So, Charlie, do you notice that the flow between your energy and mine, as expressed through our paddles, has just gotten a bit better?"

"Yes."

"And may I remind you that you can paddle in any way that you want—that the Committee has given us just three rules, and that there is no instruction about paddling in any one of them?"

"Yes."

"So you and I have made a free choice. I would like to invite you to notice that we've made a good choice. But *why* is it better? How do you know? Are there sensations and thoughts now coming into your awareness that were not there before? Is there some intuitive part of you that just *knows* this way of paddling is right for this moment, this context?"

"I think so. I can feel what you're talking about, but it's hard to put into words."

"Wonderful. This capacity to know what's right and to find the line forward is already in the Field. It's a capacity that can be accessed, trained, and that you can come to trust," he said. "It all starts by noticing, Charlie. How do you know what's better? How do you feel the 'yes'?"

I settled back into my rhythm in the bow seat. The pain in my arms had lessened. I was moving more water with less effort, and wasting less energy changing sides. I stopped trying to show off and began to help move us along without fanfare. I could feel the good balance. The canoe was more stable and was moving in a straighter line.

This new way of paddling was so much easier that the rhythm soon took over and only a small slice of my attention was required for me to do my part. I now had free space to look around. I began to watch the sky. I felt the same sense of early springtime and eagerness that I'd felt on the first day in the wilderness; only now I was a deeper, different self. The earth had turned only six or seven times since I'd left Chicago, but I felt much older. I'd made a dozen important mistakes and a couple of important choices in a very short period of time. I tried to find a way to analyze whether I was doing the right thing, and then quickly gave up the exercise. Too much work. My intuition said that I could trust Moses. Trusting him felt good. *I'm learning*, I thought. I am learning to find the right groove.

Our wilderness journey had begun, and the wheel was turning for me, the fool.

24: The Pearl

Being who you are and becoming who you are is the infinite loop that dances.
> ...*The Field Book.*

WE TOOK A SHORT PORTAGE out of Ribbon Lake. Moses carried the boat, and at the end of the trail he walked knee-deep into the water and off-loaded the canoe noiselessly. I again had a sense that a pair of eyes were on me—that I was being watched from the forest. It was an odd sensation, but not frightening. I turned, but again saw nothing.

We paddled through a series of narrow lakes which soon opened into a vast, interconnected lake system filled with thousands of small islands. Moses was guiding us through the labyrinth, so I had nothing to do except put the paddle in the water and look at the towering white clouds that built higher and still higher as the day progressed; huge columns and anvils piling atop each other, with wisps of white cirrus way up high. The part of me that had been drifting and spinning in Chicago—cut off from the life-current—was now waking up.

Ribbon Lake is a puddle on the sidewalk compared to this, I thought. A different, huge, and more complex wilderness was opening up. I was struck silent by its vastness. *We could move a thousand miles north to the pole and a thousand miles down the other side and not see another human being*, I thought. *This place could swallow us alive.*

We moved without conversation, and in just an hour of quiet, my focus began to shift. I began to notice more. The shoreline ahead was a slightly darker green than its background, which meant that it was an island separated from a further, lighter shore. A good return stroke of the paddle threw droplets of water away from my paddle-tip that caught air for an instant, then separated to become tiny prisms in the sun which fell to bounce and drum the lake's surface before merging back into the water's depth and quiet. When Moses and I were perfectly synchronized, the sound of the bow cutting water had a distinct timbre; a musicality of the metal surface slicing the lake that gave me the sense that I was sitting atop a gurgling fall of water. Just this looking, this listening, was calming my feathers and stroking me down. I was moving away from thinking about myself and the tension of my imagined future. The wilderness was inviting me to focus outside of myself on the real.

I looked at the tiny amount of gear we were carrying and the few pounds of food. With every stroke of the paddle we were going further out and deeper in. I had the distinct sense that we were moving toward the source of the Field Book. Only later would I find out that we were moving deeper still to the source toward which everything in the book was pointing.

BY LATE AFTERNOON the towering buildup of the clouds began to produce thunderheads, and one of them dropped a squall that moved across our lake with a heavy roar—laying a column of water on us so dense that there was no place around us that was not boiled white. Moses was ecstatic as we were pounded by the burst from the sky.

"Another sign that the wilderness loves you, Charlie!" he shouted over the noise of the downpour. "Nothing like a good cleansing to mark a transition and begin a new journey!"

I looked over my shoulder at him as he opened his mouth to catch some of the falling torrent, holding his hat in one hand and raising the other palm upward. I huddled in my rain jacket, trying to protect the few square inches of torso that were still dry. The squall lasted less than nine minutes, but left three inches of slosh in the bottom of the canoe.

As the rain moved on, the sun began to pierce through holes in the clouds, beaming distinct rays through a sky that was filled with motion. A broad rainbow began to emerge on our right, with a second, fainter bow above it.

In another context, I might have been able to appreciate just how beautiful it all was. But my body had decided that it was quite uncomfortable sitting in wet pants with my boots covered in muddy slosh. It was still springtime in the far north, and those beautiful rays were not nearly warm enough.

Moses paddled on just as before, showing no intention of slowing down or pulling over to dry off. I was not sure where we were headed, but could see no reason to continue to travel through the rain. Back in Chicago, we went inside when it was raining. I swiveled around, hoping to get some more information out of Moses.

"Do you mind telling me where we are going through all of these storms?" I asked. "Now that I'm out here with you, I sure would like some more information about the program."

"Yes, the 'program.' Interesting word. Implies that what we are doing will be a fixed and predictable sequence of events. I could see how that would appeal to you, Charlie. Quite comforting to be following a program, I should think. Unfortunately, I don't know of any program that will get us to where we are headed."

This was another of the shocking statements I was beginning to expect from Moses.

"You don't know how to get to where we're headed?" I asked. I began to experience a sinking feeling that I'd made a terrible mistake.

"That's not what I said," Moses replied. "I said that there was no 'program.' I can only offer life at the edge of discovery, moment by moment, Charlie. We are strange voyagers, Charlie, you and I. On the one hand, it could be said that 'where we are going' is a place that is already here, and therefore can never be a destination. On the other hand, it could be said that we are going to a place that has never yet existed; a place that we are creating for the first time together, moment by moment."

I must have looked confused. Moses stopped paddling and tried again.

"There have always been some people who believed, no ... who *knew* ... that we are inside something very vast and very beautiful. If all of our ways of being separate can be cleared away, we fall back into an awareness of this beauty. Some have described this kind of awareness as the 'peace which passes all understanding;' the 'pearl of great price.' It's a freedom, for just a moment, from the demands of the separate sense of self; a moment in which we can remember who we are; a moment of 'seeing' that changes everything. We can never again believe that all of our schemes and projects are the center of the world. And as that moment passes, we are still here, Charlie, with a job to do, a future to create that requires our total attention and commitment. That's where we're going."

The canoe was wallowing deep with its load of water, and it seemed to me that we were in danger of tipping from the slosh. "So, I'm not sure I understand. We're going out here to get a pearl?"

Moses looked at me like I was a total idiot.

"You're a 'word man' aren't you, Charlie. You like things explained to you in words."

I'd never thought about this as a preference. I always thought that most everything *was* learned through words. After all, I'd been going to some form of 'word school' for the last twenty years.

"I guess that's right," I said, starting to shiver. "I'm used to people explaining things to me in words. I'm feeling like you might be a better 'soul friend' if you'd just come out and tell me exactly where we're headed. Everyone back at the Initiative seemed to think that it was pretty important to know exactly what your goal was, and to have a workable plan to achieve it. As part of this team I think I deserve to know something more about what our strategy is to get to this 'pearl' you're talking about."

Moses looked at me, as if deciding.

He then smiled at me with a smile that was so winsome and full of mirth that I was taken off guard. In an instant quicker than the eye, he grabbed the gunwales, rocked once, then flipped the boat over one hundred and eighty degrees, right in the middle of the lake! Packs and paddles were everywhere, bobbing around. The packs were empty enough to contain air pockets to keep them afloat, but I came up sputtering, desperately trying to tread water with my raincoat and heavy boots on, and grabbing the slippery underbelly of the canoe that was now pointing skyward.

"What in the hell did you do that for?" I cried, panicked that I had no life jacket.

The water-soaked head of Moses came up slowly on the other side of the canoe. The cold lake water was draining off of his beard, and he had an impish smile on his face. He took hold of the overturned canoe and pulled himself up onto it. I glared at him.

He put his sopping rag of a hat on his head, then cocked his chin and spoke in a mock formal tone as the rivulets streamed down his face.

"I am endeavoring to provide an answer to your question about our 'strategy' for obtaining the pearl."

25: Making Fire

> Seek not the power to create things under your control. Seek rather to manifest that which is beyond the limitations of your control.
> ...*The Field Book.*

I WAS FURIOUS at Moses for dumping us in the middle of the lake. For his part, he seemed delighted with himself, as if he had just made a winning move in a game that he very much wanted to play. He was exultant as we slithered into the swamped vessel, sitting chest-deep in cold water with our butts on the keel as we gathered our bobbing packs around us. Moses calmly instructed me on the proper use of the 'pull-stroke' in this situation, holding our paddles parallel to the water and pulling them toward us in a motion like a reverse bench press. We slowly pull-stroked our way toward shore.

I hadn't secured my pack against full immersion, and was sure that some water had leaked in to soak my sleeping bag. I was wet to the bone and could look forward to a cold night. *Who cares about the goddamned pearl?* I thought. All I've been trying to do is learn the stuff I'm supposed to learn, and here I am with this strange guy laughing and dumping me in the lake. *No one else has to endure this.*

I was feeling like it was time to dump Moses and all of his talk about rules and pearls. I couldn't figure out what he was talking about half the time. If he wanted me to see some goddammed thing, he should just show me and shut up about it. I released my anger by taking huge swipes at the water, wheeling the paddle up overhead and pulling hard in just the way he'd taught me not to do, and making sure that I splashed a good bit of the cold lake water right back at him.

We reached the shore of an island and took everything out of the canoe. Standing shin-deep in the water, Moses told me to put my right hand on top on the bow plate and my left hand on the keel. Moses put his left hand, opposite from mine, on top of the stern plate, and his right hand on the keel. We rolled the canoe, and then lifted it easily keel-up out of the water. I watched the muddy water drain out. Then in a swift motion, we flipped the canoe back upright. There were probably a dozen ways to empty water from a canoe, but by doing it this way the task was done in thirty seconds with no strain to our backs. It was the best way.

I turned away from Moses, whining and tearful; angrily wringing out my shirt. It seemed to me that *I* was supposed to be the customer, the person who was receiving the training. Maybe I should register a complaint with this 'Committee' Moses kept talking about all the time. I was ready to end this humiliating episode and head back home.

Moses sensed my frustration, and just smiled at me as he poured water out of one of his boots. He peeled off his sticky wet undershirt, wrung it out, and put it over the gunwale. I was in no mood to talk to Moses or even look him in the eye. He began to speak.

"Words are *at best* a form of partial truth, Charlie. They are signs that point to something; that is all. They are never the thing itself. You have no idea what I'm talking about because you've never experienced the thing to which my words refer. We are here to rectify that situation in the most direct way possible. Full immersion, Charlie; full immersion into a larger reality with all of the lights on. I propose to set the conditions where you can be shown a reality that's larger than any conception you might have, so you can realize who you are, and what you're doing here. Then, and only then, can you know 'what to do' with the small part of yourself that can set a course of action.

"You are going to live a long life, Charlie, and dozens of different ways to engage the world will present themselves over your lifetime. But First Things do come first in our camp. A clear vision of who you are will be of great use to you. You will have a vision before it's over. I will promise you that!"

Moses turned and walked into the forest, then returned in a few moments.

"There's a flat spot under some pines at the dome of this little island. It looks big enough for the tent. We can make our fire on that granite outcrop," he said, pointing. "We'll camp here tonight."

OVER THE NEXT NINETY MINUTES, I was to learn Moses' procedure for making camp; one which we would repeat many times during our journey together. His woodcraft was a training in focused attention, efficiency, and quality; a no-frills approach exactly suited to the task at hand.

It was about two hours before nightfall. Moses carried the canoe up to the granite outcrop and turned it over. We leveled it with rocks and logs to form a table, with the keel-side making a clean surface for the preparation of our evening meal. Moses had converted the big Alaskan into our supply pack, which now carried our food, tent, and cookware. The Alaskan was placed upright against a tree, with a slotted canvas pouch holding utensils tied above it. A smaller Duluth pack (a round canvas sack designed to ride low in the canoe) carried our sleeping bags and what little personal gear we had.

With the table set, we walked to the center of the island with the tent and the Duluth pack. Moses proceeded to set up the tent in a way that was likely to withstand any storm coming out of the west. He'd found a slightly domed spot that would drain water away from the tent on all sides. Tent stakes were useless in the rocky ground (as if they would have survived the sorting) because the soil was only an inch deep. So instead of stakes we tied ropes to the corners and tent-sides, looping the ropes around sturdy sticks to make 'deadmen' which we pulled taut and pinned to the ground with big rocks. There was a proper knot for the ropes, the taut line hitch, which Moses showed me. The short end of the line went under and around the long taut line once, forming a loop, then under and around again, followed by a half hitch on top of the loop. This made a knot that would hold fast but could be easily slid to tighten the line.

I discovered that Moses had repacked my gear, putting it all inside two heavy plastic pack liners that had kept everything perfectly dry. And in place of the big, heavy Dacron-filled sleeping bag that I'd bought at the discount store, there was a compressed package about the size of a football that weighed a little over four pounds. I opened the compression sack and began to pull out foot after foot of blue, mummy-shaped sleeping bag. It was an expedition-quality bag, with Hungarian goose-down clusters providing the insulation. I laid out this new addition to my gear, and the bag began to magically inflate on its own, plumping in the cool air.

"A gift from the Committee," Moses said. "We'll be sleeping naked on the ground, and it can get a *bit* cool here. I should tell you that we're heading further north. This bag is rated to minus ten. Overkill, perhaps, for a northern summer, but you can always unzip it if you get too hot."

"Thanks," I said, realizing that I was already damn cold in my wet clothes and starting to shiver whenever I stopped moving.

We went back to the shore. No one had ever camped at this spot before. Moses began to scour the waterfront for flat stones, which he carried up and began to arrange in a modified 'U' shape open to the prevailing wind, but downwind from the rest of the camp. The front of the 'U' was narrow, with flat rocks close enough together to support a frying pan with the back wider and built up higher to support a wet stick on which a cooking pot was suspended. Moses cleared dead twigs and leaves from a six-foot radius around the 'U.' This was to be our fire pit.

We went out and looked for wood. An axe or saw was in violation of The Rule, so the wood was gathered with our bare hands. Moses wanted 'squaw wood'—branches no more than an inch or two around that could be snapped into short pieces, along with a bunch of smaller stuff.

This island had been drenched by the downpour. The pines were dripping, and the mossy ground was soaked. Spines of fallen pines littered the island. The ground here was nothing but granite, so instead of relying on deep taproots, the trees stayed upright by balancing on a large fan of roots that spread and gripped the rock surface. When a pine reached a certain size, the weight of the trunk became too much for the shallow roots, and the tree just fell over. Underneath several of the fallen spines we found wood that was surprisingly dry—dead but still on the tree. We broke off several dead branches and carried them back to camp.

Moses began to snap the sticks on his knee, arranging them in three neat piles. One pile was made up of branches with diameters no bigger than a pencil; a second pile of branches no bigger than a finger; and a third pile made of wood up to two inches across. All of the piles were within easy reach of the fire, with the smallest sticks closest. Moses insisted that I go back into the woods a second, and then a third time to look for more. He wanted piles that were at least three feet high or higher.

"We gather all of our fuel in the daytime; enough to last tonight and tomorrow morning," he said. "The forest is no place to be stumbling around at night, looking for wood. Night is not our time in the forest. We're day creatures, if you've noticed—there are other creatures that rule the night. Besides, someone left his headlamp in a tarp a few miles back."

Yes. I remember only too well. Right now I was more than happy to get enough wood to get a fire going and dry off.

In the fire pit, Moses laid two of the larger sticks parallel to each other in line with the prevailing wind. Over the parallel sticks he meticulously placed a couple of dozen tiny twigs no bigger than a matchstick side by side to make a platform. "Fuel, plus heat, plus oxygen equals fire," he said. "We make a platform so that the air can flow under the fire and feed it from the bottom up."

Out of the inner pocket of his rain jacket Moses produced my waterproof map case. It was stuffed with dry birch bark. I'd noticed the bark on the ground as we portaged out of Ribbon Lake, but had not thought to gather any before the storm rolled in. "This and the cedar bark," he said, "beats having to make a pile of shavings. The cedar is better, but this birch will work. You should watch for good kindling throughout the day. Always take it from the dead trees that are already recycling, not the living ones."

He put a big mound of bark on the platform. He then picked up some of the smaller sticks, rolled them in his fingers, and decided that they were still too wet. He took out his knife, and quickly stripped the sticks of their wet bark; then split them down the middle, drawing the blade of his knife toward his chest. He placed the dry centers of the split twigs against the kindling, forming a teepee with a small opening facing the windward side.

Next, he picked out the driest of the little sticks, which he did not bother to split, and expanded the teepee. Some of the larger wood was put on as well, forming a structure of carefully placed wood about a foot and a half high that filled the fire pit.

To my surprise he didn't light the fire, but rather took out the cook gear and brought water up from the lake in the big pot, then measured four cups into a smaller pot, adding two cups of rice. He mixed up a batter, and put some oil in a pan. I followed Moses down to the waterfront where he rigged a rod and tied a white 'swim jig' onto a strong braided line. He cast about a dozen times and landed three walleyes that he threw up onto the rocks. "A drop-off here," he said. "Always a good place to fish." Within ten minutes he had filleted the fish and rolled the meat in the batter. He cast the carcasses out into the lake.

He cut the jig off the line, and put it back in a small case with the other lures, then packed the rod and reel away. "Lures off in camp, and the rods stowed so we don't stumble into one of the hooks or break a rod. Awfully hard to get that barbed hook out of your skin," he said, showing me a scar on the fat part of his hand between his thumb and forefinger. I winced, thinking about a backwoods extraction with the tip of the bloody fillet knife that he'd just put back in its sheath.

"Check," I said.

"Good idea to keep the boots on in camp, too," he said, "unless you're completely still or in your sleeping bag. A foot cut means that I'm carrying you out. It won't heal in all of this wetness, and an unhealed cut is the *best* result we can hope for. Losing a foot or your life would be worse. The swamp is alive with things that can infect a foot wound like you wouldn't believe," he said casually.

"Check, again."

Moses returned to the fire. Before his match was struck, Moses was on his knees, his body hunched over the unlit wood with his coat unbuttoned as a windshield. He raked a single 'strike anywhere' kitchen match across the dry underside of a stone, and tilted it so that there was about a half-inch of fire on the matchstick. Moses inserted the little flame into the small opening of the teepee and held it under the platform. The flame licked up through the tiny twigs and began to smoke the birch bark. Moses held the matchstick for as long as possible, right to the tips of his fingers, to build heat in the kindling pile. A small dirty ribbon of orange flame began to lick up against the split twigs. Moses then turned sideways to the fire, exposing it to the wind flow coming in from the west. His face then went down into the combustion, just inches from it, and he made a very soft, long blow through pursed lips right at the base of the flame. The kindling pile burst into a ball of heat. He turned his head up and away from the fire like a swimmer taking breath, then back again for another long soft exhale. Ignition.

The twig platform collapsed into tiny red coals. Moses carefully placed another small stick onto the teepee anywhere that the flames licked through, positioning the wood so it could dry in the updraft and reach its flashpoint. He carefully arranged every stick, never throwing wood onto the fire despite the growing heat. More glowing coals began to gather on the granite, and Moses came in close to blow a harder, concentrated stream down on the ingots, causing the coals to turn nearly white. The tip of the flames reached a height of two feet, and the fire began to live on its own.

Moses now began taking from the second pile, placing the 'squaw wood' cross-wise on the crumbling teepee, building crosshatch levels. Each level provided a new base for wind flow to the underside of the next. He continued to add fuel this way without suffocating the fire underneath. In twenty minutes we had a pile of glowing embers an inch thick, hot enough to combust the small twigs almost instantly, to boil the rice in a pot suspended on a wet stick across the back of the pit, and cook the fish in a pan on the front. The walleye fillets sizzled as they hit the oil, cooking quickly. Moses ladled out big chunks of fish right out of the pan. The batter was crispy and sweet, and the fish were flaky and delicious. It was just the meal I'd hoped for at my miserable camp that first night on the domed rock.

We ate everything (which was a lot), but yet 'everything' was not quite enough to feel completely full. This 'unfilled' feeling would become a constant companion in the days ahead; a feeling that came from burning every available food calorie and a bit more.

We scraped the dishes into the lake, washed and rinsed them in hot water, and put everything away. We stowed the food pack under the canoe. Moses then built up the fire with much of the remaining wood, producing a blaze hot enough to singe our cheeks from a few feet away. The last glow of daylight was on the western horizon behind the trees, and a wind had come up in the west, gusting hard enough to send sparks up and out over the water. Moses untied the bow-line from the canoe, and fastened it between two trees to make a clothesline in the wind and smoke. We stripped naked and stood without socks in our wet boots as we smoked our clothes dry. "The Gun picked out some pretty good gear for a tenderfoot," Moses commented as he noted how quickly my trout shirt and pants dried in the heat. My socks would take a bit longer as they steamed on a rock next to the fire.

We put our clothes back on. Moses settled down for a smoke, pulling a brand out of the fire to light up one of his home-rolled. He'd just showed me how to make a one-match fire in a forest that had received three inches of rain only a few hours ago. *That has to be a sign of quality*, I thought. I might have been more alarmed, perhaps, if I'd known that we carried only two slender tubes of dry matches, each about an inch around, for the entire journey that lay ahead.

I began to nod off in the warmth of the fire, just gazing at the flames that were both constant and shifting. My mind began to roll over the promise of Moses. "You will have a vision before it's over. I will promise you that!" *A vision ... a vision....*

There was a pop of wet wood, and the soft crunching of sticks collapsing into embers. My head had fallen onto my chest. I lifted my head, opening my eyes, and there, just beyond the firelight, were a pair of blue eyes, looking straight into mine.

26: First Things

Intention is not a thought, a wish, a hope, or a state of mind. A true intention is not even your own. Intention is a force from outside yourself, a clarity that calls you to walk through walls and become someone different, better ... more.
...*The Field Book*.

THE EYES WERE SIMPLY THERE on the edge of the firelight. I looked over to Moses, who was sitting with his spine straight and his hands folded quietly in his lap. Moses looked back at me, meeting my startled gaze with his own calm and quiet one—simply looking as if nothing at all was happening—as if he had nothing to do and nowhere to go. I looked back toward the edge of the firelight. The eyes were completely disembodied as far as I could tell, except for a faint sound of breathing. The body of whatever creature they belonged to was completely merged into the dark background of the forest. I had the sense that the eyes had come closer as I drifted into sleep in order to conduct ... well ... an *inspection*.

I was being held in the cross-beams of blue eyes; those in front, and those of Moses to the right of me. I was unable to move. The eyes were beholding me with a combination of full attention, curiosity, and care—I felt as if I were lying on a gurney and looking up into the eyes of good physicians who were deeply interested in my well-being. I had a sense that these physicians were in possession of powerful tools, and they meant to make a careful diagnosis before they prescribed.

Then, in the next instant, the creature in the forest and Moses reached an agreement. I can't tell you how I knew this, except to say that there was a palpable shift in the field between them; they were somehow communicating without words. The eyes in the forest began to fade backward, still hanging luminous in the dark, but growing smaller. Something else was coming out of the forest into the firelight.

It was being led by the hand, although I couldn't tell for certain if it had hands at all. But it was led forward nonetheless, right to the edge of the firelight.

What emerged into the light had a golden body that was shaped like a luminous egg. It was not a physical being. That is to say that it was not *biological*—not made of blood and bone—but of some other substance that was nonetheless fully real and potent. I'm tempted to say that it was made of energy, which was true (in part), but only in part. Perhaps the clearest way to say it is to say that I was witnessing a being that was made entirely of *intention*.

I felt a deep sense of familiarity with this odd apparition. *It's part of me that lives in another dimension*, I thought. *How odd that I should think such a thing.* The golden body appeared as empty space. But as I looked deeper, I saw that the body was consciously *made of emptiness*, as strange as this sounds. It was enclosing space—almost infinite space—to hold any intention imaginable. The emptiness was like a vacuum that attracted intention into itself.

"—This is the body of your intention," I heard the eyes say, speaking now in a woman's voice inside my mind. "A part of your soul. It's a being made entirely of images. You could call it an 'Imaginal' if you like."

I looked at the being in the firelight. At first I saw nothing but the golden light. But then, I began to see that the being in the firelight contained dozens, hundreds, no—*thousands* of personalities, all of which could be said to be part of me. This Imaginal began to rapidly change color, and display different versions of me, Charlie Smithson.

One after another, in rapid succession, came visions of every potential person I might become. The visions were clear, brutally clear.

Each 'self' was carrying some human dignity. But there was plenty of disaster there as well.

I saw myself at the Thompson Firm, endlessly processing the same type of information over and over again, completely absorbed and never escaping the loop, like a worker cutting and harvesting a field that went on forever. There was the self that belonged to the Initiative that was engaged in an endless positive push forward along one line, gathering up all his energies and using them as fuel to launch a megalomaniacal rocket. I saw myself thrusting skyward and holding others in awe as I constantly displayed wealth, success, and my compelling six-pack abs. And there was myself as the Turk: sitting as a drunken victim in my own life.

Then came more versions of me, many more.

Whether they came from the past or future I couldn't tell. They were all familiar, yet clearly not part of my life this time around—at least not so far. There were versions of myself sitting still and watching my thoughts for so long that the whole world turned into an illusion. I saw myself trudging in the snow with frozen feet and a gun, with no will of my own, stopping when I was told to stop, moving when I was told to move, and killing when I was told to kill. There were many versions of myself that had almost no intention at all who required some external force to move them. I was swept up in huge crowds bent on destruction, and in other huge crowds kneeling in prayer. I did what the crowd did; that was all. And there were many versions and sub-versions of myself that were devoted to nothing but mindlessly following my stone-age instincts, over and over and over again.

The images came faster, then faster, each carrying an essence, the seed of a possibility that I could nourish and grow into a life. *The Imaginal is demonstrating the power of intention,* I thought. But yet, the Imaginal itself was free, and no longer identified with the 'selves' or their stories. It was outside of them; able to witness them all.

The Imaginal wanted to show me every possible story, each in its fullness, without judgment as to better or worse. It wanted me to see the powerful spells that my imagination could cast. It wanted to give me a gift: the freedom that comes from witnessing the creative power of my own mind.

FINALLY, the images began to slow, and the blue eyes behind them began to grow larger and come forward again. I could again feel the presence of Moses, who sat calmly on the ground to my right. The images in the egg flickered and grew still. The Imaginal returned to its original golden color, pulsing slightly, like some impossibly powerful machine that was sitting quietly in 'ready' mode. The eyes in front of me came back to the edge of the firelight, and I again felt them examining me with a curiosity that was now even stronger than before.

My companions were waiting. I had a sense that they were waiting for me to reveal how I intended to guide my future, now that I had witnessed so many of the possible lives of Charlie Smithson.

I didn't know what to do next. I glanced over at Moses.

"The Imaginal is here to give you information about what might be possible using the gift of your intention during this current life," Moses said. "Although all of us start with a set of givens, our futures are vastly more fluid than you now realize. Our inner consciousness, our intentions, can shape the future. When we change our insides, then, over time, everything on the outside will bend to more closely align with our inner reality."

"I'm still not sure how I go about changing anything. How do I begin to bend my life toward something better?" I asked.

"If you want some good information, you have to ask a good question," Moses continued, "a powerful question. Is there a question, Charlie, that's so important to you that your entire life would change if you knew the answer? Do you have a powerful question about the most pressing problem of your existence here? An open-ended life-altering question? Go ahead. Drop the question into the Imaginal field, and see what happens."

I thought about this possibility for a minute. *It shouldn't work this way*, I thought. *Someone should do this for me.* If I'm the one responsible for the question that will change my life, I might be responsible for how my life turns out. I might screw it up. *It seems easier to just follow someone else and blame them if things don't work out.*

I sat there in the firelight. We waited.

Then I heard Charlie Smithson say these words:

"If I were to become a vessel for the Divine in this life, how would I do it? Who would I become? How would I live, and what would I do?"

There was an immediate and palpable shift in the energy around the campfire. My friends, who were already sitting straight, sat up a bit straighter. It was as if the alignment they'd been hoping for had arrived. There was deep silence as a stick popped and collapsed into coals.

"Are you sure that this is *your* question, Charlie?" the eyes asked. "Not a question that you're coming up with because you're here with us, and that this question could be the very one that we might ask?"

"It's my question. I wouldn't be here with you now if this were not my question. I wouldn't have come this far," I said, now becoming certain for the first time. "It's my life's question."

There was a pause, and a moment of deep quiet around the fire.

"Very well then, Charlie. Thank you for joining us. It's a good question, and there may be more than one good answer. Let's see what the Divine might have in store for you."

The egg in front of me began to turn color. At its center was still a golden light, but the edges were now glowing with an electric blue. I felt that the Imaginal was about to display a vision.

THE IMAGINAL BEGAN by displaying an exact mirror image of me sitting in the firelight. I had the distinct impression that it was making a point: no matter what was about to happen, all of what was already 'me' would still be there. Little Charlie would still be there with the same teeth and hair, the same old car, the same skills at memorization, the same lack of friends, and the same job offer I had back in Chicago.

I felt an immediate and profound sense of disappointment. I don't know just what it was that I was expecting. Some kind of divine kitchen appliance maybe, something that would slice, dice, chop, and puree everything in my life into flawless perfection in one quick minute.

Again we waited. And then, out of some realm beyond my understanding, something came through into the Imaginal.

It was information.

Three strands. Three spirals. A triple helix.

What arrived were blueprints of a foundation upon which to build a new Charlie Smithson.

THE THREE SPIRALS were like DNA strands, each containing a vast amount of information and each intertwined and wrapped around my personal question: how could I become a vessel for the divine?

My attention was drawn to the first of the three spirals which glowed a deep lapis blue. This spiral contained a storehouse of information about the past. It was as if this strand contained information about all parts of me that might be conserved and preserved. There was a sense of dignity about that preservation. So much effort had already been spent. So many problems had already been so carefully solved. So much here to be thankful for.

The deep blue spiral went to work and began to search the past. Specifically, it was searching *my* past for things that would help me accomplish this new goal. In lightning succession, images flashed inside the Imaginal. With each flash, there was a capacity displayed—a solid potential that could be 'turned on' given the proper circumstances. It was as if the Imaginal were picking capacities off an infinite grocery shelf—a storehouse stretching deep into the past—and creating a conservative base from which to move. The Imaginal was interested only in the best of the past. I would never have imagined that I was connected to so much; that there were so many capacities already there, just for the asking.

A simple older 'self' appeared in the egg—an old part of me that could do little more than live in a cave. There was so much ignorance to be left behind, but also a jewel to be brought forward: the ability to stay alive and simply take one small step after the next in faith that something better could emerge. I would need this capacity for the road ahead.

The image of a monk arrived; and from this monk the blue orb took the relentless willingness to witness thoughts, and also the art of tuning thoughts to a vibration of equanimity. But it took only these capacities, and left behind any sense of spiritual elitism and all intention to escape this world.

And how could I be separated from the many selves so interested in the functions of my body? My body was a powerhouse engine, able to live on stored fuel from the sun, and designed impeccably for this world. The Imaginal wanted to conserve the body and all of its joys without the compulsion to follow every impulse.

—From the Turk the Imaginal took the qualities of loyalty and emotional intensity, but left behind the man's fixed thinking and self-pity.

—From the Initiative and the masters of 'success' it took a never-ending commitment to act until something useful was achieved. But this 'action orientation' was separated from any intention to dominate others. All the domination games were to be left behind.

And so on, and further on. There was nothing without some value. It was as if there were a golden thread and needle piercing through the heart of every existing possibility, and picking up the best of it on a new spiral that had my name on it. The Imaginal was compressing time and scanning for the best of all traits, shorn of all grasping and contraction.

There was no doubt that my question was influencing the arc of the Imaginal's creativity. Unimaginable power and capacity were being offered up on one condition: that I would use it to become a vessel for the Divine, and not bend the power away from this intention towards some smaller personal agenda.

And then a pause. I was looking now at a fully formed blue spiral of capacities so powerful, so beautiful, that it was hard to imagine that I would ever need anything more.

But there was more.

THE IMAGINAL SHIFTED COLOR, and a second spiral shimmered with a deep ruby red and began to pulse. There was power in that red spiral. It had the ability to pull energy into itself and to create something new. This second spiral contained the codes for creating a new future.

Like the lapis blue spiral, this strand was sorting information, looking for the best of what the future might contain. It began its work by displaying a modestly creative re-assembly of givens; simple re-arrangements of capacities that could already be found in what my past had conserved. There were 'selves' presiding over old rituals with some new words thrown in; and selves re-interpreting books that had been interpreted many times before. All of this was a bit predictable. My Imaginal had more in mind.

I witnessed the Imaginal pulsing electric red, in full power now, seeking a new way forward. The orb was overheating as it tried every conceivable reassembly of the past, acting like a million monkeys typing keys to make a story. And then it simply gave this up. There was to be no future for me that could be merely formed by randomly re-combining the past. If I were to become a new vessel for the Divine, my future was to be an open possibility—a future that was radically *undetermined*. It was precisely this undetermined quality that would open my life.

What the Imaginal had in mind for me was something completely new within the Field—a new dimension of complexity and beauty. It was searching for a path to take me there. And then it found it. A deep red line. An ancient line. An arc in the fabric of time that could be followed. It was a *value* that had a gravitational pull on everything in the Field. Two simple words might stand in to describe it: it might be called 'The Good.'

'The Good,' as it was revealed to me, was more than Love and more than Quality, even though it contained these; and more even than the desire and capacity to do good. The Imaginal had found a plumbline that went somewhere quite special. It had found a way to bend reality in the direction of embodied perfection.

I saw for the first time that it was possible for me, little Charlie, to bend the course of the future. I could do this by becoming The Good itself. That was all that was necessary. That alone would change everything. I would no longer have to seek good fortune: *I myself would become good fortune*. I would no longer have to seek goodness, truth, or beauty. I myself could become good, true, and beautiful! The goodness of the universe could then expand. Through me.

The Good, as I saw it there in the Imaginal, was a physical fact, and the leader of a set of values that had a gravity that could bend the fabric of space-time—at least the fabric of my life and time. The Good was a force field that could change the direction of every situation that I might create or encounter. *I can become Quality*, I realized. *I can become Love.*

This thread of The Good will lead to an embodiment of the Divine, I thought. This was my path into the future. The Good was already there, but the precise form of its flowering through me could not be seen even by the Imaginal. The Good was too powerful to be controlled or predicted, yet I could align forces with it. I was being shown my path: to choose to align with the unknown future of The Good, forsaking all other possibilities. *That's something within my power*, I thought. I can choose The Good. *That choice will change everything.*

Then, as I looked into the Imaginal, the future began to recede. I was left with the sense that I could follow perfection's plumb-line on my short watch, and let it take me where it would. This could be done despite all my faults and flaws and despite my small window of wisdom and my limited time.

The red strand of the Imaginal began to dim and grow quiet. It then began to display the third spiral.

THE THIRD AND FINAL spiral pulsed with a golden light that combined with the existing indigo and ruby red to form a beautiful jewel. This third aspect of myself was a deep and beautiful spiral strand that contained receptors for every type of intelligence. It was a guidance system that wound around the other two spirals, keeping them connected. The third spiral offered a deep intelligence that existed in the present moment; right here, right now. Without this guidance, all the powerful capacities of the other two spirals might go deeply awry.

What began to emerge were a series of 'eyes,' each one a portal to a unique perspective. There were intelligences that could smell and sense the chemical composition of another person; that knew instantly whether that person could be trusted. There were intelligences that knew how to be afraid, angry, and sorrowful. There was an 'eye' attuned to danger that was constantly scanning for threats. There was even an intelligence that knew how to die.

But further along the golden spiral were other eyes. There was the eye of reason: the brilliant capacity to examine a situation dispassionately. There was an eye that had the ability to witness every thought and emotion that passed through my mind. This witnessing eye could quiet my mind and simply watch a river of thoughts, freeing me from their grip. There were higher eyes. There was an eye of compassion that had a capacity not just to imagine the inner world of others but to also inhabit their world and feel from inside their skin. There was an eye that could see only peace, and a lens that could see only the perfection of all things.

All of these intelligences were energies; actual physical forces that could shift the entire triple helix. No single awareness was sufficient. Even the highest eyes were too narrow working alone. All perspectives needed each other.

I WATCHED as the Imaginal began its final metamorphosis: it began to flower. The top of the three spirals opened, and began connecting to something much larger. I almost laughed as I saw just how small 'I' was in the scheme of things. I was just a small part of a vast, interconnected Field. Each part of the helix was a microcosm of that larger field, already perfect but also *going somewhere better*. My new self was just one node in the vast and living field of energy and information. *The Field of limitless possibility already exists*, I thought. *All I have to do is tap into it.*

And then, reaching the end of its work, the Imaginal paused. An image of a child appeared at the center of its golden orb, the same child who had disappeared off the end of the dock at Bill and Edna's Loon Lake cabins. She was turning, beckoning me, and holding a five-petaled flower. On her arm were three interwoven strands.

"—*I am you ... made of love, and given as love,*" the child said.

The Imaginal went quiet, and in front of me stood an entirely new version of myself. The central axis of my new child-like body was a jeweled triple helix.

THE IMAGINAL WITHDREW, and once again I was looking into the firelight. But now there was something different. A place just in the center of my chest was pulsing with the most extraordinary kind of love. I felt like I was carrying the seed of a new world soul.

"Three strands are not easily broken," I heard Moses say.

"—Yes," I heard the eyes say, as if satisfied that we'd found something honorable.

There was a long silence.

"—Charlie has quite a sacred imagination, and the ability to see into the deep structure of things."

"Yes," Moses replied.

"—But no vision is complete without its enactment. It would be all too convenient just to open to visions and consider our work done when the vision arrives, would it not? No. Charlie is going to have to climb inside God's skin and do God's work in his own body if he is to be a Keeper of the Field."

"Yes," Moses replied. "Yet, there is much to hope for in this vision, don't you think? And from one so young and inexperienced."

I could feel a prickling flush rising up the back of my neck. I felt that I'd just received the most exalted vision that existed anywhere in the universe, and my companions around the fire were treating it like a child's toy. *They're putting me in my place,* I thought.

"Charlie has yet to actually help anyone, as can readily be observed," the eyes said.

She's right about that, I thought. *She?* Wait. Yes. Those eyes. . . .

"—God still exists up ahead of little Charlie, the way he sees it now. In his current scattered condition he could never actualize the forces of that vision. His character needs to become much stronger before we can trust his good intentions, do you not agree, Messenger?"

"Yes," Moses replied. "What he seeks must become a full habit, not just a temporary vision. There is much work to be done."

Moses and the eyes turned towards me, asking a wordless question.

I heard myself respond.

"Let my training start tomorrow."

27: Taking God's Perspective

> Consecrate your life to something that wants to come into existence for the betterment of all life. Take full responsibility. Then raise your energy and begin to shape the fabric of the Field toward manifestation of that Good. That's your job as a Keeper of the Field.
> ...*The Field Book*

MOSES WAS already out of the tent when I awoke snug in my new blue sleeping bag. The feeling in my breastbone was still there, but as I became more awake the sensation began to mix with feelings of doubt and uncertainty. I'd slept late—the sun was two hands over the horizon. I stuffed my bag, dressed, and went out to a meal of dark coffee and a little oatmeal.

He sat on his haunches next to the fire with a plastic bowl full of oatmeal in one hand and a charred stick in another. "About last night and the thing about the training..." I began. "I was thinking that we really don't have to go to all the effort to...."

Moses put down his bowl and held up his finger to silence me. "Let the single expression of consent you made last night stand as a marker now and forever. There is no need to re-think anything when the best part of yourself has already spoken: your rational mind must now be the servant of your visionary mind. Trying to understand it all rationally will lead only to procrastination and second-guessing that will rob you of power. Doubt is the thief of life. Let your mind turn only to the journey forward. Please be quiet now."

Moses pointed his stick and drew these shapes on the granite next to the fire pit with its blackened tip:

"Last night I had a chance to witness what your visionary imagination had to offer," Moses said. "The morning always offers a new perspective on the night vision. I've drawn this to amplify our understanding. So, Charlie, you can see the infinity loop that I've just drawn. Can you imagine that infinity loop moving, actually traveling somewhere, and not staying in a closed loop?" He extended his stick to me. "Can you draw that loop in such a way that the ends are open and infinity starts to go somewhere?"

This all seemed like a lot to do before I'd had my first cup of coffee, but I could see that Moses was not about to waste time. I took the stick and drew an image on the rock that looked like this:

"It looks like the sign the doctors use ... what is it called?"

"You've drawn the Rod of Asclepius, the symbol of the Greek god of the healing arts," Moses said. "Well done, Charlie. It's an open spiral growing larger as it goes upward, always growing. Both ends are open, as you can observe. There are two poles, but only one flow, Charlie, just one snake—one unity traveling around a quiet, conscious center. That's the nature of the spiral."

Moses touched the drawing I had just made. Perhaps the light was playing tricks on me, but I swear that my charcoal drawing started to move, with the staff beginning to grow longer and rise up toward the sky and down into the earth. The line coiled around the staff and ascended upward in a spiral that grew progressively larger with each turn.

I was wide-eyed as Moses drew a circle around the spiraling figure. The image then vanished, and in its place was my crude two-dimensional drawing.

"How did you do that?" I demanded.

Moses ignored me. "The important thing for you to see is that the snake is curling, and growing larger with each turn, making what appears to be two sides that are in fact not separate. What appear to be opposites are a single unity—one flow united around a central context.

"Last night your Imaginal showed us a vision. What I saw last night was the blueprint of the creative power of the Field. To my eyes, the three strands merged to form a single spiral, opening upwards. One side of the unity was seeking to conserve the best of the past, and the other side seeking the best of what could evolve in the future. This creative tension—this polarity between what to conserve and what to create was kept in balance by the loving observation of a third dimension, the many portals or 'eyes' of awareness. The whole thing was bound together in love.

"Your vision was a good sign, Charlie," Moses continued, "a sign that you and I have both chosen wisely. I saw your vision as a map of what the Committee calls 'Unitive Consciousness'—the creative power that unifies the tensions of the Field. Growing Unitive Consciousness within the human race is the entire mission of The Committee. You've seen one of the first principles of energy: energy is drawn toward its opposite, and the tension must be managed by a Unitive Power. Now I must ask you to remain silent for a moment."

Moses picked up some of the ashes from last night's fire, holding them high at arm's length to let them pour like an hourglass through the opening in the bottom of his fist. He watched the ashes as they fell in the morning breeze, making a pattern like a horse's tail. I watched the ashes fall.

"What are you doing?"

"I'm asking for consent."

"Consent?" I asked.

Moses stopped what he was doing, lowered his jaw, and looked at me with raised eyebrows.

"There once was a time when students could simply observe in silence. But I can see that we have reached the age where everything must be explained. Very well."

He paused and gathered himself, then proceeded.

"It's my impression that I've received permission; no, more than that ... *a command* ... from the highest levels of your soul to engage you in training with the goal of Unitive Consciousness."

I thought about this. I was not so sure that all parts of myself had given consent in the way Moses thought they had. There were still some objecting parts. I was pretty sure of it.

He continued.

"Once you receive a vision, it's essential that you find support for that vision. We must ask the wilderness for its support. This place is alive and conscious, Charlie—more alive than you now know. The wilderness is our host, after all."

I watched Moses scoop up another handful of ashes and let them fall into a growing pyramid on the ground. He did this several times. Then as I watched, the wind shifted and came out of the east. It swirled through the camp and sent the ashes in a spiral that twisted up through the branches of the trees before disappearing out over the water.

Moses seemed satisfied.

"The east wind has agreed to support your intention, Charlie Smithson," Moses said as he clapped the ashes off of his hands. "The rest of the forest will follow its lead. As we noted at our first meeting in the swamp, the place seems to be in love with you. The generosity of the wilderness is a powerful gift. Your gratitude would be appropriate."

I turned to the east and made a small bow with my hands clasped against my chest, not knowing what else to do. Moses observed this in silence, and with a nod of his head, he returned to his breakfast.

MOSES FINISHED his oatmeal and coffee without further comment, and I did the same. We went down to the water's edge to rinse out our bowls. Moses then doused the fire until there was not a single ribbon of steam. He insisted that we feel the ashes with our bare hands to know that they were out. He then scooped up black bits and pieces of wood that had not been fully burnt, and carried them away from the fire pit to scatter them in the woods. He did the same thing with the stones of the fire pit, then washed away the remaining ashes and covered our drawings and the small fire scar with pine needles, loose moss, and deadfall. We broke camp and began to load the canoe.

"So would it be too much to ask where we're going?" I asked as I heaved the big Alaskan into the boat.

"We are going to expand your capacity for Unitive Consciousness and learn to assist the flow of Divine Creativity within the context of the Field," Moses replied.

I stood there for a minute thinking about what this might mean. Moses adjusted the Alaskan, and stood leaning on his paddle.

"And just how does *that* work?" I asked.

I looked at Moses, who now had the same whimsical grin on his face that had appeared the split second before he'd rolled us over in the middle of the cold lake. He thought for a moment, then to my relief decided to answer my question with words.

"From the very first moment, the whole she-bang—everything around you," he said, opening his hand to the sky, "has been operating on a single principle. Energy becomes form, and form, energy. This literally has been true from the first moments of the Big Bang. It's the truth that's expressed in Einstein's famous equation."

"$E=Mc^2$!" I said, remembering what every school kid knows.

"Just right, Charlie. In the physical world, energy moves and becomes form according to laws that we call 'physics.' You could describe the entire physical universe as an evolutionary novelty created out of energy. I'm not talking about combinations of old things in heaps and piles, but things that are honest-to-goodness new: new 'emergents.' Molecules of hydrogen and oxygen gas get together in the soup of energy created by an exploding star and create the very lake we stand next to. Most unexpected! Who could have imagined the wonder of it! That kind of creativity is worth doing, wouldn't you say?"

I nodded.

"My work, and the entire work of the Committee, involves the art and science of 'metaphysics,' which is the study of how the energy of human thought, awareness, intention, and attention, become form. Don't misinterpret what I am saying: the universe pre-existed our humanity by billions of years. Humans haven't created the universe by our thoughts. But there is a part of the universe that *is* downstream of our attention. We are literally made of this earth, Charlie, and our intention is a force of this earth—a force of nature. Because of us, nature here no longer moves randomly. It has become sentient—self-aware—through us. Nature's thoughts—our thoughts—now guide the direction life will take on this earth."

"So our attention is a physical force—it actually creates?" I asked.

"Attention is its own force, and also directs physical forces that create happiness, sadness, wars, peace, health, and culture; not to mention houses, cars, families, governments, and money, to name a few. We have phenomenal creative powers, especially now that our attention is coupled with the power of machines and systems that amplify our strength. It seems like everything is out of control, but it's not. We all have control over what *we choose to pay attention to and what we choose to create*. This choice is our fundamental God-like quality. We are bits of stardust that can observe our own attention and therefore have power over one of the fundamental forces of the universe. Attention (or consciousness if you will) is a physical force in the same weight class as gravity, electromagnetism, the nuclear forces, and other big drivers in the universe. We can literally destroy life on the earth by our choices, or create a paradise here."

I put the Duluth pack in the boat, and Moses and I walked the camp one last time to make sure that we'd left nothing and that there was no litter.

"I'd never thought about my consciousness in just that way," I said. "So if attention is *that* important, what should we pay attention to? There must be something that we can do to make it turn out right, some kind of a way that we could help creation unfold here. Surely the Committee must have come up with some solution by now."

"Yes, they have."

"And what's that?"

"We have to get better at seeing this world like God sees it; and better at using our attention to jump the creative gap between the past and the uncreated potential of the future, thus becoming extensions of the Divine in this place."

I must have looked confused. Moses sat down on the stern plate of the canoe, and began to explain.

"Take God's perspective for just a moment. Imagine that you were a single unity that contains everything. All that will ever exist is moving within you, dancing as energy that is becoming form, a form that is now smiling and dancing and creating more energy. In your universe, everything within you is becoming more alive, and more aware. As everything within you becomes more aware, your powers grow: you can balance and contain even more energy, and can grow into ever more complex forms. You are a universe open for business and your business is creativity, Charlie. *Infinite* creativity."

I closed my eyes for a moment and began to feel what Moses was describing. I couldn't feel like I contained 'everything,' but I sure could feel that I was alive; that I was a balance of complex forces; that I had energy; and that I was capable of creating something. And I could feel the pull of something higher that had yet to come into being.

"Now also imagine that all cosmic creativity has come to the final and absolute conclusion that what's happening is a meaningless accident, that there is no purpose or direction to the creative flow of the universe, and that the best anyone can hope for out of their opportunity at life is to spend their meaningless existence looking out for number one, dominating other forms of life, suffering, fucking and fighting until nothing but a toxic, radioactive, and lifeless planet remains."

"What's that?" I asked, shocked out of my reverie. "You're kidding, aren't you? Even *I* can think of a better result than that!"

"Yes, Charlie. I'm kidding. You know intuitively that there's something better. That intuition itself is a powerful sign that God is living inside of you."

"Well, if God is inside of me, that means that God must be inside of you too," I said. "If you're God, maybe you could tell me why I'm here and what I'm here to do with all my energy."

Moses smiled.

"You're just full of good questions this morning, Charlie. I can't tell you why you're here, but I can tell you why *I'm* here. Your energy has drawn me here. I'm here because of what *you* want to create. Right now, *you* are giving my life meaning and purpose. And my purpose, right now, is to tell you this: there is a purpose to both your life and mine. Our purpose is to make more life. The universe is coming alive through us, Charlie, minute by minute. We are constructing a new reality every moment as we go along. We can't help but create something. The question is: what's it going to be?"

Moses sat there looking at me. It was one of those baffling moments that he loved to create. I had a sudden urge to pull out the Field Book. It was there in the map case, calling me like a life raft.

I unzipped the plastic case, opened the book, and read this passage:

> Instructions for persons who need a reason to live.
> We know about you. All is not lost. No matter how far down you think you are, there is something on this earth that you can make better with your attention and energy; something that you can make more alive. It could be another person, your body, a line of work, a plot of land. With your energy, you can bring this thing into a higher form. You know this. You have the exact key. The work will be hard, but it's worth doing.
>
> You may have to release all of your ideas about how 'success' is going to happen and at the same time do everything you can to create the new. The goal may be far ahead; impossible by today's standards. This is just the point.

Yet, if this one thing could happen—what would happen? Reality would expand. The world would be better. You know this. Life would grow and become 'more.' So commit. Then day by day, use the power of your attention, intention and energy to jump the gap between the imagined and the real.

As you do this, the infinitely creative God will be there at the edge with you, right at the bow of the boat that is cutting the waters of the universe, right at the edge of creation, moving energy that creates the next thing, and the next, and the next. You might feel it, and you might not. It doesn't matter. It also doesn't matter if you 'get there' or not. Even though you're confused, even though you're suffering—as you cast your energy toward a potential waiting to be fulfilled, you are expanding God right where you are. This is your job.

Do you want us to tell you again what your job is? Your job is to follow your highest impulse. Your job is to take your energy and move some part of this world higher. Your job is to make your life unconditionally meaningful by making something better.

And of course, there is the Good News. The News is that Reality (as it unfolds) will be vastly better, different, and more interesting than anything you can imagine. And the icing on the cake is that you have the ability to make more of it. The question is: What is it going to be?

I closed the Field Book and looked at Moses. It sounded wonderful and scary at the same time.

"This is saying that my job is to create God here. What you're saying is that I can shape reality. Is that right?"

"Just right, Charlie, just right," Moses said quietly. "In fact we can do nothing else. The bedrock of our shared experience as Keepers of

The Field is that we are already inside God and cannot be separated. So to say that we are God is *literally* true. We are made of God. God is not up above us, or outside of us, or on our side in some cosmic battle. We are within God, and there's more and ever more God up ahead, being endlessly created by and through us. As part of God, we have the power to bend the fabric of the Field with our intention, and change the course of life in this place."

I sat down, trying to grasp the implications of what Moses was speaking about. Although I couldn't see the God that he was talking about, I could see that there was evidence of stunning change all around me—the deep history of change was written everywhere in nature. Something new was coming into existence every instant: some new thought, some new thing, some new life. Reality was growing every second—well ... really every split, and re-split, and re-re-split of every second. Time couldn't be cut fine enough to say that there was a 'now' that contained all there is. It was changing that fast.

And then a light came on.

"If our job is to do God's work, this means that we're responsible, aren't we? Responsible for how everything turns out. Responsible for how the story of creation unfolds."

Moses nodded. "Now you see what's at stake. Creation is your *moral responsibility*, if I could use that old term. It's the moral responsibility of being part of God."

I was not sure that I wanted any of that kind of responsibility. Not sure at all.

"You're saying that I've reached a point where I can steer the process of creation with my attention, and I'm responsible for how things turn out?"

"Once you experience the Field, you'll know that you have one and only one job here, and that's to do God's work as best you can," Moses said. "The first step is to embrace your responsibility as a creator. That's the bedrock character trait of a Keeper of the Field."

"Wow," I said. "So how do we get started?"

"We start to grow up, Charlie," Moses responded. "That's how we participate in creation—by taking the journey *forward*. You've reached the famous 'point of no return' out here with me and are about to begin a new phase of your life, where you will be able to handle vastly more energy. The whole game from this point forward will be won or lost by the way that you move from fear, and the understandable desire to protect your old way of being. If you are ready to move in faith to manifest something higher, the game is won. If you seize up and contract around your little self, the game is lost. And when you move forward from fear, what are you moving towards Charlie, what do you think it is?"

"Into more ... love...?"

Moses smiled the largest, stupidest smile that I'd seen on his face since the first afternoon in the swamp.

"You're finally starting to get it, Charlie. It all grows. You can call the expansive quality of the Field 'love' if you want to. Love is what it feels like when you connect to it, that's for sure. When love expands, The Field expands. New things arrive in that new space. We're talking about emergents arising out of a field of love, Charlie; beautiful divine babies. Good, true, *and* beautiful to be exact. That's the cosmic fun of the creative flow of God."

What Moses was saying resonated with me. I was finally beginning to understand what he was talking about.

"The world around me is an emerging flow of creativity," I said, "and I'm part of it, *made* of it."

"Just right, Charlie," Moses said. "You are in a flow. What you are *is* a flow. When the flow stops, life stops moving and starts dying, Charlie. The flow stops when you seize up. It's just that simple. As a Keeper of the Field you are here to end the war against the flow, and evolve this world. Check out the teachings of any master. They will all tell you to stop fearing; connect with the God that you are within; love this world as part of your own being; and walk in faith into the new. That's the sum total of the spiritual life in a nutshell."

I stood looking into his blue eyes, taking it all in and receiving what he had to say.

"Now, are we ready to begin your training?" Moses asked.

"Last night I said I was ready. I guess I have to stick with that."

"Very well then, Charlie. I feel like I have your full consent at last. I'll do my best not to abuse your trust."

"I trust you," I said. "You've always told me the truth and led me to someplace better, at least so far."

"Very well," Moses said again, making a slight bow. "In the interest of trust, I have one more thing to disclose."

"What's that?" I asked.

"Everything I've just said may not be true in the way that you think of truth now. Our ideas about God change. My ideas about God may simply be a decoy for my simple mind; an illusion that gathers the force of my drive. It's the energy of my drive, the *movement itself toward something better*, that's the greatest gift. Energy is the hunter's portion for wild men like us," he said, adjusting one of the packs to make the canoe ride lower.

"The movement toward the goal is what I'm interested in," he continued. "You may notice that the caterpillar does all the work and the butterfly gets the credit. I am here to help you with your caterpillar work. It is my great privilege to do this."

He paused, swallowing hard and collecting himself.

"Let's focus now on one step at a time, and let the results take care of themselves."

I put my foot on the row of rivets that went down the centerline of the canoe, reached across to stabilize myself, and then settled into the bow seat. With a couple of strokes of the paddle we left the camp. As I looked back, the place looked like no one had ever been there.

28: A Journey to Somewhere

We are a tiny piece of the Field and at the same time exactly the same size as the Field. The Field is an ocean that contains all drops, and at the same time, each drop contains the whole ocean. To become a Keeper of the Field you must know this directly. That's where we're going.
...*The Field Book* .

That morning Moses and I began a new phase of our journey together. Although he had asked the wilderness for its blessing, it was Moses himself who provided the lion's share of the support that was so necessary to keep me moving and not just staring at the ground. I never really had a father, and this was a new experience for me. I never had someone spread his arms out and hold me within a field of such high intention.

Within moments after we left our first camp, I became a student within an old style, peripatetic training with Moses in the role of my desert father. My education was to be conducted through the vehicle of just moving around together. This 'old style' teaching put me in contact with Moses in a way that revealed everything about him—how he ate, slept, walked, acted, and reacted: how he lived. Moses had everything to show and nothing to hide, and he intended to show me everything he had. Moses was not like the Gun, a 'Wizard of Oz' man manipulating a big illusion from behind a curtain. To the contrary: my teacher *was* the teaching, laid bare.

My traveling companion was a simple man. He walked lightly and needed almost nothing. To be in his company was to be with a person who needed no approval, no money, no love, no security, no adulation, no agreement, no joining, and no leaving. Nothing. He was the first person in my life who did not even need me to succeed. He had one requirement and one requirement only: no matter what and no matter when, I would continue to take the next step forward.

WE TURNED NORTHWARD, with Moses paddling in the stern and me in the bow. We were geared to go fast and light. What gear we had was laid low in the canoe to cut the wind, and with two paddlers moving in perfect synchronization, we began to move so swiftly into the deep wilderness that I could see no way of return. It was here that I would be introduced to what Moses had to offer as a formal teacher.

Unlike other forms of training, the purpose of his instruction was not the accomplishment of a specific external objective. Rather, his purpose was to carry forward a very old agenda—the core agenda of all creation. This was the agenda that began billions of years ago in a cold cloud of hydrogen gas that had now progressed to a point where two men could stand on a granite outcrop smoking rum tobacco and look at the stars. This agenda was evolution. Moses believed that to continue forward from this point, humanity must become conscious of the process, and align with it moving forward. There is still a far distance to go, Moses said. This distance could be called the journey toward becoming Fully Human, reaching toward an Omega Point, or the process of becoming the True Self. By whatever name, in his presence I could feel what he was talking about. I could feel a drive growing inside me at the root of myself. It was the drive to become more, to evolve, to 'take the ride,' and to become someone quite different and much more interesting.

I couldn't refuse the trip. It was what I was made for. The fact that there were no specific 'deliverables' only meant that I was freed from the agenda of a previous and increasingly irrelevant self that was once interested in such things. I'd been outward bound for less than a fortnight, and already could barely remember the odd prizes and rankings that were so important to me back in Chicago. They weren't real, I'd discovered. This new dream was much more real.

Moving with Moses was to constantly be in the company of someone intent upon a higher level. One might ask why a higher level was important. I should have been happy to stay an ape I suppose. Moses would never criticize such a decision. But an ape is not much of a bridegroom. I had the powerful sense that Moses was preparing me to meet someone. "A wedding," he would say. Yes. He was preparing me to be presented to someone, and did not want to bring me into that encounter unprepared.

The Elements of the Teaching.

Moses did not present his teaching as a step-wise system. He had little need of linearity and was content to wait until some circumstance presented a teachable moment. He was so deeply subservient to a higher source that I don't believe that he himself knew what he would say or do next. He was content to let God handle it. But my logical, lawyer-trained mind wanted to see his teaching as a system that could be learned, repeated, and perhaps brought into the world at a scale that involved more than one person at a time. Moses was fine with this, although he would not have created such a system himself. He was concerned that writing everything down and presenting it in a step-wise fashion would lead to the misinterpretation that his teachings were fixed structures instead of fluid processes. Nonetheless, he said, "Each teacher in a lineage adds his or her own contribution based upon personality and character traits." Logical thinking was one of my traits; and so, with the permission of my teacher, I attempted to capture the essence of his teaching as a sequence of steps, and write these steps down in the Field Book with the beautiful pen he'd given me. I identified nine fulcrums that Moses felt were essential. Although he acted as if it all were quite simple and ordinary, Moses was in fact conveying *powers*. He offered a system by which I could begin to put my fingers on levers and move my future, first by leaving the past that I was carrying with me; then then by changing my body and mind on a molecular level; and finally by living into a radically new way of interacting with everything. I became a man with the capacity for a new future—a future that was open to the miraculous powers of the Field.

Here are the nine fulcrums of power, and their corresponding art forms, as taught by Moses:

Fulcrum One:
The power of the *Evolutionary Journey* and the *Art of Movement*.

Moses required an initial decision that changed everything. This was a decision to set off upon (and continue) an open-ended journey with the intention of going somewhere better. Embarking on such a journey required my utmost and highest answer to the call of something still unknown. Under the guidance of Moses, my life was on the move, and became a 'Personal Evolution Project.'

Fulcrum Two:
The *Power of a Catalytic Surround* and the *Art of Growth*.

The context of our work was a catalytic surround—a new environment so intense that it required a new and higher self to come forward to simply survive. My new surround was forcing me to confront the doubting voices inside myself, to leave my old behavior patterns behind, to learn new skills, and to fundamentally change my ideas about what was important in this life.

Fulcrum Three:
The *Power of Commitment* and the *Art of Trust*.

For Moses, commitment was the deliberate decision to go 'all in'— to stop looking back and mourning for my old captivity; to accept current reality unconditionally; *and to get about learning what I needed to learn*. This created a foundation that could be trusted by both myself and by others.

Fulcrum Four:
The *Power of Values Gravity* and the *Art of Transmission*.

According to Moses, speaking values through thoughts, words, and deeds creates a 'gravitational pull.' Consciously voicing and adopting a better set of values pulls us, and everything around us toward a better world. The world that Moses wanted to create was *this world* populated by human beings who were bringing heaven to earth. This direct embodiment was his core value.

Fulcrum Five:
The *Power of Training* and the *Art of Flow*.
To honor my commitment to become a new Charlie, I had to learn the concrete, physical foundations of a new way of being. This meant re-learning and training basic new habits—habits that involved the best way to move, eat, and relate to the environment around me. Under the direction of Moses, these habits were learned in such a way that they produced a state of *Flow*, which could be described as a meta-habit of joy in the midst of action

Fulcrum Six:
The *Power of Perspective* and the *Art of Attention*.
This was a process of clear, fearless, and 'active witnessing' of myself, using 'free attention' in the context of the catalytic surround and the journey that I'd chosen.

Fulcrum Seven:
The *Power of Synergy* and the *Art of Engagement*.
Moses taught that the value of one's life was determined by: (1) who you influenced, and (2) how you chose to influence them. For him, the ultimate form of beneficial influence was the entrainment of a field of love where Divine Energy flowed towards others and came back 'round again, creating a great current of love in all of its forms.

Fulcrum Eight:
The *Power of Cosmic Luck* and the *Art of Surrender*.
This was the practice of saying "yes" to my instincts, and to the unique and unusual openings which arose once my journey was commenced in earnest. These openings were not seen as accidents, but rather gateways to new situations where I could practice my new way of being and reap its rewards.

Moses emphasized that we possess vastly different instincts when we are aligned with higher vibrational fields than when we're aligned with lower ones. At some point, I could follow my instincts and surrender to the gifts that were flowing through me into the world. My instincts, he said, would become much more trustworthy, and my 'cosmic luck' much better, as I advanced through committed practice.

Fulcrum Nine:
The *Power of a New Identity* and the *Art of Influence*.
This was the work of the re-born person: to influence the Field in a way which shaped it and bent its fabric, so that the path toward a new and expanded life could be seen and walked by others.

MOSES SAID that none of these nine fulcrums or their art forms was new, and that practicing these powers was simple, requiring nothing but straightforward choices that were then acted upon with the full force of my being.

I would come to learn that doing such simple things is harder than one might imagine.

The first three fulcrums: Open-Ended Journey; Catalytic Environment; and Commitment.
The first requirement of the training—the first essential—was my willingness to set off and continue on an open-ended journey toward some vision of an extraordinary existence. This first essential was the 'table stake' of my new game. It's what I had to bring to the table just to have the chance to bet my life.

I'd chosen my journey three times: once when I left Chicago, once when I left the swamp with Moses, and again when I left the Initiative's encampment. I'd received a vision, even though I didn't understand what it meant. That was not important. According to Moses, the first test had been passed. I was officially on the trip. There was no question that my soul was moving.

The second essential was to place myself in a challenging context where my new self was not only invited, but required. According to

Moses, the quickest way to transform was to take a dive into the deepest of the deep ends—into a catalytic surround that would tear apart my old self, then force me to re-learn everything at a much higher level. Moses believed that the right environment could call forth almost unimaginable capacities.

My catalytic surround was not hard to find. I was traveling with Moses through one of the most primitive and challenging environments on earth. It was a wet, cold, and painful place that required my full attention to simply get through the day. Perhaps we could have chosen to take an adventure at one of the poles for more of a challenge, but the north woods had plenty in it to confront anyone.

There was also little more for me to do to move deeper into the 'third essential'—my commitment. I'd discovered that commitment was not all that complicated. Part of being committed was to simply say 'no.' Commitment began with relinquishment—a letting go.

My personal commitment to this adventure had already brought about some intense housecleaning. I'd left behind my unnecessary equipment, and the former great love of my life—my unnecessary 'success' agenda. I was now in the process of giving up unnecessary ideas about who I was.

The other part of commitment required saying 'yes.' The decision to say 'yes' didn't have to make sense. The decision just had to be made. My soul had made a decision when I left the Initiative to travel northward with Moses. All logic and prudence said that I should be back in Chicago now, or perhaps that I should never have left. Yet, I was committed northward day by day. I still was not completely sure that I'd made the right choice. But there were signs. Day by day I was more willing to trust the process to which I'd committed. A good support structure had magically appeared in response to my commitment, which included the arrival of The Rule that was forcing new and unusual habits. My body was more alive than it had ever been. And day by day, I was learning to trust guidance from a non-human realm.

I was increasingly willing to appear foolish and to 'fail forward' as I learned the basics of a strange new environment. Moses considered my active willingness to fail a sure sign that a new and higher stage of development had arrived. According to him, the more I failed and appeared foolish, the more trustworthy I became.

Fulcrum Four: The Power of Values Gravity and the Art of Transmission.
Entrainment of new values is simple: find some person or group who embodies who you want to be, and hang out with them until you've copied their signature frequency right down the line. It's not much more complicated than that. The challenge is to find the right person. My right person was Moses.

Unlike the Gun (and most other people I'd encountered), Moses was not interested in my ability to attain a goal. All of the money and power in the world meant nothing to Moses. His only interest was to bring heaven to earth in human form, and this, paradoxically, was not a 'result' that could be attained.

Yet his entire teaching was centered on the work of preparing the human form for divine habitation (getting us ready for 'cosmic luck') and the practical means by which this could be accomplished. One such means was the deliberate choice of core attributes or *qualities* that supported the main mission: those beautiful qualities and 'happy attributes' like caring, self-sufficiency, trustworthiness, and joy. Much of our work together concerned itself with the practice of these primary attributes until they became real and could be relied upon as facts, not merely good intentions.

According to Moses, the beautiful qualities, when practiced over time, could literally change the shape of my immortal soul. Moses believed that we could hang onto these qualitative gains—that we carried them out of this life, and that they became a platform for further work.

A UNIQUE FORM OF SHARED MANHOOD passed between us in the wilderness: a transmission of quality, man to man, with the intention of making our souls more beautiful. And, as we moved together, a remarkable phenomenon began to happen. *Qualities*—those amorphous intangibles—began to become real, and to become embodied right in the midst of the whole catastrophe.

Simply by holding the quality of joy in the field of our collective intention and imagination, joy began to arise. So too with perseverance, fearlessness, caring, and love. It was as if these qualities already existed in the Field, and all we had to do was act as if they were so. We were calling in miracles.

Moses called our miracles 'states of being.' The states were freely accessible, he said, and came and went to some degree like the weather. Open, expansive, and loving states were in the weather pattern, as were closed and violent ones. All states were accessible if we tuned into them, practiced them, and repeated them. The expansive states were easy to access in the presence of Moses, because he embodied them. Just by being next to him, I began to resonate at a different, higher frequency. Moses said that I was starting to experience my 'home frequency'—the unique vibration of my soul when it was responding to the call of its highest source. I felt that I was tuning in.

As THE NEW QUALITIES BEGAN TO ARISE, they started to physically create reality around us. I was *literally* inside happiness. Feelings like anger and worry simply ceased to exist.

I discovered that all of the bells, whistles, and must-haves of the modern world are not much connected to happiness. Happiness in the wilderness was a moment-to-moment phenomenon that anyone could have right here and now regardless of the external circumstances. I discovered that happiness is a way of traveling, not a destination. A light is switched on, and the darkness is no longer there.

I began to 'see' the first light of dawn from a place in the middle of my chest. I began to feel the wind come into my nostrils and circulate through my body before being exhaled. I was cutting grooves of joy! That such an experience was possible was a profound surprise to me. For Moses, it was just natural; the way things were supposed to be. Moses acted as if all of this was as common as the rain.

My newfound happiness was strange to me. I realized that what I had previously considered normal was in fact a state of chronic anxiety.

I now began to experience happiness almost all of the time for no reason at all. "A side effect," Moses said.

I also began to move like I belonged—quickly, silently, and in harmony with myself and the wilderness around me. "Another side effect," he said.

And there was a third side effect.

I began to move, think, and feel a lot more like Moses.

For the first time in my life, I felt the desire to care about someone other than myself. Just that desire alone was a gift beyond measure.

Moses was transmitting high-frequency values to me without saying a single word. In every moment, he demonstrated what might be called 'radical caring'—a practice of changing one's whole life to support the growth and life of the cared-for thing. For Moses, this caring was not a great moral act or exemplar performed with fanfare before an audience. No one was watching. It was just the way he was. And it was my great good fortune that the object of his caring was *me*. Moses taught me that I didn't have to go to a far-off land to care about someone. There was plenty of caring to do for the person right next to you, and sometimes this form of caring was the hardest.

I became more and more aware in the presence of Moses that I'd lived a third of my lifetime caring for no one but myself. Even now, I couldn't really reciprocate his kindness. My experience of caring seemed to be off in the future, tied up in some way with my vision of that child running off the end of the dock. Out of embarrassment, I tried to make something up to sound like I was compassionate. I told Moses I cared about the progress of humanity. He didn't buy it. Caring had to be "real, immediate, and specific," he said. For him, it was important to be able to touch the cared-for thing, to blow a life-giving wind into it, and to do this personally.

Moses became my sculptor, my creator who was bringing forth my potential as a gift to be unwrapped, like an artist might find a statue already existing inside a piece of marble. Moses was chiseling deep grooves of beauty into my heart and mind of stone. He put his whole life into it.

Fulcrum Five: The Power of Training and the Art of Flow.
It was unclear to me just how long we'd be staying in the woods, but it *was* clear that Moses did not intend to leave me without the basic skills to live in this transformational place. Like any good builder, he began with the foundation: the daily physical tasks.

Concrete physical tasks played an important role in Moses' idea of good training. Moses rarely used the word 'training.' That was more my word. But when he did use it, he was referring to concrete actions. Wholesome physicality grounded our work, linked it to the earth, and corrected my tendency to stay up in my head. Moses had little respect for perfumed gurus who could not support themselves on the earth. He was at heart an earth lover and a wayfarer, and his idea of a 'man' was someone who could manage himself, prepare his own food, navigate his environment, and live lightly on this planet.

Training meant the re-learning of basic things. New, good habits needed to be formed: habits of paddling, lifting, walking under load, making and breaking camp, making fire, and finding food. These habits would become core physical attributes—the backbone of my new self in this place. If you think that the physical tasks of living and moving in the wilderness are easy, it's likely that you haven't tried them. Moses had a method for making these difficult things easy, by training me to experience our challenges as 'happiness in working clothes,' as exercises in *flow*, which Moses taught as an eyes-open spiritual state of pure joy.

My flow started with the unconflicted feeling that I was doing something that was fundamentally right—at least right for now. It was right for me to be up in the wilderness on this crazy adventure, training to become a better human being. I'd come all in, and was ready to play the game.

Now, life in this new environment presented a whole new set of challenges. The game, according to Moses, was to meet these challenges while staying in flow. It helped that the risks of our game were always high. Most every moment required enough concentration to blissfully sweep the old chronic focus on my little self right off the table. Here, my attention had to be turned outward, and stay right in the present moment. Usually that moment provided immediate feedback—when I went out of sync, there were direct physical consequences. I could also feel when things clicked back into gear. I could feel the flow like I was balancing on a moving bicycle.

If I was successful in staying in flow, things would work out and be OK, Moses said. *At least the present moment would be OK*, then then next, and the next. The moments would then build into hours, and days, and lifetimes.

THE WILDERNESS PRESENTED LOTS OF OPPORTUNITIES TO PRACTICE FLOW. One such opportunity was the daily problem of our starvation

It's obvious, but food is pretty important to a human being. In Chicago, food could be taken for granted, but here, its supply could not be assumed. We are big, active, daylight animals who burn thousands of calories a day. In the woods, I was a predator, with my eyes set forward in my head, traveling light, and living off the land. My biology as predator and omnivore was not something I'd personally chosen. It was just the way it was, and had come with me as part of the pre-determined package. I couldn't survive on lichens and twigs like the woodland caribou.

Moses had brought me to the forest during the season of long light, the northern summer, and everything was alive and moving. We were to live here on a summer wayfarer's diet consisting almost entirely of fish and rice supplemented by a small cache of dehydrated fruits and vegetables, what berries we would find, rose hips, cattail root, some coffee, some rum-soaked tobacco in small quantities, and a dwindling supply of a dense and precious way-bread made of ground nuts, rolled oats, oil, honey and molasses which Moses kept stored deep in the big Alaskan. The way-bread was held in reserve, a kind of caloric savings account for days of intense cold and driving rain.

We were hungry all the time. Each morning I woke up to the powerful, rangy feeling of being inside of a body that was consuming itself until something was put inside of it to burn. This was an alert state of being. It was quite possible for this alertness to shift into anxiety, or even panic. We had brought only a fraction of the food we needed to survive.

If we wanted to put something in our stomachs, we had to hunt. There has never been a human that lived off the land in the Boreal Forest that did not eat meat, and usually that of the big four-legged moose, or caribou. This was not possible for us. We had no gun or bow or even a spear. Our hunt would be in the world beneath the surface of the cool water. There were countless thousands of fish there, a vast source of quality organic protein and oil that the two of us, moving quickly from lake to lake, could never deplete or harm. We could live on fish forever, as long as we could get to them.

I came to discover that hunting fish is the art of hunting other predators. Any fish of edible size is already an apex predator on top of an underwater chain that begins with the plankton (activated by the long light, lake water temperature inversions, and churning waves) that are in turn eaten by the zooplankton and tiny larvae of insects and mosquitoes; that are preyed upon by the leeches, creek chubs, suckers, shad, minnows, and immature fish; which are in turn eaten by the smallmouth bass, walleye, northern pike, and lake trout that we caught for breakfast. These big predators can be lured to their death by the presentation of a crippled bait fish in their midst. Every predator in nature attacks the crippled and weak. It's the way of the natural world.

There is a way to fish for predators that involves lots of gear, casts, tangles, and frustration. Moses' flow-based fishing involved only one lure, and he never made a cast. Moses' lure of choice was a large white 'swim jig' with enhanced properties to mimic a prey in distress. Experience had shown him that this lure would catch every fish present. He never spent time trying any other bait.

The lure had a heavy metal head that was fused around a very sharp red hook. The body of the lure was a soft white plastic that had luminescent qualities. After exposure to the sunlight, it would emit a faint glow as it dropped down through the water. If the bright red hook was threaded exactly through the middle of the long and wriggling body, the bait would rock side to side and its tail would throb as it passed through the water, sending out a vibrational field. The big eyes of the lure mimicked a fish fleeing in wide-eyed panic; and the red of the hook a ribbon of blood. There was a small teardrop spoon of plated silver that hung just behind the head that added flash and more vibration. Everything about the lure telegraphed a wounded body fleeing for its life in a spastic motion.

THE REFLEX REACTIONS OF ANY PREDATOR ARE FAST—built to take advantage of a fleeting moment of opportunity. When the swim jig went by a big predator, they would find themselves hooked before they had a chance to 'think' about it and realize the lure was a fake. There are certain things that hook humans in just the same way.

Moses connected the swim jig to his line with a knot called the Palomar which he considered the strongest knot ever invented. We used a braided, low-stretch line that was incredibly tough with a very small diameter. The line resisted cutting by even the sharpest knife, but required careful handling. It was so strong and thin that it could lay the palm of your hand open to the bone if you happened to grab the line with a big fish on.

The fish-line was threaded through the eye of the red hook in one direction, then back again the other way. Moses then tied a simple overhand knot with the doubled line, and passed the lure through the loop he'd just created. He cinched the whole thing tight by wrapping the line-end around a stick and pulling. He finished off the knot with a drop of superglue to hold it in place, so that the thin line would not slip through the tiny opening between the shank of the hook and the eye. The tube of high-tech glue seemed incongruous with our primitive surroundings and with the spirit of 'going light', but Moses was not a purist. His version of simplicity was to find the best and lightest functional fit for the task at hand; and that tiny drop of glue, used every day without exception, was not a violation of The Rule. The glue supported our little knot—the weakest link in our food chain—and was an insurance policy against starvation.

Moses never used my discount store rod and reel. His was a rod of exceptional quality made of composite graphite, matched with an open-faced spinning reel. The reel had an ultra-smooth drag made of nine highly machined ball bearings. I heard those bearings whining every day as Moses played out line to a struggling fish, making it pay for every foot of movement as it tired before finally giving up the fight and surrendering to the surface.

We did not cast the lure. Instead, we trolled it behind the boat in a precise way that required real concentration and that yielded immediate results if done properly. The lure was put out and fluttered to just the point where the white body faded from sight, but not so far that we lost connection with it. There was a trolling speed which Moses considered optimal: fast enough and constant enough so that the lure would continue to look alive and deceive the fish, but slow enough that the lure would achieve proper depth and vibrate at the perfect spastic frequency. Constant small changes in the lure's speed were essential to Moses' idea of good fishing. He taught me to keep a close eye on the exact vibration of the lure as its pulsations came up through the line to the sensitive tip of his rod. He kept the rod between the rear seat and his leg, and used the boat to vary the speed of the lure, making minute changes in speed and direction with his beavertail paddle. Strikes would often come when the speed changed for an instant, or when the lure bounced off a rock or log, creating a millisecond pause that triggered the bigger fish to attack the bait.

With the lure out, we maneuvered the boat along the shoreline, working drop-offs, points, ledges of rock, and other structures so that the bait would ride just a foot or two above the bottom and occasionally make contact with a rock or sunken log. This kept the lure continuously in the 'strike zone'—the short distance a fish might move away from its safe cover to ambush the bait.

His method worked. It was fish in the morning and fish at night. We ate the white and flaky meat of the walleye, and the dense and oily red meat of the lake trout (which was not a trout at all, but a large cousin of the arctic char). We took only what we needed; but the rain was cold, the weight heavy, and our movement swift. Moses and I ate four or five fish a day (each), unless we caught a big pike or trout that could feed us both. Since very little food was being stored outside our bodies, we had to go back to the old way. The old way was to store as much as possible inside. I came to appreciate how a hunting party in these lands could eat half a moose, and be hungry again in a couple of days.

I ate the fish thankfully, ravenously. If we fished poorly, we went hungry. It was just that simple. But it rarely happened. We turned our hunger into an exercise in flow. Each of the steps was clear. We hunted fish to live, and I was grateful for them and for the life they gave me. I could only hope that what I might create in the end would justify the cost.

TO SUPPLEMENT OUR DIET OF FISH AND RICE, we took advantage of every opportunity to gather other wild food. This was a different flow practice, one that involved always being awake and attentive to the nourishment that nature presented. The most concentrated sources of food were the rose hips and blueberries that could be found in the fire meadows everywhere along our route. Almost any place where the berry picking was good was a place touched by fire—new Jack Pines sprouted by the thousands there, along with the blueberries and tangles of wild roses. Jack Pines were trees with tough seeds that could only be opened in a furnace of heat. Low lying, sun-loving plants thrived in the open fire-meadows, having temporarily won the competition for sunlight with the aid of fire from the sky.

The berries were small, but full of sun-sweetness and tartness that exploded flavor into our mouths as we munched the fruit down along with small bits of stalk and the occasional leaf. Not a single nutrient was lost as we ate them right off the plants. Our fingertips were stained blue as the juice worked into the smallest fissures of our skin. Those blue molecules were tiny enough to travel into the apertures of our eyes and the smallest spaces between the synapses of our brains, bringing their healing properties, their chi force, their life. This was good food—living, raw, and wild.

For me, the diet worked miracles. All of the weakness and the flaccidness of my 'Chicago body' left me, and my flesh began to grow strong and more beautiful. I could see the distinct shape of all my muscles for the first time. I *had* muscles for the first time. And there were no 'ups' or 'downs' to my attention here. I became increasingly alert during the day, and more relaxed at night. All my mood swings left me. Without all of the sugar and processed food, it became easier each day to stay open, joyful, and alert. When I was awake, I was awake. When I was asleep, I was asleep. And when I was awake, I noticed that there were a couple of fishing lures that we carried despite never using them—a strange spoon-shaped lure with red eyes and a white in-line spinner. They seemed to be in violation of The Rule. I was tempted to ask Moses about them, but chose to stay quiet, like a good student, and wait for their purpose.

Fulcrum Six: The Power of Perspective and the Art of Attention.

Moses and I were moving day after day within a landscape that was both beautiful and deadly. I was still under The Rule—none of that had changed. This meant that there was to be only one crossing over any portage. The tortured portages of my first days were like garden walks compared to the passages we now faced. Many of the trails were no more than animal by-paths across some of the most rugged country on earth. It was true that we were 'going light,' but one of us had to carry the canoe across the portages, and the other had to carry all of the gear.

Wilderness movement under load—especially under the canoe—threw me off-balance, drenched me with sweat, and involved a level of pain that ground me to bits. The consequences of poor movement were extreme: one slip, one fall, or one torn knee could literally be the end of me. We were carrying no communication device. There would be no floatplane to take me out. The only rescue was not to have an accident in the first place.

Moses had deliberately dialed up this level of risk to cultivate the art of attention. I was sure about that. Oh, he'd pretend that moving through this country was not much of a feat for a 'man' like me. After all, my ancestors had walked through forests for thousands of years! I could learn to walk through them again as well, he said. But I had no doubt that if Moses were guiding someone else they would all be paddling in a small circle somewhere close to the road while enjoying a grand fishing trip and a lifetime of campfire memories. But no. He'd reserved a special type of trip for me; one which involved daily physical pain. Dealing with pain required the utmost level of free attention and full commitment.

THE PHYSICAL PAIN OF WILDERNESS TRAVEL forced me to change the physical structures of my mind. That was the whole idea. The only way to defeat the pain of the wilderness was to watch my old mind with a brand new mind that was coming online every hour of every day.

This practice had two parts. The first part might be called 'pure witnessing,' which, in a nutshell, was the cultivation of the ability to see myself from 'the next level higher.' I was to observe what was happening to my body, and to know that I, as observer, was more than my body; to observe the contents of my mind, and to know that I, as observer, was more than my mind; to observe the contents of my dreams, and to know that I, as observer, was more than my dreams; and so on. This 'witnessing practice' was designed to create freedom, and to put the multiple selves that make up any human being under the observation (and ultimately the control) of a vastly more expanded Author of the self.

The second part of the process (the 'active' part of 'active witnessing') was to consciously choose what lenses I would use to witness what was going on—what attitudes the new Author would take towards the thing observed. Moses gravitated towards three special lenses through which to view the world—what he called the three 'primary lenses of the Expanded Self.' These special lenses were: (1) the practice of *courageous curiosity* about anything and everything that was arising; (2) the practice of *seeing beauty* (especially under conditions that once were considered difficult); and (3) the practice of *gratitude*.

I LEARNED THE POWER OF PERSPECTIVE as I looked with curiosity into the pain caused by movement through the wilderness. I noticed that the torment of movement under a load contained none of the sharp, tearing sensations that indicated real trouble. The weight was intense and pressing—yes—but it was a pain that could be observed.

And as I observed the pain, I could also observe that I was not dying. In fact, just the opposite; I was getting stronger.

I began to witness what was happening in a state of *courageous curiosity*, the first of the three primary lenses of the Expanded Self. Moses encouraged me to be boldly curious about the pain. Any lower state of mind—like self-pity, fear, or anger—would not do. According to Moses, courageous curiosity was a fulcrum-point. If I could get to a place where I was foolhardy enough to be curious about the pain, it wouldn't own me anymore. I would literally be on top of it. Then all of the higher states—like joy and exhilaration—would become accessible, even while the pain was still there as a constant.

Moses taught me a practice of 'breaking my mind in two' to deal with the pain. One part of my mind stayed focused on the sensations of my body—monitoring them as I played the edge, to make sure that I did not pass into a state of real danger. With this monitoring in place, another part of my mind was freed to look out into the world. Moses taught me to look keenly at the path, to see the gradations of slope, slickness, light, and color; and then let go and let my body remember how to walk in the enchanted forest. It was in my genes, he said. As long as I was fully present and curious, my body would remember how to move on its own, and start to go somewhere better.

The final task was to see it all through the other primary lenses of the Expanded Self: to practice the feeling of *gratitude* and to *seek beauty* everywhere.

There was beauty available in every glance as I moved in pain. The sun moved in shafts of light through the trees; its light falling on pine leaves; the smell of those leaves coming up as summer heat from the forest floor; with glimpses of blue water and sky. All could be seen even with a canoe on my back. Even if the pain became so great that my eyes could not focus, there was still beauty in the power of the deep breaths in my body, in the feeling of strength, in the continual sense of moving into new and unexplored country. Seeing beauty protected me. Beauty put my mind into a joyful flow, and my body followed right along. All I had to do was to witness everything gratefully—all of it—all of the pain and all of the beauty—as one piece of exquisite nature.

MOSES INVITED ME TO DISCOVER a final 'viewing habit' to round out my experience with the power of perspective. This was the decision to interpret everything as part of a process that was going somewhere better. He asked me to adopt an *evolutionary interpretation* of my experience.

For Moses, evolutionary interpretation was a practice of emotional intelligence involving a conscious choice to interpret an event in such a way that the event was seen as the beginning of a future that led somewhere better. He wanted me to interpret the present as a future-in-the-making—a future that curved toward greater transparency, love, and the fundamental realization that everything is interconnected. He wanted me to see that my interpretation of the present moment was a reality-creating event that I had the power to improve.

He encouraged me to re-interpret a negative experience and see it as an opening doorway. For example, as we pushed northward, I often experienced myself as a weakling in the face of our physical challenges. Yet there was no way to grow stronger without pushing into weakness. Moses encouraged me to interpret the feeling of weakness a deposit in a kind of savings account: experiencing weakness today was an investment in tomorrow's strength. It was a matter of 'evolutionary interpretation.' Pain no longer meant I was dying; it now meant I was investing. There was nothing that could not be re-interpreted as an opening door: conflict, pain, mistakes, even death.

Moses claimed that I could go even further, and begin to interpret my experience as the exact thing necessary to fulfill my highest intention. If I began to interpret my experience in the wilderness as my unique path towards becoming a 'vessel for the Divine,' I was *creating the exact path by which I would become just such a vessel.* I didn't know just how this interpretation-becomes-reality thing worked, but I could see that I was progressively choosing to experience myself as part of something larger. And even my dense little rational mind could understand that if I experienced myself as a Divine being, others might begin to see me this way also. I would then begin to act in a way that fulfilled their expectations, and a reinforcing loop would be set up. What was once my interpretation would gradually become a fact.

I discovered that I was a man with complete authority over the interpretation of my own experience. In this much at least, I had powers.

Waiting on the final fulcrums.

For many weeks, I practiced the first six fulcrums of the system designed by Moses.

He remained mostly silent about the final three powers: The Power of Synergy, The Power of Cosmic Luck, The Power of a New Identity, and their associated art forms. At this point I only knew about them through his vague references. I would learn much more about them in the days ahead. I needed to be stronger, he said, for the specific synergy he had in mind. I was not yet clear enough, he said, to surrender to my own guidance and receive the kind of cosmic luck that came with full surrender. It would be a "different kind of luck," he said, much different than the luck of things going my way, or turning out as planned.

The final power, the elusive promise of a new identity and its power to bend the Field also remained unclear. I had no idea who I was becoming. Yet, according to Moses, this hardly mattered. From the moment I'd stepped away from the old 500 and into the wilderness, I'd been leaving my old identity behind. Perhaps I *was* moving into a new and higher stage of development here. That wasn't for me to say. But I was quite certain that some new person was forming—that was undeniable. I could see the new Charlie in my body and feel the joy of him as I moved.

I chose to trust the process, to keep moving northward, and to wait and see who I was becoming.

WE'D PASSED MIDSUMMER. I knew this because the days had grown quite long—by my reckoning at least eighteen hours of daylight—and were now growing shorter. We moved every day, sometimes going where the wind blew; and often taking long detours to investigate whatever lake was of interest to Moses. It seemed like we did not have a definite destination, and that the journey itself was the goal. If there was a general direction, it was always northward, following the arrow of the compass.

Time, in a journey like this, had a quality quite unlike time in the city. Time was denser in the wilderness and capable of holding vastly more experience in the same rotation of the earth. Over many weeks, that dense time began to extend and expand. It was impossible to count the days. Such a task would have been like trying to count waves lapping onto a sand beach all afternoon. The very act of moving in the wilderness with Moses silenced the part of my mind that could count days or even find value in such a task. It was many days, yes. Weeks. A month. More. I lost track of the date, the month, and even the year.

ONE AFTERNOON, WE STOPPED to pick ripe blueberries in one of the fire meadows—a huge sloping dome of rock a half mile square. The fruit was in peak ripeness.

Moses was smiling at me with his lips stained blue, not quite able to keep his hat filled with berries as he gobbled them down stems and all. Charcoal from burned pines crunched under our feet. Moses was shoveling in berries by the handful and rolling his eyes back in his head like they were the finest French cuisine. I'd eaten my fill, and was following after him, putting berries into our small blackened cooking pot.

I looked down at the charred ground out of which so much abundance was flowing, then back up at Moses. *He's going to leave me soon,* I thought. The preparation is almost over. *It's coming.*

I felt a sudden concern that the summer would end before I'd completed my training. I decided to make a request.

"I think I understand the first six fulcrums, I really think I'm ready to learn what you have to teach me about synergy, surrender, my new identity, and all the rest," I said.

Moses turned and looked at me with his piercing blue eyes—sizing me up. "Very well, then," he said. "Perhaps it's time. But before I show you anything, why don't you take a run at calling in some additional energy. We've gone about as far as we can with training and discipline. Something more is now required. Energy always follows your thoughts and the desire of your soul and takes the form exactly suited. We're calling energy all the time, whether we realize this or not."

This was all new to me. I didn't really know what to do, so I just let my mind go blank. I focused on a patch of the blackened fire ground out of which all of the abundance was flowing.

Moses looked at me and cocked his head as if listening intently, then his expression changed as if he'd seen something startling, almost terrifying.

"This is unexpected. Very well then. Your quickening is coming to you, Charlie. You've already called it."

I retraced my thoughts, trying to find the exact thought that was in my mind the moment Moses' expression changed.

No, I thought. *That couldn't be.*

29: The Quickening

> The human form allows us to connect heaven to earth, and earth to heaven. Agape, the love, coming down; Eros, the love, going up. Two poles, both longing for our evolution, for the quickening that makes the very dirt come alive.
> ...*The Field Book*.

THAT AFTERNOON WE MOVED effortlessly over small lakes and several short portages, and camped early on an island towards the south end of a lake shaped like a fishhook. There were two bald eagles in the sky. The site for our camp that night was compelling, the sort of place that deserved the careful, handwritten notation on the map that said 'good camp.' We'd found a small island with an unusually large flat spot twenty feet above the water. The campsite was protected by a huge white pine. It was a solitary tree, growing well north of its range. Any tree that large was unusual in this country, and this one was likely more than a century old. It must have worked a taproot through the rock into water to grow to such magnificence.

The fishhook lake was weedy and full of big pike. Moses caught and released about a dozen fish before he found one that he considered the right size. It was a specimen about three feet long with a heavy belly, and was plenty of food for both of us. We made an early supper out of the pike and watched an evening weather pattern roll in. Towering summer thunderheads played with shafts of sunlight to create a magnificent display of light-fall and cloud. In some of the clouds lightning was moving. It was as if the lightning was alive, conscious.

After our supper, I drifted into an early sleep, a deep and innocent sleep that came on almost instantly. I was sleeping again the sleep of a child.

IN THIS WILDERNESS, storms often came at night. Some were full of big energy; starting as puffy white cotton ball clouds, then building into massive thunderheads as they moved across the western plains of Canada, pulling water up from the big lakes, to send it crashing down onto the greener, wetter parts of Ontario. The tenting, deadfalls, and position of our camp were all forms of preparation for the big nightstorm. No matter how mild the weather looked at sunset, Moses insisted that every camp be prepared for the 'big one'—the tent placed on high ground that would drain water and positioned with its rear to the prevailing wind; the knots tested; heavy rocks moved against big solid sticks to make dead-men to anchor the tent; the shelter taut and well erected to be more aero and hydrodynamic in heavy wind and water. Yet the hundred-year storm had yet to arrive. I'd only heard steady hard rain on the tenting at night that made a lovely, peaceful sound. It was a simple pleasure to be warm and dry and listen to the rain on the roof.

IT MIGHT HAVE BEEN two o'clock in the morning when I felt a hand shaking my shoulder.

"Get up. Get up now."

It was raining hard outside, and the tent cloth was sagging from the weight of water. There was nothing unusual about this—it had rained hard before.

"What the hell, Moses—it's the middle of the night."

At that moment the orange cloth of the tent became fully illuminated by intense white light. I could see Moses silhouetted against the tent cloth, fully dressed. A wall of sound hit my body like a shockwave. My nerves instantly jumped into high alert.

"Now! Right now! There is no time!"

"But I'm not...."

Moses had the tent flap open, and the rain was coming in. I was sleeping naked in my bag as usual. Moses took me under the arm and dragged my naked body out into the rain. Wet pine needles were under my soft, bare feet.

Moses had his boots on, running, and was holding me up under the arm as I hopped over the prickly ground. There was a flash behind us that provided just enough light to see down the shoreline to my right.

He was there.

He was standing on a little pinnacle of rock, half-naked to the sky, his arms outstretched in a gesture of invitation. The spirals and whorls and markings on his face were matched by deep etchings on his body. The etchings were concentrated in circles of complex symbols moving up from his lower abdomen to the notch at the base of his neck. The centers of the circles were glowing with diffused light. He turned his eyes to me.

There was another flash, and Moses picked me up and slung my body over his shoulders, holding my ankle and wrist with one hand the way a fireman carries a child out of a burning building. In this position I could only look backward with my head upside down and flopping. The Shaman was moving, bounding with tremendous leaps towards me. It was then I saw it coming down out of the sky.

It was fast: at a place ten thousand feet above us, then at the top of the pine, instantaneously. I could see it move: dense, thick, and twisting strands of shaggy white fire. Three ropes converged on the pine, each pulsing strobe-like in multiple shocks. The great tree that had stood atop this island for a century was now nothing but the final extension of those twisting ropes of fire. They penetrated the heart of the pine, exploding the top of it. The formerly dark and dense structure of wood was in an instant made translucent. The conifer revealed itself in light as the carrier of thousands of gallons of liquid through countless miles of vein and root, and every molecule of that liquid was now carrying a charge of tens of millions of volts. The ground and sky were linked together, and our little tent stood white.

The pressure of the shock wave hit us before any sound. We were not hit by the lightning bolt—that was not the danger. The danger came from the ground below us, the fan-roots of the high pine, which were alive and jumping with lightning fire, electrocuting the ground.

Moses' leap may have been triggered by the shock wave. He might have left the ground just before. The current itself arrived just after the flash but ahead of the sound—there was resistance from the sap and ground that slowed it just enough. The Shaman was leaping also, a meter or more in the air with his legs wide and his arms outstretched—his face held up into the rain like he was drinking nectar from the sky. We were all in the air—my naked body on the shoulders of Moses—when the ground began to change color. The roots were boiling.

It must have been the power of the three prongs together that changed time in that instant. While riding down the lightning bolt, time slowed. In this still-time Moses was leaping high into the air. A raindrop broke apart on his forehead. The leap of the Shaman took him through the air to a place just beside me, and he turned his head so that his single eye met mine. A force, his own lightning, was coming out of the Shaman's body. I'm sure that the force was centered just below his belly and fired just as fast as the bolt from the sky. The life-force that the Shaman fired in that instant was a different color than the lightning, a golden color that put an energy field around me. The field had conscious intention. The sole intention of his field was to protect me.

It was then that I chose it, or perhaps it chose me. It was an urge, irresistible. My left hand extended downward, and my right hand pointed toward the sky. At the precise apex of Moses' leap, I could see the roots of the pine snaking and leaping strobe-white in the ground. A tiny ribbon-root of white fire lit the ground just below my fingertips. In that instant, I had the powerful impression that the ribbon of fire was the energy of a conscious being who was extending himself to me through the lightning. I watched my fingers reach out. I touched the fire.

WE WERE ON THE GROUND rolling as our ears exploded from the concussive force of air pressure which came like a single cannon-shot. Moses was instantly up and looking at the sky. The lighting had disappeared from the top of the pine and had traveled back up into the heavens. Two huge limbs had exploded from the tree, the largest barely missing our tent. Bits of bark were everywhere. The core of the tree was on fire and hissing in the rain.

The Shaman knelt down next to me. The current had passed cleanly through my body, through my heart and out the fingertips of my right hand. I felt my heart stop, and then re-start in a deeper cadence and rhythm. On my left side, where the current had entered me, was a tracing like the delicate branching of fern leaves that flowed from my fingers and flared into spirals that intertwined my forearm. I lay on the ground unable to move, with my arms outstretched, in a state of vibration that was too heightened to feel any pain.

The rain now intensified and stung as it landed. The Shaman squatted next to me, and picked up one of the burning brands that littered the ground. I couldn't move and could only follow his movements with my eyes. Moses was on the opposite side of me, holding my burned arm, with tears of compassion streaking down his face.

The face of the Shaman was calmer. He looked for a moment like an ancient ape ancestor touching fire for the first time—the first ancestor with openness and curiosity; the first one of us not to run away, but to approach what had come from heaven; the first one to pick up fire from the sky. The Shaman blew out the torch, leaving a smoking stick with a red glowing ember on its tip. The carved man then looked over to Moses.

"He will not remember this until he has fully completed his journey, and returned to the world to give his gift," the Shaman said.

"He may never remember," Moses said.

"Yes. But he must hear his true name nonetheless. There is hope. She has seen it."

"Yes."

The smoking brand moved closer to my eyes, which began to involuntarily roll upward, looking into my forehead.

I heard the Shaman say these words, like words in a dream:

"You are Cronus, the very earth come alive, a Messenger-in-waiting and Keeper of the Field."

And then the brand touched my forehead, just above and between my eyes.

I began to slip away from the world. In the small window of consciousness left to me, I watched Moses bow his head slightly. The Shaman took the brand away from my forehead, extended it toward Moses' forehead, and touched a space just above the old darkened mark that was already there. Then the coal passed back across my body, and the Shaman touched his own forehead. There were two marks there already, and this new mark made a third. The Shaman then picked a warm chunk of blackened charcoal from the ground and crushed it into his palm. He rubbed the black soot into my wound, then into the wound of Moses, then into his own.

"There will be no going back now, only going forward."

"Yes," Moses replied. "A new generation has begun."

I felt the two men lift me up. The rain was coming in torrents mixed with small pebbles of hail. The air had developed a special clean quality, and I pulled it in through my nostrils. Held aloft, I felt like I was moving through space, free of gravity, as the purified air circulated through my outstretched body. I could not walk these first steps myself. It was my two fathers who carried me.

30: The Turning of the Wheel

There is The Field and limitless fields of view—perspectives that can be taken without grasping onto any one of them as final. There is the View, that contains everything, and points of view from which to act. These polarities dance in an easy flow without grasping; with limitless potential arising. The evolutionary intelligence guides everything and knows what to do. This is what we have to teach you.
...*The Field Book.*

I AWOKE inside the tent after a deep sleep. I had slept through an entire day and the following night, and awoke with my mind clear. I could remember nothing about what happened except for the image of the Shaman leaping, and my hand reaching down to touch a rope of fire coming down from the sky.

"He was here, wasn't he?" I asked Moses.

"Yes. Here and now gone. He came in from a camp to the north of us. He will not return."

Moses would say no more about it. We rested. The scars on my hand and arm ached, but were healing rapidly, more rapidly than any wound on my body had ever healed. Something had happened to my body that had increased its life force and allowed me to heal in ways that were impossible before. I touched the new mark on my forehead, wondering where it had come from. Moses would provide no information, only pointing to the second mark on his forehead, and saying that he too had been touched by fire.

In three days I felt ready to travel again, and Moses and I set out together.

THERE WAS DEEP WARMTH welling from the forest floor, but some of the green aspen leaves were now flecked with gold, and the deltas of their veins and the circles of their cells stood out in sharp relief as I held the leaves up to the sun. *The autumn will come quickly here as the days begin to shorten,* I thought. I pressed three aspen leaves into the Field Book. I had yet to find a five-petaled flower like the one that had come out of the book when I first opened it in the living room of my brownstone. I'd looked everywhere for such a flower across the miles of wilderness, but had not yet found one. Moses said that the flower would arrive at its own chosen moment, and that "sometimes you must stop seeking to find what is right in front of you." I still kept looking.

Moses had gone quiet, running deep. The fire had changed him in some way, just as it had changed me, and he had lost all interest in communicating with words.

We spent the day moving quickly and quietly in shared silence, with no sense of awkwardness or distance to be bridged. Ahead of us was a bald of granite rock that grew progressively closer. Such a dome was a rarity in this wilderness which had been so thoroughly sanded down by thousands of years of wind, water, and glacial ice.

By lunchtime we'd reached the base of the dome, and Moses suggested we climb it to see what was at the top. I felt resistance to the suggestion. There was no trail through the woods. All walking through this country was difficult and dangerous, and an unmarked route that took us steeply uphill without any climbing gear sounded like a recipe for disaster. But Moses seemed certain that we should go up, so I went along.

We started to climb, with Moses taking big energetic strides. The aerobics of the hike seemed to release his energy, and I struggled to keep up. It was hard to move with him as he strode and pulled himself up the hill. Within moments we were above the pines and pulling ourselves upward by grabbing the limbs and trunks of aspen. The living aspens were quite strong and flexible, supporting all of our weight and making our hands sticky from their reddish sap, but the dead ones broke in our hands, letting us slide back down-hill, grabbing air.

Moses extended a hand to me after one such slide. He wrapped his powerful fingers around my forearm, and my left hand wrapped around his. The scars were nearly healed, and my grip was stronger, better than before. *I've made gains*, I thought.

We reached the upper part of the dome. A smooth granite face without trees presented itself. We found a very rough, tiny streambed that cut the face of the big rock and provided foot and handholds. Despite the heavy rains of a few days ago, the small gutter was dry. There were lichens of infinite variety and color spreading over the rocks—primitive plants of bright red, yellow, and electric orange that grew on the hard surface like rough, microscopic mushrooms. Curly grey-brown lichens that crunched and broke underfoot grew on top of their brighter cousins. I stepped carefully to avoid crushing them. We were making the first human trail up this rock face as far as I could tell, and I wanted to leave it without marks. The ancient plants were abrasive like coarse sandpaper, and provided a good gripping surface for the fingertips.

I was sucking wind and taking deep breaths as we pulled our bodies up the cliff. Moses stopped on a small ledge to catch his breath, but in less than thirty seconds he was ready to move again. We worked our way up the rock-face that grew steadily steeper until it became almost vertical.

Moses looked up the precipice, scanning for a route that would get us to the top. He had a look of intense focus and concentration, quite different than his usual open and expansive state. He seemed set now on the summit, as if he needed to see something there.

I could see no way to get any further without risking our lives. We were already taking unnecessary risks, and a way back down was already in doubt. Yet, Moses continued to press upward.

The cut that we were following snaked around the north side of the dome, and as we rounded the corner the little streambed abruptly ended, leaving us only a smooth granite face. A lot, quite a lot, could go wrong here very quickly. We'd abandoned any pretense that this was a pleasant way to stretch our legs. We were now rock-climbing. My body shifted its awareness. *Free climbing requires at least three contact points at all times with only one point moving.* The eyes move with the moving part to its new contact point, making sure the contact is secure before lifting off from another place, then the eyes lift, and another contact point is found. *Repeat.*

I had no idea where this new information about climbing had come from, but it seemed right for this situation. It had simply arrived at the needed time.

"We've reached a point where there's no going back," I said to Moses.

"We left that point long ago," he replied. "There is something that must be done at the summit."

"Very well, then."

A couple of months ago, I would have registered a complaint, analyzed my options, or searched for a way back down. Now I simply scanned the cliff face for a route across. And there it was. I started across, leaving Moses behind. I saw my fingers against the rock face, and the strong tendons in the back of my hands. The hands were etched from dirt and wind, and their scarred grooves and veins matched the weathering of the granite. My mind grew quiet and focused, and I was able to observe irregularities in the rock that created places for fingerholds. About six feet across the face there was a place where I could easily grip with four fingers and hang if I wanted. The surface was not quite as sheer and vertical as it seemed. I cleared the traverse, and Moses followed. It was then an easy scramble to the top of the dome.

I'D READ ONCE that for every thousand feet up, the ecosystem changes as if you'd traveled a hundred miles north. If you go far enough north, you reach a line where the trees can no longer grow. An even deeper simplicity begins there; a vast low quiet of tundra that circles the dome of the world.

There was a hollow spot on the top of this high outcrop that was filled with low bushes and rainwater. The moss and lichens here were of a different species than those down at lake level. We had climbed into the high and clear space of the tundra.

We could see in every direction. The sky was full of movement, with scuttling clouds and deep shafts of light powering through. There was a rainsquall far to the northeast. I focused my eyes south, and could see the lakes we'd been traveling, just as they appeared on the map. Ribbon Lake, if it was there at all, was lost in a bluing haze caused by the sun's pull of moisture up from the swamps and lakes. We were a long way from where we'd started. The wind was blowing warm across the rock face, evaporating the sweat of our exertion. I had the sense that everything was present, and that we could go anywhere from here.

I looked over to Moses. He was turning, with his arms held outward. One palm faced the ground and the other was open to the sky as he spun in the clear wind. *This is the end,* I thought. *He's ready to let me go.*

"This is a good place for your soul to decide where it needs to go for its completion. A beautiful high place, isn't it? Ahhh … look there!"

My gaze followed to where Moses was pointing. There, in a small indentation, was an aspen tree. It was no more than a second year sapling in height but I knew it was far older by the way it was gnarled by the wind. An individual aspen tree is usually just one stem of a single giant organism. This living union of trees forms a grove that can live for many hundreds, even thousands of years. Moses said there were aspen groves that have lived as a single body for more than eighty thousand years.

I looked down the hill toward a stand of beautiful aspen that ringed the mountain about three hundred feet below us. *Maybe this little sapling is their astronaut, the one they sent up to a high and far place, to start something new.*

Moses went over to the little tree and passed his hand underneath it. Four aspen leaves—each small, but still green, perfectly formed, and beautiful—fell into his hand. *He didn't pick those. That tree just gave him four fresh leaves.*

Moses took one of the leaves and twirled it in his fingers, then let it fall. He picked the leaf up again, then again; twirling it and letting it fall, twirling it and letting it fall.

Each time the leaf fell, it followed a different arc as it fluttered down. I found myself watching again; just as little Charlie had watched the ball. Nowhere else to go, nothing else to do.

I began to release into something new. There was an arc of energy between Moses and me. As teacher and student, we were two poles of one singularity.

I could feel the arc of energy between us as I watched the falling aspen leaf. I looked at Moses lifting the leaf and dropping it; lifting and dropping. *What I am experiencing now is his ordinary mind,* I thought. *He has flow consciousness—never fixed. His mind is as supple as that aspen leaf. That's why he's always so interested in everything and never seems to tire. His mind is not divided—never working against itself. It flows.*

It was then, without a single word being spoken, that I received a transmission of the eighth fulcrum—the energy teaching—straight out of the mind of Moses.

MOSES WAS EXCHANGING ENERGY with Source, and was doing this on many levels simultaneously, beginning with his physical body. His body was well aligned in ways that could be seen by any observer, but these alignments were even clearer when seen from the inside. He moved from a center that ran from the top of his head down the central axis of his body and continued like a plumb line into the earth. The natural architecture of his physique was in constant dynamic adjustment around this fluid center, allowing him to move with the grace and efficiency of a dancer. His weight was held low in his abdomen.

His body shone with a vital radiance that spoke of proper nourishment, wholesome exercise, plenty of sunlight and fresh air—a body that possessed the calm, open, and joyful sense that came from serving a mind that was flowing at ease. All the cells and molecules were working together to emerge as a single vessel that felt like it had been spoken—complete and perfect—out of the mind of the creator.

I could see and sense many nested fields of energy around him, each with its own intelligence. One was roughly the size of his physical body and close to his skin; and another was a golden orb three feet around his physical form. There were spinning openings that radiated from the front and back of his body through which he was able to receive information from other sources of intelligence.

All of these subtle fields had their individual consciousness, but were also organized within a larger field. There was a place near the base of his breastbone, in the middle of his chest, that was gathering energies and generating a field that flowed out of his heart. Moses was experiencing that field as a baseline of loving connection with everything. The field of love, what I had imagined as the pinnacle, was for him only the starting point. *Heaven is already here for him and everything is growing on top of it,* I thought.

I could finally see that Moses was a matrix of multiple intelligences and fields of light. He was a connection of many energies that were all conscious and alive. I realized now, without doubt, that I was in the presence of a master. This man had the ability to regulate the chemical state of his body; to observe and control the thoughts of his mind; and to hold the frequency of love. His profound influence arose not from his ability to dominate, but from his ability to expand his field. When there was something to be brought into alignment, he simply expanded himself, and experienced the 'problem' as a part of himself to be cared for. He then focused his internal awareness on the cared-for thing and let it be aligned by his field and bathed in the light. He had been holding me in his light all of this time. That's why the miracles were happening to me.

As I experienced the consciousness of Moses, something passed between us. It was a gift. There was a transfer of part of his awareness into mine. I don't know how it happened; whether it was the current of the lightning strike; the long days here in the wilderness; or simply another gift of his energy. But my awareness shifted, and for a moment *my consciousness could flow like his.*

Moses knew that I had seen him. Suddenly, he was finished. He stood up abruptly, took the four leaves, and cast them into the air. The transmission immediately stopped, and I was back inside my ordinary awareness. The leaves rose and intertwined, creating a twirling crown thirty feet above our heads, spinning there as if they were waiting for instructions. And then, under the power of the wind, they were taken off northward, like things alive. I watched them spinning and traveling swiftly until they faded from sight. I had the unmistakable feeling that the leaves had been called by someone, and that I was about to experience my first taste of the ninth fulcrum. Some form of unexpected luck was about to arrive.

Moses looked at me and smiled the deepest, warmest smile that I had yet seen on his chiseled face. He tipped his hat to me in a gesture of parting. He then turned and began to rapidly descend the dome.

THE WESTERN FACE of the dome offered us a long broad descent through the aspen grove. We then followed the shoreline through a stand of jack pines, and emerged where our boat was pulled up on the shore. Moses took the stern seat, and I was in the bow as we pushed off.

After just a few strokes, I began to hear moving water. It was a pleasant sound; a roar of water plunging into the lake and the gurgling of rapids. We paddled around a corner, heading into a narrows between cliffs where the lake was fed by a small river cascading in from the north. There was calm, slick water made by the wind shadow of cliff walls on the western shore. The river poured through the narrows, forming a chute rapid about a hundred yards long that funneled thousands of gallons of pure frigid water from the lake above to a deep pool below. The rocks of the chute were smooth, sanded clean by endless sheets of falling water. The rapid was no more than twenty feet wide and a couple of feet deep, and alongside the neck of moving water were long bare shoulders of smooth granite. I could see heat rising from the black surfaces, and guessed that they were thirty or even forty degrees warmer than the shade of the pines just a dozen yards away. The black granite glistened with veins and particles of quartz—a perfect place to be lulled by the voices of falling water and lie naked in the sun with warm, smooth rock against your back.

I was the first to see her.

PART FIVE:

THE NIGHT JOURNEY

31: Her

You've come here to open the gate. A larger reality waits beyond.
    ...*The Field Book*.

SOMETHING DARK was in the water, flowing down from the top of the chute. It couldn't be. I watched dark strands flowing in the falling water as it came closer. It let out a high pitched cry—an exuberant thrill-ride scream bursting into the air, which fell silent as it plunged feet-first into the deep pool in front of us. It surfaced and swam easily to the bank.

    I felt that I should not be watching, but really there was nowhere else to go. There was no way to turn the boat around fast enough to avoid seeing her body. I could have looked away, but my eyes just flowed from the surface of the pool over to the glistening black shore line and connected to her, the same way my eyes connected to the light coming down a line of trees or to the endless depth of a river of stars in a clear night's sky. The water flowed in sparkling sheets down her body, thicker in the middle where the point of her long black hair came together in a strand at the center of her back. She climbed out of the water and bent slightly to take large steps up the sloping bank. The muscles of her thighs and buttocks sprang out in definition, and her back formed a deep 'V.' She gained the bank and reached her right hand behind her to pull her hair to the front and side, twisting it to wring some of the water onto the rocks. She must have seen us then out of the corner of her eye.

She looked away for an instant, and then in a slow deliberate motion, she began to turn toward us. Her head and shoulders turned first. She was looking over her shoulder and smiling, as if she knew that something wonderful was about to happen. Then her body slowly began to uncoil towards us, her feet moving last, turning around to face us fully. Her stance was open and balanced on her bare feet. She seemed light, very light, and her hands hung loosely at her sides. She paused for a moment, assessing us. Then she turned her palms slowly towards us, raising them slightly in a gesture of complete openness and greeting; the same greeting given by the man-dressed woman who had appeared to me at dawn in the forest behind the Initiative's encampment. She looked down at us from the rock, smiling softly. Deep blue eyes. No anxiety. No shame. No fear. Just gazing at us, the same gaze as a young mother looking in love at her child running in play in the soft light of a summer's evening after the day's work is done.

I'd seen beauty before, but beauty had never before come across space as an energy force to strike me full, as this did. I felt a flow of energy, a tangible, physical current travel across the water into my body. It started slightly outside my body below my torso, and surged like a column of tingling heat, grabbing the pit of my stomach and moving up my spinal column and out the top of my head. A shiver ran across my shoulders, down my back and the outside of my arms, then out my fingertips. I felt a compelling urge to jump out of the canoe right now and swim across the pool with my clothes on and merge with the body standing there on the rock. I wanted to come home to it, to get inside it, to put every inch of my skin against it. At the same time I wanted to jump out and hide in terror under the cold water so that she couldn't see me. Someone had just turned on a blowtorch. I had to stop these feelings; but I couldn't stop them: there was nowhere to run or to hide. I was frozen in my seat, locked on to some beam that she was projecting into me. All I could do was look at her.

She was strong. Stronger than I was. Her skin was a deep, reddish brown that glistened wet from the lake water clinging to its surface, but that also glistened with a glow more felt than seen. The fall of light made it hard to see her face clearly—a background of energy lit her from behind. She had strong thighs with chords of muscles clearly visible. They were the legs of someone who had been ranging wide over rough terrain, taking big steps, and carrying bodyweight in the wilderness every day of her life. Her torso could have been cut from a stone, but it was very much alive and radiating. The cold water had tightened her skin, and her breasts were full and firm with the nipples erect and pointing slightly up and outward. The breeze was blowing the moisture off her skin, raising gooseflesh that in turn was being feathered down and fully warmed by the sun. The muscles of her stomach were cut down the middle and divided into sections with a very slight softness. She was unshaven, with small tufts of soft hair under her arms, and another soft narrow line of hair curling up to her navel. The up-curling of her body hair was unlike the triangle of other women, and added to the impression that she was elfin and otherworldly. On her upper arm was a band with interwoven strands which I now recognized as a triple helix. At her feet were four aspen leaves, each small but still green, fresh, and beautiful.

Moses maneuvered the canoe against the incoming current. Normally the bow came into a landing spot first and the bowman would extend a leg to fend the bow off the rocks then hop out knee-deep to pull the canoe parallel to the shore. Moses must have noticed that I was sitting slack-jawed, transfixed, and incapacitated, so he backed the stern into the steep granite bank, slid out, and found a place to rest the back of the boat so it would not tip as it wobbled on the keel-plate. I sat in the bow, a few feet into the deep water, and watched Moses walk up the bank. This was a man who had been in the wilderness for many months without respite, sinewy and tough, with more pain in his joints from hard labor than he would ever disclose. He walked the few feet up the bank with the gait of a person finishing a long endurance challenge—taking strong final strides that would soon be shortened or stopped in the presence of an imaginary line just ahead. Beyond that line was rest, comfort and solace—a place where the journey could end for just a moment. He walked up to her. There was a visible release of tension in his shoulders, like a burden had been put down. He bowed his head slightly and lowered his eyes.

I'd been traveling with Moses for weeks across some of the most rugged country on the planet. Rain squalls and scorching sun; stinking black swamp and slippery steep rock; the pain of the yoke and strap; and no place to rest but on the hard and open ground. I'd never seen him lower his head. His blue eyes sometimes closed, but they were nearly always open—focused intently on a task or gazing in soft focus at the beauty that he saw all around him. If there was any single word that could describe Moses it would be 'unbowed.' Yet, in the presence of this woman, I watched him take off his cap and lower his head. My body was shaking softly as I watched.

She took his head in both of her hands and kissed him deeply on the forehead below his wild and matted hair. Her left hand then fell away. She pulled back slightly and turned her right hand so the back of her fingers caressed his cheek. His right hand came forward and clasped hers. Their eyes met. Something was passing between them. No, not that. It was a field that suddenly came into view for a moment, something that they were both inside, breathing deeply into. Moses was slipping into a sensual, re-invigorating bath of her energy field, and his body had just come open to it. I had the strong impression of a meeting between beings that knew each other most intimately; but it was not a meeting of equals, or lovers, or even friends. It was more like a meeting of members of two different species sharing a deep energetic bond of consanguinity and common purpose. *This is a member of the 'Committee' Moses has been talking about*, I thought. *He's a junior member, the worker bee. She is his superior. He has capacities—hard won—no doubt about that. But she, she has* powers.

I stood there witnessing their interaction. I sensed nothing but deep respect passing in both directions; his respect for something higher, clearer, and beyond himself; her respect for what he had done, starting from scratch, with his commitment, discipline, and attention. She kept her focus on Moses, not turning to me. Yet there was a feminine voice speaking inside of my head.

"*—If you can come to sustain the Field inside a human body, even the angels take notice, Charlie. Even the angels fall quiet in the face of what's been achieved.*"

And then with her hand still against his face, she turned to me, smiling softly. I became immediately aware that I hadn't washed for weeks.

"So, welcome, Charlie. Do you plan to stay?"

It was a question so direct and simple, yet when *she* asked it, I felt at least a dozen levels in it. Did I plan to stay with the two of them in camp tonight? Was I planning to leave everything for good and join them in whatever project they were engaged in up here? Was I planning to stay in the kind of consciousness the two of them seemed to be enjoying? Or was she a beautiful woman standing in the door of her impeccable apartment, asking me if I wanted to cross the threshold into a night of the most exquisite intimacy imaginable?

I looked down at the packs. I could feel a rush and burning down my neck and across my face. I had no reply. I could only look down. She turned to Moses.

"Let's help him out," she said.

Moses broke off their embrace, and walked back to the canoe, crouching down and swinging the bow of the boat toward the shore so I could get out. I watched her as she moved with a long fluid erectness across the rock to a spot where a pair of pants and a shirt were drying on a branch. She put the shirt on, buttoning just one of the seven or eight buttons, and then turned the pants over, declining to put them on. She came down the rock face barefoot to help unload the canoe. Her slight covering did nothing but create more lines and shadows falling across her body that enhanced the sheer power of her presence. I felt a churning in my lower belly, like something solid had just turned into a roiling, stringy mass.

I managed to get up out of my seat without looking at her, and immediately misplaced my foot, causing me to slide down the steep granite and into the drop-off below the pool. I was suddenly soaked to the chest and grasping onto the slick bank to avoid going deeper. She and Moses both grabbed my wrists and hoisted me onto the bank. I felt like a raw beginner who had never disembarked a watercraft before.

We began the familiar task of unloading and setting up camp. I was thankful to be able to turn my eyes to the knots and tent poles so that I would have something to look at instead of her body. There was a beautiful flat spot just back from the falls that was perfect for the tent. It was the most air and light-filled campsite I'd seen. Moses and the woman went down to the lakeshore to bring up our canoe and the last of the packs. Her boat was already in the middle of the camp, turned over and wedged with rocks to make a table.

The watercraft sitting there in the dappled light was surely a canoe, but one *so* different than the rented aluminum boat that we'd been paddling as to deserve another name entirely. I went over to have a look at the boat. Everything about it expressed a character of quality. It was about two feet longer than mine, narrower in bow and stern, and made of glowing, beautiful bent cedar-wood covered in waterproofed canvas. The thwarts and carrying yoke were of a different, lighter wood—probably ash. The bottom showed a meticulous workmanship of steam-bent wooden ribs connected to the curved bottom planking with lines of clinched brass nails. On the bow-plate there was a polished brass plaque that read:

Mfg. by J. T. Seliga
THIS IS A GENUINE *SELIGA*
QUALITY CANOES

I rolled the canoe back over, and it snugged soundlessly into place.

There was no sign of a tent, but a quality silvergrey goose down sleeping bag was unrolled on an open spot, plumping up in the afternoon air. A Kelty pack and pack frame rested against a pine. *Maybe she didn't just drop from the sky after all.*

We began to swiftly set up camp. I was having difficulty focusing even on the simple well-drilled tasks of erecting the tent, preparing for fire, and rigging the rods to catch supper. She seemed to be everywhere just inside my peripheral vision—bending, crouching, and exposing herself. Everywhere to my right, then left, and behind me were flash-images of taut buttocks, soft curling tufts of black pubic hair sticking out from behind her as she knelt over, the dark channel of her breasts in her shirt, an erect nipple pressing through the material, the glistening of her arm band, the appealing timbre of her laughter, and a broad-lipped upturned smile. Love was in the air. I found myself crawling around, hunched and struggling with a confused mass of energy which included an involuntary erection. My body was just responding in the most natural way. I'd been in the woods a long time. *I wish she would put her pants on*, I thought. Clothing her would make me feel more comfortable. My own canvas pants were wet, cold, and confining as they continued to evaporate from the misstep just a moment ago. I really could do nothing about my response to her.

She appeared not to notice anything as she smiled and laughed with Moses, but I had the sense that she was quite aware of everything that was going on.

Again there was a woman's voice in my mind.

"—*Better get used to it, Charlie. Your body has to learn to contain* much *more energy than this if you want to hang out with us. Why don't you see if you can re-interpret your sexual feelings as energy—a deep gift of creative energy and intelligence that wants to accelerate you; to make you* sublime. *See if you can express the sublime energy out of your eyes, through your hands, and through your heart as well as where it's being directed at present.*"

I didn't know what to say. I didn't know how to respond to someone who was talking inside my head.

FINALLY THE CAMP WAS UP; the process had taken only a few minutes. She now turned her back to me and moved with hips swaying to the place where her pants were hanging on a branch. *Finally*, I thought. But she had no intention of getting dressed just yet. Instead she unbuttoned the only button she had going, and casually threw her shirt over a branch. She tossed her long black hair and turned to look at me over her shoulder.

"Are you up for a little slide?" she asked, and then sprang up away over the rocks. "Just let go and let it take you," she shouted over her shoulder. "It's easier that way."

Moses unlaced his boots, which came off with a sucking sound. He jettisoned his socks and stripped off his clothes, revealing a small white butt that had not seen sunshine in many a day. He followed her up the granite face. *Why not*, I thought. Why the hell not?

I got out of my wet protection suit and instantly felt warmer and better. I laid my pants in the sunshine next to hers. The granite was radiating an updraft of warmth, and there was a gentle cool breeze blowing up from the falls. This was a perfect place to dry out. My clothes had not been fully dry and warm for some time. It looked like her pants had been wet and cold as well, and she had simply taken them off to dry. Bare skin was much more comfortable under these conditions. Being nude was just functional—the right, simple, and wholesome fit for this situation. Airing the skin was no more than that—it had no other intention, meaning, or moral quality.

I walked up the rock face following the woman and Moses. My feet had become quite soft and wrinkly from the constant moisture in my boots, and the granite felt fabulous. The rock had been worn smooth by the tongue of water, but still had a coarse texture that provided a secure sense that I was on reliable footing. The stone was warm, and I was enjoying the parts of my feet as they came into contact with the granite. *Why not try walking like she does?* I thought. I put one foot directly in front of the other, the exterior edge landing first then rolling towards the middle to hold a center line that made my hips move more fluidly and sway from side to side. *This is softer—much less impact.*

I sashayed up the side of the water chute and watched something dark flow down from the top. It let out a high pitched whoop as it passed by me. The whiter, quieter body of Moses followed, turning sideways as it fell down the chute to disappear into the lake below.

I reached the top-point of the water slide, where thousands of gallons of water poured in from the lake above into a clear round pool below. I slipped into the current, and was suddenly taken by the force of gravity. The water was gasping cold except for an inch on its surface that might have been eighty degrees. I went down the chute spread-eagled. I tensed for a moment and made the mistake of trying to control my slide by grasping onto a nub of rock. I instantly recognized that trying to hold on was a prescription for ripping the tendons out of my forearm and being smashed to pieces by multiple G's of water pressure. I let go. There was nothing to do but to let the water take me.

I rode down the chute on my back, being twisted feet first, head first, sideways, and then back again. Any body part that touched the side of the chute came in contact with a bit more friction and became a pivot-point. My body fell down the rock like a turning leaf. The smooth granite felt fabulous on my back, pounding the muscles and popping the vertebra as I accelerated down the channel until gravity took me screaming over the ledge. I fell all akimbo into the deep, clear pool below.

AFTER HALF A DOZEN trips down the water slide, Charlie was a new man. There was something about the very cold water and the very warm air that whipsawed my system into a state of deep relaxation. It was delicious. Here, all I had to do was just open up a bit and rest. A good bit of the stress from the focused attention and training had been washed away on the first trip down the falls. Moses had put me under tremendous pressure just trying to get me ready, to get me strong. He'd succeeded; I was strong—so much stronger than I could even have imagined a couple of months ago. I doubted that I would recognize myself in a mirror.

We put our clothes on, which were now deliciously warm and dry. My shirt and pants felt much cleaner from the involuntary wash in the lake.

There were five nice lake trout suspended in a shirt hanging in a quiet eddy above the falls that had been caught earlier by the woman. No need to fish tonight. Moses prepared the trout and brought them up. Out of nowhere a miracle of fresh broccoli, zucchini, and crisp apples were produced from the woman's pack, along with a stick of fresh butter and a mountain of small ripe blueberries. There was a bit of cornmeal from somewhere, and we cooked the fish in fresh savory seasonings browned in butter. The left-over pan drippings made a delicious sauce for the vegetables. The woman piled my plate again and again—it seemed that my hunger was inexhaustible. Moses ate well too, and his face was aglow in her presence. Lines were erased from his face as he savored the food. She ate little, content to witness our enjoyment.

The sun was going down as the dishes were rinsed in the chute and the fire was built up. This was the time of night when we would typically flee into the tent against the swarm of night insects, but there was a fair breeze blowing up the chute and across the granite face. The night breeze here was even better than the wind across the sandy point on Ribbon Lake. The warm air was mixed with an occasional tongue of cold coming up from the lake pool. Each wisp of cold reminded me that despite the frolicking weather, this was still the deep north woods. Things could change here, and quickly.

I sat gazing at her in the firelight, the flickering glow making slight shadows on her face that accentuated her bone structure. Moses was quiet, looking into the fire. She moved over to me and placed her left hand in the middle of my chest, at the level of the heart, with her other hand behind my head. I rested my head on her hand. The hand on my chest was pulsing slightly, pulling deep breaths out of me. She was opening me. *This is getting dangerous, Charlie, dangerous to get much more open, to open up completely in the heart-place where she has her hand,* I said to myself. The woman sensed my resistance and sat back on her haunches, pulling her hands away. Just being next to her was enough. It was the best I could do at the moment.

I looked over to her, and for the first time could hold her gaze. "I'd like to know your name," I said.

She looked at Moses then back at me.

"I can be whoever you need me to be, Charlie—why don't you decide?"

This was exactly what Moses had told me the evening of my big catch at the ball field. Apparently members of the Committee did not have any pre-given names. *They've passed through the life of their old name into a new field of possibility,* I thought.

I recalled the old practice of naming in hope that the named would take on attributes suggested by the word. Women always had the most beautiful names—Constance, like that star above us in the night sky, Felicity ... Grace ... Joy. Yes. Joy. That had to be it.

"If I were to name you, it would be Joy," I said.

There was some moisture in her eye as she looked at me.

"I accept that name from you, Charlie. I'll hold it as a gift from the earth, and strive to be that for you."

We sat quietly for a moment looking at the fire.

"There's another question," I said.

"What's that?"

"Well, I was wondering. Why me? Why am I the one that's here? Why have you given me the Field Book, brought me all this way, and put all this effort into me?

"Well Charlie, it turns out that you have an aptitude for transformation. That's why you're here," she replied. "You have talent.

For someone who's spent most of his life being totally compliant, you are quite the little risk taker at heart," she said as she touched the brand-marks spiraling up my left arm, "and Moses tells me that you can consolidate gains faster than any candidate we have had in some time."

I looked over to Moses, who gave me a half-wink and a sidelong glance as he exhaled his rum-flavored smoke. All I had been doing was taking one step after the next under his guidance.

"I wouldn't be here without Moses," I said. "There's no way I would have taken the leap or learned much of anything without him."

"Yes, Charlie, you have that point exactly right. The process of transformation requires that you *act* on the impulse to move higher. It's good to have a friend to encourage you to act. And after the initial leap of faith, there's always a period of consolidation when you learn how to live at the higher level. You learn new skills, associate with new people, fall down repeatedly, and get up repeatedly. Learning a new level can take years, and almost no one can do it without support. But change does happen. There comes a day when someone who once only existed in your imagination is now walking around inside your skin as a daily habit: flesh and blood. Then you are ready to risk again."

"So, change is a pattern of risking and consolidating. Is that what you're saying?"

"Yes, Charlie. And I should mention that walking in faith towards a higher vision is not gambling. The universe *wants* to change for the better, and you are a bit of that universe, going with the flow. But even though the table's rigged, you still have to swim like your life depends on it, because it does."

The pine logs of the fire began to break in on themselves, producing a small circle of glowing coals.

"Very soon you will be given a chance to embrace even more, to live inside a bigger picture. There's always someone from the next higher level willing to reach a hand down, and make contact so we can feel their world, Charlie. We're not alone, you know—never really alone. And there is *always* more...."

Joy looked at me and saw the dozens of questions in my eyes. She smiled at me and glanced over to Moses who had begun to move toward the tent. "Rest now," she said pointing to the tent. "You will need all of your strength for what is to come, and it's coming sooner than you think."

With that she rocked back and settled into a cross-legged position on the ground. She closed her eyes, aligned her body, and began to breathe.

32: The Music

For those with ears to hear, the Truth is inside the music; in the space between words; or in the silence shared by two people who have traveled together.
    ...*The Field Book*.

THE STARS AND NORTHERN LIGHTS WERE WELL OUT as I moved away from the firelight toward the tent. Moses was already inside lying in his bag, back flat on the ground, facing upward. There was a silvery glint underneath his eyes. I had the feeling that he never lost consciousness, even in sleep. The lines on his face were smooth; his mouth turned up in a soft smile; his eyes closed and body still. *He's completed his part of the mission. He can finally relax.*

My body was also relaxing deep down. My eyelids were taken over by an involuntary brain that was simply and naturally closing off stimulation so that it could rest and repair itself. I lay barefoot on top of my sleeping bag with all of my clothes on. She came in last. She unbuttoned her shirt, pulled off her pants, and lay down between us.

The image of her lifting her arms over her head and pulling her clothes off was a force speaking to my body that began to ignite a bonfire in my spine. To make matters worse, she rolled up her pants and placed them as a bolster under her mid-back. This lifted her breasts up into the night air, cat-stretching her spine. She put the soles of her feet together and allowed her knees to flop open, stretching the chords of her inner thighs. I interpreted her undulating movements as an invitation to touch her. There was a thrilling tingle in every part of my body as I inched my right hand towards her—the same feeling that I'd felt years ago when I was thirteen and my hand first inched towards the hand of Elizabeth Jennings across the sticky vinyl seat in the Cosmos Theatre on Main Street in Prosperville. But Joy moved first. She rolled towards me and touched me lightly on the small darkened spot that marked my forehead.

Instantly my body was drenched by a flood of natural endorphins, dopamine, and sleep drugs of every kind. They were irresistible. It was as if she had turned on a spigot of natural wonder drugs from some bacchanal organ deep inside my brain. I was in a delicious chemical strait-jacket and was unable to lift even the first finger of my hand. The bonfire was still in my spine, but there was no reserve of tension whatsoever to even raise a wrist.

Joy propped herself up on a forearm, letting the ringlets of her hair fall across her breasts. I could feel her looking at me with the same loving gaze with which she'd greeted me earlier, the unconditional loving gaze of a mother looking at her fair-haired child.

"You are projecting too much of your energy onto me," she said. "It would serve you better to keep it for your own use until you are more fully formed."

All I could do was to let my head roll to the side and look into her blue eyes.

She continued. "I'm participating in this dance with you so you can feel energies in the depths of your body. Moses has taught you a foundation of good practice. I am demonstrating another foundation, the foundation of energy at your very root, so you don't find yourself in a house cut off from its power supply. This pure creative energy is coming from the engine at the root of your body. In your undeveloped state you are experiencing this energy as sexual, but there are other interpretations."

There was no doubt that I was feeling powerful energies. They were a gift from her, and I was sure that she did not want me to repress them. On the contrary, she wanted me to feel everything quite intensely, even *exquisitely*. Yet, she didn't want me to express those energies either. She wanted me to hold them for a while. I felt like a pot cooking in an alchemist's secret chamber.

"The last spiritual age was all about getting out of our animal condition, all about getting someplace away from the 'depravity' of our bodies—to 'excarnate' ourselves," she said. "The next age will be about incarnation; the involution of spirit to meet the evolution of the body. The whole movement of heaven is now to get here, to get embodied, as was done by the Nazarene and other great teachers of the past. Not out of here and higher up but into here and deeper in. This will be the task of the next age, the next turning. *Embodiment* of spiritual energy will be the goal of the human race. To live in this new age your body must be able to contain energies that are vastly higher, faster, and brighter—with less space between trough and crest—than you can now experience. I am initiating you into some of these energies tonight, and I've stilled your body so you don't hurt yourself, or me."

She again touched the spot on my forehead. My body went into even deeper relaxation, and I again felt the delicious, nourishing feeling of being breathed. The breath was cooling, and the bonfire lessened somewhat.

"And now, Charlie, it's time for you to meet someone. She's invited you to her home, and has a gift for you."

I began to drift, then fall into sleep with every effort to stay conscious working in overdrive at the same time. *If there was one night in my life to be awake—why now*—why am I so relaxed—so relaxed. . . . Then Joy's voice came into my mind.

"*—The aim of our sacred magic is to liberate you for action in the world. Just let go and let us guide you, Charlie. It's easier that way.*"

THE DREAM BEGAN at the foot of a high tower, a fantastic skyscraper so tall that the upper stories were shrouded in clouds. I was with Moses at the base of the tower when an elevator opened. A stream of people poured into the elevator car—business people in dark suits and dark dresses, ready for a day of office work in starched clothing. The stainlessness of their clothing was important to the people—a characteristic that was part of their identity. Still, it was hard for them to move in their stiff dress-ups. I entered the car, leaving Moses standing on the earth. People kept coming into the already crowded car, jamming each other until the elevator was packed tight.

The air was hot and dense. The minds in the car were full of formulas, plans, and strategies for gaining advantage and dominating each other. I pushed and clawed my way up the wall of the car in an effort to find a pocket of air to breathe. My body was held above the floor and against the wall by the press of tightly-packed bodies, but I couldn't reach a space where I was not re-breathing the exhaled air of the business people. The car began to rise, faster, and as it rose, the occupants of the car began to crawl over one another like worms in a bait box.

The car stopped on the sixty-second floor of the tower, and the door opened. I fought my way through the starched bodies to get free of the car, and its doors closed behind me. The pack of struggling, well-dressed people continued upward.

I found myself in an open space on a small landing. There was no railing. The tiny landing opened to a bottomless chasm filled with swirling clouds. A curving wall of sheer and slippery rock stretched up and outward, connecting the first tower to a second tower that rose even higher into the clouds, its top obscured. On the left edge of the landing was a spiral staircase that led up to the next level. I climbed the staircase and felt the wetness of mist on metal as I ascended to a narrow ledge between the towers. The slippery footpath was the only way to get across to the second tower—there was no place to go but forward. The sweaty elevator was gone.

I stepped out onto the ledge above the bottomless space. The ledge grew steadily smaller, and I inched my way along. I turned inward and tried to grip the wall, but the rock face was leaning past vertical. My fingertips were scratched raw from trying to hold onto a place where there was no hold. The ledge was now no wider than a nickel on edge, yet I was still gripping—gripping in terror. Finally, I could hold on no longer and fell backward into the abyss.

I was falling down now to my death—head downward and out of control. But wait! *I'm falling freely,* I realized. *There's no pain except the pain that my own fear is generating.*

I was falling on a column of air, and the air was gently holding my body. I stretched out my arms and began to move my hands like rudders. Suddenly I was not falling anymore, but swooping upwards. A switch tripped, and every cell in my body began to dance. I was playing in the sky; I could fly.

I STRUGGLED TO AWAKEN from the dream, but I couldn't raise my head. A full moon had risen and pale nightlight from the moon had spread throughout the camp. Deep shadows of the aspens and pines were clearly visible. The tent flap was open, moving slightly in the night wind. She was no longer in the tent, but the clean, earthy scent of her body was still on the sleeping bag next to me. I reached out to touch where she'd lain. Still warm. I tried to sit up, but had no power to do so. I fell back heavily onto my sleeping bag and back into the power of the dream.

I found myself at the pinnacle of the second tower. The crown of the tower was a temple: Grecian and graceful. There was a presence there, an essence that was expressed in light. It was a clear, clean feminine essence. The work of the presence was to pour out endless streams and columns of light in infinitely complex and translucent layers, each with its own intelligence, but bound together in a single purpose: to give. Endless gifts, endless blessings. The light was seeking reception inside the armored veil of every human being.

A voice. A voice that was the wellspring of the other voices that I'd been hearing in my head since the Field Book first arrived. I'd come to its source.

"—*I have a gift for you, Charlie.*"

Then a typewriter appeared, one of an older style with pounding keys that made an impression on the paper. I began to type, and music came from the machine. It was celestial music that carried transformative power. I struggled to awaken, to write the music down, to capture it, but it could not be captured. It was playing me. Pages and lines of music were resonating in my chest, filling me with perfect love. There was no room for anything else.

Then the dream changed. I was back in my own windowless cramped office sealed off from the light. There was a huge piano in the office; its flaccid strings inside a massive case of black wood that was ornately carved in gothic style. Its sounding board was too hard and could not vibrate. I tried to make the piano play the celestial music but it would not play. All creative effort had been exhausted in the construction of the casing; there was nothing left for the music inside. What might have been a source of divine music lived only as a garish piece of ornate and functionless furniture. I struggled to wake up, and the voice came again.

"—In order to gain the power to make music with me, Charlie, there is yet another phase of the journey you must take. The Messenger, Moses, has done all he can for you, and you have been given what strength can be given. Are you ready to take the next step, Charlie, to better hear the music, and perhaps even to play it?"

"Sure," my dream body said. "Why not?"

IT WAS MORNING. I woke up with breath falling in and out of my belly. The morning light was rose-colored as it filtered through the tent. I rolled over to see that Moses and Joy were already up. Joy's sleeping bag was over the top of me, and my bag was nowhere to be seen. I crawled out of the tent barefoot and stretched, still in the feeling of the dream. I was ready to greet my companions and tell them about my powerful dreams.

I looked about the campsite filled with morning light and the sound of water coming over the falls. There was something different about the campsite this morning. I began to run up the falls, searching frantically. At the fifth stride, a feeling in my stomach was telling me that my running was useless. There was no one here to run to—no one here to find. They were gone. Both of them were gone.

33: Alone

Giving up control will be required at one point in your journey. Your seed must be cast into the spiraling wind, to be picked up by invisible lines of higher potential and carried to the place where they will become a new reality.
   ...*The Field Book*.

RUNNING BAREFOOT over Canadian ground was an impossible risk. Any random pine cone, quartz pebble, or broken branch could puncture the skin of my foot. No bandage could keep out the bits of swamp that were always in my boots. A thousand little things had already taken up residence in that warm, wet container and were ready to invade any breach of my defenses. Bacteria would grow and thrive in a foot cut and make it red with pain, speaking sharply every step. Without walking, I had no way out. A foot cut here was serious, irreparable, and life-threatening.

I came down hard on a loose round stone, bruising my heel but not breaking the skin. Hopping on one foot, I began to turn and turn; looking. The aluminum canoe was gone, as was the big Alaskan, and two of the paddles. There was a high whining sound coming out of my mouth—the voice of tightness in my chest that was threatening to loosen into a panic and send me spinning and running again. I felt like a little boy who could not keep up; straining to hear the voice of my Mom far ahead, fading away into a distance where she could no longer hear my cries. Why would she not turn back; turn back to gather me up into her arms, knowing I was here, needing her so desperately? They weren't coming back. I was lost, abandoned.

I CALLED THE NAMES of Moses and Joy, but there was no sound except the echo of my own voice from the cliffs on the south shore. I turned in circles, looking and shouting. I shouted until I was hoarse, and each shout felt more desperate. It was no use; I'd been abandoned.

I staggered back to the open area of the campsite with my shoulders hunched forward. A very small part of me was able to register that this was perhaps the most beautiful morning of the fading summer—a morning that was already warm before the sun was even a hand high in the sky. The slanting rays of clear light were working through the boughs of pine into the scented bower where Joy had touched my face just last evening.

I was in no mood to see the beautiful morning. I put my bare feet into my boots without bothering to lace them up and stomped down to the stream. I sat down hard, clutching my knees and burying my head between them, whining through tears. *It turns out that friends can't be trusted after all,* I thought. Given the first opportunity they will sneak off in the middle of the night on some romantic date, leaving me to fend for myself. They've probably already found some cabin to shack up in somewhere. *I was an idiot to trust them.*

Wait. Wait a minute, Charlie. *Yesterday this stream was beautiful, and it's the same stream today. But now all your lights are off.* "There's no cabin around here. You're making this all up, Charlie," I said aloud. "What's happening to me?"

"*—Welcome to your new method of training, Charlie. You are now under my direction. I've decided that you're ready to walk under your own power.*"

It was Joy's voice inside my mind. She was using the same frequency that the other gentle voices had been using inside my head since Chicago. Only now, it was clearly Joy that was speaking on this channel.

"*—The time has come for you to advance by following your internal compass. Your task is to find home by following the lines of potential in the Field. Begin now by remembering what Moses has taught you so far.*"

The voice went silent.

The water continued to pour over the rock, picking up bits of sunlight as it fell.

My training. *With all of the effort that Moses has poured into me, I should be ready.* I thought. "Can you witness what's happening, Charlie?" I asked myself aloud. "That's one of the fulcrums."

I began to take inventory: there was tightness in my chest; my heart was beating faster; and there was numbness running down the outside of my arms. I was shaking slightly and felt cold and sweaty at the same time. My stomach felt nauseated. But there was also a part of me that was willing to ask a question and not just sit and wallow. There was a part of me willing to be curious. Perhaps I wasn't in such bad shape after all.

"You're in fear, Charlie," I said to myself. "Fear!" *It just blindsided you. Now name what's going on and get on top of it.*

It was undeniable that a sudden change in my chemical state had just hit me hard. I'd not chosen those feelings. They'd just happened on their own.

Moses once said that adrenaline moves so quickly into the body that we only notice that we are angry or afraid well after these emotions have become facts. The mind that thinks and interprets moves much more slowly than the hormonal mind. The thinking mind will never be in control of the initial burst. The fast and automatic chemicals are actually a powerful gift from our ancestors that has helped us survive this long. But we have control over the interpretation of that chemical response. We can stop feeding the fearful thoughts before they create fuel for a storm-cloud loop that drives the panic higher. *Maybe if I relax and look at the water, the chemicals will stop,* I thought.

I let my mind go blank and just watched the endless sheet of falling water. I wanted to regain my sanity. I pulled the breath up through my nostrils and, in a few moments, I could feel the fear chemicals start to leave my body.

"*—You could re-interpret this situation, Charlie, if you like. It might be leading to a better future, you know. Deciding that you have a future is another one of the fulcrums, as you know.*"

Being afraid is not necessarily a bad thing, I thought. *It's natural to be afraid when you're all alone in the wilderness. Heightened alertness is a good thing if I can keep the panic under control.*

Maybe being alone here has something to teach me, I thought. Spiritual masters never seem to be afraid to be alone in nature. In fact, masters actively seek solitude in the wilderness. Joy was alone here and was completely relaxed. "Very soon you will be given a chance to embrace even more, to live inside a bigger picture," she'd said last night. She also said there would always be help, and that I would never really be alone.

Moses and Joy have done this on purpose to complete my training, I thought. It's all part of their plan. Even leaving suddenly to induce the panic. What was it that Moses had said? "The whole game from this point forward will be won or lost by the way that you move from fear." That was it.

I continued to watch the water and listen to it fall into the deep pool below. My new interpretation was helping me. And there were those character traits I'd been working on. I'd spent just enough time with Moses for them to take shallow root as habits. *How about calmness, self-reliance, and the willingness to take the next step?* Moses would embody these if he were here in my shoes. I'd always known that there would come a time when I would have to stand on my own two feet. I couldn't hang onto coattails forever. That moment had now arrived.

IT MIGHT HAVE BEEN a half hour, maybe more. It was long enough for my butt to start to get sore. I got up and walked the few feet back to camp with my jaw held artificially high. *Might as well fake it 'till I make it*, I thought, still feeling that panic could well up any minute and take me over. I was not out of the woods yet. I looked around the camp and began to take stock of my situation.

I could plainly see that packs were gone, along with the aluminum canoe, two paddles, and half the cook gear. They'd taken my fishing rod, but the better one that belonged to Moses was left in its place. Also resting against the green canvas of the Seliga was Moses's beautiful beavertail paddle, shaped in a long oval. It was an Old Town made of a single strong piece of spruce wood unblemished by knots. On one side of the blade was his brand mark in the form of two interlocking circles, with the seven stars of the big dipper drawn within and pointing to Polaris, the northern star. On the other side of the blade was another mark, a circle within a circle bisected with rays of light.

Intertwining around the shaft was a calligraphic script that I hadn't noticed before. *'The Field promises nothing except itself,'* it said. *This is an instrument of power in the right hands,* I thought. I spun the paddle in my hand. It was well worn and comfortable—a pleasure to the touch.

Also resting there in camp was a beautiful watercraft made of bent cedar, waterproof canvas, and ash. I picked up Joy's canoe and shrugged it onto my shoulders. It was at least twenty pounds lighter than the metal one Moses and I had been carrying. It was beautifully balanced and rode easily on my shoulders.

There were strange markings around the canoe just below the gunwales: runic symbols and pictographs that would have been at home on the wall of an ancient cave. On the port side of the bow and on the opposite stern were hand-prints in red, just the size of a woman's hand. For just a moment I had the clearest impression that these two objects—the beavertail paddle and the graceful Seliga—were talismans that could bend the Field. *They're a circle of protection around me,* I thought. They needed only my intention to go forward—my faith—to activate them. *Perhaps I've not been completely abandoned after all,* I thought.

The map case containing the guide's map was on top of a pack. I picked it up, and the compass needle swung freely, pointing north as always. I unfolded the map. There was a small area circled at the very northeast edge of the map. A small stream came into a lake with a steep cliff on its south shore. The circle was connected with a line to a little bubble that contained the words "You are here!" written in a woman's hand. "Well, at least that's something," I said aloud.

I spread the map out on the belly of the overturned Seliga, the canoe's canvas already warm from the morning sun. There, near the bottom of the map, was Ribbon Lake and the place at the end of the road where I'd left the 500. The map showed a hundred miles in each of its directions, ten thousand square miles of wilderness. I could see the long and winding route we'd taken northward, and the spot—neatly marked with the designation 'good camp'—where the sky had poured down its fire into the great white pine. It had been a long and twisting route through hundreds of lakes and portages. It would take me another month or more to go back that way. But wait. There was something else down the western edge of the map.

I looked closely at the map, holding it up to the sun. *From where I am, I could carry the gear up to the top of the falls, then move through those two lakes shaped like teardrops to the beginning of that portage. . . .*

Starting on the western shore of the second teardrop lake, there was a long dotted line running east-west to connect with a larger lake system. The dotted line indicated a portage trail of what might be two miles. The letters 'bb' were next to the line. The cryptic notation meant 'ball buster,' in the crude but accurate parlance that Moses sometimes used. But after this, all the lakes were connected towards the west by what looked like short portages. There was a large lake on the western edge of the map; its main body disappeared off the map far to the north. Crossing such big water alone in a small open boat would be dangerous. My route would require crossing one of the big lake's southernmost bays, but it was a straight passage across; with luck I would only have to risk the big windy water for an hour at most. The route showed nothing then but smaller lakes and shorter portages. At the southern side of one of the smaller lakes were three heavy compressions of contour lines indicating steep ridges. Those ridges separated that lake from a snaking and winding line that marked a river.

The river was named after a European man, but on this guide's map the foreign name was heavily marked through, and in its place the words 'Goddess River' were hand-written next to the graceful curves of blue. The river ran southward and west, flowing into a huge lake thirty miles long situated largely north-south. The Goddess then flowed out of the big lake and westward off of the map. The southernmost finger of the big lake came within a half-mile of the road that I'd come in on. There was no marked trail to get to the Goddess, but if I could cross the ridges and gain the river, I could travel with the flow of current for most of my journey back. I could run the thirty mile lake if the wind was behind me, or paddle in the calm of night, then portage out of the southern-most tip to the road and walk back to the 500. With a bit of luck, it might be ten days of traveling, two weeks at most. I would then be back to where I'd started, and figure out what in the hell I was going to do next. "That's my route," I said aloud.

I turned to assess what other gear my friends had left me.

AFTER THE BIG PURGE in the swamp, I'd discovered the difference between what I thought was essential and what was actually needed. I had no illusions about what was coming next. My body had registered in its deep memory the pain of the first crushing days when I was alone. On the journey homeward out of here, I would be tethered to every ounce of weight as part of my own body. This was no time for the gathering of inessential things. If I was going to carry something it had better be damned important. I spread out the gear.

My clothes, an essential outer armor, consisted of a pair of boots, one pair of thick wool socks, one pair of canvas pants, no underwear, and a long-sleeved breathable nylon shirt with a fishnet undershirt. The undershirt trapped warm air and created enough space between the outer-shirt and my skin to frustrate the reach of the probing mosquito beaks. Moses had left his heavy wool over-shirt of highest quality (a Pendleton) and taken my inferior fleece jacket with him. I'd sewn buttons on every pocket of my shirt and pants, which turned the pockets into handy pouches. I had a multiple-use bandana which kept the sweat out of my eyes and also served as a hot pad, strap, and bandage. A thin but high quality rain-repellent outer coat completed the entirety of my outfit. I had no spare or second of anything.

In my pants pockets, I still carried the Swiss knife with its various attachments, a small, precious waterproof lipstick case of matches, and one small bottle of GI bug dope—one hundred percent DEET designed for the swamps of Vietnam—so concentrated that two drops was enough for all the uncovered area of my body. There was a single aluminum drinking cup, with a bent handle that allowed it to be stored on my belt. All my water came straight out of the lake; and by this time my stomach had become an efficient natural purifier. I had a pair of side-cutting pliers on the belt—ordinary pliers outfitted with a wire cutter attachment on the side. This was used every day to remove hooks from the mouths of fish, lift pots from the fire, and make general repairs to the gear.

Moses and Joy had left me a small and lightweight assortment of camping and cooking equipment consisting of a beat-up medium sized pot for fish and rice, and a smaller, slightly crushed and totally blackened pot for boiling water. I had a single plastic bowl, one big spoon, a filet knife for cleaning the fish, a small vial of biodegradable dish soap, and a scrub sponge. A single toothbrush was the entirety of my personal hygiene kit.

The map and compass were there, still in the same guide's case that had landed on my townhouse floor in Chicago. That was another life, long ago. The Field Book and the Faber-Castell pen were in the case. Moses had also left me the three lures we'd been carrying, the big white spinner, the strange spoon shaped lure with the red eyes that we'd never used, and a swim jig. There was not much food left. A little oil, the last of the dehydrated fruit and vegetables, some coffee, and a five pound sack of rice. A small vial of seasonings had been left by Joy. There was another contribution from her as well: ten large squares of high-energy way-bread full of oatmeal, nuts, honey, dried berries, and flecks of jerked meat. *One of these could last me a day in a pinch*, I thought, feeling my belly. There was not much fat left on reserve.

Joy had bequeathed to me a good portion of her premium gear, trading down for my discount store stuff which had now vanished. I was now in possession of a high quality one-person backpack with a heavy duty plastic pack liner to keep everything dry. And I had the tent we'd slept in last night. This looked like everything. I reached down into the pack to see if there was anything else. I felt a crushed plastic package lying in the bottom of the food pack. It was the unopened bag of sugar-coated orange jelly candy that I'd bought on impulse at the dead-end Texaco station. I looked in disbelief at the bag of boiled sugar and corn syrup. Moses must have been carrying this crap food in his own pack. Had I been forced to carry it, I would have left the candy to the jaybirds long ago.

The gear, with the Seliga and paddle, weighed perhaps ninety pounds, just at the limit where I could comply with every aspect of The Rule: every unnecessary thing absent; one trip only across any portage; no unshouldering a load once undertaken. And there were the luxury items: the Field Book and the pen. In all, it was less than half the poundage of the 'essential' gear I had brought up here at the beginning of the summer, and it was to be carried by a much stronger man.

I looked at the gear. Moses and Joy had left me the best of everything they had. I had the highest quality canoe, paddle, fishing rig, tent, pack, map, and pen that could be put together with any amount of resource. Every inch of it was proven and tested. It was good gear. Better than good.

I SPREAD ALL OF IT OUT, determined to leave something to lighten my load just a bit. The prime candidates for abandonment included the bag of candy which weighed two pounds, the Field Book manuscript and pen weighing a bit over a pound, and the two fishing lures that Moses never used: the spinner and the red-eye spoon. I picked the book up, and its pages fluttered in the wind, sending the fragile pressings everywhere. I immediately felt a sense of remorse as the beautiful pressed flowers scattered across the camp. A deep and unexpected loneliness rose like a weight in the center of my chest. I ran around the camp, scooping up the pressings. "Sorry-so sorry," I said aloud, as I picked them up and lovingly placed them back between the pages. There were writings in this book that had penetrated me, changed me. I felt that some of the symbol-language expressed in the words of the Field Book stood in for vastly larger elements of reality, pointing to and calling the spiritual world at the same time. I would need those words. I put the book and the pen in the waterproof map case. They were coming with me.

I weighed the bag of candy in my hand. Two pounds was a huge weight in my wilderness economy. Carried tens of thousands of steps, this bag amounted to tens of thousands of pounds of stress on my body. I was astonished to find this artificial food was here at all. There was nothing in this sticky bag that would not make me sick to the point of retching after the wholesome diet of wild food I'd been consuming under the watchful eye of Moses. It would supply no nourishment and only make me hungrier when it was gone. Yet, I remembered Moses holding the package in his hand back in the swamp by Ribbon Lake. "It might be important for reasons we cannot yet foresee. . . " he'd said. Maybe he was right. Who knows?

I took the beautiful in-line fishing spinner and hung it up on a branch where it caught the light and fluttered in the breeze. *I'll make this a gift to the Goddess*, I thought. *Let it stay here in the light for someone else to find and use.* I put the swim-jig, the red-eye lure, and the bag of candy in my pack.

With that, I loaded up, slung on the pack, put the canoe on top of my shoulders, and walked to the top of the waterfall where a lake was waiting. *The sign of a Keeper of the Field is not whether the lights go off, but how quickly they can come back on,* I thought. *I can do this.* I had no idea where Moses and Joy had gone. I was on my own now, on a route of my own choosing.

34: Potency

Each step toward one's best intention is a hammer designed to break your old heart, the fearful heart of stone, the heart of pride, so that a new heart, a clean heart, a heart of joy might take its place.
   ...*The Field Book*.

I SLIPPED the Seliga into the water at the top of the falls. It was a big canoe—at eighteen feet, the maximum end of what a single person could paddle. My immediate impression was that it was a craft built for the eighteenth century, when essentially all travel and commerce was done on water. It could easily hold enough gear for a trip across North America from the Atlantic to the Arctic, and it now rested lightly on the water carrying one-fifth of its maximum capacity. *This is how they ride*, I thought, *the great ones. Vastly more capacity than they need in the things that are important, and not a single ounce devoted to unimportant things.* I put the canoe in the water stern-first and climbed into the bow seat, closer to the center, paddling the boat stern-forward with my pack up front to help the boat stay lower in the water. Any other way would have turned the front of the canoe into a sail.

With just a few strokes of the paddle, I knew that this watercraft was something different. The boat was easy to hold on course. It had a wide 'lake keel' underneath, custom designed for steadiness across big open stretches of water. It was instantly quieter as the bow cut through the lake with no sound of water on metal—just a gentle, natural lapping sound like a wave hitting a log. This canoe felt like it was part of the water. The mood of the lake came through it. Everything about the vessel conveyed the sense that I'd found the right and proper way to move through the wilderness. I was now blending in and moving quietly like all of the other animals.

The morning breeze was picking up, with the wind coming in from behind me and to the side. Waves with small whitecaps began to build, and I was riding high atop them. The energy of the waves was transmitted to me through the cedar and canvas. I was riding well-mounted, and with each paddle stroke I began to feel better. *I can do this. I'm ready now.*

FACING ME THAT DAY were the two teardrop lakes, and then the long ball-buster trail shown by the winding dotted line. I reached the second lake by mid-morning as the weather began to change. The wind had shifted and was coming down now from the northeast, bringing scuds of low flying clouds, cold wind, and flying squalls of rain.

By early afternoon, I was on the lake where the long portage was shown on the map. I paddled the shoreline, peering into the forest, but couldn't see a trail. The wind and rain pushed the canoe toward the rocks of the shore, and the Seliga was tippy, rocking nearly to the gunwales as I paddled sideways to the wind. I slipped down onto my knees to lower my center of gravity and doubled back, peering into the dark forest.

There. It was easy to miss: a very old blaze on a pine, nearly covered over, and looking not much different than the bark. In the grey light I could make out a second blaze deeper into the woods. Next to the second blaze there was an opening in the trees that might be a trail. I got out to investigate and walked back into the forest. The blazes continued reliably every hundred feet or so, deep into the dripping pines. Other than the marks, there was no sign of a trail at all. I checked my feelings. There was no conflicting sensation in my body, no warning bells, only a certainty that this was the trail shown on the map, the long dotted line, right where it was supposed to be. *This one long portage, this single effort now will cut off days of travel*, I told myself.

I reached down and picked up a deer pellet from the moss and crushed it between my fingers. *This trail hasn't been used by humans for a long time*. I went back, walked into the water thigh-deep, and up-shouldered my pack. The Seliga rocked up onto to my shoulders easily. I took the first steps out of the water, instantly aware of the weight on my back. *Ninety pounds is still damned heavy.* Yet, if ever there was a reason for the one-trip rule this trail had to be it. Who would want to cross these miles, only to walk back empty and travel the same path again? Already, in a single morning, I had made twice the distance I'd covered my first two novice days in the wilderness. *It's different now. I'm so much stronger.*

I started down the trail at a brisk and optimistic pace. *It won't be weariness that defeats me if this goes long*, I thought. *It will be the pain.* I could last an hour without taking the canoe down, maybe longer. Within two minutes, dull pain signals began to come from the layer of muscles separating the carrying yoke from my bony clavicle as I passed the third blaze. *I can do this*, I said to myself. *I will not let the pain defeat me.*

The trail was a vague line winding around the sides of steep hills slick with the rain. No human footstep marked this passage. The wet moss on wet granite made for footing that slipped and gave way down hillsides, leaving dark skid-prints and forcing me into painful splits positions with all of the weight up-top. Time and again I went down on one knee to stop the skid and regain balance, then struggled upright under the weight. The old blazes were steady, leading me deeper in. *This must have been a route to some trapping ground a long time ago*, I thought. This might have been a highway then, with trees cleared and the walking easy. What little trail there was now seemed to lead right into the next tree, or through trees which were so close together that the sides of the canoe slammed against them, forcing me off balance to lurch and crash along like I was inside a human pinball machine staggering from bumper to bumper. I could hear steady spitting rain on top of the canoe and could see water begin to drip from the needles of the pines.

I WALKED FOR AN HOUR across the hillsides, down into small swampy creeks that made sucking sounds against my boots, then up more hillsides. The pain was building, shouting to my mind, cutting down into my shoulders, and radiating down my back. I knew that if I set the canoe down, the pain would immediately cease, but my muscles would begin to enter a state of rest and recovery. After such a break, my body would be unwilling to resume the load, and would complain loudly by doubling the sensation of pain. So I simply kept walking, obeying the second principle of The Rule, past old blazes appearing reliably every hundred feet or so.

An hour and a half. Beyond the limit of anything that the Initiative or Moses had asked me to endure, but I had yet to find my upper limit. The pain was becoming much worse, but I kept taking steps.

Two hours. I had no plan, no purpose. I'd actually entertained thoughts of a glorious solo conquest of the wilderness in the moment earlier today when I first felt the aliveness of the Seliga in the water. Now the beautiful boat was a stabbing, throbbing deadweight.

At two hours, thirty minutes, my life had turned. Life was now nothing more than the next step. I was moving, but had no sense of what the outcome of the moving might be. There: the next rise. Surely I will see the lake from there. But no, only more dripping pines and old marks through the trees. I slipped on one of the downslopes, going down on my left knee and feeling a twisting pain that added its sharpness to the blinding, building symphony of misery.

The bow of the Seliga ran headlong into a tree, knocking the yoke off my shoulders. I held the canoe up with my arms in a U shape, which provided an instant of relief. Pain crackled in my shoulders as the yoke went back on. *This is the last step, Charlie. You're finished. Drop it NOW!* I took another step, then another, then a third.

It was now close to three hours. A thousand steps ago my mind had told me a story that I was finished and at the outer limit of possibility. The feet that were moving below me were compelling evidence to the contrary: I was not finished. There was some part of me that was stronger, bigger than my mind, which was calmly witnessing everything that was happening. It knew my body could take more and still keep going. The part of me whose job was to control things and keep me safe had given me the best information it had, God bless it, and I'd chosen to ignore the message. My feet kept moving: sometimes forward, sometimes sideways, sometimes backward, sometimes behind me as I walked forward on my knees. But moving nonetheless.

I REACHED a small bottom, just a wide spot full of swamp muck. It was only twenty feet to a rocky embankment on the other side where I could again find good footing. I'd learned from Moses that the best way to get across such swamp-barriers was to build up a bit of speed and run across. To stand or go slow meant sinking. I built up speed on the downslope, and got three strides into the muck before my right leg disappeared up to the thigh. The Seliga collapsed on top of me, putting me in a short, dark tunnel full of insects.

And there, right in my face, not three inches from my forehead, was a five-petaled flower, exactly the flower that had fluttered out of an old earmarked book and onto the green-tiled floor of my Chicago brownstone. Just as Moses had predicted, the flower had arrived at its own chosen moment.

Until this moment, I'd always been in the wrong position, the wrong *attitude*, to look at a flower like this one. But this position was just the right one, the only possible one to peer across the inches necessary to see into the blossom's depth and be pierced by its impossible symmetry and beauty. The beauty was waiting in this little stink-bog for me, waiting for me to fall on my face so I could see it: five petals in the shape of a star, an impossibly delicate lavender, translucent and radiating out of a darker, deeper center. Stars within stars. The petals were an invitation to perfect symmetry and beauty. Tiny anthers on delicate filaments offered up hundreds of tiny yellow pollen grains. Each of those filaments led down to an even deeper world of perfection and consonance within the heart of the flower. *This is the Divine, right in front of me*, I thought. *This is what she has brought me here to see.*

I staggered to my feet, impossibly broken open. I was not finished. I was no longer a person who could be finished. I no longer had this thought as my limitation.

I picked up the canoe, walked around the flower and out of the little bog. Although I had been searching for a specimen since the first portage out of Ribbon Lake, one such blossom pressed into the Field

Book was enough. Such a flower should be left alive. I struggled up the hillside out of the bog, and I began to move into the colors.

MY WALK BECAME patterns of changing colors, much of it red, with long yellow afterimages of green branches and leaves which floated by and hung in my vision. There were some airy patches of blue arriving now and then. And of course the weight, the crushing weight, and the mosquitoes. On such a cold and rainy day, you would think they would be inside playing mosquito checkers. But instead they'd found a warm, dry place to hide right under the canoe I was carrying. The under-canoe environment was a perfect haven: the air was still and there was plenty of food—buckets of hot pumping blood if they could only get to it. The place was lovely and warm from the sweaty body-heat of a big mammal that for some odd reason was carrying a large overturned container. The bugs gathered in a cloud. I was spitting them, inhaling them. They were landing on my eyelids and riding along on my eyelashes, obscuring my vision, and their high-pitched whine was in both of my ears. The horde was fighting a battle with the toxic Vietnam bug dope that I was sweating from every exposed pore. They would come to the table and land on the feast, only to find that the drink was poison. But they were searching, searching every square millimeter—over the top of the head, around my eyes, up my sleeves and pant-legs. The few that made it through my defenses filled up on blood and flew drunkenly away.

Bites that would have caused a screaming, slapping fit back in Chicago were but minor annoyances now. The penetrations of little beaks were now like distant toy pop-guns amidst all the cannon explosions and rockets of the Western Front. A machine gun—the devil's paintbrush—was clattering away with migraine intensity just behind my right eye; the one that was seeing most of the colors. I was snorting snot. One step, then the next, and the next.

A new part of me was arising in the midst of this. The new part was clear. It was quiet.

"—*Take another step, Charlie. It's a curiosity isn't it? What's going to happen with the next step and then the next?*"

I sidestepped up the rain-slicked granite face of a small rise. I was fully committed. This portage would be crossed under The Rule: I would put nothing down. My last step would be the one where I simply folded up into nothing. My body would decide its last step, not my mind. I felt the true last step was close now, close.

I made it to the top of another rise. And then, there it was: a gray shimmer of water through the trees just at the bottom of the hill. I had no full step left, so I made half-steps and quarter steps down the slippery rock to the waterline.

I minced into the water, trying to find footing and not fall. I walked in waist deep and put the canoe down, rocking the vessel from my shoulders to place it gently in the water as Moses had instructed—catching it in the crook of my arm and sliding it in bow-first without a sound. The cloud of mosquitoes—my fellow travelers—were cast into the open air and carried away by the wind. There was an instant release from the pain coupled with a powerful sensation of rising up into the air, of being free. My feet were still on the lake bottom, but some part of my body literally rose four feet into the air.

"*—That's the body of your intention that's been pushing up against the weight to hold it off your shoulders.*"

I was feeling for the first time an energy body, a new capacity that had come on line for me as my physical body failed.

I unshouldered my pack into the Seliga. The last three hours had been the single greatest physical achievement of my lifetime; a marathon and more. There were no crowds cheering me on here at the finish line. Only the lake, the feel of its wind, the sound of its water, the steady fall of rain, and the voice inside my mind:

"*—Well done, Charlie, well done. You're more than your mind says you are. You are freer now from limitations. Yes. Quite a first day on your own, Charlie, don't you think? And the five-petaled flower has spoken to you from inside the Field. It's a good beginning.*"

I loaded my gear, sat backwards in the bow seat, and pulled out the paddle. On one powerface were the stars pouring into Polaris, and on the other, a circle within a circle bisected with rays of light. I moved forward, and the stroke released the stiffness in my shoulders. The pain was evaporating and now almost gone. What a gift from our creator that we remember pleasure so long and can forget pain so quickly. I took a couple of paddle strokes out into the water. The rain was steady and mist-like.

The exertion of the past hours had left me drenched with sweat, and the ambient temperature was dropping rapidly. I now confronted another problem. I was sopping wet, and the wet was already turning cold. If I stopped moving for even a moment, I would be wearing an ice vest out here all alone.

35: Deconstruction

Seek the road into the shadows where the treasure can be found.
   ...*The Field Book.*

I MOVED through a chain of small lakes. The afternoon light was blocked by low hanging clouds, and it would be an early nightfall. I needed to stop and set up camp. The pain of the long portage had triggered a huge flow of natural endorphins in my body, but now this chemical help was draining away, leaving me empty and raw. I was collapsing. A growing sense of loneliness began to saturate everything, intensified by the gloom, and the soft unceasing sizzle of the rain.

Alone now. Sadness coming from depths over which I had no control. I could no longer find a place within me where I could experience rest, connectedness, wholeness, and balance. All of that had disappeared. I pulled up on a point, found a flat spot for the tent, and unloaded the gear. I had a program, a sequence of events for making camp which I'd learned from Moses. I was glad to have the well-drilled sequence—it was like an outer shell keeping me together while my insides turned to mush. I got the canoe up out of the water, got the tent up, unrolled my bag, built a fire pit, gathered and stacked the wood, and brought water up for cooking. I was disciplined. I would make an ordered camp my first night alone.

After this summer with Moses, I considered myself an expert at wilderness camping. I'd had some of the best instruction in the world, for Christ's sake. But tonight the little programmed world that I could execute so easily in the presence of Moses was coming apart. Something fundamental had changed now that I was alone.

The long portage had knocked something out of me. I was too tired to fish and had lost all appetite despite the extreme exertions of the day. I interpreted this as a bad sign. The tent was sagging, and I couldn't find a way to pull the ropes to make it beautiful and tight. I was able to make a smoky fire in the drizzle with small sticks that would not stay lit, and attempted to get a pot of gooey rice going, knowing that I should eat something. The fire would not make coals, so I decided to heap a twig pile around the pot to get it boiling. After much coaxing, the twigs decided to all flare at the same instant. The pot became too hot and boiled over, sending sticky white curtains of rice-goop down the blackened sides. The fire shifted, and the pot lurched sideways, spilling some of the rice. Without thinking, I reached down to rescue the pot, and grabbed its wire handle. I was instantly rewarded with a deep second-degree burn the width of the wire across my palm. Ashes roiled into the pot as I cursed and dropped it at the edge of the fire. I ran down to the lake to immerse my hand in the cool water and watch the edges of the burn turn a brownish black. The welt was right across the spot where my paddle grip met my palm. With this injury, I would not be able to touch that palm to the grip, which meant paddling on the right side of the boat for the rest of the trip. I was stunned.

After all the teaching and practice of free attention, I now had a serious, self-inflicted wound that was the result of pure inattention. My hand was throbbing as I came back up from the lake. I was so immersed in my pain and self-pity that I didn't watch where my feet were going. The foot of my boot went right into the rice pot. I kicked the pot away, and sticky rice flew all over the camp, plastering my tent and pack. I looked down at the mess of my dinner, now scalding through my boot. I spun around, looking for someone to blame. But there was no one to blame. Every little painful detail of this little drama was caused by me and me alone.

The ruin of my dinner, the lash across my palm, and the deep exhaustion undid the last of my reserves. I lost it. I couldn't stop the avalanche despite all my training. I sat down on a rock and started to blubber like a baby. I cried for my mommy, for Moses and Joy, for friends I barely knew, and for everyone who had ever loved me. I'd never felt loneliness like this before, with no one here at all, not even a stranger on the street, or someone in two dimensions on a screen. I was alone here in the big quiet, with no one to depend on and no one to help me. I cleaned up the pot, sobbing. I tried to summon up my training, but my powers had abandoned me. Nothing worked. There was no help. No one here at all.

"*—You might die here, Charlie, you really might.*" She was speaking again inside my mind. "*There's more than a chance. Dying is what usually happens in the natural order of things when one is this deep into the wilderness alone.*"

Oddly, the thought of death was calming, even comforting. I'd never thought about death as a friend before. At least it would be the end of the loneliness.

"*—On the day of your death there will be no tears. You will just go under the water, be covered up, and walk through the gateway into the vastness.*"

No tears. Not even my own.

"*—Death is a simple friend, a kindly friend, a liberator. Your death will free you. There are no tears in heaven, Charlie, only joy.*"

THE MOSQUITOES were coming out, and I went to the tent without supper. I got my wet boots off and examined my feet. My heel was bruised from the idiot running earlier this morning, but the skin was not broken. I lay down on the hard ground, so exhausted that I couldn't sleep. It was still early evening, and the sun would not go down. I reached for the Field Book, which was now my only friend. The book fell open to this passage, deep in the heart of the book, a part that I hadn't seen before, although by now I thought I'd read it all. The ink of this section was fresh. I took a long exhale through pursed lips, and looked down at the writing in the book.

> There's a beauty in the wilderness which you may come to find, or rather which finds you, because it is beyond your power to will it into existence. It's the beauty of the blood

and bone, and what lies beneath the blood and bone, and beneath the dust that the blood and bone are made of. It's a beauty which is beneath and above and through everything which is inside of you and everything outside, which joins them as part of the same thing. It's already here. The wilderness will put the horn of this beauty in your belly in such a way that beauty will never leave you. Trust.

The rain began to land harder on the roof of the tent. My body finally gave in, and I slept as if dead. But something had happened to my mind. Maybe the woman in my head had cast a spell on me. It might have been the hallucinations brought on by the final pain of the portage trail or the five-petaled flower that had opened something in the middle of my forehead. Whatever the cause, when my body fell asleep in the tent that night, my mind did not follow; my mind stayed awake.

I UNZIPPED THE TENT and walked out into the night in a flowing white robe. It was easy walking, and I was light-footed and free of heavy boots. The low clouds were gone, and the moon was bright—so bright that my eyes contracted just a bit, making the shadows darker. It was a hunting moon.

She was on a small rise, a jumble of stone that was the rubble of some great castle. She sat up on the highest point with her back towards me, blending so easily with the stone that one could walk past her and never notice a presence until she moved. Her left hand rolled open at the wrist—an invitation for me to come and be seated.

I moved to the rocks. I felt that I was coming to a dangerous place—a place that held power. I was getting close, too close to her. With a leap, the figure on the rock could be atop me.

The figure turned, and the moonlight struck the side of her face. It was a face still young but chiseled, with eyes deep-set in high cheekbones. The eyes were white with light and fire, tinged only with a touch of blue. There were small twining horns protruding from her head, like those of a spike buck. I could make out the curve of a bow held in her left hand. An arrow was notched in the string ready for a single, swift motion that would send a shaft moving down the rows of moonlight. She was hunting, and I could quite easily be her prey.

I sat down. She didn't look at me directly, but continued to scan downrange—a huntress whose gaze pierced the shadows. I had the odd sense that she was protecting me. Anything hiding in those shadows would find her stroke both swift and terrible.

"It is love," she said.

"What's that?" I replied.

"It's love that brings you to death."

"Come again?"

"It is love that is helping you grow your power. You walk now on your own. You are growing up. This is good and necessary, Charlie. The first green shoot kills the acorn that has served it so well, and there's no going back. You are already an oak in the making. The oak never becomes great by refusing its growth or trying to get back to the peace and security of a little seed."

There was a horned woman talking with me in the middle of the night forest. I was quite certain she could float off of the ground. This was impossible.

As if reading my mind she said: "The word 'impossible' marks only the present boundary of your settled mind. Beyond that boundary many things are indeed quite possible."

She continued scanning the woods like she was expecting something or someone.

"The boundary of what is possible changes as we become more alive, Charlie. There are quickenings in this process. There's the quickening that began it all, and the quickening where the very dirt of this earth came alive. There was the first spark of your individual life and the moment when your mother felt you in her body and the two of you began to speak the love language. Then your first breath in this world. There was the moment when you met your teacher, and the moment when you responded to the call. And now, you are here, in this moment, with me."

"I don't know why I'm here—can you tell me why I'm here?" I asked.

"When you were dreaming last night, you came to the temple and were given your gift. To become a bearer of your gift you must be willing to loosen the identity that you've always known as 'yourself', to shatter your old shell and walk into a life that you can now barely imagine. The road to new life passes through death. It's a simple truth of this world."

She now ceased her scanning and turned her full attention to me.

"It's just a little leap—over and in and down into the water and up again. But you have to be ready to take this road. Are you ready, Charlie? Are you ready to become a larger being? Are you ready to travel the road into the shadows where the treasure can be found?"

This was a dream. I was again watching myself inside the dream. I then heard my dream body say: "I'll take the road."

36: Baptism

Wet the ashes of Pharaoh and let a flower grow.
> ...*The Field Book.*

IN THE VERY FIRST LIGHT OF MORNING, it's hard to tell the kind of day it will be. A clear blue sky may seem gray, and a storm sky no different than clear. I came out of the tent just as the last of the night insects were being blown away by the morning wind. The wind was cold, a great deal colder than yesterday, and coming hard from the northeast. I felt a sting on the side of my face. There was no blue sky. The wind was carrying sleet.

I was cotton-headed and confused. Twice now in as many days some 'dream body' of mine—a part of me that I never knew existed—had somehow taken over the program and was giving my consent. I was saying 'yes' to powerful feminine forces that were appearing as my guides. They were coming in dreams much different than those of normal sleep. I was inside the dreams with full volition, able to have conversations and, apparently, make commitments.

My body had registered the commitment I'd made last night as something very real. It knew that I had said 'yes' to something important, and was preparing. My flesh and bones had gone into a spontaneous mode of fasting that made my eyes bright and alert, and my body calm and receptive to what might be ahead. It was as if my frontal mind was no longer in charge and was simply being asked to observe and sustain my pre-determined disciplines; nothing more.

I should eat. Even though I had no appetite, I was still aware enough to know that I'd made a long portage yesterday, followed by a night with no dinner. I was losing weight at a fantastic clip, standing in the sleet.

I choked down a few bites of Joy's way-bread with no enthusiasm, and took a drink of cold water. I began to feel fear come up again on its own, and watched as it tried to take over my thoughts. *This is unfair*, I thought. I'm being taken advantage of. "Someone should ask me when I'm awake!" I yelled into the forest around me.

"*—But you are awake in your dream body, Charlie, more awake, in fact, than you are right now. Get used to acting from the best part of yourself. Your best part is finally starting to make the decisions. The larger part of you is now in charge, Charlie. Trust it.*"

"Get out of my head!" I shouted, pulling on my tousled hair.

Her guiding voice immediately went quiet. If it was possible to feel more deeply alone, I now began to feel it. A small part of me knew that I should be grateful for the inner guidance being offered. Yet even after all of my training, I just could not summon the feeling of gratitude this morning.

I loaded and launched the canoe. *These negative emotions are being triggered because I'm being tested at a higher level*, I thought. *This is a knife's edge.* I was anxious to get on the water, to move and warm up, and to make it to the Goddess River where the current might carry me home.

THE QUIET QUALITY of the Seliga that was so appealing yesterday now seemed oppressive. I wanted something noisier to keep the voices out of my head. I pushed off, moving southwest. All of the portages today were short and easy compared to the one yesterday, and I moved quickly.

Around noon I portaged my gear into the southernmost bay of the big-water lake. Only a small portion of the big lake was shown on my map; the rest of it doubtless took up most of the hundred-mile map section that joined mine to the north. *I'd probably end up in Hudson Bay in a couple of days if I turned and paddled north*, I thought. I looked northward into the big water. The sleet had turned to soaking cold rain in the relative warmth of midday. My body was responding to the new condition with a steady medium-hard shaking over which I had no control. It was then that I saw it.

It was small—small enough to be easily covered up by my outstretched thumb, but the profile was unmistakable: a fixed wing, single propeller, two pontoons. Next to the plane was a log building with smoke coming from a stone chimney.

"I'll be dammed," I said aloud. "A fish camp."

I'd read about these camps in magazines when I was a boy: exotic fly-in fishing adventures that attracted sportsmen from all over the world: luxury accommodations in the deepest wilderness at a high price; a Teddy Roosevelt adventure. They would be going out on the big water in motorized boats for huge lake trout and monster pike, then coming back from their 'taste of adventure' to cocktails and a gourmet meal. I could make out the metallic sheen of a motorboat with a deep 'V' hull. Wouldn't they be surprised to see me? Someone who'd paddled in for a hundred miles over some of the most difficult terrain in the world, out here alone. Certainly they wouldn't deny me one, or two, or even six of the cold beers they'd brought in by the caseload. There would be steak there too, medium rare. Fresh produce. Milk. Companionship. Laughter. That camp was probably where Moses and Joy were headed. *It was just like them to leave me to go off to some luxury cottage while I suffer alone,* I thought, knowing that such a thought was only a story I was making up to indulge my own self-pity.

The north wind was coming straight down the big lake, building whitecaps and slanting the stinging rain. I would like to tell you that I was strong that day. I'd like to tell you that I had the character to resist temptation, to stay on the road that the best part of me had chosen and to see it through.

The strong wind and rain were coming from my right, down from the north. To get up-lake to the camp I had to turn the canoe upwind. That meant paddling on the left side of the canoe and making powerful sweep strokes against the stern to bring the boat about. I tried. But the sweep stroke put the grip of the paddle right against the fresh blister-burn on my right palm. I couldn't put enough pressure on the paddle to move north. That's the truth of it. The boat was rocking dangerously in the waves, with water slapping the right side freeboard as I tried to turn, nearly spilling me out to port and into the big water. I just didn't have the strength. The waves were too big, the water too cold, and my injured hand too weak to power the paddle-blade.

I gave up, gave in. The bow of the Seliga immediately swung southwest like a weathervane, and all the tipping settled down. *She's pushing me to something; literally blowing me there with every breath*, I thought.

I'd said in my dream that I'd take the road. I didn't expect to get so much help. I swiveled my head for one last glimpse north. I could make out the small body of a man in a red wool shirt. Definitely not Moses. Then the camp disappeared; covered up by a rocky cliff-wall. The wind was immediately broken by the wall, and the water now became slick and calm. There was nothing but the sound of my paddle dipping and the water quietly breaking against the wooden hull. The camp had vanished like it had never existed. I would remain on the chosen road.

I CROSSED the next portage, moving away from the big lake so full of temptation, and then struck southwest toward the concentration of lines on the map: the cliffs that separated me from the Goddess River. The day felt short, like the long summer sun had been suddenly cut from the sky, and winter had arrived. The clouds, coming down from the north, grew darker and lower, and the afternoon was turning nasty. There was a change in sound—a soft whispering on the wooden sides of the canoe. Ice was beginning to accumulate on the gunwales. The freezing lake water now felt like lukewarm tea compared to the air. The sleet was again on the wind, hitting my back, and penetrating the raingear, wool shirt, and undershirts right to my spine. The shaking now grew uncontrollable.

I reached the cliff-side lake just north of the river by midafternoon. The short portage into the lake had failed to warm me, and it seemed suicidal to attempt the cliffs in the sleeting rain this late in the day. I was ready to stop. This was a small lake—three-quarters of a mile in length at most and a quarter mile wide. An island in the center looked flat enough to make camp. At least I would be safe there from any bears.

The camping protocol that Moses had drilled into me said that now was the time to fish. I was not hungry, but without fish, there would be no dinner. The cold and exertion was stripping calories, and stripping hard. I could feel my body being cut as the very last layer of my belly was consumed. I pulled out my two lures. There was the old red-eye wiggler, still unused.

It was an unlikely looking lure, probably something patented in the twenties. The wiggler was about the size of a large tablespoon, with a couple of small holes stamp-cut into the spoon for eyes. In each of the eye-holes was a large red bead which turned on a little metal wire running through the bead to hold it in place in the sockets. The lure was plated with bronze metal that was dulled and rusted a bit, and trailed a large treble hook. *Why not*, I thought. I tied the red-eye on with a Palomar knot, running the line through the eye twice, forming an overhand knot in the doubled line and passing the lure through the open loop. I made a good knot. I took thirty strokes out into the lake, and then flipped the red-eye out behind me.

The lure fluttered slowly downward like a falling leaf. Underwater, its color blended perfectly with the dark lake bottom, much like the camouflage color of a real fish. I put the rod between the gunwale and my leg, so I could feel the vibration and speed of the lure. The lure swam up and increased vibration with each forward stroke of the paddle, and then I could feel it die and flutter down on the glide to mimic a struggling, wounded bait-fish.

The cold was setting in.

Suddenly, the gentle vibration of the rod tip stopped, and the rod bent backward, pulling so hard that my rig nearly leapt from the boat. The reel snagged on the seat, a stroke of luck that was the only thing that kept the rod in my possession. I dropped my paddle and took the rod. Instantly the boat swung around into the wind, and I lost all forward momentum. I jerked the rod. No movement. "Damn," I said. "Snagged."

This had happened before, even to Moses. Usually, the lure was caught between rocks or had hit a saturated log. Generally it could be freed by getting behind the snag and pulling up at a different angle. I sculled the canoe back over to the spot where the lure had stopped, and gave it another pull. Slowly, the snag began to move, and then started swimming.

The line stripped off of my reel with a sizzling high whine as the drag released. The canoe began to move, pivoting and following the fish like a weathervane in an uncertain breeze. I was in open water with little risk of losing a fish here, so I backed the drag off a half-turn to put less stress on my line and knot. The line was tight in the water, with little beads dancing on the surface where it went in.

The sky opened, and rain now came down mixed with sleet—a November downpour come early. The ice continued its build-up on the gunwales as I was dragged around.

After fifteen minutes the fish stopped. I began to slowly gain some line, lowering my rod tip just slightly, pumping the rod and reeling, pumping and reeling, while keeping my line tight to pressure the fish. Another run. Another slow process of reeling in.

Twenty minutes. Now for the first time I could see him. The water in the lake was clear enough to see many feet down, even in the dim light. He was there, a huge pike. He looked to be at least four feet long through the blurriness and refraction of the water. This was a fish of an entirely different order than anything I'd seen or caught with Moses. His lower jaw was crooked and bent, like the jaw of a huge red salmon in the northwest. The pike had long sharp teeth clearly visible from above. I could see the red-eye. The lure was in the back of his jaw, near the hinge, and he was working on it, grinding it at this fulcrum point. Two hooks were in him. And now he was gone with a surge of his tail, spinning me around. Again the stop and the slow pulling in of line. He drifted up now, maybe ten or twelve feet under the boat. We looked at each other. All but one of the red-eye's hooks had come loose. The remaining hook was sitting loose inside what had now become an open hole in the bony jaw-plate of this old creature. If I lowered the rod tip, the lure would fall right out, and the old pike would be freed to swim slowly away. This seemed like a fitting end to our battle. It would be good to see the old pike win. *That fish is enough food for ten people back in Chicago, more than I can possibly eat. If I take him it will be such a waste.*

But just as I was about to lower the rod, something happened. The fish was the one who decided. He surrendered the fight, and drifted quietly up to me, the red-eye dangling in his jaw, right up to the side of the canoe.

He was old, and near the end of his time. There were deep scars on him from eagle strikes and fights won long ago, and he finned there slowly, just waiting. I expected him to explode again, as pike sometimes will when they come next to the boat, often breaking the line or even the rod and getting free. But he lay still for long seconds.

Once in firelight, Moses had told me this:

"One of the most important lessons of the spiritual life is learning to receive a gift. You must take the gift offered to you, to embrace it with both hands and not turn away. The currency of the spiritual world is giving and receiving, and you can't give unless you've first received. Take a gift when it's offered. Grow strong with it, so that you in turn can become the giver."

Looking down at the old fish, I made my choice. I reached my hand down toward the water without bothering to roll up my sleeve. In one swift motion I buried my arm up to the triceps, down into the hooks and teeth and fins, and took him at the top of his head. He was far too big to hold by his body or land without a net, so I took him by the eyes. My thumb and middle finger stretched wide over his bony skull and dug deep into his sockets. He trembled there in my bare hand, unmoving. I hauled him up by those eyes, his tail sliming over the side of the boat as I lifted him high and dropped him into the bottom. As I released him, he exploded in a tangle of fins and teeth and hooks, flailing and whipping my legs. The red-eye instantly came free, and I stepped on him to keep him in the boat, dropping to my hands and knees to hold him, and all but capsizing in the middle of the lake.

Then he lay quiet, with only his gill flaps moving, gasping for breath as he began to drown in the air.

This was a fish unlike any I had ever caught or seen caught. It could easily have been on an advertising poster for the fishing lodge at the big lake; or a black and white picture taken in 1956 that was still used after fifty years because there'd been no fish caught like it since. It was the type of fish found stuffed above the bar-mirrors in the old taps and watering holes in the small towns of Wisconsin. There it lay in my boat.

I didn't feel victorious. Only sadness for the old pike, gratitude for his life that I watched now ebbing away and given up for mine; feeling the strangeness of a world in which I was such a powerful predator, yet with such compassion welling up behind my eyes. *I need him to survive*, I said to myself, *especially now*. The cold rain sloshed two inches deep in the bottom of the boat and mixed with the slime of the pike. There was very little blood. The rain, mixed with sleet, was now coming hard. I could no longer feel my hands, and I was shaking everywhere. During our battle I'd stopped paddling and my heat-making engine had stopped firing and shut down. The shaking turned bone hard. I couldn't bring the convulsions under control or stop the steady shake-jumping of my shoulders as they received the driving rain slanting in from the north.

The pike was sliding on the slick cedar flooring of the Seliga. He was finished. The beautiful, green camouflage coat that had protected him from the osprey and eagles these many years was starting to mottle and turn white as he died and stiffened. I picked up my paddle and pulled hard for the island, but the little heat generated by paddling was not enough to stop what had been started.

I MADE IT to the island. It seemed adequate enough, although it was nothing but the jagged top of a black granite hill sticking up out of the water with a few short jack pines growing on it. There was no soil to speak of, just some moss, but there was a little spot under the clump of pines where I could lie down. I paddled to the lee shore of the island, where the water was slick and flat in the wind shadow, and got out onto the slippery rocks. The stones were all scattered at odd angles, loose and treacherous with rain, as if the last glacier had casually dumped a little of its billion-ton load of loose rock here and moved on without looking back.

I threw the pike up high on the hard rock, far enough so it wouldn't slide back into the water. It landed with a dull whack. Balancing on the slippery rocks, I unloaded the pack and put it ashore. Now it was time for the canoe.

I grabbed the canoe by the gunwales and tried to balance it on my thighs, aiming to flip it over my head then carry it up to make camp. Getting a canoe up onto my shoulders had become routine, something done a dozen times a day. The task was always a bit trickier, though, with water in the boat. This afternoon, there was a lot of accumulated water that ran down to one end, then the other, as I tried to balance the boat on my thighs. My plan was to flip the canoe at just the instant when most of the water was in the middle.

I struggled with the boat for a few seconds, got the water in the middle, and then started it over my head. I don't know whether it was a combination of my exhaustion, the cold, the retribution of the old pike, or part of some divine plan, but one of the slippery rocks underneath me moved. I lost my balance, staggered forward, and dropped the canoe from three-quarters height. It was something that could have happened to anyone. The usual consequence of such a slip was just the crash of the keel-side landing loudly against the lake surface, and an opportunity to try again. But that day, the drop from the small height of my shoulders had the effect of throwing the boat out into the water, where it landed with a slapping splash. It scooted about twenty feet away from the island, and sat there quietly, riding upright in the water.

I now stood thigh-deep in the middle of the glacial lake, alone inside the deep vastness of the Canadian wilderness. The only thing that could ever take me away from this place was bobbing there in the water, twenty feet away. I had no communication device, no signal flare, and no passer-by to wait for. With one little drop, I was separated from my life support, my vessel.

I just looked at it, riding high and motionless in the water. And then, as if guided by some invisible hand, the boat began to move. The stern was caught by a puff of wind there in the lee water of the island, and the boat began to slowly turn, so slowly and without sound, gliding with no friction; empty; leaving me. This little island was now a prison, a death trap. The canoe was gaining speed. Twenty five feet. Thirty.

I'm too cold now to go in, and I should wait and swim for it in the morning but the lake is freezing and the shore is too far and I will never make it in the morning or any other morning, and there's no life jacket in my gear and if I don't go this instant then. . . .

I was in the water. Full immersion. Pants, wool shirt, raincoat, boots, pliers, and knife. Everything. The water was instantly over my head, taking all the breath out of my body, and then I was up, panting in short, sharp breaths from the pain of the stabbing cold; pulling and kicking with heavy boots on, with the water thick and slow inside my wool shirt and raincoat. *I'm weighted towards the bottom, but I'm a good swimmer.* I can swim with clothes on and not panic. I reached the boat. My good left hand made a grab for the gunwale. I missed and went full under again. The dark silhouette of the beautiful Seliga, the quiet and beautiful handmade boat, was falling away above me, sinking into the sky.

37: Choosing Life

> The goal of all of our work is to become open vessels, pouring life into the world.
> ...*The Field Book.*

It was quiet, peaceful really, when the young man named Charlie Smithson gave it up. No sound broke the surface of the water. *This is not so bad. There's no real pain. I can just breathe the water. I lived for nine months inside my mother with my lungs full of fluid, and was able to breathe just fine. It will be just like that once again. It's nice here, under the surface, away from the pain and struggle of the world. There's so much work up there, especially if I have to do all the work alone. Who cares about living in a larger world anyway?*

I was suspended there in the cold water, with my legs kicking slowly.

Then another voice. Hers again.

"—*Just put your head down, Charlie. Look down at the bottom. Keep kicking.*"

This instruction was so counterintuitive that I was sure it was the voice of God inviting me home. I put my head down toward my chest, and gazed calmly at the bottom, moving my legs gently back and forth.

Where the head goes, the body automatically follows. Putting my head down instantly changed the orientation of my body from vertical to horizontal in the water. My heavy boots broke the surface, and my back was buoyed by a pocket of air trapped inside my raincoat.

"—*Now, just turn your head to the side and breathe. Exhale under the water, then take another breath.*"

I began to move my arms in a slow crawl stroke. The resistance of the water slowed everything to one-tenth speed, but even this speed was fast enough to deliver a painful bump when my head hit the narrow stern keel of the Seliga. I'd swum right into the canoe without looking at it.

"—*Now, kick hard and reach up.*"

I was able to get my hand on the stern plate, and then use the canoe like a big kickboard to maneuver it to shallow water. After three minutes, my boot struck granite, and I staggered to shore using the gunwale as a railing to keep me from falling over.

I pulled the canoe up along with me, dragging its soft canvas skin over the sharp rocks. I left it riding high, teeter-tottering on a rock, with the back end dipping into the water. I was in trouble.

THE WHOLE SWEATY cooling mechanism of a human is based on the physics of evaporation. Moisture leaving the skin cools the surface down. We came out of Africa and are rigged to survive under the intense equatorial sun by letting the cooling wind waft over our moist surface areas. But I was far from the plains of Africa. I had extended too far north, too far into the cold. The cooling apparatus was killing my body on this granite outcrop.

When a human's central body cavity reaches a temperature of seventy-nine degrees, that body is finished, no matter how strong the will inside. The body will give up the fight and go down. In a hyper-world where so many problems are caused by too much of everything, this cooling is a hypo death, a problem of too little.

The body begins its decline in stages. The first stage is shivering—the involuntary contraction of the muscles to produce heat; then gooseflesh, another involuntary movement that raises thousands of tiny welts in an effort to elevate the body-hair, expand the surface area, and pocket more of the precious warm air next to the skin. When this attempt fails, the muscles cramp and the hands and feet begin to turn blue. The body is working now to protect its central core, the heart, brain, lungs, and central organs, and is retreating in stages from its outposts, buying time. The warm blood has become too precious to risk a run through the cooling yards of veins and capillaries in the arms and legs. A weight of cool blue blood, stripped of oxygen, is abandoned in the extremities and not pumped back.

When the core body temperature reaches the low nineties, the body begins to shut down. At about ninety-three, the heartbeat slows and becomes irregular. A couple of degrees lower and consciousness starts to dim. But even as a dim light, awareness stays on right to the end. Awareness is the function, above all others, which the wisdom of the body values most highly in its survival. So the light of awareness stays on, dimming slowly, holding out for something, anything. Finally consciousness begins to fade; first with inattentiveness, then grogginess, then slurred speech as the language centers of the brain are affected and close up shop. And at last there is the warm descent. In the end, there is always a sense of warmth, finally warm again; time now to sleep, to rest, and to fall into the sleep from which one will never awaken.

WHEN MY RIGHT HAND SLID OFF the wet canoe, I was looking down a long white tube with soft and fuzzy edges. My hands were yards away—remote things on long rubber strings which I could move a little, but not control. There was no pain or discomfort of any kind. I was safe. *It's time now to sit down and rest. I've been trying so hard.* I will make camp in a minute. I just need to rest now, to rest, to sleep.

And at just that moment, he came.

It was the same force that I'd felt as a surge of fierce energy when I took my first steps out of the swamp by Ribbon Lake; my first steps under The Rule with Moses singing softly behind me.

He came out of the base of my skull on a dark wild horse in full gallop, and spoke with a tongue of fire that sent a blue-hot spark arcing into my brain. The Commander had once again arrived. He was alive inside of me and issuing his orders:

"*Wake up!* WAKE UP AND LIVE. *Wake up now.* NOW!"

I can't remember moving to my pack, but I was now standing over it, trying to get it open, using those long rubbery hands that did not work well, pulling on water-tight knots. The flap came back, revealing the plastic liner. My soft and wavy hands were groping into the pack, pulling out gear until it all lay scattered on the ground. My right hand felt for the bottom, searching for a smooth and unopened plastic bag. I found the bag, a two pound bag of gumdrop candy carried all this way; sixty-four fake orange slices with sugar crystals on the outside, bought for seventy-five cents. I pulled up the candy and ripped the bag open. Dozens of candies fell among the pine needles. I went down on my knees after them, got one in my mouth, then two, then six, inhaling them along with bits of the island. Hundreds of calories in concentrated form, thousands. They were sticky, sugary fuel sliding down my windpipe to be burned. I couldn't feel my fingers but my fingertips could push the candy down.

The huge and sudden influx of candy hit my stomach and sat there for a moment accompanied by a wretched, nauseated feeling. My internal engine had turned off and gone cold as it prepared to shut down for good, and this food was nothing but dead weight. But then, like some high-octane starter had been sprayed into an old carburetor, my system began to respond. First there was a little feeling of fire in my belly, and then my whole metabolic system roared to life. My engine turned back on and began to fire like a blow-torch. I was burning those big gumdrop candies as fast as they came down, fifty calories of sugar and corn syrup a slice, sixty-four slices in the bag. For a brief moment, a feeling of sticky sweat began to rise up the back of my neck.

The sleeping bag given to me by Moses, full of prime silver-gray goose down, was lying on the ground in its blue rip-stop compression sack. If I could gain the bag, the goose down might fluff open and begin to trap heat. The warm down-feathers were a sacrificial gift from the mighty lords of the high cold wind. I was ready to receive the gift as Moses had instructed.

I got the top of the stuff-sack open and the compressed sleeping bag began to come out. The bag fluffed and filled in the cold wind. All of the candy was now gone.

I pulled off my raincoat and shirts. My protective armor was now a wet death-suit that clung to my body. The wetness created a strait-jacket effect that nearly dislocated my arms as I tried to slough off my outer sheath. Finally, I was naked to the waist, and stooped to struggle with my boots. The laces had formed hard wet knots. I didn't have time for these. I picked my filet knife from the ground and cut the laces away. The boots came off with a sucking sound, and water poured out of the tops. I fell over attempting to remove the heavy wet socks. They were too hard for me just now, and I left one of them on. Then the wet pants were gone and away. I was naked in the wind on that little island, but strangely warmer than in my clothes. I was blue and small.

I got into the sleeping bag and stood up, pulling the mummy cowl tight over my head. On stiffened legs, I began to hop.

It would have been a strange sight, had anyone happened to pass by at just that moment. Out on a little island in the deep Canadian wilderness was a great blue hopping worm with a dirty little face stained with sugar and pine needles. A human reverted to caterpillar, an insect trying to stand and perform a spastic, falling dance step, the blue-naked caterpillar hop.

But something was happening—I was warming up.

It was the Commander on horseback that had chosen my life, not me. But now, I was beginning to choose it too; choosing the pain; choosing the effort; choosing life.

I hopped to one end of the island with my feet together in the narrow bag, falling on the rocks and struggling back up. Finally, I collapsed against one of the little bent pines. I was shivering, but fully awake minute after passing minute. *If this is the beginning of my new life, my first decision is this: to fully awaken and stay awake,* I thought.

It was then I noticed my visitor. It was a black raven, a big one with a three-foot wingspan, sitting atop one of the pines. He had no doubt come in for the fish, but was not down on top of it just yet, choosing instead to bounce on a branch and watch me. I had the distinct impression that he was there for entertainment. He was well established, and the fish could wait. No reason to pass up a good laugh. I kept up my spastic hopping under the small pine and looked up at him. He calmly turned his head and put a single eye on me. There was nothing to fear here. I was only a big blue worm.

I was still cold: blue lipped and goose-bump cold. I needed fire and something warm inside of me. The rain and sleet had stopped, and the air was growing quiet. I began to hop the rocky hilltop for firewood.

There was wood—some almost dry—on the lee side of a small pine that had died and fallen over. Slowly, carefully, I split the little twigs by pulling my knife through them toward my chest, trying to find a dry center. I carefully laid these precious dry pieces across two larger sticks placed on the ground parallel to the wind, and formed a little wooden platform above the wet ground. I'd made the mistake of storing dried kindling inside my raincoat, and now it was completely worthless. I hopped the island looking for something to burn and found a small dry strip of shaggy bark from a cedar which was growing low and alone on the north side of the island. I received the cedar strip as a miracle from the goddess.

I was still shaking, and my shoulders came painfully out of the bag and into the cold air every time I moved. I made a tepee of little split twigs on top of the cedar bark with the dry centers facing inward. Over this went small, unsplit damp twigs, the driest I could find. Larger stuff was waiting at arm's reach so that I wouldn't have to move away to gather more wood at the crucial moment when the fire was first feeding.

I crawled over to my wet pants and found the plastic match container, still buttoned into a front pocket. I thanked God for modern miracles, for thermoplastic and rubber O-ring seals, for that one square inch of completely dry space to store my matches. I turned over a rock and found a little dry area to strike up. The match lit, and I slid it carefully under the platform, holding the flame to the cedar bark until the match burnt out against my fingers. The first match. One match. Success.

The little teepee fire began to wisp a thin blue line of fragrant smoke. A tiny yellow flame curled around the shavings, and the fire sounded a pop as its heat hit one of the teepee twigs. The bigger stuff began to hiss. Everywhere the flame licked up, I gently placed another tiny split twig.

I lay down next to the fire, with my cheek touching the wet ground and my face not more than three inches from the little blaze. I pursed my lips and blew softly, so softly: a long, concentrated, straw-like stream of air right at the base of the fire. The fire reacted, and the twigs on my platform glowed bright with white centers and fell into tiny coals, generating heat. I cradled the fire with my body and gently placed sticks on it with my left hand, careful not to crush the blaze with too much wet wood. I turned my face away for a breath of air, and then turned again to breathe the long streaming breath down into the heat. The wet wood started to crack, and the larger stuff reached a flash point. The fire was growing now, a foot high. I had to back away a little as the heat singed my eyebrows. I was singed on the outside and frozen on the inside, but not for long. *The fire can live now for a few minutes on its own*, I thought, and I hopped downwind into the growing smoke. I opened up the cowl of the blue bag to let the heat and smoke curl in, warming my chest, pelvis, and legs. *I'm going to make it. I'm getting warm.*

There is nothing more human than a fire. I'm certain that fire was the first thing that began to separate us from the other animals; the thing that came before the making of symbols, the adornment of our bodies, the tools and complex language, the cooperation and divisions of labor. Fire is at the very base of human things, and every one of us is wrapped in and around it. It is the center of every camp, every home. To live without fire is to live and die as an animal. *But I am not an animal.* I am a human being. I can make fire in the north and survive. I looked up into the sky and extended my thanks to my teacher Moses, wherever he was, who had taught me how to make the fire here, and live.

I WAS NOW HUNGRY. Ravenous. My body had received a memo saying that it was now going to live, and quickly got about the task of issuing clear and immediate orders concerning just what it needed for its continuing life. I was starting to come down from my sugar high and could feel a headache coming on as my blood glucose plummeted. My body wanted fuel, solid fuel, and lots of it right now. I looked over to the fish. The raven was already there, pecking at one of the eyes. I lunged over, still in the bag, and waved a stick at the bird. It hopped a few feet away. I took the fish and dragged it across the ground by the tail. *Tonight I'm hungrier than a wild raven.* I hunched over the fish, growling at the bird. I am a big animal. *This is my kill, and I intend to have it unmolested.*

I filleted the fish quickly, and then threw its head, guts, and carcass over to my companion. The bird seemed quite happy with this cast-off lot, and cocked his head to look at me with curiosity, wondering why I'd given up the best parts. We proceeded now in peace: man, black bird, and pike in symbiosis; a cluster of old predators on a tiny rock.

I settled down next to my fire to cook. *I'll have steaming hot black coffee and pike for dinner, thank you, and lots of it.* Food had never tasted so good. I fried the pieces of pike, using half my remaining oil, and ate without utensils by holding on to the 'Y' bones in the meat as handles, eating the first pieces nearly raw, and then waiting and cooking the rest in the hot oil until they were golden and flaky.

Here, eating with a wild black raven, I discovered the genesis of table manners. Surely it was a sign of the aristocracy not to fall on your food and fight for it; to be established enough to wait a bit before consuming; and then to do it slowly, in a measured, pre-established way. "You and I don't have to put on any airs tonight," I said to the raven as I watched him clean the carcass of the pike. We were both eating to stay alive, without pretense. I ate and ate, and so did my friend. Then he departed, flapping slowly away.

When the bird left, I'd eaten all of one side of the fish, and half the second: close to five feet of thick pike filets gone in sixty minutes. I'd literally eaten an arm and a leg, but was still hungry. The fish was mostly protein with only a little fat close to the pike's skin, which I fried, folded up into my mouth, and ate like bacon.

TWILIGHT WAS COMING ON, and there was a merciful small night breeze to keep the mosquitoes away. I was without will or strength to erect the tent or repack my gear, and left my possessions scattered on the ground. I would have to risk the night-squall, and could only hope the rain would not come again. Even though I'd stopped shaking, I went through a detailed body inventory before daring to sleep. I could move my toes and my hands. I was no longer blue. I was conscious. I was warm. My bag had acquired the same clean, subtle scent mixed with wood smoke that I had smelled when Joy's body was lying next to mine. The scent of a new man, I thought. *I can sleep now; sleep in safety here by the fire under the twisted jack pine. I've been baptized in water, and I am now free.* I closed my eyes and was gone.

38: Losing the Way, Finding the Way

> To be human is to both find and make reality.
> ...*The Field Book.*

I AWOKE THE NEXT MORNING to another gray day with low, fast-moving clouds. The sun was obscured, but there was a slightly brighter glow straight overhead which indicated that I had slept 'till noon. I'd had a long, deep, and restful sleep with no strange dreams to disturb me. The rain and sleet had passed over, and the air now carried less humidity. Despite the ordeals of the last few days, I didn't feel that bad. I was stiff from exertion, and my back hurt from sleeping on the hard ground, but I was more alert, and my mood had shifted. For the first time in my life I wasn't feeling even the least bit sorry for myself.

"*—That's good news, Charlie,*" she said. "*Let's have a clean look around then and take stock of the situation.*"

"I'm glad you're back," I heard myself say aloud.

My campsite was a wreck. The canoe was where I left it, riding upright on the shore. Gear was scattered where I'd thrown it out of the pack. My little fire was still smoldering with an unwashed greasy pan next to it. A charred pot covered in burnt coffee was in the middle of the ashes, and my clothes were sitting out in the wind in a wet pile. There was a big bloody carcass of a fish with no eyes about ten feet away that was beginning to attract flies. This sort of camp was a disgrace to any Eagle Scout. I felt pretty good about it. Since sometime last evening, neatness and obedience to rules had waned as a criterion by which I would judge myself. I stretched out in my blue bag and didn't care what anyone, including the disapproving parts of myself, thought about the situation.

I was happy to be alive. The camp was honest, with no pretense. All of my whining and lamenting had given way to something new: a calm and rangy aggressiveness which viewed total chaos as the natural and expected state of affairs. I was curious about what chaotic events were coming next. I really had no idea what they might be.

The raven had been kind to me. My stock of rice and way-bread had been left open on the ground, but he had not called his brothers and sisters to a feast at my expense during my long morning's sleep. He'd taken only the pike's eyes and innards and departed. Perhaps it was the raven I had to thank for my new mind. Perhaps he'd taken pity on my plight and carried my loneliness far away on his dark wings during the night. Or, perhaps the old crook-jawed pike had come to my aid. The fish may have given me his calm strength as I ate him down pound for pound. *It's hard to know where a gift comes from*, I thought. But Moses was right—we must learn to take it when it comes.

Still naked in my bag, I stoked up the little fire, cooked, and ate the rest of the pike filets without bothering to clean last night's mess from the pan. I looked at the carcass of the pike. I'd thought that I could not possibly eat all of him. I was wrong. Breakfast would bring the tally to over five feet of big pike consumed by one man in twelve hours. Probably not a world record, but certainly a personal best. I was still hungry, but dared not reach for any of my pack food. I still had a long trip home.

After breakfast I got out of the bag, slipped on my sloppy wet boots without bothering to lace them up, and took a naked stroll around the island with my shoulders thrown back. The air was warmer, coming in now from the south. There was no sign of another human being, wisp of smoke, sound, or marker of any kind. The place had been abandoned by the entire human race. I was OK with that; content. Both my loneliness and despair had disappeared completely, and no thought, no amount of will or effort could have brought them back. Like a stray yellow dog, my self-pity had lit out for other country, finding no more scraps around my door to feed on.

I had undergone no willful psychological process to achieve my liberation. The dark feelings had just run out of me. Gone now. I had simply taken the next step and the next, and somehow walked into a new place beyond the reach of negative emotions.

I looked down at the welt across my right hand. The black edges were gone and the wound had closed to a thin red line. Some mystical regeneration was happening at an accelerated pace on this island. *It started right over there*—I thought, *thirty feet out in the cold water of the lee shore. That's where my vast new energies started to come in.*

Every square centimeter of my clothes, every inch of my body, and all of the corners of my mind had gone down and under to be immersed in the wildness and come back up again. I'd heard that it takes seven years for every molecule of the body to die and be reborn, making a whole new human. This was happening more quickly here.

I'd gone under and been baptized in the old way: full immersion, fully dressed, in cold water. Everything down to the smallest fiber of cloth and the thinnest hair was involved. All the smell of lawyer, who once claimed superiority because of his command of clever facts in neat and logical boxes, was gone. The last of the detergent residue of my life in the city was gone. All the stench of my self-absorption was also left behind in the cold water, along with old stories about myself, and all my big-man plans. Wood smoke had curled around my naked body and into the folds of my sleeping robe to lay its wood-scent on every hair. All my possessions had been left out and exposed to the night wind and the birds of the air. All had been baptized, and all had come up new.

I could just as easily have gone the other way.

The lake could have taken me and released me to another reality. I could be lying over there thirty feet under the water. Death by water. Life by water. No matter. I'm sure my soul would have taken the good of my baptism to heaven whether my body lived through the process or not. *But one thing is now undeniable*, I thought. *I'm here now.*

I stood looking at the slick water of the lee shore, inhaling deep draughts of air from the four directions. The air was clean, filling me open. *She has baptized me in clear deep water, and I am up alive. She has ordained me a man.*

If I chose, I could move now to the Goddess River.

I chose to move.

I WRUNG OUT my undershirt and put it on. It had all of the cozy properties of a hoarfrost suit. The same was true of my wool Pendleton. They say that wool is a good outdoor garment because it is warm when wet. This is bullshit. Cold wet wool is damnable miserably cold. Cold wet canvas pants went on my white legs. Thank God I'd brought no underwear. Wet underpants would never have been placed on my newly baptized body this morning. Such an absurd artifact would have been left to lie on this little glacial hill like an archeological relic for slow decomposition into nothing or discovery by some other idiot like myself.

I would have abandoned my stinking socks but for the risk of blisters. The wet sheep hair turned my feet into soft white prunes, weakening me. *One life change at a time, Charlie, you can learn to walk barefoot over rugged country another day.* My boots went back on, using laces now tied together in a dozen square knots, right over left, left over right, where I'd cut the laces away.

I broke camp, and the heat from my body warmed my clothes just slightly as I moved around. I washed the pots and put them away. All the scattered stuff went back in the pack. I took a look at the canoe. A little green paint was on the rocks where I'd dragged it, but no rib was broken. I dumped water out of the boat and flipped it back over. I got the Seliga up on my thighs, carried it into the water, and loaded my pack. I doused the fire, leaving a little scar that I covered up with pine needles and some loose sticks. I got in my boat and left the island, never to return. I was ready for another day in the wilderness and to earn the Goddess River by nightfall. The skeleton of the old pike I left lying there in silent witness.

THERE WAS NO MARKED TRAIL over to the Goddess River, but it was less than a mile away. I had good reason to believe this: both facts were clearly indicated on the quality guide's map I'd inherited from Moses.

Moses navigated in a world without the global positioning system. He was an old-school map and compass man. Moses' navigation system of choice was a high contrast topographical map that covered a lot of area—one inch on the map was three miles on the ground, a ratio of one map inch to about one hundred and ninety thousand inches across the lakes and hills. This produced a map about a yard square that depicted ten thousand square miles of lake country. A map of this scale could only present the big picture. My finger-tip could easily cover a half-day's travel. Important small information, like the location of portages, was written in by hand.

Like most things associated with Moses, his navigation tool spoke of quality. What was given up in scale was returned to the user with high resolution: lots and lots of little dots of ink per inch, printed on highest quality paper. Moses had picked this map for good reasons: it was light, highly accurate for its scale, never ran out of batteries, worked when wet, and a week's travel could be displayed in a small area the size of a waterproof map case. Along with the map came a quality water-filled compass which kept the needle steady.

This setup had one downside. A lake the size of a football field was just at the edge of what might show up as the smallest recognizable feature; the tiniest of the tiny blue-ink dots. Most of the things that could be seen from the bow seat of the Seliga were not on the map: it was a navigation tool that gave only an approximate position, so I never knew exactly where I was. To use the guide's map, I had to read the country and think like a wilderness traveler. Yet the trappers and Indians who first laid down the trails had no maps at all. Instead, they always followed the grain of the land. They always found the low point, the path where nature had already begun to carve a trail, the path of least resistance. They rarely resisted where nature wanted to take them.

I'd learned good navigation from Moses. He'd discussed the many ways to get lost, even with the best navigation tools in the world. Getting lost was easy. All that was required was a manly mix of hubris, a dash of overconfidence, and a big jigger of being right, God damn it, no matter how wrong your right might be. Men are lost much of the time. The first of the many ways a man gets lost is to believe he can find his way without help.

I WAS CONVINCED that the best way over to the river was to make a short paddle to the western shore of this lake and continue straight west overland. There was no portage to the river marked. Getting there required movement up and down three ridges against the grain of the land.

I know. No portage trail moves against the grain of the land. But it's just one mile, surely I can do that.

"—*But Charlie, you know enough about this country by now. You know that it can't be measured in miles. There are parts of it that will put you on your knees fighting and dying for yards.*"

Yes, Yes. I know I know. But crossing this small set of ridges is a shortcut that will save me a week of travel. My food's running low. I survived the long portage, didn't I? This portage couldn't be any worse.

"—*And just how do you know that, Charlie?*"

THE ROUTE REQUIRED simple navigation. Straight west for one mile. How hard was that? There was a bend in the river there, the easternmost point of the Goddess. If I missed the bend in the river, the walk could get a lot longer, true. I would be climbing ridges with a boat on my back. That was true too. *But its only one mile, and I have a whole day to do it.*

I had a pretty good idea of where west was. We'd been traveling the country orienting north, south, east, and west for many weeks. Before starting out, I checked out my intuition with the compass just to make sure. I was dead on. West: right there. I paddled over to the western shore of the lake, picked out a likely spot, loaded up, and started walking uphill in a westerly direction.

The first rise was not too bad. I had a view from the first ridge top of two more ridges, but couldn't see the river. The down-slope was slick and steep, but I made it to the bottom. Between the ridges there was a small hollow filled with water. Too small to show up on the map, I thought. I paddled across.

Crossing the pothole took only a minute. I moved along the west bank of the little lake looking for a place to climb the second ridge. There simply was none. I was learning that my map's topographical lines would show small spaces between them even if a cliff were vertical. The second ridge was vertical. Ropes and the skill to use them would be needed to get over this, and I had neither. The only way out was at the north end of the pothole where the land was not as steep. I got out at the north end and started walking; trying to make my way back southward and west. Yet with every step the land was forcing me a little to the right. Left was harder, slipperier, and more up-hill. I could not stride straight because I was walking side-hill. Every stride with my left leg was just a couple of inches shorter than one taken with my right. My mind was nonetheless convinced that I was walking straight west. That was my story, and I was sticking to it.

MOSES TAUGHT ME that a second way to get lost, even with a good map and compass, was to become convinced that all objective facts that contradicted one's predetermined conclusion were just flat wrong. When the third ridge failed to appear after about a half-hour, I unshouldered the canoe, took out the compass for the first time, and looked at the needle. I was shocked to see that I was walking nearly in line with a needle that always pointed toward magnetic north. The compass had to be wrong. I was walking *west*. Every bone in my body was sure of it.

All right. I may have walked a few steps north, but that was just to get around that second cliff. I was on track, moving west.

I shouldered the canoe, and began to walk with the compass in hand. I picked out a landmark a hundred yards west of me and walked toward it, but the bow of the canoe often dipped down and broke my line of sight. It was hard to hold the compass and balance the canoe on my shoulders at the same time. I lost sight of my marker and found a new one. I was working hard and moving quickly. I accepted the fact that today would be a long set of exhausting leg presses with heavy weight.

I hit another small lake that was not on the map. This lake had an irregular shape, and did not look at all like any of the bodies of water on my map, except the little round dot out in open country far out to the north of where I was. That dot was a long way from the river, and just at the base of a big round-top hill. I took a short lunch of waybread at the lake, focusing intently on the map and drinking warm and stagnant water.

There's a third way to get lost with a good map. That is to deny reality as shown on the map because it's so confronting. The conditions of reality can require just too much work. It's easier to stay in denial, and force the map to fit one's sense of the way the world should be. I still possessed some of the skills of a good lawyer: I was happy to bend the facts to fit my predetermined theory about what was occurring, instead of being open, curious, and fearless about the truth.

Forcing a wilderness map is easy because nature cooperates. Nature has a remarkable facility for copying patterns and making slight variations in those patterns so that millions of nature-made things are very similar, but no two things exactly alike. Take seven billion human faces, for example, or those 350,000 species of beetles, or the surface topography of the lake country.

The lake country presents itself at ground level in recurring patterns of sameness with slightly unique surface features. A big lake might have a dozen big bays of irregular size, some a mile wide. Any one of those bays has a dozen or so smaller bays of varying size, around a quarter-mile wide. Each smaller bay within the big bay has its own set of a dozen irregular shoreline features, a hundred yards wide. And so on down to a little patch, two-foot square next to the shore, that contains—well—about a dozen irregularly shaped bays of green weeds a couple inches wide. This patterning continues down to the molecular level and up to the size of continents. Similar patterns within patterns within patterns. Anyone new to the lake country says the same thing: "It all looks alike!" And they're right.

A topographical map is a picture of this look-alike land, taken from a height, showing whichever surface features can be seen from that altitude. If you fly high, you can only see the big stuff. Lower, and more of the small stuff comes into view, but you see a lot less area. A navigator who wants to force the map can easily convince himself that the small bay over there is actually the big bay shown on the map: they look so much alike. If you throw out your compass and turn the map one hundred and eighty degrees, the bay over there and the map will match up even more closely. And as the map is thus forced-fitted, there is that pesky, slightly sick feeling like the feeling felt in elementary school when you've misspelled a word in front of the class on the public blackboard, a word that doesn't look quite right and doesn't feel all that right either. *But I'll stay with my interpretation of the word, thank you.* After all, I've written it.

Alone in the wilderness, it's easy to be right, with no one there to disagree. In fact, it's easy to become so right that you're dead right before you know it.

I could not get what I was seeing to jibe with my map. I turned the map in every direction, but no help. *This little round pothole is part of that little stream that flows down to the Goddess River just to the north of the cliffs. I'm just where I want to be*, I thought. If I looked hard enough, I could make it fit.

I took a long drink out of the warm water of the pothole. *I'm sick of this fucking map.* Who needs it? It's no good for travel across land, and not that great for lake travel either. *Everything on it is just a bunch of blobs.* I threw the map into the top of my pack and tied the pack down. The river's west somewhere, that much is certain. *The best thing to do is just to cowboy-up and walk west.* I'm bound to run into the water.

IT WAS A LONG, STEEP UP-SLOPE from the pothole. *This has to be the third ridge. Those tight contour lines on the map showing something smaller and steeper have to be wrong.*

The up-slope had been ravaged by fire. The forest floor was covered with berry-bushes, and the blackened trees were scattered like some mighty hand had thrown down a small mountain of burned pickup sticks without bothering to tidy them up. Every fifth step was up and over a log. This portage was raking my shins to blood. "I'd give an ear for some good leggings," I said aloud.

Some of the burned trees were tilted and resting on each other, and I had to push the canoe over the deadfall, and then crawl under. The back of the canoe caught on the upright branches, and the bow ran into things in front. It was hard going with no trail, but at least the land was no longer forcing me north. The river had to be just over this rise.

I panted up the steepest part, holding onto trees as I climbed. I made it to the ridge top. All around me was nothing but a quiet forest. No river was in sight.

This is ridiculous! I jammed the canoe into the crotch of a tree, stepped out from under it, and threw off the pack. I unbuckled the flap and reached for the map. It was gone. I dug my hand down the side of the pack, feeling for it. Nothing. *All right, motherfucker.* A full blown unpacking, shaking everything out, looking, and looking again. Nothing. Looking a fifth time and sixth, as if looking for another time would make the map materialize.

THERE IS A FOURTH WAY to get lost with a good map and compass, a way that Moses had not spoken of. This was to lose the map and compass entirely.

Inside my brain, the blood was pounding harder. I could feel the pressure. My throat was tightening, and my body was stiff. I walked a short distance on rigid legs and then came back to the pack. I was emitting thin, whining sounds. Still, there was a stronger, central part of me that was completely calm, almost laughing as it watched my body. *More chaos on the menu. More weather to paddle through,* I thought. Something was coming up. The calm part of me was able to be curious. Then I began to remember.

It was parent's night at Boy Scout camp, and I was twelve years old. I'd stayed after the campfire to talk to my mom before she pulled away from the parking lot and headed back home. I had to walk back to our campsite alone in the dark. I'd taken the trail a dozen times. It was different, though, at night as my flashlight threw a blinding pool of light into a small area and created menacing shadows just outside the ring of illumination. In the small light-pool, the path just disappeared. I walked into a jumble of briars that tied me up and clung to my clothing. I couldn't move out of the briars, and cried and cried for help. I was lost and dying in the forest. Then my scoutmaster showed up. It turned out that I was only four feet off the path, and less than fifty yards from our campsite. But if you can't see the way home, four feet might as well be halfway across the world. You can drown in a bucket of water, you know. Lost is lost.

I can't believe that you're still crying like a twelve-year-old after all you've been through, I said to myself. But even after all that Moses, Joy, and the wilderness had given me, it was another involuntary response, another part of me that I didn't even know was there coming out to be cleansed in the light of my awareness. All I could do was watch myself. But at least now, as a matter of good habit, I could stand outside my whining body and do just that. I could be curious about the contours of this, the next self-inflicted catastrophe.

THE MAP that I'd held in such disdain just thirty minutes ago now became more important than any object I'd ever possessed. Without the map there was no way I could make it out of here. *Be calm, Charlie, just retrace your steps and find the thing.* I was sure that I'd put it in my pack at the pothole before I began the long trudge up the hill. The map must have dropped out somewhere on the way up.

I looked down the hill. There was no sign or trace of a trail. I could see a few places where the moss had been moved around, but mostly I'd been traveling uphill over rock, and had not left much sign of passage. I ran a few feet down the hill then back again. There was no way to tell the exact path that I'd traveled or to retrace my steps with certainty. But the map had to be back there somewhere. *Just walk back down the hill and find it, Charlie. You can't leave here without it.*

Going on a map-search with a pack and an eighteen-foot canoe on my back was impossible. *I can't see a damn thing from under that canoe—that's why I'm in this trouble in the first place.* I had no intention of carrying that big boat down the hill and back up again through all the deadfall. I left the canoe wedged into the crotch of a tree up on the hilltop with my pack next to it, and started down the hill. This simple and direct course of action was in violation of every tenet of The Rule as laid down by Moses. I was never to be separated from my life support system. But what had Moses said about the Rule, back there in the beginning?

"You'll come to learn that you cannot follow The Rule under your own power no matter how hard you try. You're going to need the help of something else, something bigger than yourself."

Yes that, or something like it. On impulse, I took a few steps back up the hill, fished the Field Book out of the pack, and shoved it in my back pocket. *Like it's going to help me,* I thought.

It was a wonderful relief to walk in the woods without all of that gear. It was like I'd been throwing a medicine ball for many hours and now could throw a volleyball, instead. I stopped every few feet and turned around to look backward. Within twenty-five yards, the canoe and pack had disappeared. I was looking at a wall of forest. I decided to walk back to a spot where I could see my gear and make a mark on a tree with my knife. Every twenty-five yards or so I turned and made other little marks so that I could follow them back to my pack. The day was getting old and the shadows longer.

"*—Those little marks aren't going to do you much good when the sun goes down, Charlie.*"

I walked rapidly down the hill, trying to retrace my steps, but it soon became clear that such retracing was impossible. Most of the hill was made up of bare stone and deadfall. Halfway down, I saw a black scrape where I'd slipped coming up. *This has to be pretty close to my route.* But without following the *exact* path how could I find where the map had fallen?

Within minutes I was back to the shore of the little pothole lake where I'd eaten lunch. Surprisingly, I hit the lake only a few feet from the place where I'd taken the boat out of the water: there was the smallest bit of green paint transferred from the canvas to one of its rocks. Nowhere was there any sign of the map. I walked back up the hill, intent now, fanning out like a bird dog and searching every square foot, every crevice. My sense of urgency was growing. I got to the top of the ridge and the little blazes on the trees petered out. But losing the blazes was now the least of my problems.

The canoe, and the pack next to it, were nowhere in sight. They had simply disappeared.

My head was spinning. I started to run and search frantically for the pack and the canoe. *It's impossible not to have come back to the same spot where I'd left them.*

I was now tripping, falling, and catching myself with my hands. Little sticks and pine needles were poking into my palms, leaving red indentations. My shins were scraping against the deadfall.

"—*It's dangerous to run in the woods, especially when the blood is in your head, Charlie.*"

I tripped again, landing face first on the forest floor; the wind coming out of me as my chest hit a fallen log. *That's it. You're done, Charlie, done.*

39: No Bottom, No Top

There is no greater blessing than the happy sight of one's own absurdity.
>...*The Field Book.*

THE FOREST IS A PLACE which hides things very well. Trees are perfect for making a wall through which nothing can be seen. Nature's way of overlapping the trees—planting one every ten feet or so—hides things nearly as well as a solid fifty foot wall. Something a hundred feet away can be very well hidden. Even big rivers.

I rolled over on my back, and looked up at the sky. In the final minutes of the day, the low bank of clouds had finally lifted in the west, like an eyelid slowly rising. A golden light came out from under the cloud bank. It was the setting sun in the west, just where I thought west should be.

"You're going to need the help of something else, something bigger than yourself. Finding that bigger thing is the ultimate lesson, the reason for The Rule. When it arrives, The Rule has served its purpose, and you'll be free." That's what Moses had said. I propped myself against the trunk of a pine. I just sat there, not knowing what else to do. Just sat. I'd done everything I could think of.

"—*There's nothing more to do, Charlie. You have done everything you can do and have reached the end of it. There is nothing to do and nowhere to go.*" She was back.

"That's an unsatisfying answer," I said aloud.

"—*It's not my job to satisfy you. It's my job to tell you the truth.*"

"There must be something I can do, some tool to use to get this right."

"—*There is none.*"

"What kind of a guide are you anyway, if you don't have a technique to teach me to solve this problem, something that will give me an advantage, something that will work every time?"

"*—I am a guide taking you where you want to go. You are out here moving towards God, Charlie. You are here to become an embodiment of the Divine, as you might recall.*"

"Well, yes—I guess that's right. Now that you've said it, that's what I've been seeking all along. I am trying to find the Field, and I haven't found it yet."

"*—Do you want help with your God project, Charlie, some help with your project of getting to God?*"

"You bet. And I wouldn't mind some help finding my gear as well, if it doesn't hurt to ask."

"*—Great, then. Here's what you must do next. Abandon your God project and release your attachment to everything you're carrying.*"

I sat there dumbfounded. What kind of a world was this? How did I get to such a strange place?

I opened the Field Book. They were conspiring, this Committee. There was a woman inside my mind, and a book writing itself as we went along.

Here's what the manuscript said on the page where it fell open:

> There is nothing that can be done. Really nothing at all.
> There is no trick or technique for discovering the basis of all
> reality. No way to sit, no way to meditate, no way to conduct
> a ritual, no way to read and understand a holy book in just
> the 'right' way. No, there is really nothing to be done. God is
> not a project.

I read on.

We cannot find the Divine with analysis, looking, or seeking for something outside ourselves. Why? Because fundamentally—always and without exception—the Field cannot be separated from the observer. There is nothing to look at, because there is no separate place to look from.

Your God project will lead nowhere. All it will do is create a fundamental and disastrous further degree of separation: a religion created in whole cloth out of your imagination and a desire to please yourself. Your religion will become a place to hang out and sharpen the tools of separation, and all of the tools of separation are killing tools.

Any and all of the things you might try—individually and in any sequence or combination—assumes that the Field, the thing that can really help you, is something you can lay hold of, something that you can gain power over. Please excuse us while we laugh out loud. This 'approach'—its beginning, middle, end, substrate, surface, texture, design, and plan—starts with and proliferates a *fundamental misunderstanding* of the nature and existential reality of what is being approached. The Field cannot be laid hold of. You cannot pound a stake in the sky!

I slid down the tree trunk to rest on the floor of the forest and touched the mark between my eyes where the Shaman had touched me. Suddenly I had nowhere to go; I was at full stop. All I could do was sit and breathe. I began to focus on the breath going into my body and out of my body. I now noticed how tense I was, how my legs ached from the effect of my striving, how all of my body's cortisol chemicals and adrenaline had been preparing me for desperate action. I was coming down, becoming limp and more flexible. I closed my eyes for a minute and just felt the breathing. Then I opened my eyes again.

For the first time ever, I began to look. Of course, I'd been seeing things all my life. But I'd always been seeing with an agenda, looking around to see where I was going, and comparing it to a map of shoulds and should-nots, of somewhere else to be. Even practicing 'seeing beauty' with Moses was an agenda. It was still a form of striving.

My attention turned outward. Instead of throwing something, I started catching. I received light in my eyes—images. The forest was beautiful in late afternoon. Light was slanting down through the trees in diagonal columns that had a heavy texture, carrying small bits of dust and the shimmer of insects. I was in pine, and its smell was everywhere. The rays of end-day light released scent from the forest floor, the scent of pine leaves slick against each other, dusky and warm. The trees were catching light, and all of the needles of the trees were fanning out to receive it, to bask in the final rays of summer. The woods were full of faint creakings and groanings—the sounds of living things in the wind; a brushing and soft hissing of pine. Everything was quiet. Not the noise of a machine anywhere. This small quiet was in the context of an even bigger quiet that moved along the ground and stretched out through the forest in all directions.

How absurd am I? What kind of fool carries a boat to the top of a hill? Who would park a watercraft on the summit of the highest, driest hill around, and then leave it to run around in panic over the country, notching trees, tripping, falling on his face, and going nowhere?

I stood up and looked over my shoulder. Perhaps it was the light that had changed. About thirty feet away, slightly down hill and to the right, there was a green log propped up against a tree. It had a curve on its front end and a cedar gunwale. Its mottled green paint was camouflaged with runes and markings that blended into the forest. The boat was still a living thing coming home to the place from which it had been hewn. A pack sat beneath the boat. I walked over and sat down on the pack with my head hanging down between my hands.

"*—Perhaps in this new place, a part of you that has been in shadow can come to light. There are golden parts in your shadow, Charlie. Perhaps there's a part of you that can find the way without a map. All you have to do is ask, Charlie. Just ask and what is already here will be revealed to you.*"

I opened my eyes, not seeking anything. And there, right there at my feet, a path.

"*—All water moves downhill, Charlie, and if you want to be where the water is, you have to walk down a hill. Even the smallest drop will seek a path, always* *the lowest path, and always the easiest. It's not as hard as you think it is. Follow the flow."*

There at my feet was a little wash, difficult to see until it was pointed out, but then plainly noticeable. A little wash of granite, just a shade lighter than the surrounding rock. I pitched the boat up onto my shoulders and started to walk downhill, following the little trail. I could now admit that I was on top of the big round hill, far to the north and still east of the river. The forest was growing darker and more intimate all around me. I could not have read a map in this light even if I had one. But the wash, the path of the carving water, the path of least resistance, was curling around the landscape; a path that would be easily missed in the full light of day without twilight to amplify its subtle gradation in color. Whatever had taken me up this hill now wanted to take me down.

Just then, something unexpected and pleasant arrived. I discovered that I knew a marching song, a bouncy little tune that was just right for the load and the moment. It went like this:

"Who's ... the ... leader ... of ... the ... club ... that's ... made ... for ... you ... and ... me? M-I-C-K-E-Y M-O-U-S-E!"

I had big clomping strides to take. They carried me down the western slope of the big round hill at a pace that was at the edge of a run. I finally was covering that mile to the river. The little path grew wider and more gravelly. It then grew moist underfoot. And there—unmistakable and clear: the shimmer of something moving in the moonlight through the forest and the sound of water.

40: Enlightenment

The Field is already here. It's been with you from the beginning. It is the life in which everything lives, moves, and has its being.
   ...*The Field Book.*

THAT NIGHT I CAMPED beside the Goddess River, a good name for something carrying so much life. I made camp and went down to drink at the river. Water is the only real drink for a man.

Sleeping next to a river running cold and swift over rock puts one at risk of dreaming in a new way. A river is not one body, but instead countless thousands of little rivers, brooks, droplets, streamlets, falls, fountains, backsplashes, rock splashes, swirls, and gurgles. These play on the senses, and come into the sleeping mind as voices. The voices speak the little talk of the nature spirits, the sprites, and muses. These spirits suspend the dreamer between the edge of wakefulness and the edge of sleep, so that the dreamer might remember the dream. In my dreams that night, something came in close. I could hear its breath outside the tent, lying with me. Just outside. I dared not open the flap to see what it was.

IT WAS MY PLEASURE to wake up in the new morning beside the clear and icy waters of a moving river coming downhill over rock; to finally put my craft into moving water; to ride easily with the movement; to be catapulted through the little rapids; and to walk the short portages around the cauldrons of mist and rainbow fire.

The river relieved me of all worry about navigation. I simply went where the river was flowing. I was where the river was. There was no other place to be. I was no longer tethered to a map and was free to immerse in a flow that was alive and a draw to other life.

My mind became more quiet, then quieter still. The little snippets of tunes, the fantasies, memories, plans, worries, advertising jingles, and my self-absorbed ruminations faded away and no longer filled my mind that morning. My mind could not hold onto such things any more. My thoughts went outside of me and down onto the surface of the river. All tension, worry, and effort were gone. I had nothing to do but move and nowhere to be but here.

It might have been that my new quiet mind helped me move more quietly, or perhaps that the final human scent had been washed from me in the icy waters of baptism. Perhaps the river was simply offering gifts. But at the seventh bend in the river, every creature of the forest suddenly came out of hiding to be with me. Over the summer, we'd seen animals on occasion, especially in the morning. But I'd never seen the forest dwellers in this abundance. They were everywhere and unafraid.

It began with a cow moose grazing on water plants in the shallows. I could just make out my own reflection in her large dark eye when she lifted her head as I drifted quietly past within twenty feet. In another stretch, otters slipped into the water. They traveled downriver with me, backstroking under the canoe, then getting ahead and raising up on their hind legs to otter-hiss me as I went by. I was being admonished for not coming into the river to play. There were eagles looking down from the sky, and osprey fishing. Hundreds of ducks were arriving from further north to bob in the shallow lakes formed by the wider stretches of the river. Fish were sitting motionless in the shadow of boulders, looking upstream and finning against the current—so perfectly blended with the rocky bottom that only their moving shadows gave them away. Beaver were working up and down the river, especially where little brooks merged in from the side. I could move up close beside the beavers, silent and camouflaged in my Seliga, nearly touching them before their hard tails boomed the water. A black bear with a three-quarters cub moved along the bank with the odd undulating motion caused by front legs shorter than the rear, a compromise between speedy legs and handy arms. I moved down river, breathing with each stroke of the paddle.

Past every bend I would turn my head to see. There. A glimpse. No. Just light through the trees. But I was sure—indeed certain: I was being followed. Something was moving with me downriver through the trees just out of my sightline.

What every creature in the forest knew, I began to remember. *We are all part of something much bigger than ourselves.* The bigger thing we are part of is *alive*. As a human being, I could choose disconnection with that bigger thing. That disconnection only makes the re-connection in full choice and full awareness that much sweeter. The Goddess River wanted a man that had chosen her and earned her. I was sure of this. I had chosen her, worked for her, and had nearly died to get to her. In return, she was opening up to me.

About noon, I passed the cliffs I'd attempted to portage over yesterday. The third and final western cliff was a sheer drop of three hundred fifty feet right into the river. No one coming from the river would ever start walking there. How absurd and full of hubris was the idiot who would try to move against the grain of the earth. This was not a land that would long endure such a man. I was glad to have left him behind yesterday and to have come around to clearer senses.

INDIAN SUMMER had arrived on the Goddess River with August warmth during the day and November cold at night. I moved downriver with the current for several days, moving, eating, and sleeping whenever my body wanted to move, eat, or sleep. I drank deeply out of the river. Fish were abundant everywhere, and all that was necessary to catch them was to flip the red-eye out in a rapid and let it drift down. The river was full of walleye, the same fish so prized in all of the little towns of Wisconsin. I grew stronger on their firm, flaky white meat. The river offered fish to me by the dozens every day, but I chose to eat only a few. My body relaxed its demands as it realized it could get nourishment whenever needed. I would not starve while on the river.

I learned to navigate the smaller rapids without portaging around—standing up in the canoe on the slick water above the rapids to pick the best route down—following the V's made by submerged rocks, avoiding the boiling water and seeking instead the fast flat water where it could be found. This water moved and mingled with the air in a way that enhanced the air and water both. I slept well at the river. I had not rested so well in ... I couldn't remember when. Years it seemed.

SOMETIME AROUND the seventh day, I decided on impulse to turn up a little watercourse that merged into the river from the right. The final fulcrum of Moses's teaching instructed me to trust such impulses, especially when I was curious, grateful, and able to see the beauty around me. That was a sign that my energy state was high enough to trust my intuition. I followed the water up a draw to where it widened into a smelly black bog. It appeared to be a dead end. But there was water-sign flowing dark down a rock face at the end of the bog. *Interesting.* Sometimes these rock walls were dams of granite, holding back millions of gallons of water in small lakes above.

I struggled through the black bog, this part barely easier than it was the first day—a sweaty task full of bugs and black flies. I looked calmly at a couple of mosquitoes trying to get their mean little probes through the back of my hand. Their beaks just bent pitifully. The back of my hand had become a wind-burned hide. Then I was up and over the rock face. There was a wind blowing toward me, a clear wind, and I nosed the Seliga into it through a dense grove of black alder. I saw a glimmering of blue through the trees, then plunged down a steep bank and staggered on loose stones into water. I threw off the canoe and felt the intense relief as the weight was released, coupled with the sensation of floating off the ground. I collapsed into cool water, wet up to the chest, washing away my sweat and the muck of the bog, and then looked out. The lake was there, glistening and blue, folding the wind and the sunlight into its surface, and carrying that wind and sunlight to me.

It was very good.

I stood thigh-deep in the joy of being fully alive and finding new country. Everything about the lake carried the sense that in this small place, I might be the first. In a world where every square inch was mapped, a real discovery of new country was to be a child again. There was no human sign. No dash of aluminum or paint on a rock from a canoe, no blazes on wood, no path in. The trees were tall and uncut, many having fallen into the lake from old age years ago. Broken cliffs of black granite slanted into the pool, indicating great depth in a small place. Shafts of white light penetrated the clear water and then worked deeper into the gathering azure darkness, as if they were descending into a twilight sky during midday. Trees grew right down to the water's edge. I could see no place to camp, but I climbed into the Seliga and began to paddle the lake.

I wanted to be here, to stay here. I didn't think there was anything more needed to complete me, but there was something more here. A place untouched, one of the last places. I followed the water's edge, breaking reflections of the trees with my bow plate and crossing the lines of logs fallen into the water. Down at the end was a rocky cliff offering a jumble of boulders that had fallen down its center to form a shoulder. Scrambling up the boulders was easy, and there at the top was a little flat spot in a grove of aspen.

I unloaded the gear and set up camp, then went back to the lake with my fishing rod. The lake was a crystal pool. I cast out the swim jig and within the first four feet of the retrieve it moved suddenly sideways, smashed by a glowing twelve-inch lake trout, perfect in its proportion. I put him in the boat and cast again. This time there was a fish within two feet. Then again, and again. Four casts, four fish, easily all that I could eat.

The fish here had never seen a lure.

I caught and released a few more for the sport of it, and then headed back to my camp. I ate, and then rested.

The breeze had shifted during lunch. It was now coming up from the south, pushing warm up the face of the small cliff. It was a feathery breeze that curled around my face and body—plenty of air movement in midday to keep the black flies and most of the mosquitoes away.

I pulled everything out of the pack to be cleaned by the beautiful air. The Field Book was there.

"You've sure expected a lot out of this little book, haven't you, Charlie?" I said aloud. *Face it.* From the first moment you opened it, you've had expectations. You really thought that if you pondered deeply over the little scratchings, and had some great thoughts of your own, you'd suddenly join the ranks of the world's great thinkers and emerge from this wilderness experience with a cohesive worldview. You actually expected to figure everything out and be able to explain everything in some rational and logical way. You've assumed all along that the world was knowable this way—through language, thought, and reason.

I began to leaf through the pages. It was hard to focus on the language recorded there in lines laid down by Moses with his beautiful Faber-Castell. They seemed to be written for the benefit of another person; for some hard-headed defensive egotist that needed some better thoughts at one stage of his journey. That egotist was a man that this wilderness had simply dissolved. My attention kept going out, out to the arc of beauty penetrating every inch of this place. The lake was a study in perspective.

The lake's narrowing and descending banks faded into a shimmering heat with a geometry that beguiled the eye like a Renaissance painting. The lake suggested itself as a vast body of water stretching far into the distance, and needed only a great three-masted ship under full sail painted into its middle to complete the illusion. My attention was drawn to the end of the picture, a high place where the sky, rock, and water found their apex.

I sat there gazing, looking out with a quiet mind beyond all arguments and lines of thought. The cliff face was gathering the full heat of Indian summer. There'd been no waking moment on this trip, not one, when I'd been both still and warm. There was always dampness and a mistiness rising from the depths of the lakes that kept me buttoned-up even in the sunlight. I needed my clothes for warmth and for armor. But here on the rock, the wind was coming up a long face of black granite perfectly positioned to catch the full force of the early afternoon sun. The wind was warm. I took my shirt off, then boots, then pants. The wool socks, now completely black, slopped up against a rock, sticking there to dry.

I took inventory. All of the fat I might ever have had, baby fat, belly fat, that little extra underneath the chin, was all long gone. My stomach was cut down the middle, with every muscle in clear definition. There are eight segments to the *Rectus Abdominis*, not six, and all of them were there, chiseled out of my body. My hands were a tough mass of wilderness etchings, fibrous and wind burned; and my shins were scarred tough as wood. Every place was healing from some welt or bite or impact. This was a tough and resilient organism, a body that had come alive in response to long, hard labor. I had arrived in power.

I was sure now that the wind would hold to keep the bugs at bay, and I began to risk full exposure. Inch by inch I spread out into the delicious, sensual feeling of being warm. The wind felt so wonderful on my body, caressing it, holding it warm in the updraft of the cliff. The warmth was penetrating through muscle into the bone, opening me.

Inhaling, then a long exhale with eyes closed—a willingness to be opened, to receive the warmth, the gift. A feeling in the chest and belly, filling with the beauty, connecting. I stood up and stretched out, embracing the wind and the beauty of that high place. I inhaled the lake and the blue of the sky. The south wind was breathing me.

THERE IS LIGHT in an aspen grove on a Sunday, knee deep in autumn. It moves as the wind moves. With each breath the trees stretch out their arms and supple wrists to connect to slender golden leaves pulling as wings, a thousand fingers in ballet, moving in undulations of circles and ovals, spinning the wind. And through this dance, light and shadow come falling together; a rustling rain of shafts and droplets, appearing and disappearing as footfalls and firefalls on a whirling floor of illumination.

It was the light, there in the aspen grove that finally did it.

The light on the forest floor, whirling and broken, was the final straw added to make a whole sum. The world shifted and came apart. I felt everything—the undivided—expand. The endless and infinite vastness of creation, and my substance so infinitesimally small, yet part of *this*. So vast. So beautiful. All saturated with connective energy, a vibrant, pounding, and shaking joy. Love. *Love binds everything together!*

The trees are full of it, the rocks, the air, my body, my mind. *Everything* is in a field of love, interpenetrating all and stretching out infinitely in all directions. And I was part of it, made of it, in it.

I leapt across the rocks, pounding and shaking the trees. Moses and Joy had not deceived me! They had not abandoned me! They had brought me to The Field!

Every part of my body released. Life was finished. There was nothing more to do. Everything now had an energy glow around it. It was so *alive*. I moved to the trees and listened to them, in love with them, connecting to them with nothing in between. They had voices in the wind. We were all there in the grove together, dancing in a field of deep time and timelessness bound together.

THE SUN WAS FADING as I walked back to my pack. The wind had scattered my gear, and the pack was turned over. The plastic pack liner had separated from the outer sack. "How about that," I said aloud. There, peeking out from under the lumpy bag was the corner of a plastic case. It was my map and compass. They'd been with me all of the time. The map case had somehow lodged outside the pack liner when I threw it at the pack in my frustration and had worked its way down to the bottom. My map and compass had been sitting in the wet bottom of the canoe for a week. That's why I wasn't able to find it. This was a day for finding what had been with me all along.

I picked up the map case, looked at it for a moment, and then began shaking with uproarious, spontaneous laughter. I dropped the map down on the top of the pack and let it sit there, resisting the temptation to dive into it and find out where I was. For the first time I knew where I was. I didn't need the map. I'd found home.

Epilogue: The Return of Charlie Smithson

> I'm in love with the core of life, the deep Eros that fills every corner of the world. The source of life has chosen me as her lover. She has given me the willingness to undertake the disciplines that might allow me to see the Source. I ride the Goddess River as a man.
> ...*The Field Book. First entry of Cronus, Messenger and Keeper of the Field.*

EVENTUALLY I DID PICK UP THE MAP, and relate myself once more to its lines and curves, the ones that might show me the way back to the spot where I'd left the old 500 creaking in the dust, to the rest of my life, and to whatever work lay ahead. I had no name for what I'd received, but I knew that it was a great and powerful gift, and that I had to find some way to arrange my life so that I could give a gift in return. I was stripped of all desire to do anything else.

I portaged out of the deep crystal lake through the black bog. I had to admit that trusting my instincts to turn up the little draw had led me to the most profound Cosmic Luck anyone could ever hope for.

I merged back into the flow of the Goddess River. The wind had changed and a pre-winter squall moved over the land carrying hard, cold rain, and flecks of snow. I had to work again for heat, shivering uncontrollably at every stop and point of rest. My summer gear was reaching the limit of its usefulness. The season of snow and hard water would soon be upon me.

In these final days, the weight of the canoe was the same, the bugs were the same, the muck of the swamps the same, the shafts of light breaking through the clouds at daybreak the same. But there was a difference.

Through it all was a peace, beyond all understanding, penetrating everything. The vibrating, pounding joy that had come upon me at the cliff-top did not leave me. It stayed and deepened into the sense—indeed the certainty—that I could die tomorrow, or drown around the next bend, and all would be well. I knew now that I was not separate from the Field; that I was within the Field. Love was no longer outside of me. Every moment, every leaf, stone, and shaft of light was precious beyond measure.

Time had taken on a different quality. Every moment was unhurried, languorous, and sensual, and yet a day passed in an instant. Time was bending, stretching, and breathing. There were moments when I felt like time was flowing in reverse—that I was getting younger.

In this new awareness I felt unforced curiosity about everything that was arising. Each thing I encountered was a discovery. I saw creation simply as a marvel and a miracle—not as a dream or illusion but as a flower of deep time. I saw an osprey dive onto a pike to wrestle him out of the water. The bow of my canoe nearly hit the side of a nine-foot moose that was obscured by mist as I portaged through a stand of black alder. Startled, the big bull cleared a trail for me using his ice age mass and giant horns like a bulldozer through the close-packed trees. There were steaming piles of bear scat on the path next to warm clawed footprints. Gifts of dry cedar lay like presents under deadfall to start the evening fire, the cedar's fragrant smoke bringing warmth and life.

Now, I began to see five-petaled flowers everywhere. As I peered into their depths, I felt a warming in the center of my forehead, as if something were expanding there, allowing me to see even more of the energy that radiating from within the blossoms. As I looked up from the flowers, the forest became a changing pattern of vibrant colors in hues layered over each other in ever greater depth. And through all of this was the dominant feeling of bottomless gratitude, the joy of being alive, and the impossible heartbreak of the beauty of the world.

It was another day on the river after my awakening, late afternoon. I came around a bend into a wide pool, and she was standing there on a low pinnacle of rock, with the river cutting underneath. She looked as if she'd been expecting me. She was in a state of quiet alertness, relaxed with her tail neither up in agitation nor down between her legs. Her coat was a glossy silver-grey with long strands of black on the tip of her tail. The blue eyes were there, waiting for me to look into them. The same eyes that were in Joy's face, were now set deep in the calm face of this beautiful silver-gray she-wolf; the very eyes that were in the face of the dream-wolf that had come to me the first night. This was the creature that had been following me. She'd been moving all the while, watching my struggles and my victories, and standing guard outside my tent at night to protect me like the Shaman had protected me as I traveled in my dreams.

I stopped all motion and began to glide very slowly across the water. She made no effort to move, but simply turned her head to look into my eyes. We held each other's gaze for a long moment as I drifted by. There was not a trace of fear, hostility, or separation. Her placement on the pinnacle, surrounded by the flowing water, was deliberate: it was the place of an independent and powerful creature, simply standing by her river to acknowledge my presence. It was a moment of inclusion, a graduation. I was being accepted. I had come to her world, and she, the alpha female, was acknowledging me as part of it. Her gaze was the birthright. I knew without doubt that both she and I were Keepers of The Field.

I drifted for a moment longer, and then she turned and disappeared into the forest. One step, two steps, gone.

I moved the rest of the day in an even deeper silence. I was a part of her now, and she a part of me.

It was near sunset when I found the paintings on the rocks. They were under an overhang in a flat-water section of the river where it ran deep. Red paint and drawings in two dimensions without perspective. A picture of humans standing on water, standing in canoes. Brown and orange lichens grew web-like in patterns on the paintings, making them exquisite. A red palm was placed on the rock at the height of my shoulder. I pressed my hand against it. This hand was just the size of mine. And next to the hand was the red face of a wolf, looking calmly.

BY MID-MORNING of the next day, I reached the big water where the Goddess River emptied herself. It was a lake so vast that the opposite shore was barely a line on the horizon. Even a moderate facing wind on such a body of water would defeat any solo paddler. But that morning the wind was blowing at my back. It was a hard wind—howling down from the north—churning the big lake water into a great energy system full of foam and whitecaps and making walls of water above my head. If I put the Seliga into the lake, there would be no turning back, turning sideways, or turning at all. One wrong move and the lake would have me, but with a following wind of such power, I could fly down the lake and be at the southern shore by late afternoon. I then could portage to the road, walk a mile or so to where I'd left the 500, and be on the road to Winnipeg by nightfall. I could be back across the border sometime tomorrow.

I had no anxiety about the future. Yet, at the same time, there was a bright kindling of anticipation about what might come next, a powerful optimism that I could be part of a new humanity that could bring heaven to earth, and that the time had arrived where this might be possible.

I had solved none of the world's problems here. I had simply reached the point where no problems existed. In the process, I had grown so much; indeed had grown into another type of human being with the capacity to be great: not great in what I possessed, thought, or controlled; but great in what I might make possible for others.

I sat shivering at the inlet to the lake, deciding. What was I going to do, and where was I going to go? I couldn't stay the winter here, not alone, and with only summer gear; and I couldn't see myself showing up at the Chicago brownstone with these blackened hands and a mind like flowing water. I needed someplace to re-integrate into a new life.

But what about Edna? Edna was alone there on the shores of Loon Lake. She would take me in and be glad for the company. I searched the Field for an image of Bill. I was sure that he had passed gently to the other side, and that Edna was now in a nether-world without him.

I laughed out loud, recalling the life mission 'discovered' for me by the Initiative. What was it?—"To create a beautiful retreat environment where I use the power of my friendship and my capacity for diligence to aid others in creation of their innovative projects." *You actually remembered it, Charlie. Way to go!* Maybe, despite all of their contrivances, the Initiative had hit on something. I was filled with mirth at the thought that they might be right. Maybe the cabins would be a place to stand and a place to begin to help. Yes. I would drive back to Wisconsin, pull off of the highway at the old arrowhead sign, and see if I could return some of the kindness that Edna had shown me. Cabin number six would be a good place for the world (and for me) to see what kind of man I had become. I could begin to create the future there.

But, wherever I might go, my search for happiness was over. The Goddess River had poured through me, and all I wanted to do was to pour my life back into the river; to find some way to give a gift to others; to love and to serve. Edna would be a good person to teach me how. And perhaps, just perhaps, I could come to see footfalls and firefalls of light on the shores of Loon Lake, and feel the open joy, just as I'd seen the light and felt the feeling here.

I MADE THE COMMITMENT. I sank down to my knees to lower my center of gravity and rested my buttocks on the edge of the bow seat, loose at the hips, with the paddle branded by Moses in my hands, the paddle with weathered writing on the shaft that said "The Field promises nothing except itself." I went out. One stroke, two strokes. Caught now by the wind. The Seliga rode out onto the lake, into the big water, being lifted up from behind and tossed forward, sliding down the surface of the first wave, as I ruddered to keep the bow at the exact point where it would not take on water. It was then I saw them.

They were standing on an outcrop of rock perhaps fifty yards to the side. I was already well out into the lake with the force of the wind behind me, and there was no way that I could turn and reach them. Moses and Joy stood there, beaming, fully arrayed as beings of light unmasked. They were pumping their hands, and kicking their legs—

cheering like fans at a varsity football game, laughing at their own absurdity and filled with joy.

I crested another wave and slid down it into a trough. On the top of the next wave they were thirty yards further away, and Joy held out her hands above her head in an open, wide blessing. Moses was shouting across to me with cupped hands, and his words reached me amid the sounds of the wind and waves.

"Now you've done the easy part, Charlie, *the easy part!* You're now ready to...."

His words were drowned in the wind. But I knew he was right. I could only smile. This *had* been the easy part. The hard part—what to do next, what to do now that I knew, now that I had seen the Field—lay ahead of me. *After all*, I remembered...

> "The spiritual journey starts with the realization that there is nothing more to wait for. There is no 'something else' that needs to happen before we begin. The conditions are already perfect. We start exactly where we are. Whether now or later, this is the only place we can begin."

I turned my attention southward. I was dancing on a knife's edge in the beautiful Seliga. The slightest lapse of attention, and I would be awash with water. Again and again in rhythm, I paddled up the waves and slid back down. The conditions were perfect. I was a man, riding free and well mounted into new country, surfing under the hard October sky.

The End.

The Author, Age Nine.

A Call to Action, and an invitation to Join the fieldwork school.

> Move forward. Find out who you're intended to be.
> ...*The Field Book*.

Isn't it time we did something?

One of the most powerful human experiences is the feeling of movement in a direction of positive change—a direction that one knows to be right. But at this moment, we live in a time when every human thought, belief, system, and practice has been shaken up and dumped out on the table for examination. There are hundreds of conflicting directions on that table—indeed thousands. How do we choose our path, determine what's of ultimate value, and find the power to live in a way that will bring forth the deepest, widest, and most creative future for ourselves and all of life? And what, exactly, can a person do, from the small place where one stands, to make any real difference at all in the face of life's overwhelming obstacles?

We all know that the stakes are quite high. And I believe that fourteen billion years of evolution has placed a very big bet on the creative capacity of a certain person who's reading this invitation now.

If you would like to come home to a place where you'll find advocates, protectors, and friends of your highest intention, please visit us on the web at http://fieldworkschool.org/. I hope you click through and join our tribe. We'll always have some free and useful teaching as a gift for you when you join.

As of this writing, one of our primary interests is learning and teaching the very best practices to help people change the direction of their future, and fearlessly engage in the self-authoring life. We've put together a body of teaching that we call '**fieldbending**.' Our unique approach weaves together the practice of personal evolution, the art of flow, and the power of spiritual friendship to form a trellis on which to grow. Our work dives much more deeply into the potent 'nine powers' as taught by Moses in this book. I hope you'll check us out, and enroll in one of our courses or small groups. You will always be invited to one of our infusion meditation and healing circles when you join. It's one way to engage in the work of a human being, and start creating someplace better.

I invite you to join us, and become one of the soul friends and kindred spirits at The Fieldwork School.

Now's the time. After all, there's no other time we can begin.

In Hope and Gratitude,

Ross Hostetter, Co- founder of the Fieldwork School.

http://fieldworkschool.org/

Acknowledgements

I have many people to thank for this book. No formal editors, agents, publishers, or paid staff at this point—as this has been an honest, independent work undertaken with the grace of my friends, family, and guides who have been with me for 6,000 hours of writing on the clock and the 11 drafts (not counting three first attempts that could not properly be called a draft), beginning with longhand scribbles on legal pads, later learning to type, learning to listen, learning to write, finding my story after many false starts, writing down in faith whatever arrived and not knowing where it was all leading; suffering along with me; and wrestling for years to make a story out of spiritual impulses, feelings, images, lucid dreams, memories, and a single life-changing experience of enlightenment.

Thank you to my friend and spirit brother Mark Mitchum of San Antonio, Texas, a writer with whom I once took a wild leap into the unknown and in whose company a 'download' of automatic writing arrived about the "beauty that lies beneath the blood and bone, and beneath the dust that the blood and bone are made of"—that download being the very seed and call of this book that survived underground for year after year to flower at last. This has been a quarter-century quest to discover the story in which that passage belonged (see page 350 in the initial paperback version). Thank you to my long-time friend and brother Jeff Tedford of St. Louis, Missouri, who introduced me to the world of literature and inspired me long ago with a young man's dream of writing; and who, upon receipt of the very first of the very crappy first drafts, encouraged me abandon the idea of a memoir and to "Start with baseball, and go from there" in order to find out who my main character was. I followed his advice, and it worked.

A bow of gratitude to my old bud, Dennis Strini, who taught me a thing or two about 'wordsmithing,' and who was there at the beginning as we left our jobs, ventured forth, and began to live the dream of becoming creative people in this world.

Thanks to Rhonda Jones-Hartell of Telephone, Texas, my co-traveller in spiritual community, who read my first writing at its very worst; and who offered me badly needed guidance on grammar, punctuation, and sentence structure. I have no idea why I never learned these things in school. Thank you also to my friend and fellow spiritual traveller Don Hatchett of Dallas, Texas, who meticulously edited early drafts, and was strong enough to tell me they were not anywhere good enough.

Thank you to my friend and soul brother Marc Pollock of Dallas, Texas who read two later drafts and who has never offered anything but enthusiasm, encouragement, cheerleading, real help, and good advice—especially advice about the spiritual teaching in this book.

Thank you to my first and only writers group in McKinney Texas with Jiaan Powers, Margery Clive, and especially Catherine Sjostedt who gave me such encouragement as she read and felt the story moving somewhere for the first time. Thank you also to Marcy Mallory of Waxahachie, Texas for her enthusiasm about the book.

Thank you to my many friends and fellow travellers in Boulder, Colorado. To Daune Green, who read what I thought was a final draft (there would be many more) and sent such a beautiful note of encouragement. To Loretta Milburn of Lyons, Colorado, who offered me good advice about the sexual energy in the book, and the appearance of Joy. To my friend and brother in creativity Mark Botvinick, who read a later draft as a true professional reader, and who gave me good advice about the Field Book entries and the overall structure and pacing of the story. Thanks also Mark, for standing with me through the travails of discouragement and offering words of solace when I needed them.

To my friend, brother, and partner in conscious evolution Chris Menne, who has offered me steady encouragement, friendship, and resource, and who gave me advice about a woman whom no reader has met, because I wrote her out of the story after listening to Chris and realizing that I'd not done her justice. (You will meet her in the next book, God willing, when the feminine will rise to the fore).

Thank you to my friend, Integral brother, and general partner in crime Jeff Salzman who read and loved the book; and to my friend and fellow seeker of Goodness, Truth, and Beauty, Steve McIntosh, whose philosophy strongly influenced the vision of the future contained within these pages. Thank you also to my friend and fellow Keeper of the Field, Steven McHugh, who read this thing and gave me positive support and encouragement from his big heart and from the Guides. Thank you to David Riordan who told me that the writing was good at a time that I needed to hear just that to move forward. Thank you to Johnny Thomas who read and redlined the book, helping me. May your own book flower, Johnny, in its due season. Thank you also to Kevin Stansbury, Kathy Fragnoli and Ken Chapin who read the story and offered me encouragement. Another 'thank you' to author and coach Alexis Neely, who gave the book a read and a shot in the arm when she told me the book was finished and great. Thank you to author Marco Morelli who gave me encouragement as a fellow writer coupled with good advice about the publishing path; and to authors Robin Reinach and Robert McNamara for the same. Thank you also to my friend and cover artist Bryce Widom, who read and loved this book, and agreed to create the striking image that is on the back cover.

A bow of gratitude to Adelyn Jones, who was truly enthused about the book at a time where I had no gas left in the tank at all. Adelyn, your enthusiasm and your energy to take this project forward was, and is, invaluable.

A *very* special 'thank you' to my colleague and friend Linda J. Laws, who read, commented on, marked, and edited hundreds of pages of drafts, and who really 'got' what I was trying to do. It meant so much to me to have someone to talk to about this book at the Boulder Integral Center as I travelled down to the office at 4 a.m. and stayed past midnight to make a go of it. Linda, you were that person.

Thank you so much Ken Wilber, for giving this book a terrific shot in the arm with your endorsement; and for your Integral Vision that has brought so many of us together.

A deep and reverent bow to spiritual teacher, publishing expert, and mystical traveller Matt Lacata, who encouraged me, generously advised me, and opened up contacts for me in the publishing world.

I can hardly express my appreciation for the work of my beautiful daughter, Melissa Claire Hostetter, whose talented eye found and took the author photograph on the back cover.

And to you Delynn Copley, who took this book with you on your business trips, who worked on it as a labor of love word by word and line by line while cris-crossing the country on airplanes, moving all those commas and little quotation marks, seeing the hundred flaws that no one else could see, and making this book just so much better. Your work completed this novel, so I could finally release it. It's done. Thank you *so much* for bringing my life's work across the finish line.

And now, for these:

For the unfailing interior guidance of the Divine Feminine, in all of her forms, whose many voices have been speaking to me, encouraging me, and dancing ahead of me on the path from the very beginning. I hope that this effort is good enough and this final published draft—at least close enough to the story and teaching that you wanted when, for some odd reason, you picked me, of all people, to bring your words into the world.

For my mentor and First Teacher Billy Finucane of Tennessee, the man who became the character Moses in this book, who died of exposure on the upper Missouri River in 1972, after giving me his paddle earlier that year. For you Billy, who saw a light around me; who brought out my untapped inner strength as you stood by me and forced me to confront my weaknesses; for you, who taught me to see the Beauty; and who conveyed such knowledge that can be taught about the wilderness, leaving me prepared and ready to go into the deep woods on my own, where the wilderness herself would teach me all of the rest.

This book would never have come into being without the support of my beautiful partner-for-life, lover, soulmate and friend, my wife Mary, who has been with me every step of the way as we tried to reconcile this dream with the realities of our life together with three kids. For all of her help and careful reading, for cheerfully accepting the burden of this book in our midst, and for our firm and final decision to follow the spiritual path together, to commit in full, and risk our security for the chance to bring the presence of the Divine, the great I Am, into this physical world through the vehicle of our gifts, including the book you are holding in your hands.

Finally, there is no measure of thanks that can return the gifts I have received from my beautiful sister, Beth H. Petersen Wiskochil of Bridport Vermont, whose very soul is in this book along with mine. There is no greater gift to any person with a dream than for someone to see that vision before it is fully formed, to know that it's worth doing, and then to put their shoulder in behind the wheel along with you, blowing on the little flame, and to be there full-willing to put their feet in the mud and their head in the cloudless sky right along with you. You have been that person for me, Beth, the person who has read every word of this book at least a half-dozen times, the person whom I could trust to make the right decisions about the book large and small, the person who supported this work financially, and who has offered her gift of unfailing wisdom and profound generosity at every turn. We have brought this forth together, and I am proud of what we've done.

Let all of these gifts play forward, and let this book be a beacon of hope to everyone it touches; an instrument of Divine presence; and a pathway towards the unitive life.

In Gratitude,

Ross Hostetter   Boulder Colorado; Springtime, 2014.

Start a Relationship With the Author

ENJOY 16 DAYS OF FREE INSPIRATION FROM

THE FIELD BOOK

Available only from the author at

http://www.keepersofthefield.com/

A SPECIAL 'THANK YOU' TO MY READERS AND FRIENDS:

Enter this coupon code:
Ireadthebook

WHEN YOU SIGN UP FOR THE **FIELDBENDING FORUM** OFFERED BY THE FIELDWORK SCHOOL. GET YOUR FIRST MONTH OF **TEACHING, HEALING, AND SPIRITUAL PRACTICE** AS MY GIFT.

Visit http://www.fieldworkschool.org/ for details.

We'd love to be part of your book club.

Study guides are available.
Arrange for the author to visit your club!

Contact: ross@fieldworkschool.org

Made in the USA
Charleston, SC
26 June 2014